About the Author

Jay Raven is the author of Gothic chillers and historical horror reminding readers that the past is a dangerous place to venture, full of monsters and murderous men.

He blames his fascination with vampires, witches and werewolves on the Hammer Horror films he watched as a teenager but living in a creepy old house beside a 500-acre forest teeming with bats may have something to do with it.

If you would like to be informed of new releases, enjoy bonus short stories and access exclusive giveaways and competitions, simply join the Jay Raven VIP Readers Club by visiting the website at www.jayraven.co.uk. It's free and you can unsubscribe at any time.

D1523414

CRIMSON SIEGE

BLOOD RIDERS – BOOK ONE

JAY RAVEN

Jay Raven Books

First edition published by
Junction Publishing 2018

Second edition published by
Jay Raven Books 2019

©Jay Raven 2018

www.jayraven.co.uk

Cover, formatting and design by Peter Jones
Editing by Maureen Vincent-Northam

It is the mid 19th century - a decade after humanity's narrow victory over the ravaging vampire hordes...

CHAPTER 1

TRANSYLVANIA 1857

They made remarkably little noise for such a large group. The four men and their sole female companion trod cautiously, careful not to let the crunch of stones or the snap of twigs announce their approach alongside the stream. Up ahead, the mill house and its large wheel stood clearly silhouetted in the bright moonlight.

The additional illumination was a bonus. It made the weaving, undulating path easier to navigate for the five, weighed down with nets, flintlocks and cudgels.

Milosh Drubrick stared upwards at the full, fat orb. In the countryside the peasants called it a poacher's candle. With his army background Milosh knew it by another name. To him, it was an ambusher's moon.

He looked at the others, noting their intent and the excitement in their expressions. There was tension too, revealed in a twitch of an eyebrow or a hard swallow. They may have followed this routine countless times but this night was special. It was more dangerous, the prize bigger; as were the risks.

Theodore and Johann looked straight ahead, focused. The tall duo stepped in unison, ramrod straight, looking every inch the Imperial Guards they'd once been. Although the men were edgy, lacking their normal easy camaraderie, Milosh wasn't worried. Both had proven themselves over and over and he expected this time would be no different.

Behind them, Gregor, the oldest of the group, silently mouthed prayers, head bobbing like a child's toy. It often irritated Milosh to see the grey bearded, balding man mutter his holy incantations. Tonight, however, the extreme peril of their mission meant divine assistance might be all that stood between them and destruction.

Irina, the one woman in the company, trembled. He knew for her it was ecstasy, not fear. She revelled in the tension, the anticipation of danger, the sheer nerve-tingling sensations. She often described it as the next best thing to sex. Then again, he reflected knowingly, she described everything as the next best thing to sex. It was the one word never far from her lips, or her mind.

As they rounded a bend in the track, ducking under an overhanging branch, Milosh let his thoughts switch to the sixth member of the gang - the dwarf Quintz. He'd been left behind on the roadway with the horses and the wagon. It wasn't that the little man lacked courage - in many ways he was the most ruthless and cold blooded of them all. Nor was he a problem because of his diminutive size, being a fierce fighter and expert knifeman.

He remained behind purely because he had a special task, a vital role in the attack. As keeper of their secret weapon, it was his responsibility to ensure it arrived at just the right moment to secure success. Too soon and its noise would alert those inside the mill house to the impending attack.

"You'll have no trouble telling when the moment is right," Milosh had assured him.

"By the gunfire?" the dwarf suggested.

"No, there will be no shooting. Unless we have no other choice. We need to take our prize alive."

Then how would he know, Quintz pressed.

"By the screams," Milosh replied. "Come when you hear the screams. And just hope they are his and not ours."

Recalling that conversation made Milosh grin, delighting in its melodrama, as he abruptly halted the group by raising his palm. The foaming, rippling water had caught his attention. Something floated in the stream.

He knelt, and pulled the object towards him. It was a body; face down, arms and legs outstretched like a starfish. Johann and Theodore rushed over and helped him flip it over.

The man's dead features were twisted in terror; throat gone - ripped open.

"Jesus Christ," Theodore gasped.

Milosh's irritated glare cut off any more words. He flicked his eyes up to the building fifty yards away. Thankfully, there was no sign anyone had heard the outburst.

He felt warmth as Irina pressed up against him and put her lips against his ear.

"It must be the miller," she murmured. "Poor bastard."

She indicated the ragged, gaping hole. "Look at the wounds, the butchery. Only one thing could have done that. It proves the information is correct. The creature came this way."

Probably only minutes before, Milosh estimated. Their quarry was still here. He'd bet his life on it; was betting all their lives on it...

Another shape bobbed nearby. A middle-aged woman, just as dead, just as brutalised.

"And that," Irina whispered, "must be the miller's wife."

"What about the rest of the family?" he asked, putting his mouth to her ear, breathing deeply, smelling the intoxicating mix of musk and scented soap on her skin.

"Two teenage daughters," she replied. "I can imagine he has a different fate in mind for them. Once these abominations have feasted they like to fuck..."

At that moment they heard the first moans from the mill house.

"Sounds like the evening's entertainment has begun," she observed.

"Then we had better move swiftly and strike while it is distracted," he answered, pushing away thoughts of Irina and her warm, yielding, insistent body and replacing it with a thought which excited him just as much - gold, piles and piles of gold. The gold they were going to earn for tonight's enterprise.

Gregor glared at his leader, appalled by the obvious greed in Milosh's eyes. Let the pious bastard disapprove, Milosh told himself. Tonight was the big pay-off. When they were rolling in wealth, the old bible-basher would want his share just as much as the others.

They rushed forward, daring to make more noise as their footsteps were drowned out by the carnal gasps coming through the windows.

As they reached the walls, Milosh signalled his accomplices to spread out around the building, ready to burst in through the various windows and doors. The moans grew louder, joined by the relentless splashing and squeaking of the rotating water wheel. It was difficult to separate the mechanical groans from those emanating from inside the candlelit interior.

Milosh glanced inside; the sight so stunning that he took an involuntary gulp. The three bodies were writhing, gyrating, squirming in a fluid, balletic motion - rolling from one side of the straw-covered floor to the other, the trio lost in a frenzy of sensual indulgence, hungrily biting and sucking, subsumed in an eager passion, both strangely beautiful and appallingly animalistic.

The two blonde, lithe girls were naked, eyes glazed, lips open and wet as the young, virile, half-dressed male nibbled harshly on one breast then another, alternating between the women, forcing their heads between his legs to suck and lick and bite, their tongues competing, clashing, melding around his erect penis.

Then he was mounting one girl as the other kissed him deeply, aggressively, teeth gripping his lips, grunting, dribbling, trying to devour him in her urgent, wanton grasp.

Swift, hard thrusts and he was rolling over and entering the second sister, the first lying, back arched, sated, twitching in ecstasy, her moan long and loud.

Mesmerised, Milosh watched in envy, imagining himself for a moment in the long-haired male's place.

"Magnificent, isn't he," Irina purred, rubbing up against him. "I'm told they can mate for hours on end, just imagine that. Climaxing again and again and again and never tiring."

He trembled both at that thought and at the stirrings in his loins as she sought his crotch, eagerly exploring.

For a split second, he was aroused. Then the danger, the madness of it at this most reckless of moments, made him stop.

"You just can't help yourself, can you?" he gasped, brushing her hand away.

She glared sulkily and turned back to the scene inside.

The handsome male knelt, hands between each girl's legs, pushing his fingers inside, exploring the dark, moist voids. The girls quivered as he slowly probed. Moments later, he brought the fingers out, glistening, and, crossing arms, offered them to each of the young women.

"Bitches. Whores. Godless sluts. How can they do this? It's depraved. Obscene," Gregor snapped from his vantage point nearby, as each girl sighed in anticipation and began licking the killer's long slender fingers, lapping each other's love juices.

"They don't know what they're doing," Milosh told him simply.

"They are bewitched," Irina said, "only aware of their lust and overpowering need to please him. He has total control over their bodies, their minds, their emotions,"

"And their souls," Gregor added bitterly.

Milosh gave a wry smile. Trust the old man to worry about that.

His attention returned to the inhuman puppet master and his naked playthings. The creature's casual dominance over his victims was incredible. Even after years hunting vampires, Milosh was still amazed by their raw, unequalled power; their effortless grace and ruthlessness. No wonder they instilled such terror. And such jealousy.

He gestured silently to the others. It was time to spring the trap. And perhaps, just perhaps, save the girls if the creature hadn't already contaminated them, transformed them into other damned examples of his kind.

With well-rehearsed precision, the gang burst in. From the middle of the undulating mass of bodies, the male snarled as he became aware of the intruders. Propelling upwards, he bared his teeth... long, jagged, predator's teeth.

CHAPTER 2

"This is murder. I won't do it."

Anton Yoska's words were louder, more vehement than he intended, a reaction to the splitting migraine slicing through his brain.

Across from him the visitor rocked back, podgy, well-fed countenance darkening. The nobleman was clearly not used to anyone having the temerity to answer back.

"Oh, I suggest you will if you know what is good for you," the Envoy replied, grating cut-glass voice level yet laced with restrained menace. "I did not travel hundreds of miles, putting myself through a series of intolerable hardships, for you to simply refuse. The instructions are clear. As is your duty."

Rubbing his gritty eyes, Anton looked in disbelief at the dispatch. It was dated November 16th, five days earlier, and labelled: *For the Urgent Attention of Anton Yoska, Lord Marshal of Our Dominions South of the Carpathian Mountains.*

It instructed him to immediately execute Edward and Pieter Lucens, the brothers he held in the cells of his jailhouse. No reason given, just the simple threat: 'Failure to carry out these orders without delay will incur my severest displeasure.'

Glowering, Anton examined the document. The vellum was ostentatiously expensive, discreetly watermarked and sealed with a large dab of blood red wax, into which was embedded the unmistakable Imperial Coat of Arms. Even if it hadn't contained these signs of authenticity, he would still have known the spidery handwriting, the clipped, condescending tone and the assured certainty any whim of its writer would be treated as holy writ.

"You will find everything is in order, Lord Marshal," the Envoy promised, absent-mindedly adjusting the ring on the outside of his ermine-trimmed riding glove.

The Crown Prince had obviously anticipated his reluctance, Anton understood. That was why the parchment had been delivered personally by Count Kravnik, a power player in the Royal Court. The aristocrat might appear pampered and effete but that belied the truth - he was a ruthless enforcer right down to his well-manicured fingertips, with a reputation to match.

"These men haven't been tried," Anton pointed out, the stabbing in his head intensifying. "Their case cannot be heard until the circuit judge arrives."

"And when, pray, will that be?"

Anton's attention flicked to the window. The icy frost on the glass gave its own answer. The temperature was plunging, and already the tops of the nearby brooding mountains wore a thick mantle of white. Winter, and its bitter cruelty, was mere days away.

"Probably not for months," he predicted. "The nearest judge is ninety miles away. There are already heavy drifts in the passes, the tracks north are buried. And worse is coming. It would be folly for him to set out now. The prisoners can't be tried until the spring assizes."

"An entire season's delay!" Kravnik muttered, aghast. "You propose to keep them locked up until March? For the state to feed and keep them warm for all that time? That is preposterous. Totally unacceptable."

The Envoy's tongue flicked angrily over his thick, moist lips. "It is little wonder crime is out of control in your territory, Lord Marshal, if this is how you treat criminals and ruffians. The cut-throats must think you a wonderful fellow, running a hotel for them. And do you provide any other comforts for their delight and convenience?"

Anton bit back his reply. It didn't do to act rashly with Kravnik, no matter how much the goading sarcasm riled. Especially not with everything else Anton had to worry about. For a moment his thoughts strayed to the bedroom where Sofia was lying sick, before reluctantly forcing her from his mind. No matter how much he worried about his wife's fever, he had to stay focused on Kravnik's needling accusations.

He'd noticed the Envoy had stressed the word Lord in Lord Marshal, underlining that it was merely an honorary title and any true nobleman would view Anton as no more than a simple thief-taker, a jumped-up watchman.

But watchman or no, he was still the guardian of justice in the community of Brejnei and its surrounding lands and had vowed that all - high born or commoner - would receive the protection of full judicial process.

He didn't trust himself to look at the Envoy, choosing instead to gaze through the window at the roughly dressed men in the muddy thoroughfare, hurrying home to their weary wives through the chill, grey twilight. It was barely 4pm, and already the ramshackle settlement was being grasped by darkness. Across its half dozen narrow streets, pale yellowy lights appeared in first one small window then another, threadbare curtains hurriedly shut against the approaching night, heavy shutters banging into place as fires were piled high with scavenged wood.

Often it seemed to him the crudely built timber-planked homes leant forward even more in the darkness, their overhanging upper storeys almost touching, as though huddling together for warmth and protection.

Brejnei was a harsh place to spend winter, he mused, an unforgiving place to be poor. It had once been a thriving settlement, populated by thousands, back in the glory days before the nearby silver mines played out. Now, robbed of the mineral riches, the barren land and unyielding forests tested the remaining few hundred men to breaking point, leading them to reckless desperation.

"The Lucens brothers are not cut-throats or ruffians. They are accused simply of poaching," he replied, twisting back to his unwelcome visitor. "And, by statute, they are innocent until a court has found them guilty."

With an impatient sigh, Kravnik stood, picking up the glass paperweight from the desk.

"Innocent, you say," he repeated, rolling the sphere in his fingers. "I was informed they were captured in the act of hunting stags on Royal land?"

Anton agreed warily.

"And it was indeed you, Marshal Yoska, who detained them?"

He winced, knowing where this was going. "Yes," he conceded.

"Well," the Count observed, holding the orb to the oil lamp and grunting in amusement at the spectrum of colours dancing from it, "what can be the problem? You know with complete certainty they are guilty."

"Of being hungry. Of needing to feed their families."

11

"Ah, a bleeding heart. Compassion for the common man. So rare in a law officer. Nevertheless, they were caught red-handed, and slaughtering deer is a capital offence. A trial is a waste of time... and Crown funds. So you will follow the instructions I've brought you. Without any further excuses."

"Executing men for stealing a few sides of venison is barbaric."

"Perhaps," Kravnik agreed. "However, these are harsh times. And it is the law. The law you are sworn to uphold."

Anton felt his anger about to explode. There was a knock at the door. It was Tomas, his serving boy, carrying a large tray piled with food and a pot of coffee - the meal demanded by Kravnik on his arrival in the Marshal's study half an hour before.

"Ah, refreshment," the man grunted. "About time. Well, don't just stand there, boy. Bring it in, bring it in."

Tomas looked nervously at Anton, who beckoned him come forward.

Shifting on his chair to gain a better view, Kravnik watched intently as the servant crossed the room.

"What is your name, boy?"

"Sir?"

"What are you called?"

"Tomas, sir," the boy replied, placing the tray on the table. "Tomas Lakri, sir."

"And how old are you?"

"He's fourteen," Anton said warily.

Kravnik smiled thinly at the boy. "Tell me, Tomas Lakri. What do you think of our great Marshal?"

The boy bit his bottom lip. "Sir?"

"Is he a fair employer? Does he treat you well?"

Colouring, the lad looked at Anton for help, unsure what to say.

"Don't embarrass the boy," Anton warned, voice tightening. "How can he possibly answer that?"

Kravnik ignored the question, pulling off his gloves, and poured himself a cup of coffee. He studied the food with disdain as though it was no more than the scraps he'd expect in a crude, rural backwater like this.

"I merely thought if he were unhappy, we always have need of good servants in the Royal Court." The Count picked up a knife and began slicing the salami, letting his index finger stroke its length in a way that made Anton queasy.

"Tomas is happy here and is well treated. You have my word," he insisted, jerking his thumb for the lad to leave. "Check on the mistress," he instructed the boy. "I'll be up to see her shortly, when I've dealt with this *gentleman*."

Tomas was at the door when Kravnik poked the meat slowly into his mouth and said casually: "Not so fast. Boy, come here."

Hesitantly, Tomas approached the Envoy. Kravnik picked up the paperweight again, placing it on the lad's palm.

"This is for your trouble, young man. Consider it a token of appreciation. Before you do your master's bidding, fetch my things from the stables, and have a room made up for me."

"You're staying?" Again the words came out more forcibly than Anton intended.

"Of course, Lord Marshal. We still have much to discuss. And it is too dark and too cold for me to commence my return journey. Besides, I intend to remain to ensure you carry out your instructions."

"Wouldn't you be more comfortable in the local tavern?"

Letting a cube of cheese hover near his lips, the Count's expression hardened. "Are you refusing me your hospitality? Am I not to benefit from the kind-hearted largess, which seems to be provided without hesitation to any criminal?"

"I simply meant we're not set up for guests, especially not visiting dignitaries," Anton answered carefully. "And with my wife's illness..." He gestured helplessly.

"Quite."

If Anton was expecting more empathy, he was sorely disappointed. The nobleman didn't even bother enquiring about Sofia's condition. He barely waited until Tomas had left the room before purring: "Now, Yoska, before that enchanting boy interrupted you were telling me why you hold the law in such low regard. A curious standpoint for a man in your position."

Anton remained silent, resisting Kravnik's baiting.

"You were telling me why these guilty men must have their day in court. Do go on. I insist. Enlighten me."

"Because it's the only moral thing to do," he replied. "Otherwise we are no better than savages."

The nobleman's eye glinted triumphantly as he drained his coffee cup. "Ah, I see. So now you're saying the Crown Prince is a savage. Dangerous words..."

"That wasn't what I meant, and you know it."

Anton's anger welled up again, the throbbing in his skull doubling.

"Don't play games with me, Count," he snapped. "I'm not in the mood for tricks and traps. If you have something to say, just spit it out."

"Something to say? I thought I had been quite clear already. Was I not articulate enough for you?"

"Look," Anton said, meeting the messenger's amused gaze. "There's something else going on here. Why is Leopold suddenly taking an interest in poachers? Especially in a God-forsaken corner of the country like this? Surely he has more important matters to worry about?"

"*Crown Prince* Leopold," the Envoy stressed, correcting Anton's impertinent over-familiarity, "believes an example has to be made. To maintain order. To keep the rebellious populace in line."

"To keep me in line, you mean."

Kravnik laughed icily. "Ah, Yoska, I can see why you vex the Prince so."

"I'm a lawman... not the Prince's poodle."

If the Count sensed an implied insult, he chose to ignore it. "You are a Crown representative and as such will do as you are told. And I am here to see you do."

He raised an admonishing finger, indicating all debate was over. "These men die tomorrow. I saw a large oak tree in the main square. Strong, wide branches. It will do nicely for the hangings."

"Don't you mean lynchings?" Anton said, barely able to hide his disgust.

Kravnik's expression chilled further. "The executions will take place at first light," he said, flint edged. "Just be a good fellow and make the arrangements."

Anton shook his head, more in incredulity than defiance. "I have only two deputies, and the accused men have friends, families - dozens of supporters who would like nothing better than to show what they think of the Crown," he cautioned. "There's been simmering resentment for months and it only needs one spark to set it off."

Kravnik wasn't listening, now absorbed in slicing more cold meat, heaping it onto his plate.

"Really, Lord Marshal," he murmured. "I am so disappointed. I would have thought you of all people would be able to deal with a handful of disgruntled yokels. This is not what I would have expected from the fearless Anton Yoska, the renowned hero of the vampire wars."

His next words were barely audible through his chewing yet no less chilling for that. "And they are condemned men, not accused men. I would take care to remember that, unless you want to find yourself joining them."

CHAPTER 3

Even in his excitement, Milosh Drubrick remembered the ultimate law of the vampire hunter - never aim where the creature is, aim ahead to where it is going to be a millisecond later. The speed of these beings was unbelievable.

The first net fell short, dropping ineffectually over the spot where the male had been, partly trapping the two stunned girls. Fortunately, Milosh had made the exact calculation and the second net found its target.

The male tipped over, caught in mid leap, and crashed to the floor. He thrashed about, roaring in anger and frustration; spitting and hurling curses; evil threats pouring out in a torrid.

The netting wouldn't hold him entangled for long and Theodore and Johann were immediately upon the writhing bundle, holding it down, grabbing at the creature's flailing limbs.

Phlegm-flecked teeth tore at them through the thick rope, each bite closer and more determined, ripping at the hunters' thick clothing and gauntlets.

Then Milosh was standing there, club in hand.

"You've had your fun," he whispered to the thrashing creature, "now it's time I had mine."

He swung the club hard, again... and again... and again.

As each blow landed with a wet thud, he could hear the miller's daughters wail in sympathy for their hurt lover, crying in animal distress for his pain.

He turned, about to tell the others to shut them up, just in time to witness the elder daughter throw off the netting and charge forward.

Something in Milosh's horrified expression alerted Irina, because she ducked just as the girl flew at her. It was a close thing. The attack missed by mere inches, the teen caught off balance and falling.

Without compulsion, Irina kicked out, catching the girl a sharp glancing blow to the chest, then kicked again - this time aiming at the throat.

The girl gurgled like a hollow drain as Irina ground her boot into her attacker's windpipe, pressing harder and harder.

"Gregor," she yelled, beckoning for assistance.

The old man twitched, seemingly unable to take in what was happening then rushed over, fumbling frantically in the pouch slung over his shoulder.

Although small, the crucifix did its work. It seared with a sizzle; smoke and the smell of burning flesh filling the air as he pressed it on the writhing female's forehead. The girl howled and Gregor struggled to help Irina keep her pinned as the teen bucked and convulsed.

"Well, that answers one question," he informed Irina grimly. "We're too late to save them, God forgive us."

He brought out a sharpened stake, no longer than six inches, and a heavy hammer.

"Do it, do it now," Irina urged. "I can't hold her much longer."

Whispering a prayer, he placed the stake against the girl's left breast and hit it home with as much force as his arthritic fingers could manage.

It dug deep and she shuddered, letting out a banshee yell that made his stomach lurch. Nearby, her sister under the net let out a matching shriek - just as forlorn and furious.

"It's said they have a psychic link," Irina muttered, as the staked teen fell silent and still, "and from the sound of that I can believe it."

She motioned to the other girl, now staring malevolently at them through the netting.

"Should we dispatch her as well?"

Gregor didn't get to answer. Across from them the male became more agitated, his desperate thrashing so intense the other gang members struggled to contain him.

"Come help," Milosh yelled to them. "It's about to break—"

As the word *free* left his lips the bundle burst open, the force sending the men flying in different directions. Milosh hit the wall with a bone-crunching slap, lungs emptying with a whoosh.

Groggily, he saw the creature rise, dark eyes blazing, grunting, head turning from side to side, deciding who to attack first.

Quintz, Milosh thought frantically. *Where the hell was Quintz? He must have heard the commotion. How many screams did the dwarf need to hear?*

Johann was out cold - head cracked against the edge of the table. Theodore wasn't much better, getting shakily to his feet, swaying, vision glassy and unfocused, fumbling for his gun.

In a trice the creature made its decision. Perceiving Theodore as the more active threat, it pounced, knocking the flintlock from his grasp. The weapon clattered loudly to the floor, as Theodore was propelled upwards in a smooth, effortless hoist.

He yelped in shock.

The *infernal* held him clear off the floor, using only one hand, his fifteen stone as insignificant to it as if he was made of straw. He spluttered as the iron grip tightened around his throat, and the creature jerked him towards its eager mouth.

The thick collar provided only a second's protection. Then the fabric gave and the incisors plunged. Blood pumped out in a spurt that catapulted across the room.

Irina rushed forward, only for Gregor to intercept, holding her firm with the warning: "No. It's too late. You can't help him."

He was right. Ripping a sizeable chunk out of Theodore's neck, the creature discarded the tall hunter with a dismissive throw, his twitching victim landing in a heap on top of Johann.

Quintz! Milosh thought frantically. *For the love of God, where was Quintz?*

Nerves jangling, the gang leader realised it was all over. The fiend focused its malevolent, burning stare on him and spoke.

"You are all going to die." The voice was refined although made guttural and low by anger. "And you will be last. I will make you watch while I feast on the others. You will have to listen to their screams, knowing your turn will come."

With that he leapt.

On impulse, Milosh rolled, as fast as he'd ever moved in his life. He spun away just as the creature swooped, missing him by a hair's width. Smashing to the floor, it was momentarily stunned.

The vampire growled, fury giving it a volume that twisted Milosh's nerves. Yet, even as its incensed clamour filled his ears and he felt his bowels spasm, there was a sudden louder, deeper, more violent roar.

As he looked up, he saw the source of the new din and burst into high-pitched laughter, grinning in relief.

Salvation! Quintz had come!

The tiny man was straining to hold the chain around the neck of a dark, bulky shape that slobbered and bellowed. The muscular outline lifted itself to its full eight-foot height, put back its head and roared again - even more aggressively - and, tugging Quintz along with it, bounded determinedly towards the vampire, enormous claws ready.

The Undead male - their lethal adversary, their prize; only seconds before a creature of immense power and fury - opened its lips again. This time to whimper.

CHAPTER 4

The bedroom felt cold, the last embers of the fire low in the grate. Fortunately, Sofia wouldn't notice the chill, Anton reflected. Touching his wife's cheek, he felt its own fire raging within it.

She was drenched in sweat, hazel hair lank and plastered to her forehead, nightshirt strained and clammy. Moaning in her semi-conscious state, she murmured incoherently.

"Shhhhh," he whispered, pulling back the covers she'd pushed away in her fight against the boiling torment. "It's fine, it's fine. I'm here. It's going to be all right."

He didn't know if she could hear, but he needed to say something; to sooth her and to battle his growing sense of helplessness as her condition worsened.

It was the third day and the fever hadn't broken. And it had been ten long hours since she'd last woken, opening her eyes only for an instance - pained and lacking any cognition.

Anton didn't know if Sofia was having nightmares, or if the fevered thoughts in her head made any kind of sense. He hoped she was unaware, because then she wouldn't see how close he was to despair.

Glancing in the dressing table mirror, he hardly recognised the man staring back, sallow skinned and haggard. Although Anton was barely forty the last weeks had taken their toll and he could now pass for ten years older. His dark brown hair was greying, the once luxuriant locks thinning and lifeless; his eyes dull and watery.

He'd hardly slept in days - locked in a cycle where lack of rest brought migraines, and the searing pains guaranteeing any sleep was fitful and inadequate.

He'd forgotten when he'd last eaten. Even the sight of the Envoy's food hadn't stirred any appetite. It was no wonder the clothes that had once struggled to contain him now hung loose.

Running fingers over his stubble, he realised that he'd let himself go. Another day or two and he'd have a full beard. And that would never do. Sofia hated him to be unshaven.

"You are Lord Marshal and you should look the part," she'd insist. Although he couldn't see why being a lawman meant he had to worry about his appearance, he knew enough about being a husband to sigh and go along with it, changing his shirt or putting on a much smarter waistcoat.

At this moment, he'd have given anything for her to be nagging him.

The door opened quietly. Tomas stood there with a fresh bowl of water and flannels.

Thanking the boy, he took a cloth, dipped it in the cooling liquid and placed it on Sofia's forehead. She groaned and shivered. A bad sign.

He could see the concern in the lad's eyes.

"Is she...? Is she going to...?" The boy couldn't bring himself to say the word.

"I don't know," he said, heart heavy. "The physician has done all he can. The potions seem to have no effect. The typhus is winning."

He gently stroked Sofia's fiery cheek. "If she has the will and the strength to fight, she might yet recover," he said softly. "Though I fear she may simply succumb."

Tomas breathed in sharply, loud and snotty, a shiny tear at the corner of his eye. "She looks so frail. I shall pray for her," he said, with an earnestness unusual for someone so young. "Pray for God's tender mercy."

Anton sighed. He was long past believing in the mercy of God, or that God even knew or cared he existed.

"You do that, Tomas," he said, squeezing the lad's shoulder. "You pray for her and pray for us all while you're at it. We could all do with his blessing."

Plus, his forgiveness, he told himself. Forgiveness for the cruelty of men. Forgiveness for the cowardice of those who know better and stand aside while evil is done.

He held the rag and bowl to the lad. "Take my place here. Cool her brow. I have matters to attend to. I won't be long."

As he left, Anton paused on the landing. A light shone under the door of Kravnik's bedroom. He considered making one last plea for the reprieve of the brothers, but knew it was futile.

Instead, he headed downstairs, along a narrow panel-lined passageway and through to the far end of the building where the cells and stables were located around an inner courtyard.

He didn't usually spend much time in the jail, preferring to leave his deputies, Pavel and Nicku, to guard any prisoners. The cellblock depressed him - the bare, whitewashed walls, stone floors and rock hard cots reminding him of the military barracks he'd lived in for so long.

No matter how high the fires were built the jail always held a chill, the badly-lit corridors making it permanently dingy, while the lingering stink from the piss and shit pots provided a sickening backdrop.

There were five cells - more than Anton required - a throwback to the silver boom era, when the imposing residence complex had been built as a jail-cum-courthouse-cum-judge's lodgings, before Brejnei's overnight decline made all that superfluous. He couldn't remember the last time all the cells had been occupied.

Four were unremarkable eight-by-ten stone cubicles, their fronts a line of floor to ceiling iron bars with inset door and stout lock. The fifth cubicle was a different matter altogether. It was the maximum security cell. Totally enclosed, it had a solid, blue-grey steel door, a small peephole allowing the guard to watch the captive without risking getting close.

Its internal dimensions were smaller too because of the thick layer of padding on the walls - a precaution to thwart those liable to be violent, to others or themselves. It lacked a bed and anyone unlucky enough to find themselves thrown in there usually slept huddled in a corner, as comfortable as the cramped space and straitjacket would allow.

There was one other major difference to the cell - it had no window, always in perpetual darkness.

Anton hated the chamber, sad that it should be necessary to treat anyone like that, but aware that some hard cases were too dangerous to handle any other way.

He carried on along the cell corridor to the deputies' room, which served as an office and recreation area, with a cot where the night guard would sleep. The space was dominated by a large desk where the deputies were supposed to process paperwork when not dozing through the hours of numbing boredom. The room wasn't much better than the cells, despite possessing large windows, a wooden floor and a pot belly stove in the corner, pumping out some heat and keeping the coffee pot steaming.

Even before he stepped inside, Anton's nose wrinkled at an awful smell - not night soil, something almost as bad, the aroma of cheap, pungent, cloying tobacco. It could only mean one thing. Nicku was on duty. The man was never without the stained, long-stemmed clay pipe hanging perilously from the corner of his mouth.

He looked up with lazy, hooded eyes as Anton walked in. "Evening, *boss*. Didn't expect to see you here so late. What's wrong, couldn't sleep?"

There was always a hint of dumb insolence in Nicku's tone and measured stare to let Anton know just what he thought of him.

The man had been a deputy in Brejnei most of his adult life, a local man with important friends on the council, and had expected the Marshal's job when it fell vacant five years earlier. The Crown Prince, however, had other ideas.

"Where's Pavel?" Anton asked. He had expected the younger deputy to be there too.

"Out on last rounds," Nicku replied. "Checking all's quiet. Chasing the last drunks home. When it became apparent you were entertaining an important guest, we figured you'd be too busy to carry out curfew patrol."

Ah yes, resentment *and* curiosity. The grizzled, uncouth veteran was itching to know about Count Kravnik and his unexpected arrival.

Well, he wasn't going to give his impertinent underling any information. Let him stew.

"I want to see the poachers," he instructed, and was greeted with the inevitable pained sigh.

"They'll be asleep."

"I don't care. I want to speak to them."

For a moment Nicku seemed set to refuse. Then, making a sucking noise through his yellowing teeth, he lifted the main cell block keys off the rack behind the desk. Letting them dangle on one finger, he offered them half-heartedly to Anton.

For the umpteenth time since taking up his post, Anton felt the urge to punch the deputy, to wipe the gloating look off his wrinkled mug.

Instead, he snatched the keys, saying: "I have an errand for you. Go find the undertaker."

Nicku recoiled. "What?"

"I need the undertaker. He must be brought here. Within the hour."

"Is it your wife? Is she...?"

Anton didn't answer, simply jerked his head. Scowling, the man grabbed his coat.

"What do I tell him?"

"Tell him Lord Marshal Yoska sends his compliments and says that we have two men who are in urgent need of his services."

Nicku's visage filled with horror, but Anton was already unlocking the cell corridor and, lamp held high, walking into the darkness.

Both brothers were deep in slumber. He swung the lamp, letting it clatter against the bars, watching them grumbling, blinking uncomfortably in the intrusive illumination.

"Whh-at's the matter? What is it?" Edward, the older, barked.

Anton's voice was filled with urgency and a sense of awe at what he was about to say.

"Shut up," he told them, "and listen. I don't have much time and you need to pay attention. Heed my words carefully. You need to do exactly what I tell you or you will go straight to Hell."

CHAPTER 5

Kristina Modjeski paused behind the curtain, drinking in the intoxicating essence of fear. Apprehension permeated each corner of the grand hall. Some hundred petrified souls awaited, nerves twisted, hearts racing, dreading what each second might bring.

They were convinced they were about to die, struggling to ignore the pleading voices in their heads telling them to flee. Instead they sat, smiling awkwardly through frozen muscles, clumsily gulping wine from the ornate goblets, pretending nothing was amiss.

Above the enticing aroma of dread, Kristina could smell another odour, more stringent and pervasive - the unmistakable stench of greed. It was the desire for wealth and influence keeping her guests pinned to their seats, rocking slowly, hiding their trembles under clipped small talk, insincere bonhomie and politeness.

No matter how afraid, they would stay and listen, for they knew she - leader of the most powerful vampire clan in the whole of Eastern Europe - was about to offer them the world, and all its riches.

She focused her thoughts. Time for the grand entrance. With a tug of her slender fingers, she pulled aside the drapes and appeared dramatically to a round of applause.

Surveying the hall, she took in the sights in a rapid, forensic scan. Tables of nobles, political leaders, financiers, industrialists, regional governors - all standing, clapping madly lest they offend their deadly hosts, their auras sickly yellow and pulsating with foreboding.

Behind them, in the shadows, bodyguards - men with crossbows and swords, slit-eyed, motionless; tense and ready for action, alert to any sign of treachery, ready to counter any hostile move - their auras black as night and just as alive.

At the top table, leading the applause, her husband Viktor dominated, looking as handsome, poised and threatening as ever. He nodded encouragingly, the movement so rapid few would have noticed.

She gave silent thanks to finally have his support. She knew he would have preferred they simply feasted on the assembled dignitaries, drinking deep of their bloated blood.

It would be a fitting revenge for the decade of humiliation her people had endured since their defeat in the last great conflict, for the ruthless subjugation of the nosferatu, their banishment to the remote and hated reserved lands. It would send a terrifying message to the world: we are corralled, but not beaten. We are still to be feared and obeyed. Tremble before us; beg for our mercy and forgiveness.

Although a massacre was appealing she had other plans, schemes that went beyond a mere moment of vengeance; beyond an instant of sweet hedonistic indulgence and fatalistic pleasure. She had an audacious design for the future of The Brethren - the squabbling federation of nosferatu families. She, Kristina Modjeski, was going to unite them, forge them into a cohesive and unstoppable force. Through her determination she would create a unified vampire nation. The time of being hunted, shunned and reviled would soon be over; she was going to bring her kind into the light.

She grinned sardonically... bring her kind into the *metaphorical* light. And for that she needed the help of these pampered mortals.

"All-out war did not work for us. Dominance requires a more long-term, pragmatic approach," she'd explained to Viktor when he raised objections. "We must adopt a more diplomatic strategy."

"Fear has always worked perfectly well for us in the past," he'd insisted.

Yes, but it hadn't brought an end to the persecution of their kindred, she pointed out. A new tactic was necessary. They must charm to disarm.

They had, she argued, to infiltrate, insinuate themselves into every level, and sphere of society. They had to befriend...

"So you're saying the wolf should embrace the sheep," he observed dubiously.

"Only as a means to an end. If the wolf is cunning he'll never hunger again; if he forsakes the hunt and becomes a shepherd. Then he simply controls and harvests the flock."

"It is a bold tactic," Viktor agreed, "except I doubt the sheep will be so obliging."

Yet here they were. Clapping, co-operating, ensuring they helped usher in their own eventual doom.

"Friends," she said, motioning for silence. "Welcome. I bid you welcome, and thank you for giving up your evening to hear what I have to say."

She waited for them to take their seats, scanning each table to ensure everything was as planned. Yes, there were members of the family dotted in amongst the guests -

captivating them, answering their questions, reassuring them; close enough to maul and maim should anything go wrong.

She spotted one empty chair. Stefan wasn't there. Her brows furrowed. This was typical of him. He knew he was her favourite, that she looked upon him as a son and was ready - all too ready - to indulge him. Even so, she had made it clear she wanted him here tonight. It was important.

Forcing her irritation aside, she held her palms wide to the guests as a sign of openness.

"This is an epoch of progress and change," she began, "and we accept we must embrace this transformation and recast ourselves to fit the modern era. The dark ages with their ignorance and superstitions have passed, and despite the Church of Rome's continued insistence on persecuting our kind, we feel the hand of destiny is upon us. It is time for us to join with Mankind to put aside our mutual hatred and distrust, to banish the suspicions of the past and work together to shape the future - to create an age of prosperity and security for all."

The room applauded, and she beamed. Waves of relief washed off the delegates, many visibly relaxing, refilling their glasses and drinking deeply.

"In this year of our Lord... *your* Lord... 1857, I am asking in all humility to allow us to join with you, to tender our sincere friendship. As you are all aware, we have immense wealth - our longevity has enabled us to wisely gather and increase our funds over decades, centuries indeed - and we are now prepared to free these funds, to invest in expanding your businesses, to launch new endeavours and enterprises with you, and place capital behind those political movements led by men of vision."

The greed level in the hall instantly increased and she took a moment to steady herself. It was saddening how much these fools were enslaved by worthless money.

It was difficult not to let her scorn show. If only they knew, she thought, if only they comprehended what pathetic puppets they would become. They would never know the dizzying scope of her ambitions until it was too late. For what she hadn't revealed was she'd already been busy - planting funds with groups who would cause chaos, anarchist cells and revolutionaries who would spread mayhem, bloodshed and dissention across Europe in the coming years. While the continent tore itself apart, The Brethren would take over - and its agents, those here tonight, would do their insidious, secretive work unchallenged and unobserved.

She swayed even more, increasingly giddy. The emotions of the assembled crowd gave off more psychic energy than she'd anticipated. It was making her light-headed.

Then, abruptly, she gasped as an intense, excruciating, throbbing bolt of agony stabbed into her.

The guests all looked stunned, muttering between themselves anxiously, bodyguards twitching unsure whether to reach for their weapons. Viktor was on his feet, concern clear.

Another pain - in her stomach, a fierce, cruel, searing stab of icy torture.

This time she couldn't help herself. She doubled over, puzzlement vying with suffering for possession of her numbing senses. Dumbfounded, she frantically scanned the room for an attacker, for the weapon, although no one had dared move. All were frozen, rooted by consternation.

The pain... oh the pain... it was unbearable...

What? What was happening? Who was doing this?

Viktor dashed towards her, his movement blurred and jerky. There were yells, confusion, worried shouts from all corners of the petrified and panicking crowd.

Except, those weren't the shrieks she was hearing. She was hearing female screams - far away, miles away - and a roar of anger and anguish... a male voice. One she knew so well.

He was in danger. Her son was in danger. The pain, the torment was his. There was a rapid, disjointed explosion of images, swimming in her mind - the psychic bond tugging at her, snatching her strength and sanity.

He was being attacked, fighting against several men. She could see momentary glimpses of faces, filled with hate, of fists poking and hitting. They had chains, manacles, and worse...

As she collapsed the full extent of his agony engulfed her, drowning her own senses and emotions.

Viktor cradled her head. She couldn't feel his touch or hear the words he was frantically mouthing. All she could see was the dark, growling, salivating shape coming towards her son, intent on tearing him apart. The beast reared... and she felt herself jolt and recoil as the mental link abruptly severed.

She couldn't help herself. The cry came from deep inside her heart, from the very essence of her being and burst from her lips as a marrow-chilling howl...

"Stefan!!!"

CHAPTER 6

Anton climbed the stairs unsteadily. A blurry glance at his fob watch revealed it was long past midnight. Although he knew he must sleep, he couldn't stop thinking about the rashness of the wild ideas forming in his imagination.

He'd left the cellblock with the men's curses ringing in his ears. The gaunt, black-hatted undertaker, looking more like a cadaver than many of his clientele, had carried out his duties with practised efficiency, measuring both prisoners for their coffins with a cold, appraising glance.

"A rush order like this will cost extra," he'd said, licking the end of his pencil before scribbling figures in a small, black book. "I'll have to work through the night to have the caskets ready."

"Simple plain pine is all I need," Anton had instructed. "No frills, no fuss. Keep the expense to the minimum."

Neither man had abused the undertaker, reserving their venom for the Marshal.

"Just as you stand in judgment of us so will you stand judgment in the fullness of time," Edward admonished. "And God will not forgive, not forget."

For a second, Anton considered the irony of having two people praying about him at the same time - the condemned man urging he be damned, Tomas pleading the Marshal be helped.

It would be a difficult outcome to predict, he thought with a wry shake of his head.

Tomas! He remembered he'd left the boy tending to Sofia hours ago. The lad must be going frantic.

"It's all right, Tomas," he began, opening the door, "I'm sorry I was—"

He stopped; puzzled. Sofia was alone, deep in a troubled slumber, the bowl lying on the floor, filled with rags nearly dry.

Anton felt a surge of annoyance. How dare the boy leave her side! Then, as rapidly, it dawned on him something wasn't right. Tomas was conscientious and devoted to his mistress.

A yelp brought Anton to. It came from the nearby bedroom, and he recognised the voice.

He covered the distance between both rooms in three strides, grabbing the handle. The door wouldn't budge.

"Tomas," he yelled, shaking the locked door violently. "Tomas!"

Another yelp, and the sound of a slap and something crashing to the floor.

"Kravnik," he bellowed. "Open this door. Open it right now. If you've—"

"Master!"

A single word, the fear it contained chilling Anton to his core.

"Open this bloody door or I'll break it down," he repeated.

Kravnik's voice, tense, also fearful, boomed. "This does not concern you, Yoska. Go away. Leave us alone."

Anton raised his boot, kicking hard. The frame quaked but didn't give. On the second determined attack the wood around the lock shattered and he fell into the room.

Fury doubling, he saw Kravnik, nightshirt hoisted over his hips, on top of the struggling boy. He had one hand over the lad's mouth and was fumbling with Tomas' breeches with the other.

"Get off him, you bastard," Anton roared, grabbing the nobleman by the shoulders and hurling him bodily across the room.

"Are you all right, Tomas? Are you all right, boy? What has this depraved bastard done to you?"

The lad was trembling, eyes brimming, teeth chattering. "He... he... he tried to..."

The words wouldn't come out. The lad dissolved into sobs. Closing his eyes, Anton hugged him, feeling the boy's body shake and sag.

Across the room, Kravnik glared. "It was not my fault," he declared, flustered yet defiant. "It was the boy. He led me on. He came to my room. Offered himself. Wanted money."

"That's not true!" Tomas gasped. "He dragged me here. Said I had no choice." The boy sniffed loudly. "He said he'd tell you I'd been stealing if I didn't... didn't..."

Anton didn't need to hear any more, telling the boy to leave. Gratefully, Tomas fled, pausing only to give the Count a look of pure hatred.

"You do not seriously believe," Kravnik blustered, "that I...? The boy is obviously a liar. You could see—"

"The only thing I can see," Anton said, voice low and threatening, "is it was a gross mistake to let you into my home."

He threw the Envoy hard against the wall. The man grunted in pain.

"I ought to beat you into a pulp," he barked into the aristocrat's alarmed face. "You deserve a good hiding. And I'd like nothing better than to give it to you."

Kravnik gasped. "Only you won't, will you, Lord Marshal? Not if you want to keep your position. Not if you want to keep your head attached to your shoulders."

The nobleman's expression filled with contempt. For a moment, Anton felt a burning violent impulse. Then, bitter reality intervened. He wasn't going to hit the man, no matter how much the degenerate's actions justified it. For that would be suicide. It would be his word, a humble lawman, against the Crown Prince's favourite; the court darling.

"You know, Yoska, you are a fool. You never know what is good for you," Kravnik observed, as Anton let go of the expensive silk nightshirt and stepped back. "You never know when to look the other way, when to learn to go along with events, when it is politic to please your betters."

"Like standing aside and letting you molest a boy?"

The man didn't reply, merely rubbed his shoulder.

"Or do you mean, acquiescing when Leopold extorts extra taxes from his starving subjects, or exterminates them on a whim?"

The Count snorted contemptuously. "Have you ever wondered, Lord Marshal, why you are stuck in a poor, shit-splattered, forgotten outpost like this? Why a man of your talents and reputation has every request for transfer refused?"

Kravnik stretched across to the bedside table and took a sip from the glass of sherry. Anton noted in irritation that the Envoy had helped himself to his drinks cabinet. Just like he'd tried to help himself to other things he had a desire for.

"Do you know what the Crown Prince says about you? *'I have Anton Yoska exactly where I want him.'*"

The Count swirled the liquid. "And he does, does he not? Under the thumb. Rotting away in obscurity. Safely away where you cannot cause any trouble."

Anton regarded him frigidly. "Is there a point to this?"

"Merely that you are man who is out of favour at Court, and that is a very lonely place to be."

"There are lonelier places," Anton countered. "Especially for people with unnatural tastes. People who wouldn't want those tastes made public."

The threat registered. Kravnik gave a half nod. "Tonight's misunderstanding was *unfortunate*," he agreed. "It would best be forgotten."

"And what if I don't want to forget it?"

The Envoy took a gulp of sherry, relishing its flavour before responding. "I thought you might overlook tonight's *indiscretion* because you need a friend at Court. Someone to represent your interests, someone with influence."

Anton gave a bitter laugh. "A friend at Court? You? Why would you think I'd want a friend like you? You disgust me."

Neither said anything for a moment, then the Count sighed heavily.

"It is not a proposition I will repeat," he confirmed, making it clear the conversation was at an end. "I will expect your silence regardless. Anything less and I can promise you, it will be particularly unpleasant."

With that, the nobleman began climbing back into bed.

Migraine flaring again, Anton stormed out of the room. Re-entering Sofia's bedroom, he noticed with relief she seemed quieter, her anguished murmurs silent. Kissing her clammy forehead, he sat, head dipping.

He knew two things with unwavering certainty. He was so agitated sleep would be an impossibility and, more importantly, he would have to tell the undertaker to construct an extra coffin, luxurious and expensive... fit for a nobleman.

CHAPTER 7

Her giddiness had passed, yet the memory of the acute pain lingered. Nothing Kristina Modjeski could do diminished her anguish or the indignation growing with each passing hour.

She glided along the riverside path to the mill house, convinced wherever he'd been taken, Stefan was in extreme danger. Vampires were more difficult to destroy than mortals. Even so, it didn't make them impervious to attack, or to torture. Stefan had been suffering horrendously when the mental link between mother and son had abruptly severed.

Sending her puzzled, badly shaken guests home with excuses she'd suffered minor stomach spasms from ingesting impure blood, Kristina had rested until the psychic shock had faded. Then she'd let her heightened psychic senses search out for him, unsuccessfully. Stefan wasn't dead, she'd have felt it, but he was unconscious or some distance beyond the range of her powers. That meant his abductors were professionals, aware of the mental rapport, and had drugged him, spiriting him away as swiftly as possible.

She paused, closely examining the two bloated bodies in the stream. Their injuries were brutal, frenzied and lacking in finesse. Stefan's trademark.

No matter how much she tried to impress on him the need for secrecy and stealth, he was headstrong and hedonistic, taking his pleasures blatantly, without regard for the consequences. It was this passion, this single minded instinct and lack of restraint that endeared him to her. It was also what made him so dangerous to the clan.

She'd tried countless times to explain the vital importance of not drawing unnecessary attention, of avoiding repercussions.

"Why worry," he'd mocked, "when we are untouchable; invincible? We can pick the mortals like fruit from the trees and there is nothing they can do about it. It is our right to indulge any whim, satisfy any hunger or desire. We are gods."

Although seductive it was a perilously naïve view, she reminded herself as she hurried along the path. The Brethren were parasites, and Mankind would only tolerate parasites to the point where they became a real threat to the host and then, she knew, the humans would stop at nothing to eradicate them.

The open doorway beckoned. In the candlelight, shadows danced as those inside moved about silently, going about their search.

She noted the wooden surround was badly scratched and smeared with fresh blood. Running her finger across the red stain she brought it to her tongue and tasted.

It was Stefan's. His image came into sharp focus in her mind. She concentrated, pushing her mental faculties to their limit. Still nothing. His mind was blocked to her.

She stepped inside, taking in the devastation in an instant. There were all the signs of a pitched battle - furniture toppled, crockery smashed and scattered, food strewn around, straw and discarded clothing everywhere. Stefan had obviously put up a desperate struggle. Her son was immensely strong, capable of bestial fury, so the gang must have been large or very well armed.

Then she saw the walls and understood. More scratches; deep, raw, long, gouged. Not human, not nosferatu, something else; something immensely powerful, possessing fierce, slashing claws.

"Over here," Viktor summoned. "There's more."

Her consort and his men were staring at two naked corpses lying in the debris. Females: blonde and once beautiful, now frozen in grimace, bodies twisted, the obvious results of dying in agony.

One had a short wooden pole projecting at an angle from her blood-stained chest, the wood whittled and tapered. A prepared stake. A slayer's tool. On her head was an ugly burn, a scar in the shape of the cross.

The other, yards away, was staked too. That was where the similarities ended. This one was gagged, arms bound to the legs of an overturned table, legs splayed, her breasts bruised and bitten, thighs cut and battered; stained red up high where her private parts were ruptured and torn.

Kristina fought the bile surging up from her stomach. Trembling, she pictured what had happened. She didn't need psychic powers to tell the degradation, violence and terror the girl had been through. She'd seen countless similar atrocities like this over the decades, the unspeakable defilement that befell lone female *nocternus* captured by their foe.

"They were very thorough," Viktor said, voice hoarse and filled with revulsion.

"As shall we," Kristina promised, "when we take our revenge."

She ordered the bodies to be taken outside, saying: "The dawn's first rays will take care of them."

With a last scanning look, she decided to depart. There were no clues here, nothing physical that pointed to where Stefan had been taken; the location also barren of psychic residue.

Back outside in the cool night air, she scanned the darkness. Which way? Which direction had they gone? Towards the Capitol? Deeper into the dense countryside? Or were they headed for the border?

The gang were obviously more than common assassins, she deduced. If so they'd have slaughtered Stefan right there and chopped off his head to use as evidence to claim the customary vampire bounty.

No, they were more than the usual mindless slaughtering scum. They understood Stefan's importance; aware of his true value.

So, where would they go? What would they do?

The faint shimmer was so low mortal eyes wouldn't have registered it. To Kristina it was a beacon.

Veering, she headed towards the bushes.

Glimmers of dirty white flickered through the tangled undergrowth - the fading aura of a man recently expired.

In an instant, her anguish and doubt evaporated, replaced by an icy pleasure.

Professionals - but not infallible.

The body was badly mauled, most of the throat missing. In addition, it bore other signs of extreme violence - injuries that hadn't been inflicted by Stefan.

On the left temple a round bloody hole showed where the musket shot had entered, powder burns testament to the closeness of the gun. On the right side of the skull, four inches higher, a gaping smashed flap splattered with grey mush, evidence of where the lead ball had exited with explosive force.

"A powerful weapon," Viktor observed, as he joined her.

"Used with precision," Kristina agreed.

By ruthless men, they both understood.

Rather than leave behind an injured comrade, they'd executed him in such a way to ensure maximum damage and guarantee he couldn't be re-animated.

A pity. A great pity. She'd have enjoyed the delicious cruelty of keeping him on the edge of death, in a torment beyond human endurance, sanity destroyed in a frenzy of terror.

Still, there was one way he could be of use.

She reached down, thrusting through his chest and tugged. The still warm heart tore out easily, bringing dangling, dripping nerves and blood vessels with it.

Holding it aloft like a trophy, she savoured the alluring smell. Then, positioning it above Viktor's open mouth, squeezed with might. The dark, crimson liquid cascaded over his lips, his chin, his clothes.

He moaned in appreciation.

Then it was her turn. Gulping greedily, she felt it pour down her throat. The taste was exquisite, distinctive, a rare indulgence. Hunter's blood, the very best. Rich, gamey, full bodied... and tinged with regret.

CHAPTER 8

Anton squinted in the bleak lamplight, carefully examining the curls of rope strewn across the table. The coarse jute cords felt rough, the fibres tightly matted and unyielding. They wouldn't snap, wouldn't fail. Perfect for the gruesome task ahead.

A shadow fell over him. Pavel, the younger of his two deputies, stood in the storeroom entrance. He looked past the Marshal, at the twin lengths of rope and the nooses Anton had just fashioned from them.

"I've never been to a hanging before," the young man said, voice quivering. "Never seen a man executed. They say - they say it's a horrible way to go."

"They're right," Anton agreed, wishing he hadn't been to dozens of chilling executions over the years. "It's ugly and cruel, and there's no dignity or nobility about it - not for the man who's dying or the poor wretch who must be hangman."

Pavel gulped, acne-spotted face wan and tired. Anton suspected, like himself, the deputy had barely slept, thoughts plagued by hideous images of what lay ahead.

The boy was barely twenty, hadn't properly seen life and now he was going to witness death, Anton thought bitterly. Violent and senseless death.

"Marshal? Have you ever... ever hanged anyone before?"

The question made Anton's heart miss a beat. He looked out the window at the darkness, fought to push away the irresistible swell of memories; the terrified faces, the screams, the accusing ghosts.

"Yes," he replied, feeling self-loathing. "And I promised myself I'd never do it again."

He coiled the ropes and put them over his shoulders, grunting with the weight, ready to head out to the courtyard. Pavel didn't move, staring distractedly.

"They say it is agony," the deputy murmured, half to himself. "A man can twist and swing for half an hour, choking, twitching, the rope burning in."

"If you do it right, the neck snaps instantly," Anton informed the young man. "However, if that doesn't happen it takes a long time to choke to death, and yes, it's messy and it's bloody and there's no worse way to die."

He was going to add he'd do his best to ensure the two brothers expired instantly, but Pavel wasn't listening. The deputy was in the corridor, throwing up.

Anton watched, stonily, pushing away thoughts of sympathy for the novice lawman. There wasn't time for weak stomachs or doubts.

"Finished?" he asked as, coughing, Pavel raised his head and wiped his glistening, soiled lips.

The deputy nodded.

"Good," Anton replied, "because I've got a task for you. And you need to hurry."

Something about Anton's piercing glare prevented any questions and as he explained the errand to Pavel, the Marshal thought his underling might throw up again.

"There can't be any mistakes, any slip-ups," he stressed, grabbing the youth's shoulder so hard his fingers dug into the skin, "because it'll be the most important thing you've ever done."

The wagon bucked alarmingly as Quintz jerked harder on the reins, the horses sliding in the mud as their hooves fought desperately for purchase. The whole rig vibrated violently as they sped along the uneven forest track. The wheels bounced, wobbling over rocks and treacherous ruts in the ground, the dwarf refusing to lessen the breakneck pace. The gang had been running half the night, cutting deeper and deeper into thickly wooded territory, racing dangerously between the trees, narrowly missing them in the impenetrable darkness; racing for the dawn and the comparative safety it promised.

They had to burn the miles, he knew, they had to keep up the speed. Even now the creature's kin would be on their tail, devil riders hammering after them in uncontrollable fury, covering the ground faster on their blazing-eyed hell steeds, and more surely than the mercenaries with their lumbering, loaded cart.

If the *infernal* pursuers caught up before first light...

Shivering at the thought he let the horses feel the lash. Their galloping increased, heads bobbing, nostrils wide, breath coming out in flaring puffs.

Beside him, Gregor held on frantically, being jostled and thrown around the seat.

"You've got to slow down," the old man yelled. "You'll kill us all."

"I won't need to," the dwarf said, out of the corner of his mouth, "if the Modjeski get their hands on us."

Quintz flashed a questioning look at Milosh who was riding alongside. The gang leader's expression was set hard, determined. He gestured back for the small man to keep using the whip.

Maintaining her position at a steady gallop just behind Milosh, Irina appeared anxious, whether from their immediate predicament or her annoyance, Quintz couldn't tell.

She'd been unhappy back at the mill house. Not because of the appalling atrocity Johann had performed on the captive girl, him leering, rushing back inside, unfastening his belt buckle just moments before her screams rent the air. No, that didn't cause her any concern - to the point where she'd ignored Gregor's disgusted pleas to intervene, with the impassive response: "She is no longer human. No longer deserving of any pity."

"But, as a fellow woman," Gregor argued, "surely, you can't just stand back and let—"

"She's no longer a woman. She is a thing, an object," she'd stated icily. "Beyond compassion. Why should I care what happens to an object?"

No, Irina's annoyance was that they'd lost a gang member. With Theodore gone, they were down to only five and that put the venture in jeopardy. As if the dangers weren't extreme enough already.

Some twenty or so yards forward, Johann kept his body low, leaning in close to the head of his galloping mount. Riding point, he'd been leading the way through the murk for nearly two hours, occasionally shouting back warnings about protruding tree roots or unexpected twists in the path.

His voice clearly betrayed exhilaration. He was relishing the adrenalin surge, the drama, the relentless pounding pace; digging in his shiny, army-issue spurs, making his horse flinch. Quintz suspected the scar-faced rider was reliving memories of old cavalry charges and past glories.

What was it Milosh had once said about his young, restless, rake-thin protégé? Johann was too unstable for the Imperial Guard. Too impulsive. He enjoyed the violence just that little bit too much, his glee unnerving the other troopers and terrifying the officers.

He attacked on a whim, taking offence at the merest slight, whether real or imagined. Only the influence of Theodore had kept him under control, and now Theodore was gone.

Most chillingly, Johann had absolutely no conscience. Just like the rest of us, Quintz reminded himself. All except Gregor. All except the preacher man.

He risked a glimpse upwards, seeing the first hint of light far in the distance. It was hardly luminosity - not in the sense of white, welcoming illumination, more a black less dense and huddled than the surrounding inkiness. Encouragingly, it was a promise of the growing redness to come. He allowed himself a moment of hope. Maybe they might just get away with it. Just maybe their pursuers would call off the chase, turning back or at least taking shelter from the sunlight's deadly rays for a few precious hours... the vital head-start the gang desperately needed.

A shouted order from Milosh had Quintz yank back on the reins. The rickety buggy slew sideways, rear wheels swinging out to the left as the horses responded, slowing abruptly. He pulled on the large handbrake, having to stand precariously on the bouncing seat to get sufficient leverage. The pads rubbed against the wooden wheel rims, a flurry of small sparks leaping into the night, the acrid stench of burning assailing his nostrils.

Even with the brake on full, the contraption careered onwards for more than fifty feet, nearly toppling as it swung to a complete halt where two forest roads intersected.

"Shit!" he exclaimed over the noise of the panting team of stallions. "I thought we were going to tip over there. That was too close."

Gregor gave him a filthy look. Making a show of muttering thanks to the Almighty for his deliverance, the old man examined himself for bruises.

"You're demented, little man, you know that?" he grumbled. "You drive like a lunatic. It's a fully-loaded wagon, not a damn chariot."

Quintz grinned dismissively, telling him: "If you don't like it you can always ride on a horse. Though I doubt at your age you'd be able to keep up. And you know what happens to those who fall behind."

"Make him walk if he doesn't like it," Johann shouted over, with a disturbing grin. "See how long he lasts."

Ignoring the tense exchange, Milosh slowly circled the immediate area, warily searching into the darkness.

"We'll rest up here for a while," he announced. "It's too exposed for my liking, but they say *infernals* are loath to approach crossroads."

Irina rode to his side. "Even if it's true, we're not safe anywhere," she insisted. "We've got to keep going."

"Not at this pace," he answered, dismounting and taking a long swig from a hipflask. "We'll wear out the horses. They need rest. We've got to stop for a few minutes."

Quintz felt the vehicle rock. Under its heavy, dark canvas there was movement.

"Get back there and find out what's going on," Milosh ordered Johann. "If it's our guest, give it another dose of the potion. We can't risk him breaking loose."

He threw the young man a club. "Use this if necessary."

"It'll be a pleasure," Johann replied menacingly, giving it a test swing.

Milosh jerked his head to Quintz. "You go look too. Make sure your little pet is okay, only don't feed it. I want it starving and inches from him."

With a brusque nod, Quintz clambered awkwardly from the running board and headed around the back. He heard Irina tell Milosh: "If we've got to stop, we should put the time to good use. We should get Gregor to say a few words. For Theodore. To mark his passing."

Beside him at the rear of the cart, Quintz sensed Johann's body tighten. Johann and Theodore had been like brothers. No one had dared broach the subject of their comrade's death in front of him until now, worried what reaction it would provoke.

At the mention of Theodore's name Johann twitched and the ex-trooper quickened his stride, pulling back the canvas flaps angrily. He raised the club to strike their captive.

"No!" Quintz protested. "Don't!"

It did no good. The cudgel struck repeatedly, clanking through the metal bars of the cage concealed under the heavy drape. Its occupant recoiled with each blow. Quintz knew the chained and bound male nosferatu was already too far gone - too badly mauled, scratched, gashed and beaten - to register more pain. Nevertheless, that didn't mean it couldn't be fatally wounded.

"That's enough," he rumbled.

Johann ignored him, landing two more cruel thuds.

"I said, that's enough!" Quintz repeated, more insistently and Johann halted in mid attack, startled, looking down to where a knife point now jabbed into his belly.

"Don't make me," the dwarf warned.

Johann sucked in sharply. It made his stomach contract, not enough though to present any safety from the cold steel.

"You're a treacherous little bastard," he said, just above a whisper.

"A treacherous little bastard with a big nasty blade," Quintz corrected. "Plus the guts and skill to use it."

The larger man regarded him with loathing and grudging respect, spitting contemptuously at the other's feet. "Funny, I never had you down as a vampire lover. All freaks together, is that it?"

Quintz ignored the insult. He'd heard worse, far worse, from those who swiftly learnt to regret their jeers - some merely losing their tongues - others not so lucky.

"I'm just safeguarding my investment," he replied, pressing the knife harder so his fellow bounty hunter grimaced. "The reward is for the bloodsucker alive - or as alive as these things can be. You kill it and we get nothing. Understand?"

His companion didn't answer.

Quintz jabbed harder, drawing a thin line of blood. "Theodore is dead. Just accept it. Destroying the creature won't bring him back." He paused as a pleasing thought dawned on him. "Maybe you should be grateful. Thanks to it, we all now get a bigger split."

Except for the fact the ex-soldier would have been impaled by any sudden move, Quintz knew Johann would have throttled him without compunction.

"I should break your puny little body into bits," he rumbled, so vehemently Quintz felt the full blast of his hot, angry breath.

"Any time you want to try, I'll oblige you," the dwarf answered, unfazed, "and my sharp friend here and I will make sure it becomes a four-way split."

Johann's eyes flared but Milosh's noisy footsteps stopped any further action.

"Break it up," he ordered both men, tapping the butt of his firearm meaningfully. "I don't want to hear another squeak out of either of you. Just sort the bloodsucker so we can get rolling again."

With a cold grin, Quintz withdrew the knife. Johann didn't move for a moment, looking like he'd still like to maim the dwarf. "Know what, half measure, you're not worth the effort." He threw the vial of opiate to Quintz. "If you care about the leech so much, you take care of it."

It took a few moments to dose the captive, and check on his other cruel charge. Satisfied both were adequately sedated and wouldn't be giving any more trouble for a while, Quintz gazed at his blade, inspecting the shiny wetness of Johann's blood.

Reaching inside the two separate sections of the large cage, he wiped the sticky crimson residue on the bars at each end. Grunting with amusement, he watched both his passengers snuffle, nostrils curling searchingly, as they slumbered.

"Remember it well," he urged them, words soft and lilting like the sweetest lullaby. "Remember the smell, my deadly darlings, and dream - dream of its promise."

Gregor was flicking through his bible, looking for a suitable passage, as Quintz re-joined the group.

"We should have given him a proper Christian burial," the old man said, reproachfully.

Quintz almost laughed. What a crazy thing to worry about. They'd all been content to let Milosh shoot their critically wounded companion; even Johann had acquiesced. It was what they'd agreed must happen if any of them became severely injured and put the entire group in peril. Yet, ironically, not stopping to dig a grave offended the God-botherer more than the hastily expedient execution.

"Look," Milosh grunted, unconcerned, "there wasn't time to drop his sorry carcass into a hole in the ground. Theodore knew the score. You can bet if things had gone the other way he wouldn't have hung around long enough to bury any of you."

He sniffed, adding: "Our comrade's gone, just food for the crows, and it makes no damn difference to him or us what fancy words you want to read out of that story book. So forget the sermon, and saddle up. We've a long way to travel and precious little time."

"We're still going ahead with the original plan?" Irina asked, her incredulity obvious.

"Of course," Milosh replied.

"Only, with Theodore dead, I thought..."

"You thought?"

"We'd cut our losses, head for the Capitol, make a dash for it. Try to outrun them."

He looked thoughtfully at the rickety, ancient signpost at the far side of the crossroads. "That's what they'll expect. They'd cut us down before we even got half way."

Striding purposefully through the mud and puddles, he approached the tilting, weather-beaten post and jabbed his finger at the crooked wooden arm pointing north east. It would take the gang into the dark heart of the country, as far away from the city as possible.

"Nothing has changed," he announced. "We head this way."

"To where?" Gregor queried, revealing their leader hadn't trusted everyone with the details.

"To call on an old friend," Milosh replied, with a strange smirk, unnerving in its iciness.

"To call on an old friend?" the old man repeated. "I don't understand. Why?"

Milosh gestured for one of the others to answer.

"To take care of some unfinished business," Johann volunteered cryptically.

This still didn't help. Gregor's lined forehead became even more puckered. "What are you talking about? What business could possibly involve seizing an *infernal*?"

"The most deadly of all," Quintz explained softly. "The most thrilling, satisfying and profitable of all possible businesses..."

He sighed wistfully.

"Vengeance."

CHAPTER 9

For generations the challenging geography of Brejnei had been, depending on your point of view, a blessing or a sinister trap. Located on the north bank of the slow, meandering Mosna River, the settlement occupied a teardrop-shaped promontory created by a pronounced loop in the wide, lazy waterway. This natural moat meant anyone approaching from the woodlands of the south had to cross a rickety wooden bridge to gain access.

Those travellers approaching from the bleak north faced a barrier even more daunting - a range of inhospitable granite peaks that, together with their flinty foothills, wrapped around the rear of the settlement on three sides, as much a city wall as any structure built by man.

Most of Brejnei's inhabitants appreciated the forbidding topography, seeing the river and mountains as protectors, keeping those inside in an encircling hug, safe from the prying eyes of outsiders who'd force change and question the inhabitants' fervently-held beliefs.

For Anton, the combined effect of water and stone made the place feel more like a prison. He considered the icy crags as intimidating giants keeping the town trapped in time, dark watchers staring down with stony hearts on those poor ignorant, superstitious souls they held in their unbreakable grip.

Now, with the first crimson rays of morning silhouetting the jaggedly looming outlines and painting the snow-crested ridges a sickly cerise, he knew he was right. They may be majestic, but there was nothing benign about the summits.

Shivering at the biting wind howling down from their desolate slopes bludgeoning along the frosty streets, he pulled his coat more tightly around him. Narrowing his eyes, he watched as a solitary hunched figure trudged along the main thoroughfare, boots squelching through the churned-up mire, coming closer with each passing tread. The man walked tiredly, a stooped silhouette in the watery sun.

"Is it done?" Anton asked, as the figure eventually drew level with him.

His deputy nodded.

"And no one saw you?"

"No," Pavel replied.

"You're sure? You're positive you weren't seen?"

"It was deserted. Not a soul around."

Relaxing a little, Anton gave him a pat on the shoulder, muttering: "Good lad" and bundled the young man into the jailhouse's cobbled courtyard, both of them shoving the gates shut behind them, dropping the heavy crossbeam into place.

"I did exactly what you asked," Pavel told him, as they headed back into the storeroom, "I didn't expect it would be such hard work. I'm exhausted." He stifled a yawn. "What I don't get is why you—"

The Marshal paused in mid stride, and immediately put a finger to his lips, motioning for silence.

Although the approaching footfall was soft, deliberately stealthy, Anton had good hearing, especially when it was the unmistakable squeak of expensive leather boots.

Raising his voice, he immediately grabbed Pavel's arm and shook him violently, the deputy almost stumbling in surprise.

"I won't have it, do you hear me, boy?" he scolded. "Fetch a mop and a pail of water. Get rid of it. The stench is disgusting."

Appearing from the shadows Kravnik didn't acknowledge either man, instead approaching the pile of congealed vomit on the floor.

"Ah, now that is embarrassing," he observed, with a scornful sigh. "I thought lawmen were supposed to be tough, with ice in their veins and stomachs of iron. It seems I am mistaken. How depressing."

Anton's nerves tightened. Had the nobleman overheard them? Had he spotted Pavel's furtive return to the Marshal's residence?

For several moments, Kravnik said nothing. Circling the large stain, he paced like a cat, with deadly elegance.

Anton went taut. Come on, you bastard, say something, he thought fiercely. If you saw, if you heard, just say. Don't play games.

After twenty agonising seconds, Kravnik stopped, exhaling in disdain, telling Pavel: "I would get to it, as the Lord Marshal says. Clean up this filth. We do not want anyone else learning how delicate you are, now do we?"

Damn it, Anton reflected as Pavel scurried away. That had been close. He'd hoped the Count would stay out of his way until it was time for the executions. Apparently Kravnik wanted to oversee every detail, drawing sadistic enjoyment from the growing tension.

He studied the aristocrat for signs the man felt remorse for last night's outrage and saw nothing. Kravnik was well slept, alert, and had obviously eaten a huge breakfast. Even now, he clutched a half-full coffee cup in his podgy fingers.

"The arrangements are progressing well, I trust?" The innocent question crackled with implied threat.

"Everything is going to schedule," Anton answered, motioning to the nooses hanging on the heavy hooks. "You'll get your hangings, don't worry."

"And the prisoners? They had a satisfying breakfast?" Kravnik enquired, taking a noisy slurp.

"Yes."

"Good, good. I am a great believer in the traditions, in doing things correctly. The condemned man had a hearty meal, that sort of thing."

With a mental picture of what Kravnik had put away into his cavernous belly just minutes before, Anton murmured: "Yes, I couldn't agree more, Count. The condemned man should enjoy a hearty last meal."

There was silence for a moment and Anton feared he'd said too much. Thankfully, Kravnik didn't respond.

"As for my own repast, it can best be described as adequate," he complained. "You keep a humble table, Lord Marshal. I thought with me here you would have made the effort." He grimaced. "It was served to me by some sour-faced cook. I was disappointed not to be looked after by the boy. What is his name - Tomas?"

Anton looked searchingly at the man to see if he was deliberately trying to provoke. The Count's expression was inscrutable.

"I thought it best if Tomas rested," he answered. "He was badly shaken."

"Probably very wise," Kravnik agreed non-committally. He tapped the side of his mouth, thoughtfully. "I must say,

Yoska, I am pleased to be spared you making some tear-soaked, heart-tugging last-minute clemency appeal for the poachers."

"There's no point. They are doomed. You've made that clear."

Anton hefted one of the two nooses off the metal clasp and held it to the Envoy. "So let's get on with it."

The nobleman regarded the rope for a second as if it were a coiled snake.

"I would love to assist you, Lord Marshal. Alas, as you can see..." He gestured to the now empty cup. "...my hands are full."

His head swam. Inside his befuddled skull images danced and tumbled, colours exploded, sounds collided in discordant battle while myriad pulsating shapes and forms merged and twisted into a kaleidoscope of random meaning and sensation.

In the whirlpool of confusion, a tiny part of him - in his battered and besieged inner core - fought to regain control; knew he'd been drugged and that chemicals were scrambling his thoughts, making him hallucinate.

There was more - pain; intense, remorseless, merciless pain that stabbed, clawed and stung. Bruises, gashes and rips in his flesh all throbbed in torment, made even more unbearable by the unrelenting pounding to his bones as he was bounced and jolted repeatedly.

Wherever he was, whatever was happening, he felt his body in motion; shaken violently. Every few moments, there would be a jar from below rippling agony through his whole frame.

A wagon? Was he on a wagon? If so, why was it going so quickly?

The firework display detonating inside his cranium distorted his vision. It seemed dark. Pitch dark, unnaturally dark. Not the gentle, cocooning black of night, but something man-made and sinister. No matter how much he tried to prise open his throbbing eyes and look, he couldn't pierce the impenetrable gloom. Yet, he could sense light above - blinding, hungry, remorseless sunlight - searching for him, desperate to engulf and destroy him with its deadly warmth, only inches away on the other side of the dusty material.

There was a bewildering smell too, a rank animal stink, the odours of fur, rotting meat and fetid breath, combined with the choking stench of piss and shit. Even as he recoiled and struggled, he realised he was shackled - sharp iron digging into his already abused and weakened body. He couldn't escape, couldn't even move.

He stretched his fingers, feeling more steel. First one smooth strong bar, then a gap, then another, repeating as far as he could reach. A cage. He was in a cage.

Focusing, he remembered - disjointed fragments emerging despite the opiate's dizzying, powerful, mind-altering effects.

Bounty hunters, an ambush, the agony and terror as they manacled and beat him.

He was Stefan. He was special, superior, and glorious. He was nosferatu. He lived to hunt and feast. He instilled fear and awe.

Yet all that was secondary, a mere detail compared to his true magnificence. He was Modjeski!

Willing the churning shapes and colours to still in his mind, he focused. He must regain control, cut through the delirium, think clearly. He had to summon help, make contact.

He reached out with every fibre of his consciousness, projecting his thoughts.

A picture of Kristina appeared, and he targeted his mental emanations towards her, calling to the woman he considered his mother, his protector.

THEY ARE HOLDING ME LIKE AN ANIMAL. I'M CAGED, BATTERED AND ALONE. I DON'T KNOW WHERE I AM AND IN CERTAIN DANGER. SAVE ME, MOTHER. COME AND GET ME BEFORE IT IS TOO LATE. SAVE ME, SAVE YOUR SON...

Despite the dullness and drowsiness, the dampening effects of the potions, he pushed the emotionally potent thoughts out for miles. Although the psychic cry travelled straight and true, he couldn't feel her receive it. He began to panic. Why wasn't she connecting? Why was there no soft, reassuring presence in his mind? Why wasn't she there?

MOTHER, he pushed harder, *HEAR ME. HEAR ME NOW. I NEED YOU. I NEED YOUR HELP.*

As his pleas went unnoticed, his apprehension magnified, and Stefan Modjeski knew his terrifying ordeal had just begun. For across the tar-dark cage, he sensed the other occupant - sedated for the trip – stir, sniff the air and growl: low, deep and ravenous.

CHAPTER 10

Frowning, Anton pressed his ear against the gates. It didn't make sense - there was no sound on the other side. He'd expected an excited clamour, the racket of a large crowd gathering, buzzing with anticipation, eager to witness the coming spectacle and to jeer and shout. Not this eerie silence.

He glanced at the large clock high on the courtyard wall, its ornate brass hands pointing ominously to the last quarter of the hour. Fifteen minutes to nine. Surely word of the impending executions would have spread by now, the undertaker's gossiping lips guaranteed to do their work?

"You look perplexed," Kravnik said, breaking into his thoughts. "Is something amiss?"

Anton didn't know how to respond. "Perhaps. I'm not sure." He stroked his chin in thought. "No. It's fine. I'm just being jittery."

Ignoring the Count's scornful expression, he focused his attention on the two men in front of him, both tense, gripping short barrel flintlocks. "All set?" he asked.

Nicku grunted coarsely while Pavel gave a thumbs-up, jerky and nervous.

"Okay," Anton said, "get the prisoners out."

The brothers stood, clutching the bars of their cells, knuckles white. Pieter, the younger brother, had been crying, eyes puffy and red. Edward looked stoic enough, but Anton suspected he could burst into a rage at any moment.

"It's up to you," Anton explained. "We can do this with the leg irons, chains, handcuffs - the whole rigmarole. Or I can simply tie your wrists. It's up to you. Are you going to give me any trouble?"

Pieter stared at the floor, shaking his head.

Edward met his gaze, expression unchanged. Anton sensed the condemned man was looking inside his captor's soul, trying to comprehend what kind of cruel, callous being could do something like this.

Don't look for my soul, Anton thought, because you won't find one. I lost it a long time ago.

"Edward?" he prompted after long, awkward moments.

The poacher inhaled deeply. "Does it make any difference?"

"Your families..." Anton began, "it would be less distressing for them. If you weren't chained and manacled."

The man curled his lip. "What does it matter? We're to dance the hangman's jig. Do you believe my wife will be any less devastated just because I'm not wearing chains?"

No, Anton agreed, yet it might at least give the men a shred of dignity in their last few minutes. Edward's cold, unflinching stare showed the man cared little.

He came to a decision.

"Only bind their hands," he instructed Pavel. "I don't want this to be any more of a circus than it needs to be."

He sensed Kravnik behind him.

"Is that wise, Yoska? I would consider a degree of caution to be in order. I would not wish to be in your position if something happens. If they escape..."

Anton met his challenging stare. "If you'd like, I'd be happy for you to fit the manacles on them personally. If you feel our security precautions aren't sufficient."

The nobleman didn't feel the comment worthy of response, gesturing in irritation to get on with it.

Nicku unlocked the cellblock and they walked through to the courtyard in single file, Kravnik and Pavel in front, the two brothers in the middle with Anton behind. As soon as he'd locked the door behind them, Nicku joined the Marshal at the back of the group.

Six horses waited, already saddled, wooden steps in place beside the steeds to be ridden by the prisoners. With tied wrists the brothers would struggle to mount the horses. The blocks were necessary to give them extra height.

Kravnik had suggested using a cart to transport the brothers. Anton vetoed the idea. It was cumbersome and slow, he'd argued, and too easy for any restive crowd to block.

Although a powerful argument, the Count had looked bemused, asking: "And afterwards? How then will you transport the bodies?"

Anton's voice had become sterner. "Don't you worry, Count. Leave me to deal with dead men and the consequences."

The lawmen opened the gates, blinking as much in surprise as from the daylight flooding in. There was no raucous waiting crowd, just an empty, windswept street. Something wasn't right. Where were the gawping onlookers, those who wouldn't pass up the spectacle and vicarious thrill?

"We should call this off," he declared to the envoy.

"I fail to see why," Kravnik challenged.

"It's too quiet. Something's brewing."

The Count gave him a withering look. "Last night you warned we risked a riot. You painted pictures of a blood-hungry mob, awaiting just one small spark to burst into a conflagration of violence and rebellion."

He pointed along the deserted road leading to the square where the hanging tree waited ominously - wide boughs like outstretched arms. "Yet, see for yourself. There is no danger to our person, no gauntlet to run. Your beloved citizenry clearly do not care."

Every nerve in Anton's body tingled with alarm. He motioned Pavel to take point, with the warning: "Keep your eyes peeled."

With every shop and business closed, each home locked, windows boarded and shuttered, Brejnei looked neglected and forlorn. The growing gusts of bitter wind served to reinforce the feeling, blowing scraps of paper and other rubbish across the dusty street in a whirling dance while making the raised walkway boards rattle and shake.

What was the expression? A one-horse town. To Anton it felt even more hopeless; lost, poor and fly-flown.

Whether edgy on his own account or picking up on the Marshal's uneasiness, Pavel edged his horse forward gingerly, his head constantly moving as he scanned the route.

Sixty feet on, he halted, gesturing it was safe to follow. At that instant it began. A single jarring clank rang out from an upstairs window, followed rapidly by a second and third.

Pavel gave a start, almost falling from his steed, reaching for his weapon, unsure where to aim.

"No!" The Marshal's voice was shrill. "Don't fire."

With that, he dug his spurs into his mount and swiftly joined his deputy, eyes flitting from one building to another seeking out the threat.

Another metallic clank, even louder.

Bringing up his own gun to shoulder height, Anton frantically searched for a target, trying to determine both the nature of the attack and its source. But he could see no one.

The next boom was only feet away and Nicku shouted, pointing to a set of shutters above the general store. As Anton looked, the thick wooden panels rumbled again, hit with such force from inside they seemed ready to burst off their hinges.

"Stay here," he instructed the young man and circled back to the party guarding the prisoners.

"We need to call this off, right now," he told Kravnik.

The Count made a face. "Out of the question. Tell me, are we under attack?"

"No, not directly."

"Then why ever should we be deflected from our task? No missiles have been thrown. No shots fired. No one has even dared show their faces. Surely, you do not propose to allow a few childish noises to frighten you."

Anton's face darkened. "It's not the bangs that worry me. It's what they signify."

Kravnik looked puzzled. "Signify?"

"They're a signal. We're about to be ambushed."

CHAPTER 11

Telling both deputies not to open fire unless they saw definite movement from the upper storeys, he looked imploringly at Kravnik. "I haven't got enough men for this."

The Count's expression tightened. "That is not my concern. The executions go ahead. Nothing has changed. The sentence will be carried out. I will not be deterred by any imagined threat."

Imagined?

For a second Anton thought he'd heard wrongly. Even now he knew attackers were working out the best moment to spring out and overwhelm the small execution party.

Swiftly he calculated his possible courses of action. Kravnik wouldn't countenance returning to the jailhouse so it was a straight choice between edging forward slowly, trying to keep all angles of approach in his line of fire, or risk making a dash through the funnel of storefronts.

The decision was made for him, as a fresh round of crashes erupted just yards away. Immediately he discerned the method and purpose to the din. The tinny banging was moving ahead of them building by building announcing their progress to those who waited with ill intent.

"We're going to have to make a run at it," he whispered to the Count. "I'll need your help."

Reaching into his waistband, he drew a loaded flintlock and tried to pass it to the noble. Kravnik made no attempt to accept the weapon, asking: "And what on Earth do you expect me to do with that?"

"Cover the prisoners. Stop them making a break for it. I'm going to be occupied keeping us alive, making sure no one attacks from the side streets. Pavel and Nicku need back-up. I can't do two things at once."

The aristocrat showed no sympathy. "Much as I am sure it would amuse you, Lord Marshal, I have no intention of becoming one of your minions. Dealing with this is your responsibility. I am no common gunfighter, nor do I have any intention of learning how to be."

For a split second, Anton made eye contact with Edward Lucens. He thought the condemned man would be taking comfort from the confusion and the Marshal's obvious humiliation. Instead, he saw hopelessness.

Cursing, Anton swung to the rear of the group, putting himself behind Kravnik and the two brothers, ensuring he had them in sight constantly.

"At the next crash we ride as fast as we can for the oak," he said loudly. "Whatever happens, don't stop for anything."

Speaking directly to Edward, he warned: "Try anything. Fail to co-operate and I'll put a musket ball in the back of your head and save us all the trouble of hanging you. Got it?"

The prisoner grunted an insult.

Certain that the entire group had got the message, Anton wrapped his horse's reins around his left hand, grasping tightly while holding the flintlock in his right.

A crash louder than any so far made the entire group jump, and digging in their spurs they took off at speed, resembling a shambolic cavalry charge.

Anton just had time to glance to the sides, seeing figures rushing forward on foot from behind water barrels, others running across to block their path, but the attackers weren't fast enough.

Looking forward he saw the hanging tree now only fifty yards away, the oak looming large; the designated branch clearly visible, awaiting the deadly ropes. Standing underneath, at least nine members of the Lucens family formed a tight circle, arms linked, blocking access to it.

Pavel yelled and pointed towards them, agitated, gripping his musket so tightly his veins stuck out. Next to him, Nicku had his gun pointing straight up to the sky, the weight taken against his shoulder, his expression a mixture of contempt and amusement.

Anton commanded the men to keep charging and the circle broke as the deputies approached at speed and took up position beside the hefty trunk.

For a moment the crowd vacillated, unsure what to do, giving the prisoners and escort vital time to join the other lawmen inside the cordon.

This was it, Anton thought, scanning the agitated features of the family and their yelling, cursing supporters. This is the moment when they'd make their move.

Cantering back and forth, forcing the onlookers even further back, he ordered the two deputies to lift the lengths of rope, curled around the hooks on their saddlebags, and throw them up over the strong bough.

Although Pavel trembled, he succeeded, the thick cord whipping over in a clumsy throw. The noose hung eight feet from the ground. Just the right height to go around the neck of a man on horseback.

Anton waited for his other deputy to do the same. However, Nicku had other ideas. He scanned the crowd, spotting friends, flushing at their personal pleas to him to let the men go.

"This isn't what I signed up for," he whined. "I'm a deputy, not an executioner. I don't want any part of it."

The mob cheered.

Anton had half expected this. He jerked his head in Kravnik's direction. "See that pitiable excuse of a man? He's determined this is going to happen, and if you defy him, interfere in any way he'll have you dragged to the Capitol in chains. That's if he doesn't just have you shot on the spot."

The deputy glanced towards the rabble, then towards the Count, and ran his tongue anxiously over his upper lip as he assessed who intimidated him more.

"Well, Nicku?" Anton pressed. "Decision time. What's it to be?"

Cursing, the truculent deputy spat on the ground and threw the rope upwards, a round of catcalls and booing accompanying the move.

Two nooses. Side by side; waiting.

It was time, Anton told himself, for his plan to work.

He took the reins of the two prisoners' horses and led them towards the dangling loops. Firearms levelled, both deputies swung their guns in an arc, watching the seething crowd edging nearer.

Slowly, deliberately, Anton placed a noose over each brother's head - Edward first, then the weeping Pieter.

"Hurry up," Kravnik barked. "Get on with it."

Anton wasn't going to rush. It was too important. Methodically, he took the other end of each rope and tied them tightly around the sturdy trunk.

Inhaling heavily, he prepared to slap the rear of each of the prisoners' horses. He took one last look at Kravnik, who waved furiously at him to finish the job, and was flabbergasted as a lone figure unexpectedly dashed out from the throng.

It was a woman, Pieter's wife, wailing, pleading for them to stop.

For a moment Anton thought Pavel was going to shoot her in fright, until Nicku grabbed the younger deputy's gun, shoving it skyward.

Everything turned to chaos.

Pieter yelled out "Marie!" and tried to struggle just as the woman crossed the last few inches of open ground, grabbing Kravnik's reins.

"Please, My Lord, don't kill him," she begged, "for the love of God, spare him. My husband's a good man. He doesn't deserve this. Please God, don't do this."

The Count looked stunned, and in a reflex action tried to pull his horse away. Its rump swung and hit the woman full on.

She was falling... the circling, excited animal's feet stamping dangerously close to her head. And the milling crowd gasped and poured forward, yelling, arms outstretched.

A shot fired into the air, over the heads of the advancing throng - Nicku's gun. In reply, stones flew towards them and Anton knew he had to act quickly.

Roaring, he slapped the backsides of the two steeds bearing their doomed riders. The horses yelped and bolted.

Both prisoners jerked violently off as the ropes tightened, and were instantly dangling; swinging, twirling, twitching like demented puppets.

Despite his promise to Pavel, the Marshal saw neither brother's neck had snapped. They were strangling, eyes bulging, the death-grip ropes choking. Each man kicked in agonised panic, legs flailing.

Which was exactly what he wanted...

...to put maximum pressure on the branch; which immediately cracked and began to split, giving way seconds later with an angry snap.

It was difficult to say who looked more astonished - the two brothers who found themselves unexpectedly falling to the ground, nooses now harmless around their necks or Count Kravnik who'd witnessed it and was trying to work out what had just occurred, while at the same time moving back in panic from the mob trying to get at him.

"Do something, Yoska!" the nobleman bellowed, trying to find a way of escape just as spectacular as that of his now freed prisoners who, nooses ripped off and discarded, were staggering frantically away, puking and coughing.

Pulse racing, Anton raised his gun.

One shot.

One shot to finish it.

And aimed...

...at the Envoy's head.

He'd rehearsed it in his mind, what he'd say in his report. *A terrible tragedy, a stray shot from the mob. I'm still investigating, however, it may be impossible to identify who the shooter was. In all the confusion, it's difficult to tell exactly what happened.*

There'd be official castigation, messages of reprimand. However, Anton knew no one at Court would be overly upset at Kravnik's untimely demise. He was a poisonous influence, and his removal would open up opportunities for other Royal hangers-on. And Anton knew Leopold would comprehend the clear and chilling warning. Here's your perfumed lackey returned to you in a body sack. Don't send any more or they'll end up the same way.

The scene dissolved into bedlam - just what Anton needed. But although it gave good cover for what he was about to do, it also made getting a clear shot at Kravnik maddeningly difficult.

Twice, he went to pull the trigger only to have the nobleman swerve and wheel at the last second to avoid grasping, shouting citizens.

Then Anton had it, the perfect line on the back of the Count's head and, lips pursed in hatred, targeted the weapon.

The boom was resounding.

Reverberating.

Loud.

Too loud.

For a moment, Anton thought his gun had somehow gone off accidentally; discharging before he could pull the trigger. Then he looked up, saw the cause of the noise and felt the colour drain from his face.

Some hundred feet away a figure on horseback sat stock still, exuding silent menace. The grinning, barrel-chested man looked straight at Anton and bowed in mock salute. He had an experienced killer's ice-cool demeanour, a smoking shotgun and two bodies lying on the ground near his feet.

CHAPTER 12

The silence was total, unnatural. Not a soul moved. They gawped at the stranger and Pieter and Edward sprawled lifeless by his feet. The gunman's blast had caught both brothers at chest height, slicing through them like artillery fire.

Anton inhaled dizzily, unable to take in what had happened. Twisting in the saddle, he stared accusingly at Kravnik, assuming the Envoy had guessed about the escape plan and taken steps to thwart it. It took only one glance to see Kravnik was just as astonished, open mouthed, stunned.

If not him? Who? How?

Remembering he still had his gun pointed at the aristocrat, Anton swiftly lowered it, motioning for his two deputies to join him, Pavel even more ashen than before.

"What's happening, Marshal?" he gasped. "Who is that? What does he want?"

"I don't know," Anton replied, dumbfounded, "but I'm damn well going to find out."

Instructing them to keep their weapons trained on the stunned rabble, he cantered towards the mysterious newcomer, mind whirring. Kravnik didn't budge, apparently preferring the peril of the mob to this new, unknown threat.

The stranger didn't budge either, content to make the Marshal cross the distance between them, his bulky figure relaxed yet upright in the saddle; alert, ready for action.

There was something about the pose that reminded Anton of a coiled predator.

His foreboding grew as he sensed the man sizing him up, a gunslinger's expert evaluation, and he tightened his white knuckles around the trigger of his own pistol.

As he drew closer, he noted the other's firearm was more than a simple shotgun. It was a weird-looking weapon with a large circular body six inches across, housing nine individual barrels; quite unlike anything he'd ever seen before. A custom-built contraption, capable of inflicting huge devastation. Lethal and expensive.

The implications sent a chill through him. He had only a single shot. There could be several chambers of the cannon unfired.

The gunman's bullish, close-cropped head inclined challengingly, his fierce, deep set eyes glowering with barely concealed menace.

Halting three feet away, Anton felt his apprehension and puzzlement turn at once to astonishment. It couldn't be. It wasn't possible.

"You!" he gasped.

"What's wrong, Marshal?" The man grinned contemptuously, revealing two gleaming gold teeth at the front. "You look like you've seen a ghost."

"I have," Anton whispered, feeling reality slide away. "I'd heard you were dead!"

"Sorry to disappoint you, old friend. I'm very much alive." The rider motioned to the bodies at his feet. "Unlike these two wretches."

The reminder of the doomed Lucens brothers hit Anton like a slap. He was supposed to have saved them. How could this calamity have happened?

"You need to do exactly what I tell you or you will go straight to Hell." That's what he'd told them. And like fools, they'd trusted him, to their doom. Like so many others in the past.

"There was no call to do that," he said, sickly regarding the bloodied, broken bodies discarded in the mud. "They weren't armed."

"They were escaping."

"On foot," he snapped. "They wouldn't have got far."

"Perhaps," the gunman agreed, disinterestedly. "Though their friends looked like they were more than enough to keep you and your deputies occupied. These two would have gone to ground in the woods. It could have taken you all winter to catch them again, if ever." He chuckled dryly. "Especially as I doubt there'd be many volunteers to form a posse."

Anton's eyes narrowed. "They were under my protection. You had no right!"

"They were on the run, fleeing justice," the gunman countered. "Under the law that made them fair game. You should be thanking me. Come to think of it, you should be paying me."

Anton felt a wave of disgust. "You haven't changed."

"Neither have you," the stranger responded. "Still self-righteous, still bleating while those under your charge die horribly. At least these two went quickly."

Again, Anton's mind struggled to keep up with the unfolding events. Was this deadly intervention planned? The gunman was giving nothing away, an impassive, taunting gleam in his intimidating eyes.

"I doubt kindness was ever on your mind," Anton said scornfully. "Just the reward. That's all it's ever about with you. The money."

A noise behind made him stiffen. Kravnik approached, having decided the newcomer posed no immediate threat.

"What the devil is going on?" he asked, sharply. "Who is this individual?"

"Drubrick." Anton made no effort to hide his loathing. "Milosh Drubrick. The self-styled Angel of Death."

Kravnik scowled, unsure if he'd heard correctly. "The angel of what? What are you blabbering about, Yoska? Speak plainly!"

The newcomer smirked. "I'm Milosh Drubrick," he said, tapping the side of his forehead with one finger in mock salute. "At your service, Your Honour. I'm what you might call a freelance law enforcement officer."

Anton snorted. "What he means is he's a bounty hunter. A sadistic, trigger-happy, money-grabbing, mercenary for hire."

Milosh beamed as though the description was the most fulsome compliment he'd ever received.

"And an effective one, if the last few minutes' work are anything to go by," Kravnik observed curtly. "It appears we are in your debt, Mr Drubrick. It is fortunate you happened to be passing. Heavens know wh—"

A sudden wail interrupted. Marie Lucens, the woman who'd moments before had been brutally transformed from wife to widow, was stumbling forward, arms opening in shock, head thrown back in a primal howl of grief.

Over the Count's shoulder Anton saw several members of the crowd abruptly startled from their daze.

"It appears fuller introductions will have to wait," Kravnik said anxiously, watching as more of the onlookers came back to life, muttering angrily, pointing in their direction. "Lord Marshal, you have some serious explaining to do, but for now I require you to get me to safety, and be quick about it."

Those nearest were already stooping to gather sticks and stones, keen to continue where they'd left off. For a moment Anton considered riding away to leave the preening aristocrat to their clutches. Bitterly, he reflected, he couldn't. Not with Milosh as a witness.

"But the bodies?" he began. "We can't just lea—"

"Now, Marshal Yoska!" Kravnik snapped. "Without delay. If any of these inbred oafs as much as touches me, I will have his hand chopped off and yours too for allowing it."

Telling himself there was nothing more he could do for the corpses, Anton beckoned his deputies to join them. "Quickly. Get the Count back to the jailhouse," he instructed. "He can't come to any harm. Understand?"

Pavel looked puzzled. "You aren't coming with us?"

"I'm staying behind to make sure our homicidal visitor doesn't eradicate any more of our citizens," Anton answered firmly, gesturing for them to get going. "I'm going to send him on his way before he spills any more blood."

Nicku didn't need telling twice to save his skin. "Come on," he urged Pavel. "Let's get out of here."

"We can't leave the Marshal!" the young man insisted.

The older deputy gave Anton a look of undisguised repugnance. "Leave him. He can take care of himself."

"Yes, indeed," Count Kravnik agreed, voice laden with clipped venom. "I am certain of that. And it is a tempting prospect to abandon him to the quarrelsome populace so dear to his heart. Alas, we need him, and his mysterious friend, if we are to get out of this in one piece."

He made direct eye contact with Anton, pupils contracting to tight balls of ire. "I expect maximum protection from you. No tricks. No mistakes. And this bounty hunter looks a useful fellow to have around. He comes with us. You can expel him from Brejnei later once I have got to the bottom of what has just transpired."

With that, the nobleman dug in his spurs, and took off at speed, the others having to gallop to catch up, their steeds' thudding hooves sending up wild splatters of soil.

The only way back was through the furious horde and as the gallopers approached it became clear the solid mass of humanity wasn't going to part, even if it meant being trampled.

The riders stopped sharply, horses rearing in alarm. They looked frantically for another means of escape. All at once the rabble was surging around them, sticks swinging.

"Fire your pistol," Anton heard Milosh command, as eager, snatching fingers tried to wrench Pavel and the others from their saddles.

"What?"

"Fire your damned weapon. Now. High into the air!"

There wasn't time to argue. Anton's flintlock boomed reassuringly as he pulled the trigger. The shot had the intended effect, the echoing report causing the rioters to halt in mid attack.

"Listen up!" Milosh's voice roared dramatically. And, glancing sideways, Anton saw the bounty hunter had the cannon levelled, ready to use. "Heed me well. Any man so much as twitches and I'll end him where he stands."

Some of the men angrily worked out the odds, knowing Milosh couldn't shoot them all. Still, there was an unwavering, dark sincerity in his tone making them unwilling to take the risk.

"I know what you're thinking," he went on, scanning the hate-filled faces. "I have only a few shots left. True, but I guarantee I will use them to maximum effect."

With that, he turned and took aim straight at Marie Lucens.

CHAPTER 13

The crowd reeled.

"Either you all back off or she gets the full blast between the eyes. She will join her poor departed husband in his coffin," Milosh promised. "It can be a joint funeral. All very neat and poetic."

"You wouldn't dare!" a voice challenged.

"Wouldn't I? I'm an exterminator by trade. I enjoy it. What's one more to my tally?"

"Marshal," another yelled. "You've got to stop him."

Milosh laughed coldly. "I think not. Your dashing Lord Marshal has scruples, a strong moral code. What he doesn't have at this moment is a loaded gun. I made sure of that."

Shocked, Anton looked at the flintlock he'd just discharged and tasted ashes in his mouth, realising he'd been played. The same old Milosh - manipulative: the master of deceit.

"Well? What's it to be? Do I kill the bitch or are you going to let us pass?" Milosh's voice hardened.

The mob's revulsion was raw, volatile. It was impossible to predict their next move. Nevertheless, one by one they began to disperse, stumbling to the margins, dropping their makeshift weapons into the mud.

The riders edged forward, Anton tensed, ready for any sudden aggression. Beside him, Milosh swept the mob with his devil gun, letting it line up on one man then another as he silently mouthed 'boom'. Anton sensed the gunman's exhilaration, Milosh yearning for someone to make a false move so he could send them to the next world.

The group of lawmen tightly encircled the Count, their passage maddeningly slow and it took several tense moments to trot clear of the last of the throng.

They'd ridden just a few yards beyond when a shout of "You bastards are all going to die!" screamed after them.

"No doubt," Kravnik muttered, relief washing over him. "But not today. And not by your grubby pauper's paws."

As they broke into a canter, the Count beckoned Milosh. "It appears I am indebted to you for a second time and I promise you shall be handsomely rewarded," he said. "However, for now if you would guard the rear and prevent any of these unruly peasants from coming after us, I would be greatly reassured."

Milosh bowed theatrically, and turned his horse around. Heading back the way they'd come, he took up station some fifty feet behind.

"I should be the one doing that," Anton complained.

"Indeed, Lord Marshal. There are many tasks you should be performing. Whether I can trust you to carry them out is another matter," Kravnik retorted. Then, sighing disdainfully, he said: "Spare me your tiresome indignation. I sent him back there to be out of earshot. I would learn more about this mysterious bounty hunter who has appeared in our midst. Tell me all you know."

For an instant, Anton was flummoxed. Where to begin in the litany of betrayals, murders, robberies and psychopathic havoc that made up the thug's existence? It would take hours to recount all his crimes and outrages. Yet there was, in truth, only one important fact to impart.

"He's the most dangerous man I've ever known," he answered bluntly.

Kravnik raised an eyebrow, as though questioning the hyperbole. "Although he is clearly a thug, he seems no more threatening than any other brute I have encountered, especially in these godless parts."

"I mean it. He's more callous and evil than the criminals he pursues," Anton retorted. "In a world of back-stabbing, homicidal scum, he's the most treacherous."

He risked a wary glance back at the gunman, who had stopped and was lovingly re-arming his multi-barrelled weapon. "You've seen what he's like. For Milosh Drubrick there is *no Wanted dead or alive*. He always brings them in stone dead, no exceptions."

"You sound frightened of him."

"As I would be of a rabid dog. And you should be too. He's no respecter of rank. Or privilege."

"Well, you have that in common, at least," the Count murmured icily. "What of his background? I sense a military bearing under the ruffian swagger. You served together in the vampire wars? He is a former comrade?"

Anton stiffened. "We served together, yes, but he's no comrade of mine. He was an insult to the uniform and all it stood for."

An image raced across Anton's mind. Nine years before. A stark, desolate military prison, the stench of sweat and despair, the rattle of keys and shackles and Milosh, face crimson, spittle flying as he screamed through the metal bars: "You're a dead man, Yoska. You hear me. A fucking dead man. You won't get away with this. I'm going to kill you. If it's the last thing I ever do I'll see you six feet under."

Forcing away the unsettling picture, Anton answered: "I am the one person on this Earth he'd most like to see broken and destroyed."

"Yet paradoxically this man just saved your life," Kravnik pointed out, mouth pursing in bemusement. "He could have murdered you several times back there and there would have been nothing anyone could have done to prevent it. Intriguing. Perhaps the animosity between you is not as toxic as you believe."

Or is worse than you could ever imagine...

Anton calculated: "If I'm still alive, it's because it suits him to keep me that way. He'll have something much worse planned for me than a simple quick death."

But what?

And why now after all these years?

After a while, Kravnik judged it safe to reduce to a gentle trot and the riders carried on slowly through the empty streets lost in their thoughts, the only sound the mocking kaah-kaah cries of the rooks on the tavern roof.

Glancing sideways, as he reloaded his flintlock, Anton noticed Kravnik was oblivious to their surroundings, attention still focused squarely on the bounty hunter.

"He seems a most resourceful fellow," the Count pronounced with fascination. "Quick thinking and with such vicious impulses. I was just thinking what an ideal Marshal he would make."

Until then, Anton had considered it impossible to detest the aristocrat any more passionately. Now he felt he'd barely dipped into the deep well of abhorrence.

"Yes," Kravnik mused. "Someone the locals would fear, not troubled by the tedious soul searching and misplaced decency that seems to blight your judgment. A fellow who could be trusted to follow orders faithfully and not question his betters."

Anton scowled. "Any time you want to give him my badge, you're welcome," he said, touching the battered metal star on his jacket, fingers brushing against its coarse, pitted surface. "It's only brought me heartbreak."

"It is a tempting prospect," the Count admitted. "Especially as I suspect he would make a far better job of it."

"Then what's stopping you?"

"And relinquish the hold I have over you? Where would be the satisfaction in that?"

Without warning he grabbed Anton's reins, bringing both horses closer. "Especially now you have played right into my hands."

"I don't know what you mean," Anton fired back, but Kravnik waved away his denial like an irksome insect.

"You must take me for an imbecile, Yoska, if you think for an instant I don't know you sabotaged the executions."

Anton felt the noble's stare burn into him. "It wasn't my fault it became a farce," he protested. "Perhaps if you'd waited, given me time to build a proper gallows and send for a professional hangman then things would have gone smoothly. Maybe if you hadn't been in such an indecent haste, weren't so determined to put on a public show."

"Oh, you are being too modest, Lord Marshal," Kravnik purred dangerously. "So many masterly touches - summoning the undertaker at midnight so he could alert the families, electing not to manacle the legs of the prisoners, not using a proper conveyance as I suggested."

The aristocrat sighed to register how tedious it was becoming. "And the unlikely coincidence of the branch snapping?"

He jerked his head in Pavel's direction. "Shall I ask the impressionable and eager to please young deputy what he makes of it? Perhaps, when this little sideshow has ended, the three of us should go back and examine the branch. I would be fascinated to discover if it bears the marks of a saw."

Anton felt his Adam's apple bob.

"You're guessing," he replied, the words sounding hollow. "I did what I was bidden. You saw me hang the men, as per your instructions. I have dozens of witnesses, people who wouldn't lie to save me."

Kravnik leant in so near Anton felt angry specks of spittle hit him wetly on the cheek.

"You are pushing your dwindling luck right to its limits," the nobleman warned, voice dipping menacingly. "You have managed to thwart me twice now, standing in the way of what I desire. There will not be a third."

He flicked his eyes to Milosh positioned behind them, the menacing cannon cradled easily across his arms. "Provoke me again and I will take more than your badge - I will take your head. From what you say of him, I am sure your sadistic friend would be more than happy to obl—"

The rest of the threat went unsaid as a shout interrupted and both men turned to see Nicku pointing excitedly ahead to the jailhouse. And in a heart stopping second Anton knew, in this day of horror and dark revelations, his troubles were only just beginning.

CHAPTER 14

There were four of them - a woman, two men and a child - attempting to reverse a tall covered wagon into the jail's courtyard. Despite lacking co-ordination, and yelling annoyed instructions between themselves, the adults were succeeding in inching the wide load backwards through the narrow wooden gates, just missing the walls on both sides. As they pushed and guided the wheels, the child ran around the team of four muscular horses hitting them with a stick, the animals whinnying in protest as they edged back step by step, skidding on the slick cobblestones.

Cursing, Anton turned to Milosh. "Your gang?"

The bounty hunter broke into a wide grin. "My associates," he corrected. "Fellow travellers with an interest in making a profit."

"What he means is they're more felons," Anton told Kravnik, "here to back him up."

He glanced anxiously at the figures, their forms becoming clearer with each approaching yard. It was immediately apparent one of the two men was considerably older than the other, his balding pate glistening with sweat at his exertions. He was slight, stooped, frail and puffing, complexion flushed. His clothes looked no better than rags, threadbare and ill-fitting, plain brown cloth bare of adornment, reminding Anton of a monk's habit.

He seemed an odd character to be one of Milosh's hired killers, and Anton wondered what use such a fragile old man could be to the bounty hunter, especially as he was struggling to manhandle the protesting wheels.

Yet, there was an even more baffling figure. Drawing closer, Anton became aware of what he'd assumed was a child wasn't a youngster at all. It was a tiny adult no more than four feet in height.

Any resemblance to a child ended there, he quickly noted. The dwarf's visage was pinched, hard, skin sallow, etched with years of bitter experience, eyes hooded and dark, like small bottomless pools of tar. Unlike his companion, he moved rapidly, whole body rolling with brisk, clipped, staccato steps. And unlike the old man, his clothes were brightly coloured, well-tailored, expensive. The patterns and hues seemed like a costume, designed to dazzle and impress, his tightly curled black hair theatrical.

The two couldn't have been more different or more incongruous. An old man and a dandy hobgoblin? What was Milosh playing at?

Still puzzling, he switched his attention to the remaining man - in his early thirties, cadaverously thin, chewing tobacco slowly and deliberately, the movement defiant. Exactly the type of callous thug Anton had encountered countless times before. Quick in a fight and even faster to start one.

The brute was dressed in a long canvas trail coat, which swung open to reveal a holster slung low on his bony hips, and had a cold lizard's stare and a diagonal scar running from his left ear to the corner of his mouth. Anton had seen scars like that before, made by sabres. So the rider had been in the military. Not an officer, not a gentleman. No, the ferret face was too cunning and sly to have ever been more than a foot soldier. Then, spotting the rider's shiny spurs, Anton corrected himself. Cavalry. He'd been a horse soldier.

However, it was the woman who most held his attention, slender and slight, yet not in any way delicate or vulnerable. He judged her to be in her late twenties or early thirties. More striking than beautiful, features sharp, face angular, she was pretty in a way that would attract men who desired women with character and spirit.

She was dressed in riding britches shoved deep into knee-high boots, her coarse, woollen jacket tied loosely over a white linen blouse. Two leather holsters crisscrossed her chest, each holding a pearl-handled flintlock. Her long, flame-red locks were held in place by a black head-band. Beneath that, deep blue eyes constantly scanned; a warrior's trait.

Anton became aware that he must have been staring, for the woman smiled knowingly, making no attempt to hide the fact she was evaluating him with the same appreciative attention.

He was also aware of Milosh watching the silent exchange, face darkening. So *his* woman? *More than just another hired gun. Useful to know...*

As Milosh introduced his accomplices, each acknowledging their names, his interference in the executions suddenly made sense. It had been a diversion designed to distract attention while the bizarre group and their vehicle slipped into Brejnei unobserved.

"I see you haven't forgotten what the army taught you," Anton observed acidly.

"Never go for a direct frontal assault if you can sneak around your enemy," Milosh concurred happily, adding: "It appears you've been outflanked, old friend."

"Will someone tell me what in damnation is going on," Kravnik demanded.

"We're delivering a prisoner," Milosh reported, "into Lord Marshal Yoska's tender loving care."

Bemused, the Count looked questioningly at the Marshal, trying to reconcile what he was hearing with Anton's claim that the bounty hunter always eradicated those he pursued.

"Is he alive? This fugitive?" the Count quizzed.

"In a manner of speaking," Milosh replied, with a wink.

Kravnik's puzzlement magnified. Anton's confusion immediately converted to apprehension.

Oh Lord, it couldn't be.

The wagon was nearly a third through the gates. Under its heavy purple velvet covering, no doubt pillaged from a grand house, he could just make out the outline of bars revealing a cage fastened on the back. It was standard kit for many bounty hunters, although no others he knew bothered to hide their captives under wraps.

Unless...

"Stop!" he bellowed suddenly. "Stop that wagon! It doesn't move another inch!"

"What?" Irina asked.

"I said to stop. Right now."

As he reached for his flintlock, Milosh whistled, short and shrill. In a silent, fluid motion, each member of the gang produced a weapon - a well-rehearsed manoeuvre: deadly and efficient.

"And who's going to stop us?" he scoffed, gesturing to Anton's frightened looking men. "The old lag with the pipe who keeps giving you the evil eye? The trembling man-boy? Or the over-fed aristo enjoying every moment of your discomfort?"

He chuckled, mouth opening wide enough for the gold inside to glint in the sharp sunlight. "Wise up. You're outflanked and outgunned."

Without breaking eye contact, Anton levelled his own pistol at Milosh. "Outnumbered or not, I'll make sure I take you with me," he promised.

His own words replayed in his head. *If I'm still alive, it's because it suits him to keep me that way. He'll have something much worse planned for me than a quick death.*

Now he prayed his intuition was right, gambling Milosh wouldn't simply execute him on the spot.

For several nerve-shredding moments both confronted each other, stares locked, until Kravnik rode between them.

"Enough!" he announced curtly. "Everyone will lower their weapons or they will answer to me." And dismounting his horse, he inhaled deeply. "I fail to see what all the fuss is about. Good grief, what prisoner can possibly be worth all this hostility?"

Kravnik marched towards the wagon. Without looking back, the nobleman grabbed at one of the ropes holding down the drape, pulling it free. "I see I shall have to investigate for myself," he announced and ducked underneath the canopy.

"You better stop him, before he gets himself killed," Milosh warned.

It was too late. Before Anton could react, a muffled shriek came from underneath the drape followed by the deadliest of roars.

CHAPTER 15

Pacing the grand hall, Kristina Modjeski glowered at the giant shutters covering the castle windows. The jeering daylight, the only thing in existence her kind feared, held her impotent, taunting from outside, making her as much a prisoner as her kidnapped son.

"With each passing hour Stefan's abductors move farther from our grasp," she scowled, picking up a goblet and dashing it against the wall, "while we linger here, doing nothing, powerless."

Across from her, Viktor remained silent, waiting until the surging flush of her wrath subsided.

"It's true we cannot venture out until nightfall," her consort conceded calmly. "Nevertheless, no matter how far and fast the gang travel, they cannot escape us. It is only a matter of time before we hunt them down."

Calmly, he scooped up the dented metal cup and placed it softly beside the large calfskin map, spread wide across the banqueting table.

"We know which way they went," he pointed out. "Their vehicle slows them. Our steeds can cover the ground many times more swiftly."

Halting her fevered tread in mid stride, she spun. "And if they become conscious of this and slaughter Stefan in the meantime?"

He didn't reply.

Exactly, she thought darkly.

Leaning in, she pored over the ornate map, scrutinising the chart's details that outlined every district and municipality in the country, each river and range of hills.

"It makes no sense for them to have gone north east," she insisted. "It takes them away from any possibility of safety."

"Yet, bizarrely, that is what the mortals have done," Viktor replied. "The trackers followed their trail for miles before they had to pull off the chase and take shelter."

To avoid the damned dawn! To avoid instant immolation under the sun's merciless rays.

She ran her slender fingers over the chart's contoured surface, trying to discern what devious plan the loathsome kidnappers could possibly be following. The escape route took them in the opposite direction to the Capitol, deeper into the interior, far from shelter and protection.

"There are only woods, scrubland, and mountains, no settlements of any consequence," she muttered, perplexed. "It is desolate, a wasteland."

"Perhaps they have panicked and are fleeing headlong without thought," Viktor suggested. "They may not be aware they are bound for the badlands."

For a moment she considered the idea, then - remembering the care and skill the hunters had gone to, the cool ruthlessness of the execution of one of their number and the significance of the deep claw marks on the mill walls - she discounted it.

"Every detail of this outrage has been planned to the most miniscule degree," she replied evenly. "There is a clever strategy at work. If they are headed into the interior, it is for a purpose."

"To hide out?"

Unlikely, she thought. They would know she would stop at nothing to rescue her son. There would be no point at which the hue and cry diminished and it would be safe for them to emerge from concealment. She could wait months... years...

Her attention jumped to a corner of the map and a random idea jumped into her mind. It was too incredible. The bounty hunters couldn't possibly expect *that* to stop her.

Brejnei? Smack in the most remote corner of the wilderness.

Scolding herself, she dismissed the ridiculous notion. She was tired, overwrought, letting her imagination and concern cloud her mind.

Maybe that was what the scum intended. To cause confusion. To muddle and bamboozle. It was possible, of course, that they had simply strapped Stefan to a horse and ridden south. The cumbersome cart could be a decoy. The gang was cunning, more than capable of such a deception. They could be holed up anywhere.

"As soon as dusk falls I want scouts searching in *all* directions," she instructed. "I refuse to be tricked. Deception or not, these scum will not elude my wrath."

"They won't get away," Viktor pledged and wrapped his arms around her, pulling her in close. "You must rest. You must sleep in order to be fresh when darkness falls and we resume the chase."

His voice was soothing, comforting, and she knew he was right. She was exhausted. She must give her drained body time to recuperate from the punishing psychic exertions.

Surrendering herself to the drowsiness washing over her, its welcome numbness seeping into her being, she barely registered as Viktor scooped her up and carried her towards the bed chamber where her silk-lined coffin was placed upon its marble plinth.

As Viktor laid her down, and gently brushed the hair from her forehead, Kristina felt herself dropping into the beckoning darkness. Yet a last nagging thought hammered in her skull as she sank into oblivion.

Brejnei - the one town no nosferatu would dare enter.

Brejnei - where *he* was.

Kravnik flinched, heart pounding like a blacksmith's hammer. His yell had been a reflex, the sound escaping his lips before he could prevent it, and he chided himself for being spooked so easily.

He'd deduced there was some sort of animal in the darkness as soon as the appalling zoo house stench filled his nostrils. And he'd been in the act of placing a scented handkerchief over his nose when the black stillness erupted as a large paw swiped at him, the claws clattering across the iron bars of the cage.

It roared, lurching forward with malicious intensity, and for a brief second he thought himself about to be gripped by its drooling jaws, but fortunately the beast stopped as its restraints held firm, causing it to bellow again in frustration.

This time Kravnik was prepared for the deafening bellow, and muttered: "Let's see what we are dealing with." He fumbled in his tunic until he found the small enamel tin of matches and, trembling slightly, lit one of the tiny sticks.

The illumination was pitiful. He could just make out a large bulk, the momentary glint of moist eyes filled with malevolence, then the match fizzled out plunging him back into impenetrable murk.

A large animal? Why would bounty hunters have gone to all this trouble to smuggle a wild creature into the town? And why bring it to the local jail? It made no sense.

The second match flared, and he became aware the beast wasn't all the cage contained. On the far side, something white and pale lay half prone, attached to the bars with manacles.

Shuffling determinedly along the side of the wagon, forcing himself under the voluminous folds of the heavy covering, he edged closer to the second occupant. Just as the flame extinguished, he glimpsed enough to tell him it was a young man, half naked.

The third match lit with a crackle and this time he could see clearly. Although the captive's clothes were tattered, there was no disguising their finery. Nor the grooming that had gone into the long, flowing locks before they'd become dishevelled and full of straw. Even bound, the figure had dignity, a quiet, natural poise; almost a stateliness.

The pallor was deathly white, the thin lips burgundy - stark against the porcelain complexion with its fine blue veins. It could have been a woman's face for its symmetry and exquisiteness, except there was strength too: raw masculine power.

He noted the man was badly injured, gaunt body riddled with vicious cuts and bruises; chest hair matted with dried blood, angry welts showing where a whip had been used without pity.

Whoever this was, the bounty hunters had clearly taken out their fury on him - or had he merely been the object of their sadistic sport?

The Count remembered what Yoska had said about Milosh Drubrick's reputation. Yet this prisoner hadn't been executed, was still alive, albeit in this abysmal condition.

"Who are you?" he murmured. "What have you done to deserve such treatment?"

At the sound of his voice, the pale figure stirred, head lolling to one side as if in a swoon. The hair fell away, and bruised and battered lips parted revealing glistening flesh-ripping teeth - and in one chilling instant Kravnik understood.

This time he couldn't control his nerves, and stumbled backwards in panic, his footing going from under him. The heel of his riding boot caught in the edge of the thick, dense drape and he felt himself falling, arms flailing, as the sliding, dusty material began to wrap around him.

He had one last glimpse before the tumbling curtain covered his eyes - of sunlight, bright eager sunlight, flooding the corner of the cage.

CHAPTER 16

Leaping from his horse, Anton landed heavily, putting his head down and sprinting. He knew he had bare seconds to avert a catastrophe as the velvet cloth fell swiftly, carried by its own weight, exposing more and more of the cage to the daylight.

Behind him, he sensed Milosh riding hard to catch up, with the same frantic thought: protect the vampire, get to it before the merciless sun set it alight.

Underneath the fabric Anton heard Kravnik's muffled yelping as he thrashed about.

"Stop moving," he shouted to the panicking nobleman, grabbing two large handfuls of the dusty material and holding tight, trying to arrest its fall. "You're pulling the covering off. Stand still, stand still, you wretched idiot."

He didn't know if Kravnik heard him, the frantic movements continuing regardless. Looking up in dread he saw one deathly white manacled hand now fully exposed to the sun's beams and immediately crumple and blister as instantaneously a high pitched, inhuman sound rent the air.

"Milosh!" he yelled, urging the bounty hunter to act. "Quickly. We're going to lose it."

In horror he watched the prisoner's hand blacken then burst into flame, the screech intensifying so loudly the startled onlookers covered their ears.

Then Milosh was there, reaching between the bars, beating at the orange tongues of fire. He extinguished the singeing threat before snatching at the rapidly disappearing edge of the curtain, arresting its drop and, teeth gritted, attempted to yank it back.

It took three strong tugs before the brightly covered canopy gave up its resistance and was manhandled back, scar faced Johann helping Milosh secure it into place.

Anton's mind whirled. What in God's name was Milosh and his gang up to transporting a live vampire? There was a standard bounty for hunting the nosferatu who ventured off the reservations. Slayers need only produce evidence of the kill, the creature's decapitated head or the torn-out fangs. Hauling one of the demons alive around the countryside was illogical; dangerous beyond all reason.

Stumbling from under the cover, Kravnik was ashen, yelping: "It's a vampire. A damned vampire, I tell you!"

Brushing himself vigorously, he straightened, glaring at Anton.

"I detest the abominations," he declared. "They are an affront to all that is decent and Godly and you allowed one of them to get close to me. You put my life at risk!"

Anton said nothing. If only it *had* attacked you, he thought, all my troubles would have been solved.

"Look," Irina said unexpectedly, pointing back along the main street.

Following her outstretched hand, he saw the townsfolk were filing back, marching forlornly behind two groups of men carrying the bodies of the Lucens brother on planks, balanced precariously on their shoulders.

They were only moments away. He had to think quickly. He couldn't risk another confrontation, couldn't allow the gang to add more to Milosh's bloody tally.

Plus, he had an even greater fear. If the inhabitants of Brejnei learnt there was an *infernal* in their midst they'd stop at nothing to destroy it and anyone who tried to stand in their way.

Seconds before he'd been ready to send the bounty hunters packing with their deadly prisoner. Now the only route out was blocked by the returning throng of humanity.

"All right," he instructed, making an unhappy decision. "Get the wagon inside, on the double. Nicku, Pavel, help them."

The deputies looked stunned, as did Kravnik. "You're not seriously considering giving sanctuary to a monster!" he demanded.

"I have no choice. If these people get wind of what we've got here, they will go berserk. They'll burn the place down, with us inside."

Kravnik flinched as the implications rapidly sank in. "Of course," he replied, and turning, urged: "You heard the Lord Marshal. Put your backs into it."

All the gang sprang into action and, with the extra muscle power of the deputies, the lumbering cart went unceremoniously through the narrow gap, wheels protesting as they scrapped against the gates.

Milosh grinned triumphantly, yet that wasn't what unnerved Anton. It was Gregor, the old man, who now staring up at him, shaking his head in pity and despair.

CHAPTER 17

The heavy oak gates crashed shut, sending up clouds of choking dust.

"That should do it," Anton said, as the deputies dropped the hefty crossbar into place, seconds before the first volley of rocks thudded against the woodwork and muffled voices outside bellowed insults and threats.

Transfixed, Kravnik studied the now barricaded entrance as if he doubted it would keep out the rabble. "Are we safe?" he asked dubiously.

"With this lot in place the jailhouse is as impregnable as a castle," Anton reassured, brushing his grimy fingers against his britches.

"What about the other parts of the residence?" Kravnik pressed. "They must be vulnerable to attacks? Surely there are weak points?"

"All the doors are reinforced, treble dead-bolted, and the ground floor windows have heavy iron bars over them," Anton reassured. "My predecessor took the precautions of converting the entire building into a fortress. One of the legacies of being the representative of a deeply unpopular regime."

He studied the disturbing newcomers dismounting beside the wagon and said with foreboding: "It's not the people out there you should be worried about. It's the ones we're locked in with."

Kravnik's attention switched to the strangers, assessing the ill-assorted misfits as they tethered their horses, stretched and studied their new surroundings.

"A disreputable bunch," he agreed. "And though not the type of companions I would choose, I fail to see what we have to fear from a dwarf, an old man and a woman. They resemble a rag-tag troupe of travelling players more than reckless desperadoes."

Anton's expression hardened. "Don't be fooled by appearances. They are vultures without morals or conscience. They'd slit anyone's throat for the coins in their purse."

Kravnik thought about it for a few seconds. "You may well be right, Lord Marshal, however, for the present, I am more concerned with their alarming cargo."

Both looked in the direction of the wagon. With the gates closed the courtyard was shrouded in semi-darkness and the cart had been safely pulled to one side away from the grudging light trickling from the skylights high on the far wall. Although there may be no immediate threat to the supernatural prisoner, he reflected grimly, the Undead captive posed a real and chilling threat to all those trapped with it.

"Why have they brought it here?" the Envoy asked pointedly. "What do they hope to achieve?"

Anton rubbed at his gritty eyes. "Whatever it is, it won't be good, you can bank on it."

Milosh beamed as the lawman approached, the burly man's features creasing, making him appear like an amused walrus. "Trouble with the blue-blood?" he scoffed. "He doesn't look that happy with you, old comrade. Not a man to tolerate incompetence, I'd wager."

The gang members smirked, and Anton felt himself flush. "You let me worry about Count Kravnik," he fired back. "You just worry about telling me exactly what's going on. What are you doing with a live vampire?"

The hunters all looked at Milosh. "Let's just say we brought it here as a gift," he teased.

Anton's migraine flared. "I'm in no mood for riddles. What does that mean? Tell me."

"It's as Milosh said," Irina explained, coming up close behind him, murmuring warmly in his ear, "it's a very special gift. One you've waited years for, dreamt about possessing."

With that, Johann and Quintz each grabbed a rope and yanked back the heavy drape, revealing the prisoner.

Anton couldn't help himself. The instant his eyes settled on the bound hostage, he muttered: "Oh my God," and staggered backwards. Even in the deep gloom, he identified the pale, battered face and fought to stop the flood of emotions suddenly overwhelming his senses.

"Ah. I thought that would get your attention," Milosh said dryly.

CHAPTER 18

Anton recoiled, his mind refusing to accept what was before him.

"What the Christ have you done?" he gasped.

Milosh ran his fingers mischievously along the length of the metal enclosure, heavy signet ring clanking against the bars in a triumphant tattoo.

"The unthinkable," he answered gleefully. "I've captured a prize beyond imagination."

"You must be out of your mind!"

The bounty hunter grunted proudly. "Why? Because no one else would dare go after him, of all the vampires in the world?"

"Because you can't hope to get away with it," Anton replied with a shudder. "Because it's going to bring the wrath of Hell crashing down on your head."

"Who is it?" he heard Nicku ask in a hushed whisper. "Who have they snatched?"

Anton couldn't bring himself to say the name out loud as though denying the fact could somehow make it a fantasy and in a moment he'd awaken to find out it had all been a sick and twisted dream.

"Stefan Modjeski," Gregor volunteered from the sidelines.

"The prince of bloodsuckers," Quintz added, as if any of them needed to be reminded of the nosferatu's rank and reputation.

"Good Lord," Kravnik exclaimed, covering his mouth. "It can't be!"

Anton's reply was tinged with disgust. "It is. Trust me, I of all people should know." And glowering at Milosh, added: "I said you were the most dangerous man I'd ever encountered, and this is exactly why. Only you would have the arrogance to abduct a member of the Modjeski family."

"Or the balls?" Milosh suggested, puffing up his chest. "The audacity to do what others only fantasise about? Caging a demon, isn't that what most would call courageous?"

"No, it's what they'd call suicide," Anton retorted. "A short cut to the afterlife."

The creature moaned deep in its troubled slumber, its injured and blackened hand twitching.

For Christ's sake, how much sedative had they forced into it to maintain the fiend's torpor even when it was in such pain.

"This is lunacy," Anton declared, eyes darting between hostage and captors, trying to figure out which presented more immediate danger. "Even if it doesn't awaken, tear those bars apart and rip you all to shreds, his clan are guaranteed to do much worse when they catch up with you."

He was aware of Pavel edging away from the wagon as though the vehicle itself might try to attack him.

"It's just stories about the Modjeski. Isn't it? It's all made up," the young deputy said, unable to disguise his concern.

"Of course it is," Milosh agreed reassuringly. "Marshal Yoska likes to scare people; to make his former exploits sound more exciting. It's all fairy stories, exaggeration."

Anton kept his voice low. "Fairy stories? Exaggeration? There are entire graveyards filled with reckless fools who went up against the Modjeski. Cemeteries filled with the mass pits of what scraps were left to bury afterwards."

His words hung ominously in the air.

"Why have you brought this abomination here?" Kravnik demanded, trying to reclaim his authority. "What possible reason can you have for exposing yourselves and us to such unwarranted peril?"

No one replied; a furtive glance passing between the bounty hunters.

"It will involve money, you can rely on that," Anton surmised. "A lot of money."

He paced purposefully between the gang, scrutinising each in turn. "You wouldn't do this for glory alone. You wouldn't put yourself in such jeopardy unless there was a big pay-off," he said shrewdly. "So what's your angle?"

Milosh grinned. "You work it out."

"Yeah," Johann challenged. "C'mon, lawman. You're supposed to be so smart. You tell us."

"Ransoming him back to his family? I'm sure you've abducted plenty of victims in the past and been paid handsomely," Anton reasoned. "But you must know that won't wash with the Modjeski. They'd rather let Stefan be destroyed than be bested by a bunch of cut-throats and bandits."

He sensed the old man inhaling sharply, annoyed at being called a bandit. Even so, the elder didn't rise to the bait. None of them did.

Anton slowly circled the dwarf. "What else could you be planning? Eh, Quintz? Selling him to the family's enemies? Auctioning him to the highest bidder?"

The small man's smile widened but he didn't answer.

"An intriguing notion," Anton speculated, "except no one would be rash enough to take him. Thousands have reason to hate the Modjeski and would love to see them humbled, but they know it would be signing their own death warrants to act."

So what scheme had they hatched?

A chill spread through his veins as he spotted Irina beaming knowingly.

Her words rewound in his mind. "It's a gift, a special gift... One you've waited years for."

No!

"I see you've worked it out," she said, eyes twinkling. "There is one person who is going to take him off our hand. You, Lord Marshal Yoska."

"And you're going to make us wealthy into the bargain," Johann promised.

"What do they mean?" Kravnik spluttered.

"I have no idea," Anton replied anxiously, "and I'm not going to wait to find out."

Jabbing his finger at the cage, he told the hunters: "That's it. The games are over. I want you out of here. Now. Take the wagon and go. Get that monster as far away from here as possible."

"Not so fast, Marshal—" Johann began, but Anton cut across him, voice tightening.

"I don't care what twisted scheme you've concocted. I'm not getting mixed up in it or allowing you to drag this town into a private war with the deadliest demons to ever stalk the Earth."

Again, the gang exchanged a silent look. Milosh gave an exaggerated sigh, murmuring: "I feared that might be your attitude, old comrade."

He sidestepped as Quintz reached into his tunic, produced a knife and hurled it determinedly in the Marshal's direction.

Anton reacted automatically. He dived, snatching for his gun as the spinning blade whizzed over his shoulder. It missed by less than the thickness of a hair, the draught like an angel's kiss as it sped past his ear, embedding into a thick post just behind him.

Fury swelling up, he took aim at the dwarf just as Milosh intervened, telling him: "Relax, lawman. Relax. You weren't the target."

"If I'd been aiming at you, you'd be dead right now," Quintz agreed. "I never miss." He indicated the Marshal should look around.

Exhaling in anger and relief, Anton saw the stiletto had dug two inches into the wood, pinning a large piece of dog-eared, yellowing parchment that Gregor had only a moment before been gripping. The metal projectile had landed precisely between the old man's wrinkled second and third fingers, not drawing so much as a single drop of blood.

"Read it," Milosh said, more command than invitation.

Carefully re-holstering his pistol, Anton got back to his feet, and approached the pillar as Gregor shuffled hurriedly out of the way.

Giving the dwarf a spiteful look, Anton switched his attention to the crumpled paper. The edges were torn, and in the gloom it was difficult to make out all the words printed on it, but on closer inspection he saw it was a Wanted poster.

Even in the murkiness there was no mistaking the patrician visage sketched upon it, or the bold words: 1,000 CROWNS REWARD.

"It says the vampire is wanted for multiple murders," Johann explained, tilting one of the oil lamps so its pool of illumination cascaded across the dirty, dog-eared sheet. "He's worth his weight in gold to anyone who can hand him over to the authorities."

Irina grinned, adding: "So we thought: who better to deliver him to than the famous Anton Yoska, scourge of the nosferatu nation."

Anton looked from one bounty hunter to the next, searching for any sign this was a cruel, malicious jest.

"This is a fake," he declared. "Something you've fabricated to trick me. I don't believe it."

Milosh sucked through his teeth. "It doesn't matter what you believe. You're not exactly in charge anymore." With that, he ordered Johann and Quintz: "Search the place. Find out if he's got any more back-up."

As the dwarf and the scarred thug disappeared in the direction of the main residence, Milosh suddenly put his beefy arm around Anton. The contact lacked any warmth or camaraderie.

"Read on, old comrade. You'll see it instructs law officers to provide all possible help and shelter to anyone capturing the leech."

He squeezed hard, making Anton wince. "Which means you're not going to send us packing. Quite the opposite. You're going to make us welcome guests and lavish us with as much hospitality as our little heart's desire."

He waited a half beat, before whispering: "And when we're rested enough to hit the trail again, we'll be leaving with saddlebags full of gold and that foul devil safely locked up in your cellblock."

And, sniffing dismissively, added: "Whatever happens after that will be your problem, old friend, not ours."

CHAPTER 19

Anton flexed his shoulders, muscles tensing as he angrily broke free from the big man's grip.

"This is bullshit," he declared. "I don't know anything about a bounty on the head of Stefan Modjeski. This is one of your crooked schemes."

Milosh pretended to be offended. "No trick, no deception. It's all perfectly legit. The bloodsucker is a wanted man. You've read it for yourself in black and white."

"On a forgery."

Anton snatched the poster free of the blade, even more of the paper breaking off, leaving a gaping hole in the middle.

"You can't expect me to accept this tatty note," he said, waving it angrily. "Just look at the state of it. The paper could crumble at any moment and the bottom half is missing completely. Even if it were genuine—"

"Which it is," Irina purred.

"—I'd need to see who signed it. I'd be mad to take responsibility for that monster on your say so without knowing who authorised the warrant. That section is conveniently absent."

The gang leader gave a long-suffering sigh. "You shouldn't be so suspicious," he chastised. "I can supply that information quite easily. It was signed by The Crown Prince personally."

Anton snorted.

"Now I know for sure you're lying," he declared. "I'm all too familiar with Leopold's scrawl and I'd be able to tell if the signature was faked. You couldn't risk that, so that's why the bottom of the poster is missing. Nice try, but it won't wash."

As Anton went to turn, Milosh motioned towards Kravnik. "Do you really want to go against our most gracious ruler's wishes, with one of his courtiers here to bear witness to your defiance?"

The lawman looked meaningfully at the Envoy. "Well? Do you know anything about this?"

"I must confess to being as much in the dark about this as you are," the Count replied after a moment's deliberation. "However, there are certain matters in which the Crown Prince does not see fit to confide in me."

He waved his well-manicured hand vaguely. "It could be argued that if there is any possibility, no matter how remote, that the Modjeski has a price on his head, then co-operating would be the prudent course of action."

"Even if it's a set-up? Even if leads to disaster?" Anton retorted.

Further discussion was brought to an abrupt halt by Johann's reappearance, Quintz behind him, struggling to keep up with the taller man's stride.

"Well?" Milosh prompted.

"He hasn't got any more deputies. Only a fat, squawking pig-ugly cook. I've locked her in their pantry with the rest of the pork. She won't be giving us any trouble," Johann reported with amusement.

"And there's a child looking after some sick woman," Quintz added.

At the mention of Sofia, Anton felt a jolt of self-loathing. He'd been so bound up with the mysterious arrival of the bounty hunters he'd forgotten about her. How could he have done that? he thought bitterly.

"Your wife?" Milosh asked.

He nodded, heart heavy.

"What's wrong with her?"

"A fever," he replied, voice unsteady. "She has typhus."

Milosh made a face Anton couldn't decipher. He suspected the gunman was considering her value as a potential hostage. Thank the Lord that was denied him. She was too far gone for him to do anything worse to her.

"The child?" Milosh pressed. "Yours?"

For a second, Anton didn't answer, picturing a young girl's face, wrinkled in laughter, eyes shining under her tight, auburn curls. And then visualising the headstone that marked her grave. Gone from the world at just seven years old. Was it truly two years since Gretchen's passing?

"He's just a fool serving boy," he answered, putting as much contempt as he could into his voice. "He's of no consequence."

He studied the other's expression to see if the big man had spotted the lie. Tomas could only be protected if the newcomers thought Anton cared little about him.

After a moment Milosh grunted, clearly disappointed not to have more bargaining chips.

Forcing the tension to drain from his shoulders, Anton announced: "I'm going to check on my wife. I won't be long. When I come back you and your *associates* will be leaving, no arguments, and you'll be taking that evil creature with you."

His voice hardened as he instructed the deputies: "In the meantime, Nicku, Pavel, no one goes near that wagon."

Marching towards the main house, he waited until he was out of sight of the gang, then raced upstairs, not pausing to take off his greatcoat or fur hat. Kravnik followed, less agile yet with the same sense of urgency.

Tomas looked relieved as Anton pushed his way into the bedroom.

"There was a man," the boy began anxiously, "with a scar—"

"I know," Anton said soothingly. "It's okay. He's gone now. How is Sofia?"

The lad's head dipped and he motioned to the shivering figure under the bed clothes. "She is fading," he said sadly. "Each hour she is growing weaker. I'm sorry," he sobbed. "I don't want her to die but I cannot—"

His eyes went wide as he spotted Kravnik and he flinched, stepping back several steps.

"Don't be afraid," Anton assured him. "You're safe. The Count knows if he tries to touch you again I'll break his neck."

Kravnik coloured, lips pinching.

"I have faith in you," Anton assured the boy. "Stay by your mistress's side. We have some trouble downstairs so I don't want you to come out for anything. No matter what you hear, keep the room locked. Okay?"

As Tomas repeated his instructions to prove he'd understood what was expected, Anton bundled Kravnik out into the corridor, saying: "Come with me."

"Where are we going?"

"My study," he answered briskly, heading back to the ground floor. "We don't have much time."

Inside the small office, he headed over to the desk and began yanking out the drawers, pulling out papers and scattering them across the top.

"What are you doing?" the Count challenged as Anton snatched one page then another, discarding them in irritation.

"There has to be some paperwork," he answered tersely, not stopping for an instant in his search. "If there was a reward that large posted for the apprehension of any criminal, I'd have been informed."

"So the poster is a ruse? The bounty hunters are attempting a swindle?"

"They had better be. Because if they are telling the truth we're in more trouble than you can imagine."

Not finding anything in the desk, Anton grabbed a large metal box in the corner of the room and, swinging open its lid, emptied its contents on to the floor.

"There'd be a poster, or a letter, or an official document of some kind," he grumbled, rummaging through the disorganised pile. "There'd have to be for something that important."

Even though Kravnik shared the lawman's growing sense of unease, he couldn't help a disparaging observation: "I see paperwork is not your forte."

"I'm a marshal," Anton sniped back. "I'm hired for how well I handle a gun, not a fountain pen."

After a few moments, he exhaled, straightening up. "This is hopeless. There are bills, receipts, instructions on how much I'm allowed to spend feeding prisoners, requisition orders for new weapons, and a dozen missives from the Royal Court telling me how to do my job and how much Leopold is disappointed in the results I'm getting. No wanted posters, nothing about any warrant for the arrest of Stefan Modjeski."

"Is it possible you simply did not receive notification?" the nobleman suggested.

Anton fired him a scornful look. "You know what a bureaucracy the Royal Court is. Every decree, instruction, or idle thought our ruler has is written down, and transmitted to us by weekly courier; usually recorded in triplicate. Sometimes," he added pointedly, "they even send a Court official in person all the way out here to ensure I get the message."

A loud crash reverberated, followed by shouts and the sound of horses complaining.

"I suggest you get back to the courtyard at once," the Count counselled. "It sounds as if your untrustworthy guests are taking matters into their own hands."

Anton swore and shoved past him.

Bursting into the courtyard, he took in the scene in an instant. Nicku was nowhere to be seen and Pavel was staggering, dazed, holding a handkerchief to his nose, the rag barely stemming the flow of blood.

"I tried to stop them, Marshal," he said, plaintively, eyes brimming. "You've got to believe me."

The cage was wide open and, standing before it, kitted out in thick gauntlets and heavy protective garments, Irina, Quintz and Milosh were about to venture inside.

Anton didn't need an explanation of what they were attempting. It was obvious, as was the identity of the person who'd punched Pavel. Johann was grinning triumphantly, slowly rubbing the back of his knuckles.

His immediate reaction was to take a swing at Johann. The bright, defiant leer of the man suggested that was exactly what the thug wanted.

Instead, Anton pointed to the cage and declared: "I didn't say that thing could be unloaded."

"No," Milosh agreed, without conviction. "The way I figured it you'd eventually come around to my way of thinking. So I decided I'd save time."

He indicated to Pavel. "Don't blame the kid. He put up a good struggle. Impressive - he looks such a mummy's boy."

No, Anton, thought. He didn't blame the young deputy. The fault lay with the other one.

"Where is Nicku?" he snapped. "What have you done to him?"

Irina ran the tip of her tongue over her lips teasingly. "Why, nothing, Marshal. Nothing at all. We didn't need to. He took off the moment your back was turned."

Kravnik appeared in the doorway. Anton flashed him a piercing look, warning not to get involved.

"He's probably still running," Quintz added. "His look of fear was something to behold."

"I reckon he's shit himself," Johann joked. "Maybe that's where he's gone - to hide in the outhouse."

The gang all grinned.

Despite the stinging sneers Anton was more concerned by their supernatural prisoner. Even in its comatose condition, it was leaning towards Pavel, lips parting, sensing the proximity of the young man's oozing crimson life-force.

"That's enough," Anton said brusquely. "Fun's over. Come away from the cage." Gesturing to Pavel, he warned:

"Move right back, lad. While you're bleeding, you're in extreme danger. Get out of here."

Before the youngster could respond, Kravnik wrinkled up his nose and asked loudly: "Do you smell it?"

"What?" Milosh asked.

"Smoke. I smell smoke."

"That will be Nicku's pipe," Anton replied, anger doubling, promising himself he was going to make the elder deputy's life a misery.

"No," Milosh exclaimed, jumping from the running board. "It's not that - there, look."

Following where the big man's arm was pointing, Anton now saw the cause of the stink and, trembling, immediately yelled "fire!" as black clouds billowed out of the cellblock towards them.

CHAPTER 20

"Close the cage. Bolt it shut and don't take your eyes off the creature for a second," Anton told Irina and Gregor as he broke into a run, shouting to Pavel: "Water - now, fetch water."

The various figures scattered across the courtyard, panic building. As he raced, Anton sensed Kravnik behind him.

"Is it the townspeople?" Kravnik pressed as they hurried through the smoke towards the cells. "If they have found out about the vampire!"

"It can't be," Anton snapped back, waving away the acrid, sooty cloud. "There's no way they could know."

The smoke was issuing from the deputies' room, billowy ripples pouring out from under the door. Each thick, choking, swirling wave rose higher up than the last, wafting upwards towards the courtyard ceiling.

Coughing, eyes stinging, Anton grabbed the handle, wrenched it around and pushed. The well-oiled metal swung easily and he half fell into the room, Kravnik following a step behind, silk handkerchief clamped over his nose and mouth.

The Marshal paused for a half beat, taking in the room with a rapid, probing glance and swore.

There were no flames, no raging inferno, no hungry tongues of orange lapping at the walls; none of the roar and fury of a blaze, just dense acrid smoke filling the room and, partly obscured behind it, Nicku. He was leaning over the stove, its door wide open, pouring oil on bundles of papers and forcing them frantically into the red glow of the coals.

"What the—?"

The deputy twitched in fright as he saw Anton. The kerosene can fell from his grasp, rolling, spilling its viscous yellow contents across the floor.

"Look, boss, I can explain," he said, raising his hands in defence. "It's not how it looks. I didn't mean to—"

For a moment Anton struggled to take in what he was seeing, then understood what the deputy was doing.

"You bastard," he spat.

Shaking, and desperate to destroy the last of the evidence, Nicku grabbed what remained of the papers and thrust them towards the open mouth of the stove.

Anton heard Kravnik yell: "Stop him, Yoska!" and the lawman instantly dived, trying to cover the distance between himself and the stove.

He knew, right from the moment he threw himself forward, that he wasn't going to make it in time. The bundle went onto the coals with a sizzling, crackling, rush.

Hands now free, the deputy swung a punch, but too slowly. Anton anticipated it, ducking under the arcing fist and barrelled full-pelt into the man. They both crashed to the floor.

Anton landed on top and the deputy cried out as he felt his arm being twisted up high behind his back.

"Let me go," he grunted, teeth clenched.

Anton had no intention of releasing his grip and forced the man's head to the floor, his wiry grey hair smearing through the spilt oil.

"Get the papers, quickly," he shouted, but the Count was ahead of him and was already half way to the stove.

Anton had never seen the aristocrat move so quickly. With a gasp, the Envoy reached the open stove, grabbed the sheets still protruding and pulled them out.

The ends burnt fiercely, the red glow racing up the rolled papers - threatening to turn them into a blazing torch.

For a horrifying instant, Anton thought the nobleman was going to drop them on to the oil-soaked floor. Just then Pavel ran in with two pails of water and Kravnik thrust the burning bundle into the water. The flames extinguished with a satisfying hiss.

"Right," Anton told Nicku, twisting the man's arm so hard he yelped. "I want answers. What have you been up to? What were you trying to get rid of?"

Nicku swore, refusing to say anything else.

"I think I can solve that little riddle," Kravnik said, glancing at the sheets he'd unpeeled. "They appear to be your missing Wanted posters."

Anton felt astonishment and anger surge through him. "The bastard must have been opening the courier's weekly despatches and removing them."

"Why would he do that?"

"To sabotage me," Anton answered. "To make me look incompetent."

"To show the world how useless he is," Nicku muttered, between pained gasps. "What a fraud the great almighty Anton Yoska really is."

He coughed hard, both from the pain and the smoke.

"Ah," the Count said, holding the sheets away from him to stop the wet ends dripping on his clothes. "I suppose that accounts, in part, for the disastrous results you have been having, Lord Marshal."

"How long?" Anton demanded, face up close to Nicku's. "How long have you been doing this?"

Nicku grunted unrepentantly. "A year... maybe eighteen months."

Both Marshal and the Envoy came to the same thought at once.

Kravnik rifled through the pile of papers, searching... and after a few seconds gave a loud yelp.

"It transpires," he announced, "that your Mr Drubrick has been telling the truth after all."

Sighing, he held up an exact copy of the Modjeski wanted poster, singed but complete right down to the Imperial Seal on the bottom.

Gregor winced, forehead wrinkling in pain. His stomach was growing worse, the corrosive acid gnawing at his guts.

He rubbed his side to ease the throbbing caustic sensation, making sure he kept his largest crucifix steady, held high, directly facing the prisoner. Its silvery glow shimmered in the gloom, casting strange and magical shadows.

"You all right, old man?" Irina shouted across to him.

"My insides," he replied, "are agony. I'm suffering torments."

He belched loudly, feeling little relief from the burning within.

He was too old for this, he told himself as he looked to the deputies' room where the lawmen had dashed minutes before and where there was an ominous silence after the yells and loud crashes. Too old for this stress, disruption and dread. Too old to be missing his sleep and snatching meals on the run.

Certainly too old to be bounced around for hours on end as the mad dwarf made the cart career dangerously over the rutted and uneven track.

"Take your medicine," Irina advised, her tone lacking sympathy. "Your special elixir, that herbal muck that stinks of dead cats."

Oh yes, take my medicine. Why didn't I think of that? he thought sarcastically. For a woman she had remarkably little compassion.

This was the final straw, he vowed, as awkwardly he swung the pouch off his shoulder and, one handed, opened the flap. Regardless of what Milosh wanted or planned, Gregor promised himself he was getting out of this anarchic band of mercenaries as soon as he could manage. This was his last adventure, his final encounter with the forces of Satan.

He just hoped Milosh could get enough gold to make it possible. It wasn't certain, he reflected soberly. Although Milosh was supremely confident he could get this Marshal to dance to his tune, he wasn't so sure. There was something about the lawman, if you looked deeply enough, looked past the beaten, world weary exterior.

Mumbling to himself, he rooted around in the bag. The elixir bottle was in there somewhere, hidden in the jumble of items. Annoyingly, there were so many vials, packets, pamphlets, crosses, stakes and bibles stuffed inside that it was difficult to locate.

After a moment, he found the small blue bottle and brought it out, eager to swig the indigestion remedy. Yet, even as he grasped the bottle and unscrewed the cap using his teeth, he looked into the disorganised bag and made a discovery, a chilling discovery, that meant no amount of elixir could still the new, urgent, churning in his belly.

CHAPTER 21

Kravnik regarded the poster for a third time. Memories flooded back. Of course, this explained it all.

"A terrible business. Truly horrific. I had forgotten... how could I forget such a thing?" he muttered, noting the Marshal's puzzled expression. "It was more than three years ago."

He showed Anton the handbill listing the names of six victims. All women, all cruelly and spectacularly slain in sexual sadism of unbelievable depravity.

"It lasted nearly a week. The Capitol was in terror," he recalled. "Each night another one, mauled, desecrated. It caused widespread panic amongst the nobility. The murderer was obviously targeting aristocrats. It knew who they were, was able to gain access to the places they dined, the gambling houses, their places of entertainment."

"Because it was an aristocrat too," Anton ventured and Kravnik agreed, marvelling at how swift the lawman was on the uptake for a plodding constable.

"We never identified the fiend responsible. There was not enough evidence. There were plenty of candidates, members of the grand nosferatu families, all with certain connections, as well as appetites..."

"Yet I never heard a thing," Anton said in amazement. "Six deaths caused by a vampire, and I didn't know anything about it?"

"Brejnei is remote, a benighted rural backwater. I doubt you are aware of a tenth of what happens back in civilisation," Kravnik suggested. "Besides, it was decided not to unduly alarm the populace at large by letting the news spread more widely."

He saw Anton's flabbergasted expression and guessed what he was thinking. *Not to unduly alarm?* The Marshal probably thought they should have screamed the news from the rooftops.

"It is not wise to give the most important people in the country the idea that The Brethren can simply venture off their reservations, feasting on whomever they choose. It is bad for morale," he elaborated, noting the lawman's incredulous look.

"There was some discussion at Court about availing ourselves of your services," he disclosed. "However, it was agreed your methods, although effective, were less than discreet."

"Plus, I'd have told Leopold I wasn't for hire. Not against a foe like that," Anton pointed out.

"Quite so."

Six aristocrats slaughtered. A deliberate affront striking at the heart of the establishment, reminding all that despite Mankind's victory in the war the corralled vampire clans would never be controlled; never be truly tamed.

Shamefully, Kravnik recalled he had argued no action be taken. The state couldn't afford to rekindle the animosities between the *infernals* and humanity, he'd counselled. It was politically dangerous to give the squabbling sections of The Brethren a cause to unite.

He studied the Marshal for signs the man was somehow pleased it was nobles who'd suffered and not his beloved common people. However, he saw only despondency.

Perhaps Yoska's reputation as a closet revolutionary, a man who couldn't be trusted as 'one of us', was exaggerated.

Yet, even as he began re-evaluating the lawman, Anton remarked: "Do you know what's most appalling about this? Even in the midst of death and terror you care most about safeguarding privilege and wealth. If a vampire kills a peasant or two it is only worth the standard modest bounty, but if one of these foul creatures kills a member of the aristocracy then there's a huge price on its head."

Kravnik allowed himself a weary smile.

"You must try not to let the chip on your shoulder show quite so openly," he cautioned. "You have to learn a peasant's life is worth nothing. It is a simple fact of economics. Ordinary people are so... ordinary. There are so many of them."

Anton glared.

But why had Leopold decided to issue a warrant now after all this time? the lawman probed. What had finally convinced their ruler that Stefan Modjeski was the predator responsible for the blood spree?

"I cannot speculate," Kravnik answered truthfully. "I have no idea. Perhaps missing evidence has come to light. Some new clue or witness. Or more likely Leopold's patience has become exhausted and he has selected Stefan as the most likely culprit."

An intriguing possibility entered his mind. Or perhaps The Sovereign now deemed the time right to act against Kristina Modjeski; to prevent her extending her sphere of pernicious influence far beyond the country's borders. Executing her son would be the most brutal reminder to the ambitious bitch of who held the true power in Transylvania.

Why 1,000 gold crowns? Why so much? Anton pressed, interrupting his musing. It was unheard of, even for the most heinous and brutal criminals.

That part of the mystery, Kravnik knew he could answer.

"To attract the attention of your friend Drubrick and his ilk," he explained. "To ensure The Brethren, especially the Modjeski family, got the message that there is a limit to what we will tolerate."

He tapped at the poster, at the last name on the list of victims. "To underline that one cannot rape and butcher The Crown Prince's own God-daughter and hope to escape retribution."

CHAPTER 22

"Holy shit! Would you look at this," Milosh declared, taking in the first- floor parlour in one appreciative sweep. "This building is huge. I've stayed in smaller hotels."

"It's not as grand as it appears," Anton quickly countered. "They intended it to be a regional governor's house or some such but it never happened. Apart from my office, the kitchens and the dining room, nearly all downstairs is closed up or used for storage. We all live up here on the first floor, and that includes the servants' quarters."

Milosh mused. "Still, look at it all - drapes, fine furniture, carpets! Who'd have imagined a humble sheriff would lead such a pampered life."

He strode across the room, snatching the brandy decanter from the shelf and sniffed the amber liquid before putting the crystal container to his lips and taking a deep swig.

"Yes, indeedie," he said, sinking with a grunt into one of the armchairs and putting up his muddy boots on the other. "You're living in the lap of luxury, old friend. Servants. Soft sheets. Regular wages and three square meals a day. I envy you."

"I doubt that," Anton replied evenly, trying not to show his annoyance as the large man produced a dog-eared cigar from his waistcoat and lit it with great ceremony, blowing large shimmering smoke rings up towards the ceiling.

Both men had left the others to air out the cellblock, opening all the windows to banish the thick, acrid fumes. Now it was becoming as bad in here, he reflected, as the cigar smoke spread across the room.

Kravnik's words still rang in his mind from half an hour earlier. "This poster changes everything. As much as it appals both you and I, you must take the vampire into custody without delay.

"Crown Prince Leopold's wishes are obvious. He will want Stefan Modjeski put through a show trial. Our master will insist on a public execution, the maximum amount of humiliation. It will be a demonstration of state power."

"You mean it will be a sop to Leopold's vanity, an excuse for him to repair his damaged pride," Anton had retorted.

"And as such," the Count pressed on, ignoring the treasonous remarks, "it will be your duty to see the vampire remains safe and undamaged; your responsibility to ensure nothing untoward happens to it until arrangements can be made to transport it to the Capitol under heavy escort."

With that pronouncement, Anton's world had turned on its head.

"I could do with a cushy number like this," Milosh went on, snapping Anton's thoughts back to the here and now. "Maybe I should get the blue-blood to make me Marshal instead of you. It can't be hard to keep the peace in a third-rate dump like Brejnei. What'd you think?"

Anton regarded him coldly. "If there was any way I could swap places, I would. Right now, I'd like nothing better than to ride out of here and never look back. Only I can't. I have solemn obligations to discharge, and a crisis blowing up. All thanks to you." He gave a bitter laugh. "Besides, the idea of you being Marshal is ridiculous."

"Because I'd be the biggest crook around?" Milosh prompted jovially, letting ash fall carelessly from his smoke.

"Because you enjoy hurting people too much."

Visualising the badly injured and abused body of the vampire, with its multitude of raw slashes and bruises, he added accusingly: "Because you enjoy torturing prisoners."

Milosh sighed, bored, taking another swig, amber liquid dribbling, staining his shirt. "All right, I admit it. We gave the bloodsucker a good hiding. He had it coming. He cost me dearer than you can imagine."

Anton couldn't keep the repugnance from his voice. "Nothing you can say justifies that kind of savagery."

The bounty hunter was unmoved. "I don't see why you're acting so high and mighty. You used to do much worse," he reminded. "That's what scared the leeches so much. You were ruthless. Brutal. You used to get the job done."

"That was in the war. A long time ago. I was a different person."

"A better person. Not some whining milk-sop do-gooder. You never used to be so squeamish. All this fine living has softened you, turned you into a pen pusher."

The words hit home. Anton swallowed. He'd never considered it before, but Milosh was right. These days he *was* nothing more than a glorified civil servant.

"And you of all people shouldn't care what happens to that particular fiend," the bounty hunter continued. "After what happened, what it did..."

He didn't explain. He didn't need to.

Neither spoke, tension twisting, then unexpectedly Milosh leapt to his feet, shaking himself vigorously like a dog emerging from water.

"I'm bored with all this prattle about duty and honour and other pious nonsense. It's depressing," he boomed, with a lop-sided grin. "Tell me, what do you think of my merry compatriots? Aren't they a beguiling band of rascals?"

Rascals? Vipers more like, Anton thought.

"I haven't encountered a group like them," he replied honestly.

"Hand-picked every one," Milosh enthused. "Each has a different talent. Especially Irina. She has many skills. Oh yes, quite a woman."

He leered, making his carnal meaning clear. "She's been with me for some time now. I slew her husband - he was extremely upset I'd cheated him at cards. I had to put a musket ball through his heart. It was the only way to shut up the whining fool." Chuckling, he added: "Of course, it left her a widow so I took her on. It seemed the only decent thing to do."

"Very charitable," Anton agreed sardonically. "Although I imagine it wasn't exactly a chore. She's certainly eye-catching—"

"And off limits to you!" Milosh warned.

"But it's the old man that truly intrigues me," Anton said. "He seems an unlikely bounty hunter."

"Ah Gregor. Our resident holy man and pain in the arse."

"Holy man?"

"Father Gregor Mathias. A priest." Milosh waved a finger to contradict himself. "That should be a *former*

135

priest. Nevertheless, still handy with the crucifix and holy water."

"And an expert on vampire lore," a voice announced from the doorway.

Turning, Anton saw the old man watching them, a bible under his arm.

"Yes," Milosh said mockingly, "he's a fine teller of vampire tales. Keeps us all entertained around the camp fire. When he's not too busy bothering God and preaching to us about the evil of our ways."

The old man gave Milosh a sour look, regarding the bottle with distaste.

"Perhaps I should preach harder if it stops you abusing God's creatures," he suggested, crossing the room.

The gang leader's laughter boomed scornfully. "God's creatures? They are God's creatures now? I'd have thought The Almighty more than anyone else would take delight in seeing them tormented. Aren't they the spawn of the devil?"

"No," the old man replied. "You are."

To Anton, he said: "Much as Drubrick pours scorn on my faith, he needs my services and he knows it. I still have contacts in the church, know techniques for subduing the abominations. I am familiar with how they think, how they'll react, what they'll do. I have my uses." His sharp look intensified. "Even if it does mean I have to keep company with hoodlums and thieves."

Anton was fascinated. "You're a *former* priest. What happened?"

He couldn't hide his curiosity. The church had waged a war centuries long against The Brethren. Surely, Father Mathias would have been a valuable asset. It wasn't as if he was too old - he was still battling vampires, even now. So why get rid of him?

Before Gregor could answer, Milosh jumped in, declaring: "He was too fond of the novice nuns and the communion wine."

He chortled at his own wit and Anton tensed. Sober, Milosh was unpredictable. Intoxicated, he could be lethal.

"I went against the orders of the Holy Father," Gregor said slowly, ignoring his leader's jibes. "I allowed a vampire to live."

Anton's eyebrow shot up.

"Helena was my friend... before The Brethren took her, before they transformed her. We had grown up together. I felt pity." He paused, lost in memory for a moment. "To my eternal shame I let her escape."

"What happened?" Anton asked, although he could guess.

"She went on to slaughter half my village."A wave of pain crossed his face, replaced immediately by anger and determination. "It's a mistake I never intend to repeat. I won't rest until the abominations are wiped out." He looked pointedly at Milosh. "Nevertheless, that isn't a licence for sadism and cruelty. They should die swiftly and with as much mercy as we can muster, God willing."

Milosh sighed loudly. "Gregor, you're full of shit, you know that. I've had enough of your religious clap trap to last me a—"

The door swung open. Irina stood there.

"The smoke's gone," she announced. "We're ready downstairs." She glanced at Anton, eyes lingering just a second too long.

He didn't meet her gaze, looking instead at Milosh, who took a long final puff on his cigar and, face hardening, mouthed "Off limits" with a determination that made the Marshal's mouth go instantly dry.

CHAPTER 23

Over the years Anton had deplored the darkness of the jailhouse's courtyard. With the outer gates shut, the interior was thrust into the densest gloom, making it difficult to unload prisoners, often having them stumble and fall. The small amount of sunlight allowed by the meagre skylights left much of the cobbled floor in perpetual dimness, adding to the sense of claustrophobia.

Now, as he surveyed the covered wagon, Anton thought with irony that today the courtyard needed to be even darker, any trace of solar rays banished from its inky interior.

Above him, Pavel swayed on a ladder hammering loudly, banging in the last of several rows of nails to secure blankets over the windows. Around the walls, hastily attached oil lamps threw out a peculiar illumination; frantic shadow shapes dancing as the flames flickered powerfully in the draughts. With the last vestiges of daylight screened out, Anton judged it would soon be safe to move their photosensitive captive into the cellblock.

And as Irina, Gregor and Johann pulled the heavy drape from the remainder of the cage, revealing its other contents, Anton couldn't stop a loud gasp escaping his lips.

"Good Lord above, a bear," he exclaimed.

"A brown bear," Kravnik agreed, edging away, the memory of his earlier fright still raw. "And a nasty looking brute. A man-eater, I'll warrant."

139

As if proving it could hear them, the animal lurched around and bellowed, the gut-wrenching sound ricocheting around the stone walls for several moments.

"Magnificent, isn't it?" Milosh commented, joining them. "Our secret weapon. Mean as a swindled Cossack and just as violent. And he gets even grouchier when he's been cooped up for ages. We need to let him out to exercise."

Anton's face clouded. The idea of letting the burly animal out of the cage troubled him as much as moving the vampire.

"Don't worry," the bounty hunter said, motioning to the dwarf. "Quintz will look after him."

"An eight-foot bear being supervised by a four-foot midget," Kravnik marvelled dryly. "This I have to witness for myself."

Giving a sharp whistle, Milosh signalled Quintz to bring out the animal. The mountain of fur roared again, and bared its teeth as the small man began to unlock its chains and free it from the side of the bars. Then, swiftly, it charged.

Instinctively, Anton averted his eyes, not wanting to see the carnage about to happen. However, there was no scream, no shouts of alarm.

Turning back, he saw the colossal beast was licking the dwarf's face!

"I can scarcely believe it," Kravnik muttered.

"It's his bear," Milosh explained to the two men as Quintz put a collar around the animal, attached a short chain to the band of leather around its neck, and coaxed it down as though it was a pet dog. "It would tear the head off anyone else, fortunately it dotes on him."

Pointing to the next building, Anton ordered Quintz to take the hulking brute into the stables, warning: "Put it in the farthest stall, away from the horses. And the instant you've finished exercising it, chain it up. We've got enough to worry about already."

The animal and keeper prowled slowly across the yard, a picture of companionship - the beast still taller than its handler, even when it was on all fours.

"Why bring along a bear?" Kravnik puzzled. "Surely it hampers you?"

"The animal is useful," Milosh explained with pride. "Vampires hate bears. They are terrified of them. They are one of the few creatures the Undead cannot control."

That made sense, Anton conceded. It also explained how the hunters had been able to overpower the mighty nosferatu male.

"So that's why you have Quintz in the gang," he suggested.

"It's not the only reason. He is also a good fighter, smart, and as you've seen for yourself, highly skilled with a knife."

True, Anton reflected, the dwarf was a dangerous opponent. Accurate. Even more worrying, fast, incredibly fast.

Milosh's voice tightened. "And, by the way, we're not a gang. We are a team of legitimate bounty hunters." He gave the Envoy a half nod. "All legal and sanctioned by our esteemed ruler."

Yes, Anton reflected bitterly, feral killers sanctioned by an even more pitiless murderer in a crown.

The bear safely led away, the group prepared to unload their deadly cargo. This was it, he apprehended sickly, his last chance to influence the terrifying events unfolding.

He pulled Milosh to one side, declaring: "Look, this is lunacy. Call it off. Take it somewhere else. I don't have the men, firepower or the facilities to deal with a vampire."

Milosh's face was impassive. "The jail seems okay to me," he replied, flatly. "Solid stone walls. Sturdy cells with thick iron bars. Enough chains and shackles to keep the parasite bound securely. Besides, you're resourceful. You're the famous vampire slayer. You'll cope."

"Except the Modjeski will already be searching for him. If they find out he's here, we haven't a hope of holding them off."

Anton kept his steadfast stare upon the gunman, searching for a flicker of indecision or pity. He saw none.

"Don't fret, old comrade," Milosh said gruffly. "The bloodsuckers haven't a clue where we are. They'll be running in circles, getting more and more confused. It's a big country and this God-forsaken dump is the last place they'll look." He added: "Send word to Leopold and he'll despatch half the army to your assistance. You can be the big hero all over again."

"Not if I'm dead."

"No one is going to die. There's no need to make a song and dance of it. All you have to do is sit tight and keep the creature heavily drugged so he stays docile until the cavalry arrives."

His beefy palm patted Anton on the cheek, with all the force of a slap, as he scoffed: "Even you can manage that."

Yawning, he sauntered away. Behind him, Anton glared. The insult stung, yet not as much as the knowledge that no matter how easy the ruffian had made it sound, what Milosh had suggested was impossible.

Even if Anton had anyone he could trust to convey the message to Leopold, it would take more than a week for the round journey. The troops wouldn't get to Brejnei in time.

For all his glib, empty reassurances, Milosh must know this. In fact, Anton sensed, the gang leader was counting on it...

CHAPTER 24

There was no putting it off any longer, he reflected heavily, it was time to move the ogre to the maximum security cell.

Wiping his wet palms, Anton advanced slowly across the cobblestones towards the wagon, each step a thunderclap in the tense silence.

The horses had been uncoupled and led away, the bear was safely housed in the stables under Quintz's watchful care, and Anton had positioned the bounty hunters around the vehicle, muskets trained on the prostrate, comatose vampire. Milosh was up close, his widow-maker shotgun aimed straight at its head, while Gregor fidgeted around the perimeter with his tall, metal crucifix, bending under its punishing burden.

Well back from the line of fire, Pavel stood by Kravnik's side, both pallid and excited, staring at the spectacle unfolding with keen, shining eyes.

Anton had got as much firepower as he could muster. It did little, however, to still his nagging dread.

The transfer had to run without a hitch. If they lost control for even an instant, they were doomed. A virile male vampire was the most formidable predator under God's Heaven, and if it got loose it could dispatch them all in seconds.

"Are you sure it's drugged?" An anxious voice behind him whined. "It looks like it's pretending. It's awake and just waiting to attack. Christ, I just know it."

Anton grabbed the owner of the voice roughly and thrust him forward, sending the figure skidding towards the cart. "Well, that's for you to find out, isn't it, Nicku," he prompted icily. "You get the honour of checking. Your antics with the fire have earned you that plum job."

Earlier, Milosh had suggested Anton break every bone in the double-crossing deputy's body. "If any of mine had done me over like that, I wouldn't hesitate," he'd declared.

The idea had been seductive, Anton thought, but he needed as much manpower as possible, no matter how poor the calibre of the man.

Stumbling, Nicku pulled up less than a yard shy of the cages, looking back with naked resentment.

"You'll need this," Anton announced and flung a bunch of large, heavy keys at him. "And this."

The straitjacket fell short and Nicku had to bend to snatch it. His expression hardened as he tucked it under his arm, exhaling noisily as Irina giggled at his discomfort and Johann shook his head in disbelief.

Muttering, Nicku inserted the key in the lock and, venturing up the three wooden steps, swung open the cage door which protested; screeching like a scalded cat.

Anton shivered, recalling how the bounty hunters had madly tried to unload their captive just an hour before without the necessary precautions. If he hadn't got back to the courtyard in time to stop them... The prospect was too terrible to contemplate.

Nicku stopped, unwilling to step inside.

"No hesitations. Do it now," Anton told him harshly, "or I'll lock you in there with it."

"You heard the Lord Marshal," Kravnik instructed loudly. "Get to it."

Nicku knew better than to let the Count see his anger and rebelliousness. Muttering a silent oath, the sweating deputy reached out gingerly, brushing the slumbering nosferatu's face. It moaned softly and he flinched.

He looked back to Anton pleadingly. His boss's expression didn't soften, miming for Nicku to pull up the vampire's eyelid. Swallowing hard, he carefully moved back the fold of skin.

"Well?"

"I can't tell. I can't tell, dammit. He seems out of it, but..."

"Slap its face," Irina suggested.

"What?"

"Hit it," Milosh exhorted. "Hard. It won't be able to fake anything if it's inflamed."

Licking his lips anxiously, Nicku drew back his hand and slapped - the blow a faint, wet, glancing contact, devoid of aggression.

Kravnik rolled his eyes. "Ridiculous," he said, scathingly.

Suddenly Johann was dropping his gun and rushing over. "For Christ's sake, hit it," he rebuked, climbing into the cage, shoving Nicku to one side.

"Like this." The bounty hunter landed a solid, stinging blow on the comatose captive.

"Hard as you can," he instructed and swung again. The sound increased as did the severity of the smack.

"You've got to show it who's in charge," he said, voice rising giving the creature a cuff that smacked its head back with a sickening crunch.

"You've got to show the bastard it can't slay your friend and get away with it." The fingers balled into a fist and

146

jabbed as he bawled: "This is for Theodore, you fucking animal."

Instantly Anton was pushing his way through. "That's enough," he yelled. "It's had enough, stop it. The prisoner is under my protection."

"Protection? Your protection? Good. He's going to need it."

Johann's fist pulled back as far as he could stretch, building up for a lethal uppercut. However, the unmistakable click of the shotgun being cocked made him halt, frozen in mid action like a brutal statue.

"You heard Marshal Yoska," Milosh said, voice low. "The bloodsucker has taken enough punishment for now. We need it alive."

For an instant Johann didn't respond, warily eyeing the shotgun, then slowly broke into a sly grin and stepped back, hands high in mock surrender. "Sure thing. No more. I get it."

Anton looked questioningly at Irina. "Theodore?" he mouthed, bemused.

She looked downwards, eyes clouding. "He didn't make it," she replied softly.

"God rest his soul," Gregor added, crossing himself clumsily under the weight of the cumbersome crucifix.

So there had been another member of the gang. That's what Milosh had meant about the creature costing him dear. Stefan Modjeski had fought with lethal fury during his capture, and being outnumbered hadn't stopped him slaughtering a heavily armed, experienced fighter. That thought made Anton even more determined to move the vampire quickly.

"Unlock his chains and get the straitjacket on him," he ordered the deputy and sadistic bounty hunter, now holding Stefan's slumped body between them. "Make sure it's tied tightly. Put some muscle into it. I want him trussed up like a Christmas goose."

They worked swiftly, jerking the anaesthetised vampire's arms backwards, pulling buckles shut, tugging cords to breaking point, apprehension making each motion fast and brutal. Presently, the creature was bound, hefty manacles fastened to its legs, arms wrapped tightly around its body by the jacket's layers of thick canvas.

Grunting, the men manhandled the now bound prisoner like a sack of corn, not caring as its legs thumped painfully against the sharp edges of the steps.

Drooping, Stefan Modjeski appeared subjugated. Anton wasn't going to take any risks. "Wait," he cried, rushing forward.

"One final precaution," he said, producing an iron object from the satchel fastened around his waist. "A souvenir from the war."

It was a mask, a cumbersome medieval device guaranteed to subdue the unfortunate victim forced to wear it. It had slits for the eyes, tiny air holes around the nosepiece. Crucially, the aperture for the mouth was covered by a grid of interwoven bite-proof mesh. The whole contraption opened at the rear, where three hinged flanges were welded, the brutal headpiece held closed by sturdy padlocks.

"Prop him up," Anton instructed, hurriedly unlocking it. "Hold him still while I fit this."

Johann whistled appreciatively. "Now that's more like it," he encouraged, pulling the creature's lolling head fiercely upwards by the hair.

Advancing, Anton thrust the mask forward, lining up the cumbersome apparatus with the vampire's features, and pushed, fingers edging closer. Metal made contact with its nose, and Anton placed a palm on each side of the device, forcing it around the skull. But he didn't get to complete the manoeuvre.

Later, he'd learn that in an overpowering psychic burst he'd lost all sense of his surroundings; time, space, the sounds and smells had been cut off from those around him as his hands magically stuck to the cowl.

All he knew in that split second was unbelievable pain as a thousand bolts of agony pulsated through his body and he was held captive - juddering, lips foaming, convulsing like a man possessed.

CHAPTER 25

Screams...

The stench of cordite...

Weeping...

Isolated musket shots, followed by the sound of ripping flesh...

Shuddering, he knew it was Ossiak, and somehow he'd been transported back to his most terrifying nightmare.

Forcing open his eyes he saw the battlefield littered with the dead and dying, blood-drenched uniforms sprawled in a seething moaning mass of suffering and helplessness. All around towering figures in black ripped, mauled and drank, moving greedily from body to body.

In the pile of corpses, Anton lay, paralysed, unable to raise his head or reach to stem the rich stream pouring from the gaping wound in his torn neck. He coughed in ragged spasms, shivering as the coldness of the grave crept relentlessly through him, harbinger to his inevitable fate.

Into his eye-line, a lone nosferatu commander trod triumphantly through the charnel house chaos and laughed, exhorting the others to more heinous acts of viciousness, bellowing: "Feast, feast, my brothers. Drink deep. Celebrate. Rejoice. Don't stop until you have drained every last drop."

Then it turned its attention to Anton with cruel amusement.

"And what do we have here?" it asked, examining his uniform. "A lieutenant. A dashing young officer. The pride of *the Imperial Cavalry. And so brave, so determined. Even now I see defiance in his dying eyes."*

The creature knelt by him. "Shall I watch you fade away?" he mocked. "Shall I see if I can detect the mystical moment when your soul departs its feeble shell?"

Anton tried to curse his tormentor. The words wouldn't come through his dry and cracked lips; only a gurgling rasp.

"No," the male said, debating with himself. "That would be a waste. It would be a travesty to allow such a pretty soldier boy to become food for the worms. No, my fine martial friend, I have another fate in mind for you. I shall keep you for myself."

He ran a long nailed finger across Anton's cheek, in a chilling caress. "You will be a welcome addition to my noble house."

With that he slashed the nail across his own wrist, and howled in elation as he pushed the wound against Anton's open mouth, forcing in droplets of crimson-hued infection.

"There will be pain, confusion, terror and sickness," the creature said soothingly, as Anton's back arched and he convulsed uncontrollably, "however, that will pass and then you will know eternal bliss. You will know the gift of immense power. You will learn what it is to be a god amongst m—"

"Marshal!"

"Yoska!"

"Snap out of it, man. Quickly, someone pull him free."

Anxious voices called through the fog of recollection, pulling him back from his subconscious, as he sensed his shaking pain-filled palms prised free from the mask.

Instantly the battlefield was gone. Vanished. Evaporated like an evil magician's illusion. But not the apparition of his tormentor; the nemesis whose face hadn't aged a day in eleven years. The old adversary who now gawped at Anton through the metal mask, eyes wide in shocked recognition, watching in rapt fascination as the lawman's legs buckled and he went crashing into the beckoning darkness.

CHAPTER 26

"Drink this," Gregor urged, thrusting the glass of water towards him. Gulping, Anton drained it in a single swallow and held out the vessel, mumbling shakily: "More."

He took longer with the second glass, feeling its coolness caress the back of his raw throat, dowsing the fire below.

"Are you all right?" the old man asked, as Anton coughed, wincing as the nagging migraine crept back.

"I feel like a horse kicked me in the head," he replied gruffly, "Give me a moment or two to get my wits together."

Blinking, he discovered he was lying under a blanket on the couch in his parlour.

"What happened?" he asked groggily.

"You passed out. Johann and Pavel carried you here. You were blabbering on about the creature. Most of it didn't make sense."

The cleric dipped into his bag and brought out a small potion bottle. "Here, take this. It will help with the shock."

"What is it?"

"Mostly herbs. It's a medicinal compound of my own devising. It will calm your nerves and reduce the nausea."

The green liquid looked unappealing, thick and greasy. Anton sipped it hesitantly. It tasted like the bottom of a stagnant pond.

"The prisoner?" he asked anxiously, trying to sit up. "I must check on—"

"Taken care of," Gregor reassured, gently forcing him back. "The creature is in the maximum security cell, securely shackled to the walls. Nicku is guarding it. And Johann is guarding Nicku."

Well, at least that was something, Anton thought.

"And Sofia? My wife?"

"No change, I'm afraid," Gregor answered wearily. "I checked with the boy, Tomas. He wouldn't let me in. I had to converse with him through the locked door. He says she is sleeping fitfully. The fever still holds her in its grip."

Anton fought to stop melancholy washing over him, drowning him in its despair. He knew it was foolish to hope for some miracle. He had to accept the inevitable.

"The boy said you both drank from a contaminated well," Gregor reported, interrupting his train of thought. "Yet you were unaffected. I don't see—"

"I spat it out," Anton explained. "I sensed the water was tainted. I tried to warn Sofia but it was too late. She'd already swallowed too much."

"And you have shown no symptoms since?"

"None that I am aware of."

"Remarkable," Gregor said, half to himself. "Even a few drops should be enough to guarantee infection. You obviously have a strong constitution, or..." he stroked his chin thoughtfully, "...a guardian angel. Whichever it is, the good Lord above seems to be watching over you."

Anton doubted it.

The door opened and Kravnik entered, flanked by Milosh and Irina.

"Ah, I see you are back with us." The Envoy's tone betrayed relief. "You have been under for almost an hour and a half. I feared, at one point, we might have lost you."

He flicked his eyes meaningfully at Milosh who was loudly munching on a chicken leg and Irina who had obviously bathed and was now wearing several items of Sofia's jewellery. "As you can see our guests have taken the opportunity to make themselves at home."

Forcing back his irritation, Anton stared meaningfully at Milosh. "The creature? Its eyes opened?"

Kravnik nodded. "It was truly impressive. He viewed you with such unadorned hostility. It was clear no matter how much you despise Stefan Modjeski, he loathes you more."

Pausing in mid chew, Milosh chuckled. "He has good cause. Trust me, Your Highness. Which is why we brought him here, of all the jails in the land."

"How long?" Anton pressed.

"What?"

"How long were its eyes open?"

"I fail to see what importance that has—" Kravnik began as Milosh cut across him.

"A few seconds," the big man answered. "A heartbeat or two. No more. Nothing."

"That's all it takes," Anton reminded.

He saw puzzlement cross the Count's face.

"To communicate with his kind. To summon help," Anton explained, watching Kravnik's expression transfer from bemusement to apprehension.

"The creatures can project their thoughts?" the noble asked worriedly. "Speak to each other in their heads? I thought that was a fallacy."

"It's a fact. They can link their minds, sense each other's emotions," Anton confirmed. "We just don't know how they do it or over what distances it is effective."

"So you are telling me the Modjeski may already know their kinsman is here?" Kravnik's face paled.

"No," Milosh declared forcefully, as he finished the chicken, flinging the leg bone into the fire and wiping his greasy fingers on his coarse trousers. "The bloodsuckers haven't a clue where he is. They'd have to be close by to form a psychic link and we're a long way from the nearest reservation." He sighed. "In case it escaped anyone's notice our captive is so heavily drugged he's unable to think straight. He might have recognised Yoska, but he was back in his coma a moment later. No harm done."

No harm done? You're willing to gamble all our lives on that?

The bounty hunter snorted, as though he too could read thoughts, and chided Anton: "Stop being such an old woman. We're safe. I guarantee it."

A chill gripped Anton's body as he muttered: "I wonder how many people have that empty promise engraved on their tombstones."

CHAPTER 27

A face, an indistinct visage, swimming through her disturbed slumber; features at first unclear then becoming stronger, more pronounced. Kristina Modjeski fought the drowsiness, the fog clouding her ravaged mind as she slept.

She moaned in frustration, trying to concentrate, forcing the face to become tangible and whole. It was a man - handsome, noble, brave though troubled.

Stefan? No, no... not Stefan. Her son's face was clear in her mind and her heart and this was different, a face that triggered vague, distant stirrings of fear and discomfort.

Oh, why couldn't she see clearly?

She pushed upwards with all her mental power, clawing her way back from the depths of unconsciousness. She must fight to focus, drive away the stupor paralysing her.

For moments she despaired, thrashing, as helplessness engulfed her again. Then it began to clear; the veil started to lift. She could see.

With a mighty hiss, she sat bolt upright, awake.

The face was in sharp relief, features clear, the man's dark expression and determination rendered with sickening clarity.

It wasn't a dream but a vision.

A vision seen through her son's pained eyes.

A vision of the old enemy...

Yoska!

"You have no faith in Drubrick's assurance about our safety, do you?" Kravnik insisted, looming over Anton as the Marshal splashed cold water from the washbasin over his face.

"No," he replied, regarding his wan reflection with a growing sense of futility. "It's a lie. Or at best, a naïve hope."

Grabbing the towel, he scrubbed at his cheeks much more roughly than needed. "Even if we have providence on our side and the abomination didn't communicate with his clan, we've simply bought ourselves a little more time. They won't rest until they locate him. As soon as darkness falls the creatures will be scouring the countryside, looking for tracks, torturing anyone they find for information. Eventually they'll work out he's here."

"Surely the Modjeski will not dare come to Brejnei," Kravnik interjected, touching his throat absent-mindedly as though checking it was still intact. "Not with you here. Your reputation..."

"Won't deter them for a moment." Anton gave him a pitying look. "They will stop at nothing to rescue Stefan. They won't let anyone stand in their way."

The Count's lips pinched. "There must be something you can do."

"I'm open to suggestions."

"Commandeer the gang's vehicle. Have your deputies transport the creature somewhere else, to another jurisdiction. If the Modjeski knew their kinsman was no longer here they might leave Brejnei alone."

Anton laughed bitterly. "I can't tell you how many ways that could go wrong. Just supposing my deputies could smuggle the cart past a populace who'd happily drag the vampire into the daylight and watch it burn, how far do you think they'd get before Nicku saw his opportunity to overpower Pavel and make off? And if Pavel put up any kind of struggle that treacherous bastard would murder him for sure.

"I'd have one dead deputy, another on the run and a comatose prisoner stranded on the open road. And God knows what would happen if night fell and the bloodsucker got free from the cage."

He glanced anxiously at the clock. Five past two. Half the day gone, only a few hours until twilight.

"Anyway, moving the prisoner is out of the question," he continued. "As you said, Leopold will expect me to keep the thing safely locked up here, not risking it in some half-baked attempt to get it off my turf. Losing Stefan Modjeski would be just the excuse he needs to act against me."

Both fell silent as the implications sank in.

"You talk like a doomed man," Kravnik observed.

"If I do it was you who sealed my fate the moment you allowed Milosh Drubrick and his crooks to come into town."

The aristocrat looked away for a second. "I had no idea…"

"You have to hand it to Milosh," Anton said in bitter admiration. "The set-up is a work of evil genius. Whatever happens, I'm done for."

The Count bit the side of his face, lost in thought. "I perceive the plan is fiendishly clever," he allowed. "Nonetheless, the nosferatu will surely still want vengeance on the bounty hunters, will still pursue them wherever they go?"

"Most certainly. The Modjeski won't rest until they've butchered the entire gang as a warning to others. But Milosh will have determined that he can run an extremely long way on 1,000 gold crowns. And he's arrogant enough to think he can outwit them."

As he's outwitted me...

"You could run. Save yourself."

Anton gave him a weary look. "I don't run. As you so pointedly reminded me - I'm the fearless hero of the vampire wars."

He jerked his head towards Sofia's bedroom. "And I can't leave. Milosh couldn't have known my wife would be sick, but it's given his plan an extra sadistic twist."

Kravnik ran a hand over his chin. "She is dying," he pointed out. "No one would blame you if you left her behind."

"I would blame me. It's out of the question. I'm not forsaking the woman I love, not for anything or anyone."

"Then you are a fool."

"Of that, there is no doubt."

"So you intend to simply give up?"

For the first time in hours Anton felt his grasp on events firming. "It's obvious that as well as knowing little about the Modjeski, you know even less about me," he replied sternly. "I never give up."

"Then what on Earth do you propose?"

"I have an idea how I can get Milosh and his gang to leave and take their prisoner with them."

The nobleman's tone was dubious. "And how, pray, will you achieve that miracle?"

Anton's face became chill and cunning. "There's one thing Milosh Drubrick has overlooked."

The Count raised a quizzical eyebrow.

"Brejnei is a very small town," Anton replied cryptically.

CHAPTER 28

His low, soft singing filled the stable block, each beguiling note wafting towards Heaven like a divine offering. Luxuriating in the melody's enchanting resonance, feeling the magical words swirl around his tongue, Quintz lay back against the welcoming pliability of the dense, musky fur.

Beneath him, the bear slumbered, relaxed, inert; its mighty chest rising and falling gently as it snored, enthralled by the ancient lullaby's intoxicating rhythms.

He stroked the giant beast, stretching as far as his short arms could reach, fingers digging into the warm fleecy pelt, the caress loving and tender.

"Rest, my mighty darling," he cooed. "You have earned your repose. Sleep deep. All is well. Our tasks are complete... for now."

He closed his eyes, recalling the lyrics to another ballad, even more beautiful and enthralling than the one he'd just finished and began to sing, pitch perfect, even though his mind was focusing elsewhere - on the stable door that had just furtively opened and the stealthy footsteps approaching.

His right hand moved fluidly from the smoothness of the fur to the rough inside of his coat, a cold blade sliding effortless into his palm.

"You will have to be much quieter than that if you hope to take me unawares," he challenged, breaking off the song. "Or maybe you have a death wish."

Opening one heavy lid, he aimed along the glistening edge of the stiletto, straight at the intruder hiding behind the stall wall, face obscured behind hanging saddles.

"You can die by my knife or be torn apart by the claws of my ferocious friend here. It's your choice," Quintz announced, as the hidden figure unexpectedly yelped and leapt out.

"Don't hurt me! I didn't mean any harm!"

The face was white, eyes startled and moist, raised hands trembling alarmingly.

"Don't throw the knife," the figure begged. "Please don't throw the knife or set the beast on me. I'll go. This instant. Look, I'm going." And he backed up shakily.

"Wait!"

Quintz regarded the terrified young face with amusement. "Not so fast, Pavel. Stay where you are. I want to know who sent you to spy on me."

The deputy's face went even paler. "Spy on you? No one sent me to spy on you!"

"Not Yoska. Not Kravnik?"

"No, no one. I told you, no one sent me."

"Then you decided to spy on me all for yourself."

"What! No - no. It's not like that. I wasn't spying." He gulped. "I just wanted a look. I've never seen—"

Quintz tilted his head, questioning. "A freak? A half man? A poor feeble dwarf?"

The youngster looked about to wet himself.

"A bear," Pavel spluttered. "I've never seen a bear. Not for real. Only in drawings. I wasn't looking at you, I swear."

Quintz resisted the temptation to torment the gullible young man further. It was far too easy and that robbed it of any real satisfaction.

"Come here," he instructed, beckoning with the knife.

For a moment Pavel didn't budge, then his dread of the diminutive man overcame his reluctance and he edged forward, one careful step at a time.

"How is it you've never seen a bear before?" Quintz enquired. "This region is famous for them. The woods overflow with thousands of the beasts. Even if you hadn't encountered one in the wild, you'd have seen performing bears at the cities, on market days, at the festivals."

Pavel looked down, the blush fetching some colour to his chalky cheeks.

"I've not been to a city before," he confessed. "Not been to a market or a festival. I've never been more than fifteen miles from Brejnei."

"Never?"

"Never," he confessed. "Most people here haven't ventured much beyond the town. They've never seen the need."

"Not even for courtship? Weddings?"

"No."

Quintz whistled softly, smiling to himself. "Well, that explains a lot," he murmured. "I imagine Brejnei isn't over-blessed with scholars. Or beauties."

"Sorry?"

"It doesn't matter," the small man dismissed amusedly, noting that the deputy's look of befuddlement was all the evidence anyone could want.

"Do you want a closer look at my companion?" he offered.

Pavel's head bobbed eagerly. "Of course! If it's all right? If you don't mind." He eyed it warily. "If it's safe?"

"He's asleep. You've nothing to fear. Moreover, he won't attack you while I'm here." He flashed the boy a wicked grin. "Not unless I tell him to, of course."

That joke did little to reassure the deputy. Quintz noticed the young man trembled even more as he stepped across the straw-covered floor.

"It's huge," he whispered, as he halted inches way, gazing in admiration at the slumbering animal.

"Some two hundred and eighty-five pounds - three times my weight," the dwarf estimated, "which is only right, as he is three times my stature."

"Does he have a name?"

"A fitting one too for a creature so powerful. He is called Samson."

The deputy's wide eyes moved over the amber fur, and the moist, black snout, taking in the ears and the short tail, coming to rest on the curved yellowed talons.

"The claws look so dangerous," he whispered in awe.

"More than just dangerous - lethal," the dwarf said proudly. "Three inches long and sharp as any razor. He could take off your face with one swipe."

On impulse Pavel leant back.

"Don't you want to come closer, touch the beast, feel his fur?" Quintz coaxed.

The young man waved his hand warily. "I can see well enough from here."

"Ah, Samson, our young visitor fears you." The small man ruffled the brown pelt playfully. "He doesn't understand you as I do. Doesn't appreciate how magnificently malevolent you are. How alike we both are, my beautiful fiendish brute."

He blew, a gentle ripple parting the fine hairs like waves. Pavel watched spellbound, also puzzled.

"You have questions? Something perplexes you?" Quintz prompted.

"I-I just won-wondered how you can exert s-such control over it," he stammered. "I don't get why he l-lets you handle him like that, like he's your p-pet."

"Oh, he is no one's pet," Quintz replied emphatically. "I can assure you. He is a friend, a companion, not a plaything. We have a special bond, a trust built up over years. He knows I would never allow anyone to hurt him and he would destroy anyone who tried to harm me. We are like brothers. Fellow travellers."

"But how? How did you win his trust? How did you ever get near him without being torn apart - or eaten?"

Quintz gave an enigmatic smirk tinged with sorrow.

"We have a friendship forged in suffering," he said, bitterly. "We both know what it is like to be beaten and abused, to face the wrath and scorn of men."

He grimaced, remembering. All those years ago. The canvas billowing high above his head, the music of the fiddlers and drummers, the roars and shrieks of terrified animals in cages, and the crack of whips - always the crack of whips.

"We were both in a travelling circus," he said softly, half to himself. "Myself from the age of six when my parents rejected me because they could no longer endure the shame of having brought an evil sprite into the world and Samson after being trapped and captured in the woods to replace another bear that had been worked to death."

His voice hardened. "Balthazar, the circus owner, was a cruel man, sadistic and drunken. A bastard of the first order. He took delight in tormenting all those in his charge, all those creatures too weak and powerless to prevent it. He employed all manners of violence. His favourite instrument of punishment was a long, wicked bullwhip, which he used on anyone or anything that sparked his ire."

Pavel's throat twitched. "And he used it on Samson?"

"Every wretched night, without pity, without exception. Until he drew blood. Until Samson wailed in pain, crimson matting his fur."

"Why?" Pavel insisted. "Why would he do that?"

"To make Samson perform. To make him dance for the jeering crowds throwing pennies. To prove no matter how fearsome and strong willed the bear might be, Balthazar could bend it to his will. To prove his dominion over all his belongings."

He paused, noting the young deputy's fists balling in empathy, knuckles turning white.

Oh, my young friend, your sense of indignation does you credit, but you have no idea, no inkling of what it was like - what I had to witness, what I had to endure.

"Did he... Did this man hit you?"

Quintz thought for several moments, trying to banish the spiteful images circling in his mind.

"Not at first," he recalled. "That came later. When I turned twelve, when he began to train me to perform in the ring. I thought he'd use me as a clown, most circuses employ dwarfs as clowns, but Balthazar had a more cunning idea in store for me. What more of a crowd pleaser would it be to have a midget as a knife thrower, what an attraction that would be.

"Alas, I was clumsy, uncoordinated, no aptitude at all. I couldn't hit a target no matter how closely I stood to it. Nevertheless, he had a solution, a way of rectifying my mistakes. For every knife I dropped, for each blade that missed its mark, he'd slice my legs, a single slash across the calves."

"That's horrible! Barbaric!"

"Yet effective," Quintz said. "You'd be astounded how quickly I improved, how proficient I became."

He let a look of cold satisfaction cross his face. "And how useful that dexterity proved when I finally decided to dispatch him from this world."

"You murdered him!"

"I had no choice. One night, he was drunker than usual, and flew into a maniacal temper, bellowing that he was going to teach Samson a lesson he would never forget. To my eternal shame I watched as he whipped my poor beauty a dozen times, then something inside me said 'no more - it ends. It ends now' and I intervened."

He gave a bitter sigh. "Or at least I tried to. When I grabbed at his arm, trying to wrestle the whip from his grasp, he brushed me off as though I was no more than a playful pup. I was dashed to the ground. If he'd stopped the beating then, if I'd succeeded in assuaging his fury, Balthazar might have lived."

There was silence for a moment, save the steady sonorous snore of the recumbent bear and Pavel's agitated breathing.

"What did you do?" he asked finally, voice tense.

"The only thing I could. I threw two of my knives. One into each of his eye sockets."

He rubbed at his legs, feeling the rough lines through the material, scabs that refused to heal, still hard, angry and puckered after two decades.

"I didn't miss. Each throw was perfect. Each blade sinking an inch into his brain. Balthazar taught me well. It was his gift to me." He sniffed harshly. "My gift, in turn, was not to let him suffer longer than necessary. He was dead before his miserable carcass hit the ground."

If Pavel had looked frightened when he first crept into the stable, he now appeared terrified.

"W-w-what happened then?"

"I fled and took Samson with me," Quintz replied. "For years we toured villages, performing, living on scraps, always on the run. Always looking after each other. Then, eventually, fate intervened and our paths crossed with Milosh Drubrick and we joined his gang."

He looked at the gleaming thin stiletto as though just remembering he had it in his clasp.

"However, that's an arrangement that's about to come to an end. After this grim adventure Samson and I are going to be free of him," he promised, and running his thumb lovingly along the wickedly keen edge, murmured: "One way... or another."

CHAPTER 29

Scowling, Nicku peered through the cell's spy hole. He could see the detested *infernal* was safely chained up, immobilised and drugged, door treble locked. Despite that he was still uneasy.

It was crazy having it here. Suicidal. You kept as far away from vampires as you could. Any moron knew that. So why, he asked himself, was he standing just feet away from one of the heathen creations, with only a few inches of steel plate as protection? Guard duty, Yoska called it, except Nicku knew it was revenge, punishment plain and simple; petty retribution.

He rubbed his shoulder. Christ, it hurt. That bastard had nearly yanked it out of its socket.

He had a good mind to quit and leave the Marshal and his scum criminal buddies to their fate. That would teach them. Leave them in the lurch, show them they couldn't treat him this way.

YOU DON'T NEED TO TAKE THIS ABUSE!

He didn't need to take this abuse, he told himself. Didn't need the almighty Anton Yoska looking down his nose at him, pushing him around like he was shit.

YOU ARE WORTH MORE THAN ALL OF THEM!

They had no right to sneer at him, Nicku thought, his sense of injustice burning. He was worth more than all of them.

170

Engrossed, he watched as Stefan Modjeski slumbered, occasionally moaning as he endured some opiate-fuelled dream.

I hope it's a nightmare, he thought savagely, just like the bloody nightmares he gives me.

"Are you afraid?"

"What?"

He turned to where Johann was sitting, stretched along a wooden cellblock bench, watching him with a smug self-assured look.

"I asked if you were afraid, friend," he repeated, gently stroking the length of his scar, fingers tracing the contours. "That is the seventh time you've looked in on the demon in as many minutes."

"No, of course not," Nicku snapped. "It's just regulations. I have to check prisoners on a regular basis. To make sure they're all right."

"Well, you are certainly very conscientious," Irina added, winking at Johann. She moved past Nicku, disconcertingly close, her hips tight under the riding britches. He dithered, unsure whether to look again through the cell spy hole or watch the woman's shapely progress as she sauntered up and down the corridor, Milosh's customised shotgun over her arm.

God, she was a turn-on.

"The thing could take ill. I'm supposed to monitor his condition," he explained weakly.

He sensed the woman's amusement and felt himself colour. "And if it wakes. It could try to escape," he added.

"And you'd be the one to stop it," she purred. "How brave. How reassuring to know you're on the case."

"Yes," Johann concurred, dryly. "I feel so much safer."

Fuming, Nicku went again towards the cell, then halted aware they were noting his moves. Oh, why don't they just bugger off? he thought irately.

Well, why doesn't that swaggering thug go? The woman could stay. He was prepared to put up with her. In fact, he reflected, she'd be just what he needed to take his mind off his deadly charge, and the sense of grievance gnawing away at him.

YOU CAN HAVE HER!

She was obviously up for it. Everything about her - her teasing walk, pouting lips, the come-hither eyes and the husky voice signalled she was available; more than available. He knew she'd be good; unforgettable.

ALL YOU HAVE TO DO IS REACH OUT. SHE WON'T RESIST.

He visualised what it would be like to have her there, right in the cellblock, on the floor, up against the wall, forcing himself into her - her holding on to the bars as he thrust... What a turn on that would be - fucking her, knowing the demon was slumbering right next to them.

SHE DESIRES YOU.

Sensing himself stiffen, he glanced down to see if his arousal was evident.

"So, my brave Nicku, have you been a deputy long?" she asked him, abruptly snapping him out of his erotic daydreams.

"Nine years," he replied, hiding his crotch behind his hands.

"So you know the Marshal well? You've served alongside him for a long time?"

He couldn't help his lip curling.

"I was here before him," he grunted. "Years before."

The woman raised an eyebrow.

"I was just wondering, what he's like," she prompted. "I've never known a legend before, especially not a hero of the vampire wars. He intrigues me."

YOU NEED A SMOKE.

"He's no hero," Nicku fired back, the intensity of his venom surprising even himself.

He pulled his pipe from deep inside his jacket and began pushing tobacco into the ceramic bowl. He lit it with a match, sucking in greedily, feeling the welcome tangy smoke instantly calming him.

"What I mean is few people around here view him as a hero," he corrected, trying to sound more reasonable. "You'll find precious few souls in Brejnei who look up to him."

"Oh yes? Why's that?" Johann asked.

"Because we all know he's a spy - for the Crown Prince. He was forced on us. You don't employ a man like him unless there's something going on. Yoska thinks we don't know, but we're not stupid. He's not on our side. He never has been. It's all an act."

"I find that difficult to believe," Irina said, giving him a dubious look.

"And there's more," Nicku continued quickly. "Ossiak. The massacre. His so-called finest hour."

"What about it?"

"Don't you think it's suspicious he was the only man to survive out of an entire cavalry troop? How did he stay alive when so many others died?"

He took a deep puff on his pipe, watching the smoke rise, reminding himself for a moment of the earlier incident in the deputies' room, the indignity and shame making his embarrassment multiply.

"There are rumours," he revealed with relish. "People talk. They say he betrayed his men, made a deal with the bloodsuckers to save his own life; was probably in league with them all along. No one trusts him."

At that, the bounty hunters exchanged a knowing look. *THEY DON'T BELIEVE YOU.*

"I only speak as I find," he insisted, feeling even more uncomfortable. It was as though he was under scrutiny. Screw these newcomers and their nosy questions.

"How long you going to be here?" he questioned, keen to do some snooping of his own.

Johann shrugged. "A few more hours. Maybe we'll stay overnight and rest up. Why are you asking, friend? Eager to get rid of us?"

"No," he lied, replying too quickly. "Just curious. That's all. I didn't mean anything by it."

"It all depends on your employer," Irina volunteered. "If he coughs up the reward without any fuss, we'll be on our way. If not, we'll need to stay awhile and help convince him."

Her tone was soft, reasonable, yet there was a hint of cruelty lurking just below the surface.

"It's not as if your shitty little town has much to offer in the way of diversions." She grinned teasingly. "Unless, of course, we count your handsome boss."

Any lust Nicku had for her vanished instantly.

"He is devoted to his wife," he said pointedly.

"That may well be. She is, however, on the edge of death. And after she's gone…"

"He wouldn't even look at you."

174

"Don't you think? Men can be so vulnerable when they have just been bereaved. They need a soft sympathetic shoulder to cry on." She pouted. "And I have my attractions. Be assured few men can resist me, especially when they are grieving and need comfort."

"Shut up!"

Johann's unexpected words boomed in the confined space.

Startled, Nicku saw the anger in the man's intense glare and instantly understood that the woman's wanton flaunting had been aimed at her fellow bounty hunter.

HE'S BEEN FUCKING HER BEHIND DRUBRICK'S BACK.

Nicku grinned lewdly as it all became clear. The slut was two-timing Milosh, pretending to be his woman, and his alone, except it was all a lie.

"Shut up," Johann repeated. "I don't want to hear any more."

Irina made a mocking face, and laughed, her whole body quivering with delight.

Yes, scar face was screwing her but only when she let him, Nicku surmised. She loved the sex but he could see she got even more pleasure from the sensual power of keeping her illicit suitor dangling, wanting, begging...

YOU CAN STOP HER LAUGHING.

Nicku frowned. That last thought felt strange, alien. He was enjoying her mockery, savouring Johann's obvious discomfort. Why ever would he want her to stop?

THIS WILL WIPE THE SMILE FROM HER TROLLOP LIPS.

He paused, puzzled. What would? A finger of ice gripped his heart as he looked up and saw that, indeed,

Irina had stopped laughing, and both she and Johann were staring at him in shock.

Neither spoke, mouths open, aghast. He instantly knew something wasn't right. They were staring at his hands.

Shaking with trepidation, he let his own eyes slowly pan downwards - to where he had casually emptied the entire searing contents of his pipe onto his open palm, the skin already reddened and raw under the glowing embers.

His mind wouldn't take it in. He thought it an illusion, a trick, some sort of witchcraft. He did a double take, unable to understand what was happening. It wasn't possible.

Then he heard a voice inside his head whisper: *THIS IS BUT A TASTE OF THE AGONIES TO COME.*

In an instant the numbness ended and Nicku shrieked as his blistering, weeping hand curled in waves of excruciating pain.

CHAPTER 30

"What the hell is this?"

In the Marshal's cramped office, Milosh thrust his finger irritably into the small pile of coins, pushing them in incredulity across the desk top.

"A down-payment on the bounty," Anton replied. "A hundred gold crowns."

"And this," Count Kravnik added, sliding over a sheet of paper, "is a promissory note for the remainder. Signed in my name."

For a moment, the bounty hunter seemed unsure how to react. He'd clearly assumed collecting the reward was a mere formality.

"What kind of trick are you trying to pull?" he demanded, his challenging stare darting between both men.

"No trick," Kravnik answered levelly. "The note is perfectly valid. You simply take it to the Capitol and present it at the Royal Exchequer and payment will be made to you in full."

Milosh snatched the sheet and scanned it furiously.

"An IOU? You're palming me off with a frigging IOU! Where's my money? Where's the gold?"

"There is none," Anton told him. "What you see is all there is."

"I don't believe you!"

Under his desk, Anton let his fingers hover near the drawer where a weighted cosh lay.

"You've got gold. I know you have," Milosh accused, balling the parchment and flinging it to the floor. "You wouldn't have a strongbox if you didn't have gold to stash in it."

"It's for documents. Important, confidential documents," Anton answered carefully. The bounty hunter was shaking alarmingly, and Anton was convinced it was only Kravnik's presence in the room that had so far prevented Milosh from trying to throttle him.

"Leopold keeps a tight rein on finances," he explained. "I hardly get enough from him to keep the jailhouse running. As far as he's concerned, this small outpost isn't worth the candle."

Milosh whirled to Kravnik, spittle on his lips. "He's lying! He's making it up!"

The Envoy sighed philosophically before getting up and walking over to the fire.

"What Lord Marshal Yoska says is correct," he confirmed, warming his ample backside against the flames. "This is a small, unimportant backwater. What you see on the desk, those one hundred crowns, represents a year's allowance from the treasury."

"But the poster says—"

"The reward poster states the Marshal is obliged to take your prisoner, and he has done that. However, it says nothing about him having to pay you the bounty in person, or in cash for that matter."

He raised his finger, to prevent any interruption. "It is clear the Crown Prince's intention was always for the captive to be delivered to the Capitol, not to be dumped in the middle of nowhere. The clause about lawmen being required to supply assistance and shelter is meant solely to deal with emergencies."

"Isn't this an emergency?" Milosh challenged.

"Perhaps," Kravnik conceded. "If it is, it is one of your own making. One you could still rectify."

Anton could sense the bounty hunter working out the angles.

"I get it," Milosh said, menacingly. "I get what's going on here. This is a ploy to make me take the vampire and leave."

"On the contrary," Kravnik refuted. "No one is asking you to do any such thing. We are simply saying there are insufficient funds to pay you in cash. Be assured you have the note and my word it will be honoured."

A sly look passed over Milosh's face. "If I take your note, I'm taking you with me to make sure there's no funny business," he warned.

Kravnik smiled amicably. "By all means. These are perilous lands and I would be greatly reassured to have your protection on my return journey. I am as eager as you are to leave this dreary place. Although..." He paused thoughtfully. "...I cannot guarantee what kind of reception awaits you. I would not like to predict what the Crown Prince's reaction will be to one of his envoys being held as a virtual hostage. He takes an especially dim view of that type of behaviour."

The threat hit home. Anton noted that, even in his fury, Milosh was re-evaluating the Count, comprehending how dangerous the nobleman could be.

"Look, there is an alternative," Anton ventured. "If you don't trust the Count's word. I'll dispatch Pavel to the

Capitol with the note. Leopold can send the reward money back with the soldiers."

"That means staying here six, seven days?" Milosh said, appalled.

"It could be ten." Anton suggested. "Don't worry. You are all more than welcome to stay on as my guests."

Milosh's eyes blazed. "No! No way. I won't remain here a minute more than I need to. I want out of this stinking dump before nightfall. I want my gold. Give me my gold!"

"I have to concur with Marshal Yoska," Kravnik purred, disturbing the logs with the poker, sending up a stream of sparks just as crimson as the bounty hunter's complexion. "It seems the only reasonable compromise. You have a straight choice: either take your captive to the Capitol and collect the reward in person or remain here while we arrange delivery of the bounty."

Milosh surged forward, thumping the desk with such force the coins bounced into the air.

"This is a stitch-up!" he rumbled. "You sons of bitches are pulling a con."

Anton didn't balk. "No one is trying to cheat you," he replied, voice measured. "It's just how things are. You picked the wrong town to bring your prisoner to."

Milosh thumped the desk even harder. "Don't fuck with me," he warned, running a hand over his face.

"You!" He jabbed his finger at the Count. "You're some sort of official. A tax collector? That's it, isn't it! You're here to collect Leopold's loot. He bleeds all his subjects dry. You must have thousands..."

The finger swung across towards the safe. "...all safety locked up in there!"

He jerked his head. "Open it!"

Neither man moved.

Kravnik gave the hunter a patronising look. "I can assure you I am not a tax collector, nor would I ever lower myself to that level. Even if I were, I doubt Brejnei and its shabby inhabitants would yield more than two hundred crowns if we seized every piece of tat they possess."

"Well, Your Worship, if that's the truth, you'll have no objection to opening the strongbox and letting me see for myself, now will you?"

For several agonising moments both hunter and noble locked malevolent stares. Anton had no idea who would blink first.

Then abruptly a figure burst into the room, breaking the malignant spell.

It was the first time Anton had seen Johann rattled, as the scar-faced hunter gasped: "Come quickly. Something terrible's happening!"

CHAPTER 31

Nicku's teeth were clenched, lips pulled back in a taut grimace. "Christ! Be careful, you stupid bitch. It hurts like hell!" he moaned as Irina grabbed his injured limb and thrust it into a pail of water.

"Your thanks are noted," she replied, with scorn. "Any time I can help, just say the word." And walking away, muttered: "Pity you didn't burn both hands."

On the other side of the deputies' dayroom, Anton frowned. "Tell me again," he instructed Nicku. "Convince me you didn't do this deliberately to get attention."

The deputy fixed him with a look of undisguised derision. "What do you think I am?" he challenged. "Some sort of idiot child? Of course I didn't bloody well do this deliberately."

"It wasn't an accident?"

"No. I told you already. Why won't you listen? No accident. No cry for attention. It did it to me, that fucking devil." He jerked his head angrily towards the vampire's cell. "It got inside my head, forced me to..."

"Perhaps," Anton said, chilling at the implications. He snapped his fingers. "Your hand. Let me see it."

Groaning, Nicku obeyed, lifting it from the water and holding it out, fingers curled around the blistered palm.

It was a mess; puckered, raw, the top four layers of skin burnt away, the flesh deformed and ulcerous. There was no way anyone could have inflicted that upon himself.

"Have you got anything to help with that?" Anton asked Gregor.

"An ointment. It will soothe the pain, though I doubt it will do much to heal the burn," the old man replied, starting to fish in his satchel. "This needs the ministrations of a proper physician."

"Maybe later. For now, patch him up the best you can," he instructed, and beckoned to Kravnik. "Come with me. There's something I need to check."

They left the room, and hurried along the corridor, the Count pointing out: "In case you have forgotten, Drubrick is on his own in your study."

Anton waved it away. "I'll worry about that later. We've got much more to be concerned about right here."

Tensing, he stopped outside the maximum security cell and peered through the spy hole.

Stefan Modjeski was still sedated, lying on the floor, in a foetal position, all shackles solidly in place. All the same, something had altered. He couldn't tell what, couldn't clearly pinpoint the change, but knew he should be alert, and afraid.

"Tell Irina we need the shotgun," he said urgently. "I have to open the cell door."

Kravnik paled. "What!"

"I need to see properly. I need to go in there. Get the gun now."

Kravnik reappeared seconds later with Irina; flanked by Johann and Pavel, both edgy, pistols cocked.

"Everyone stay back," Anton ordered, "and be ready for anything."

He operated the lock, pulling back the heavy metal door. Venturing a couple of feet inside, he stopped, heart racing, the sound crashing in his ears.

The creature didn't respond to his closeness. There was no discernible movement or variation in the low, guttural breathing behind the confines of the mask.

Yet something about the vampire was different. As he studied it for several nerve-jangling moments, Anton sensed what it was. The creature was giving off waves of crackling psychic power, its mind radiating malicious energy, seeking to invade his thoughts; pushing, teasing, probing.

RELEASE ME!

Despite the drugs, it was regaining its wits, fighting up through the layers of befuddlement; growing stronger with each passing second.

UNDO THESE CHAINS.

"Get Gregor, tell him to hurry," he said over his shoulder, unwilling to relax his scrutiny of the creature for even a heartbeat.

He closed his eyes, fighting the powerful voice now inside his head, exploring with its chill fingers, scratching at his mental defences, trying to bend his will to its own.

"What's wrong?" Gregor asked, pushing into the cell beside him.

"The creature is surfacing from its lethargy," Anton answered. "The potion is wearing off. You need to administer another dose."

The old man didn't respond.

Prising his attention from the now stirring nosferatu body in front of him, he glared forcefully at Gregor. "Now, before it awakens."

The former cleric made no attempt to obey. Instead, he bit his lower lip, eyes casting down.

"Gregor!" Johann shouted.

"I cannot," the old man replied, voice quivering. "I cannot. There has been a terrible mishap."

With nausea rising in his throat, Anton heard him say: "It is Quintz's fault. He ran the wagon too fast. I tried to stop him. I warned him to slow down. He just wouldn't, and now it's too late."

As he opened the satchel, Gregor's shaking liver-spotted hands produced two smashed bottles. "The vials are broken," he announced despondently. "None of the draught remains."

CHAPTER 32

Head pitched forward, the heavy metal mask resting against its chest, the creature showed little signs of life. The onlookers knew it was an illusion.

Anton could hear them inhaling as one, the sense of apprehension in the confined cellblock corridor suffocating.

After several agonising moments, the caged head jolted and began to lift. Inside the straitjacket the body slowly tensed and stretched; buckles and straps creaking as they strained.

"Oh my God," Irina whispered.

"Quick, man," Kravnik urged from the back of the group, "close the door. For pity's sake, close the cell door!"

Frozen in morbid fascination, Anton didn't move. The mask continued its ascent, degree by degree, until it came horizontal and halted. Its occupant growled deeply, its eyes snapping open; a flare of blazing intensity behind the metal slots.

From his standpoint, just inches away, Anton felt its power and its malicious curiosity. The stare burned into him, making him sway.

The head tilted slightly, one way and then the other as it regarded him and then it hissed; a long, low, sibilant sound that made the watchers flinch.

"Yoska..."

It licked its lips, as though tasting his blood.

"Anton Yoska..."

The lips curled.

"The slayer…"

Anton held its magnetic stare.

"And you are Stefan Modjeski," he replied, barely above a whisper. "Predator, creature of the night, murderer…"

He paused for a half beat. "…monster."

The vampire laughed icily, the timbre deep and rich, edged with scorn.

"Some would say you are the monster, slayer. To my kind you are the killer - the ungodly who must be feared and hunted."

Anton gave a nod, to acknowledge the truth of this.

"Perhaps. Except, I am not the one with a price on his head. I am not the one trussed up in a cell. I am not the prisoner."

"No," Stefan admitted. "You are correct. I am captive, kidnapped, dragged here. Bound like an animal. Tortured."

He strained again flexing against the binds.

"But I shall not be dominated for long. When my family learns where I am, they will come for me and when they do, your reputation won't save you."

The vampire took in the audience in a contemptuous sweep. "Nor will it save any of your treacherous companions. All here will perish. Those who abducted, drugged and beat me and those who sheltered and protected them. You will die in exquisite agony."

"Do they know?" Anton probed. "Do your family know where you are?"

"I cannot say," the voice behind the mask reported with haughty indifference, "and it matters naught. You must know - deep in the most forlorn and most tormented corner of your soul - that it is only a matter of time. They

187

will come. And their vengeance will be indiscriminate and total.

"You are all doomed. None will be spared. None will survive. You may have me at a disadvantage. A temporary disadvantage for now, however—"

With that, he unexpectedly surged forward.

Startled, the knot of terrified watchers stumbled back, falling over each other, crying out in alarm until the creature's advance was pulled short, as the chains holding the back of the canvas jacket to the wall snapped taut and mercifully held.

"Kill it, shoot the bloody thing," Anton heard Pavel exclaim, the deputy's panicked outburst high pitched.

Relaxing, smiling through the metal grid, Stefan Modjeski stepped back, the chains going limp again.

"It is good workmanship," he conceded. "You know your trade, master jailer. The restraints seem professional, robust, yet will they be enough? Will they hold?"

"They will," Anton promised, still standing exactly where he had been, outwardly unshaken.

"We shall see. Or maybe your young friend is correct and you should destroy me now while you still can."

The head arced, slowly studying the frightened group. "Should Yoska do as the virgin boy suggests? What do you think - Irina?"

Anton heard the woman gasp. "How - how does it know my name?"

"Or you, Nicku, who seethes with rancour against Yoska, a hatred even deeper than mine. What say you?"

One after another, the vampire spoke to each, making their dread build.

"And you, Count Kravnik, Royal favourite, a man so confused and conflicted he does not know his own mind. Annihilate me or save me? You cannot decide. Amusing."

"I am not confused," the Envoy answered, anger clear. "If it were my choosing, you would be staked this instant. I would have the Lord Marshal show you what made him the scourge of all you foul, loathsome parasites. Unfortunately, we need you alive, for trial and public execution. The Crown Prince expressly wishes to watch you die."

"And anything the Prince wants, you ensure he gets," Stefan agreed sardonically. "At least, for the time being."

He part closed his eyes, focusing. "What's this I see in your thoughts? A kernel of disloyalty, raw ambition? You are his man - yet you harbour dreams. My, my, Count Kravnik, such dreams of greatness. Usurping the monarch? A dangerous notion, my Lord, even as an idle fantasy."

Anton couldn't help himself. He twisted to look at the Envoy, who was stunned, mouth half open.

"It is a lie," Kravnik replied with a shudder. "I do not... I would not..."

"Wouldn't you?" Stefan challenged. "Your aura suggests otherwise."

Confused, the Envoy backed up several steps. Then, with a momentary burst of uncertainty, he scurried away, pushing the others aside to make his frantic exit.

"Leaving so soon," the vampire said, with a cold laugh. "Wouldn't you like to hear what else I can see?"

Anton regarded the being with renewed respect and trepidation. The creature was trapped, tethered, facing extermination. He should be humiliated, subjugated, yet he looked upon his captors as mere playthings.

"What about me?" he asked softly. "What do you see in my aura?"

The creature's eyes narrowed. "Aura?" it questioned, puzzled for a moment, then replied darkly: "I don't need to read an aura to tell about you, Anton Yoska. It is written on your face for all to see."

It grunted thoughtfully as it studied him. "I see a man who is hiding, a slayer who has lost his fire and passion. Who prefers to shelter behind a lawman's badge. A man who is running..."

Anton swallowed hard. He knew he should bring an end to this alarming demonstration of the nosferatu's power, but found himself mesmerised.

"Running from what?"

"You know the answer already."

"Tell me!"

The demon creature glared scornfully.

"From yourself," it announced. "From your destiny."

CHAPTER 33

Anton stumbled out of the cellblock, sweating, Stefan Modjeski's words reverberating inside his head.

Hungrily sucking in air, he bent forward, grasping his knees, staring at the courtyard cobbles but seeing a picture of the battlefield instead.

Yes, he'd escaped his predetermined fate but for how long? How long before the grave that should have marked his final resting place at Ossiak was dug here in Brejnei? How long before the eternal damnation that lurked in the darkness, waiting impatiently, triumphantly claimed him?

He'd barely been able to hold his nerves together long enough to slam the cell shut and bar it. Now he needed alcohol, oblivion from the nightmare unfolding around him.

Damn Milosh Drubrick, damn him to eternity. It was no co-incidence he'd kidnapped the one nosferatu guaranteed to create the maximum mayhem. He'd carefully selected his prey - to bring back the past, to dig over old memories, to reopen old wounds.

Reopen old wounds? Absent-mindedly, Anton reached up, touching his neck, feeling the roughness of the mottled skin under his collar.

"You look like death itself," Milosh observed as minutes later Anton finally made it back to his office.

"Your sympathy is touching," he replied, noting that he'd interrupted the bounty hunter tampering unsuccessfully with the dials on the strongbox. "It makes me feel so much better. You'd look like this too if you'd just been through what I've experienced."

He gestured to the safe. "There are more than ten thousand possible combinations. You'll be fiddling with those dials for weeks. You might as give up now."

Anyone else would have had the good grace to look embarrassed. Milosh merely crinkled his nose philosophically.

"You can't blame a man for trying," he said wistfully, giving the nearest dial one last hopeful twist.

"And it was too good an opportunity to pass up," Anton agreed cynically. "We both know you don't like to let a good diversion go to waste."

Closing the door, he moved towards the desk, opened the drawer, and took out a bottle of vodka; noticing the cosh had been removed in his absence.

"The bloodsucker got much to say for himself?" Milosh asked, as Anton filled a glass unsteadily and downed it in one.

He poured himself a refill and sloshed some into a second glass, shoving it across to the bounty hunter.

"Plenty, and most of it about what it intends to do to you when it gets free," he replied. "He's extremely keen to meet you again."

"I'll bet."

Anton rubbed his eyes, sensing another migraine lurking not far off. "Why weren't you there? I could have done with the back-up. Frightened?"

"Just allergic to cells," Milosh answered, lips pinched. "I've seen enough of the inside of prisons, and I have you to thank for that."

Again the picture of the bounty hunter's younger self popped into Anton's mind. The Milosh of nine years ago screaming violent abuse, raging uncontrollably, telling him he was a dead man.

"You're fortunate it was only prison," Anton retorted, letting the vodka burn its way down his throat. "For what you did I'd have happily put you in front of a firing squad."

Milosh's face was impassive. Any casual observer might have considered him unmoved, save for the vein twitching at his temple.

"Five years," he said with rancour. "Five whole years of my life. Locked away. Sentenced to hard labour."

Anton sighed. "This is what this is really about, isn't it? Settling the score with me."

The bounty hunter made no attempt to deny it. "Of course," he agreed, gold teeth showing in a tight grimace. "You have no idea how long I've planned this, how many nights I've lain awake imagining this moment."

He drained the glass, smacking his lips. "Johann thinks we should have just ridden in and shot you dead on the spot. I reckoned this way was so much better. I love the poetic irony. I've signed your death warrant and it's all legal. I'm being the perfect loyal subject."

He got up and snatched the bottle. "If you eliminate the vampire, both sides will take their retribution against you. Besides, you wouldn't contemplate it; not even for a moment. Not the noble Anton Yoska. You'd never harm a prisoner, even one whom you had good reason to want to destroy.

"What else can you do? Surrender him to the Modjeski and the Crown Prince will have your head. Keep him alive, chained up in your cellblock and the creature's family will go through you and your useless deputies to get him back."

He sloshed more vodka into his glass and, making a mock toast, said: "I wish I could watch how it all pans out, only I'll be long gone before the fun starts."

"Just like always," Anton replied savagely, "Just as you always do." And, with a surge of anger, remembered...

He fought to close his lips, to stop the crimson droplets dropping into his mouth, struggling to prevent the foul infection sliding down his throat. But he was too weak, too far gone. Anton could feel it seeking out his stomach, on its malevolent mission to change every atom of his body; reshaping it to its evil end.

Above him he could just make out a deep, male voice murmur: "There will be pain, confusion, terror and sickness, but that will pass and then you will know eternal bliss. You will know the gift of immense power. You will learn what it is to be a god amongst men."

A voice inside his head urged him to give in, to let the strange metamorphosis run its sinister course. This is better than death, it whispered coaxingly, this is better than the chill darkness of the grave.

Yet the last vestiges of his mortal self fought back, and thrust him upwards on to one elbow, staring straight at the omnipotent being recreating him in its own image.

"No..." he gasped.

The nosferatu laughed.

"You cannot prevent it. You cannot stop the celestial change taking place within your veins. It is foolish to even try."

Coming up close, it whispered: "You cannot run, soldier boy. You cannot escape your fate."

With that another spasm overtook Anton.

Nearby, he heard screams - the last of his comrades being dispatched, each trooper eviscerated - and, in his fading thoughts of resistance, he envied them.

Then out of the mayhem he heard another sound, the high-pitched whinny of a terrified horse; hoof beats stamping as it pawed the ground desperately, rebelling against the urges of its rider.

The vampire turned at the unexpected noise, and Anton glimpsed over his shoulder a soldier, face ashen, watching the scene with horror and repulsion. The callous eyes had seen much over the years yet were still clearly appalled by what they were now witnessing.

For a fleeting moment, Anton felt hope.

Rescue.

"Shoot," Anton wanted to shout. "Kill it! Now! Before it reacts! Put a musket ball in its head."

The horseman made no attempt to attack. Instead, the soldier's expression hardened and he circled, the three stripes on his arm flashing into view on the tattered uniform.

The rider didn't even bother looking back as he dug in his spurs and let the horse have its head. With a bone-shaking bound, the steed leapt over the nearest pile of bodies and hurtled away.

If he'd been able to, Anton would have sobbed, weeping for the deliverance that could have been, so cruelly snatched away. No moisture came to his reddening pupils.

195

But he did manage to raise a hand pleadingly towards his fleeing saviour, whispering one pitiful last plea to the distant figure of the sergeant now fleeing the nightmare battlefield.
"Milosh... Come back. Save me."

CHAPTER 34

Gregor flinched, covering his face.

"You're a useless sack of shit," Johann stormed, grabbing him brutally by the arm and dragging him across the cellblock. "I told Milosh you were a fucking liability and we should have ditched you back at the mill."

"It wasn't my fau—"

"One task. That's all you had to do. Keep it drugged. And you screwed it up. You stupid, senile old fool."

Gregor flushed, breaking into a spasm of coughs, alarm growing. He'd seen Johann angry before, but never with this unbridled hatred.

"Irina!" he gasped plaintively, looking for support.

The woman showed no compassion. "You knew the vials were broken," she mouthed coldly, "And you said nothing."

Behind them the vampire chuckled, its glee as chill as deep winter and just as unforgiving.

"Well, we've got no use for you now." Johann grasped his throat, digging in his thumbs. "Shall I put you out of your misery, bible-basher? Shall I just snap that scrawny chicken's neck and be done with it? C'mon, speak up, old man. Tell me why I shouldn't just finish you where you stand."

Gregor's mind whirled, desperately seeking words, any words, that would placate his furious comrade.

"The draught," he whispered, the words a strangled gasp. "I could make more of the sleeping draught."

"And what bloody good would that do us now?"

"We could try... try to sedate it again. Perhaps we could—"

Spinning him, Johann thrust the old man towards the cell, jerking his head so hard Gregor yelped.

"Who's going to administer it? Hey, preacher man? Who's going to get close to that thing? You? Are you volunteering? Because I'm not going anywhere near it!"

Gregor spluttered, dizziness overwhelming him, knowing this was it. He was about to die.

The suggestion of preparing the draught had been a desperate ploy. There was no way he could brew up another batch. He lacked most of the ingredients, and even if he'd had them it would take days to distil all the necessary elements to an effective potency. None of it mattered now. He knew the deception had failed.

"You're always bleating on about how God's got a room reserved for you in his Heavenly mansion," Johann scoffed. "Time to find out if it's got a good view."

He squeezed as tightly as possible.

Gregor tried to plead, as the throttling fingers blocked his throat. All he managed was to pray silently in his head, beg the Lord for forgiveness, as stars exploded in his mind and filled his sight, a final firework display.

"Stop! Take your hands off him!"

The words were quaking, tinged with fear, yet determined.

"I mean it. Leave him be."

Instantly the grip was loosened and Gregor fell to his knees, retching, coughing up phlegm spattered with blood. Looking up woozily he saw Pavel, shaking fit to bust, holding a pistol at Irina's head.

198

"Do as the boy says," she advised Johann carefully, motioning slightly towards the gun six inches from her left temple. "He's trembling so much I doubt he'd hit me. All the same, I'd rather not take the risk."

Johann studied the boy with new respect. "I'd have thought that the smack on the nose earlier would have taught you not to mess with me, boy," he said, spitting a greasy splatter of tobacco juice on to the stone floor.

Speaking directly to Irina, he added. "He's got balls this one. Even if he does look like he's about to piss himself."

He moved a step back from Gregor. "You can put the gun down," he assured Pavel. "I only wanted to give the old git a fright."

Reaching, he yanked the old man unsteadily back to his feet, dusting him off. "See. He's okay. Nothing broken. Not a rosary bead out of place."

Irina spoke softly, calmingly. "You've made your point, Pavel. Everything's fine now. You can point that thing somewhere else."

She turned and, as the deputy began to lower the shaking gun, moved it gently sideways with two fingers.

"What is it with men and their weapons," she murmured, letting the fingers slide suggestively down the barrel.

"You're a lucky bastard," Johann told the old man. "See that kid, he's worth ten of you. I'd rather have him on my side than you and your bag of useless potions."

He jerked his head towards the main residence. "Make yourself useful. Get us some coffee. You can do that without mucking it up, can't you?"

Gregor glared, humiliation burning as much as his raw throat. "But the boy?"

"I won't touch him. I promise. Take him with you."

The bounty hunter jerked his thumb. "Go with the God-botherer," he commanded Pavel. "Make sure the old sod doesn't get lost."

The deputy began to edge away, gratefully.

"And, kid..."

Pavel stopped; rooted to the spot, trembling.

"Pull a stunt like that again and I'll make you eat that pistol. I'll shove it right down your fucking throat. Is that clear?"

The young man nodded, the movement so rapid he almost knocked his chin on his chest.

CHAPTER 35

There was no time for delicacy or precision. Kravnik yanked open the dresser drawers, grabbing his perfectly folded, beautifully ironed clothes and thrusting them roughly into the canvas travelling bag not caring that the expensive garments instantly wrinkled and crushed.

All that mattered was speed; getting away from this benighted shithole and putting as much distance as possible between him and the monster.

The encounter with the vampire had unnerved him much more than he'd dared admit. It wasn't the party trick of the *infernal* reading his aura that worried him. He was confident there was no evidence of his treason. He'd been careful to make sure no signs of his plotting were committed to paper.

No, it was the terrifying certainty that with Stefan Modjeski fully awake and able to transmit his whereabouts to his ungodly brood, any hope of remaining safe was gone. It would be certain death when the nosferatu over-ran Brejnei even for an innocent bystander like himself.

He had to escape. Without a moment's delay. And in secret because neither that fool Yoska nor the feral gang leader would allow him to leave. He was too valuable a bargaining chip to lawman and criminal alike.

There was only one opportunity to save his skin. He must saddle up and slip away while the lawman and bounty hunter were arguing and distracted. The likelihood was he'd be miles away before they missed him.

Except, a sudden unsettling thought occurred to him. The gates! It had taken both deputies to drop the heavy crossbeam into place. It would need as much manpower to lift it again.

Damnation!

He shuddered and looked at himself scornfully in the mirror, observing the dread and hopelessness in his own features.

You are smart and resourceful, he told himself sternly. Nothing is beyond your cunning. Think. Think.

Then he saw it, the reflection in the looking glass smiling, his lips forming a triumphant sneer, and he felt a moment of genius inspiration. He had a solution. Oh yes, a way out no one else would ever have dreamt of.

Both deputy and holy man hurried across the courtyard, keen to get away before Johann changed his mind. When they were safely in the main residence, Gregor stopped, telling Pavel: "That was brave, also unbelievably foolish. You didn't have to do that for me."

The young man blushed. "I couldn't stand by and do nothing." He grinned awkwardly. "Anyway, I was being selfish."

Gregor gave him a questioning look.

"I want to know about vampires and no one else will tell me," Pavel admitted sheepishly.

For the first time that day, Gregor felt like laughing. "What do you want to know?" he asked, as they headed through the building towards the smell of cooking.

"Is it true what they say? That vampires live forever? That they can't be annihilated? What about crucifixes? They're supposed to be afraid of them. And what about holy water and—"

Gregor held up his palm. "Whoa! Slow down. One question at a time." He mused, for a second. "Most of the stories you've heard about the nosferatu are untrue, or at least gross distortions. For instance, vampires aren't indestructible. They can be destroyed: by a stake through the heart, by decapitation, immersion in running water, explosion. These are the tried and tested methods. Of course, exposure to sunlight is the quickest and most effective way of dispatching them."

"What about guns? Crossbow bolts?"

He thought about it for a moment. "Ah, now that is more complex. There are many ways to incapacitate a vampire, but although one can inflict grievous harm on the creatures with poison, guns, crossbows and the like, the effects - though temporarily successful - may swiftly wear off."

He watched a look of bafflement cross the deputy's face. Mmm... how to fully explain one of creation's most inexplicable and darkest miracles?

"They can be injured just as easily as we can," the old man began. "They feel pain, they suffer, they bruise and bleed. The difference is the rapidity with which they recover. Their metabolisms are phenomenally accelerated, many times faster than that of a mortal. It's what gives them their incredible speed and strength."

Immediately Pavel's look of bewilderment deepened.

"Metabolism?" he repeated, trying the new word around his mouth as though it had a taste. "What's a metabolism?"

"It's too complicated to exp—"

The old man sighed, then he had an idea. "Look, my boy. You saw the injury to Nicku's hand."

"Yes. It's awful."

"And how long do you suppose it will take to heal?"

Pavel considered. "I don't know. Weeks, maybe months."

"Very well. Let's consider what happened to the prisoner. The creature's hand was injured just as severely by being exposed to sunlight. Amazingly, by tomorrow there will be no traces of the burning. It would be as if its maiming had never happened. Do you grasp what I'm telling you?"

"I think so."

"To answer your question: yes, it is possible to kill a vampire with guns, although it can take many shots to end its life; as our troops found out to their cost in the war. Despite the fact that a single musket ball can bring it down, the abomination will have regenerated and repaired the damaged tissue within minutes."

"What about garlic? Doesn't that wipe them out?"

"No, it merely acts on their systems to delay the recovery time. It hampers the clotting of their blood. During the war our troops learnt to smear it on their musket shot."

The young man went silent for a while, letting the information sink in. Glad of a respite from the eager quizzing, Gregor led on briskly, presently coming upon the two tall glazed doors to the kitchen.

"What about holy water?" Pavel pressed. He didn't get a reply.

Gregor had opened the handle and entered, the unexpected sight that greeted him eliciting a thoroughly ungodly profanity.

CHAPTER 36

"You left me to die," Anton's words dripped with disgust. "You rode off and let that thing do what it wanted with me."

Milosh sniffed, unmoved. "You were a goner. Any fool could see it."

"And the rest of the troop?"

"They'd all been slaughtered. The leeches were feeding off them. What was I supposed to do?"

"You deserted!"

"I saved my own skin. I did what any sane man would have done. The battle was lost so I rode for my life."

Anton pointed to himself. "And yet, as you can clearly see I wasn't a goner. I survived. I escaped."

"And that's something I'll never understand," Milosh fired back. "Why you didn't perish. I saw you. You were drained, a bloodless husk. Another few seconds and you'd have been wormfood."

He paused, expectantly, inclining his head for an explanation.

Anton held his intense look, refusing to oblige.

"You know the crazy thing about this?" Anton said, after several tense moments. "You made no attempt to rescue me, and yet you feel you're the victim."

Milosh glowered. "All I did was leave you behind. As far as I could see you were just another corpse. Anyone would have done the same, but what you did to me was personal."

"It was my duty."

"Hunting me down, dragging me back in chains? Giving evidence at my court martial? That wasn't duty! That was you ensuring I suffered for what happened to you." His jaw clenched. "Don't give me that man of honour bullshit. You wanted to see me in front of a firing squad."

Anton thought for a second. "Only as an example to others. Not for my own satisfaction."

Milosh suddenly smiled. "It must have been a shock when the Colonel intervened at the last moment and made that plea for clemency. Oh yes, I can still remember the stunned look on your face when he stood up. Sergeant Drubrick doesn't deserve this fate. How can any of us say what we'd do in the same circumstances? A split second wrong decision in the red mist of battle... blah, blah, blah."

"You blackmailed him into speaking up for you. You coerced him."

"Of course, I did. He was weak, greedy and perverted. I got word to him I'd reveal all his grubby little secrets."

Except it didn't do the whole trick, Anton thought with a stab of icy satisfaction.

"You still got five years," he pointed out. "The great plan to cheat your way to an acquittal didn't go the way you intended."

Milosh's expression hardened, his eyes clouding as he recalled. "Do you have an idea of what I went through?" he muttered, lips tightening. "Woken each day at five am with a bucket of freezing water thrown over me. Three snatched mouthfuls of cold gritty gruel then dragged outside, shackled to a chain gang, marched six miles to the quarry. Twelve agonising hours breaking rocks in all weather - hail, snow, blazing sunlight, teeming rain. Always chilled to the marrow or baked so dry my skin flaked off in sheets."

His pupils glazed as he remembered. "The work could kill the strongest man. It claimed many of the other damned souls I was locked up with. We were nothing more than walking skeletons. I could feel death at my shoulder, watching, waiting, counting off the minutes till I succumbed.

"Do you know what kept me going, what made me fight to live? The thought of what I was going to do to you. The suffering and torment I was going to inflict on you, my dashing Lieutenant. Night after night I lay shivering on my cot, my belly empty, muscles aching, ears filled with the sobs of the other wretches and I planned. Silently, patiently, inside my head, I planned."

It was as if a switch had been flicked. The bounty hunter's face relaxed, his expression regaining its earlier sadistic amusement.

"Eventually it came to me. The most wonderful vengeance I could devise. A reunion - me, you and the bloodsucker - back together again. The only three who know what happened at Ossiak. Three deadly enemies, all with unfinished business, brought together for one final confrontation. Only this time guaranteed there'd be only one winner." He prodded his barrel chest.

Anton marvelled. Only now did he truly appreciate the depth of his former comrade's hatred. A scheme for retribution nine years in the making. And yet, he reasoned, for all Milosh's scheming and ingenuity, the plan was already unravelling.

"I pity you," he said. "Not for your suffering. You deserved every last moment of it. But for the futility of what you've tried to do here and the fact you've failed."

"Failed!" The word was like a gunshot.

"Yes, you've messed up again. Back then you over-estimated the Colonel's influence and now you've miscalculated by coming to a penniless community looking for riches."

He absent-mindedly twirled the empty vodka glass. "Poor Milosh, things don't seem to work out for you, do they? All those long nights plotting my downfall and all for nothing."

He got up and knelt by the safe, spinning the dials, the tumblers clicking loudly as they aligned and the locks sprang open.

With a flourish, he swung open the strongbox. "Because, as you can see, I wasn't lying. Have a good look. There's nothing. No treasure. No hidden stash of cash."

Milosh's mouth opened and closed silently as he refused to believe the evidence of his eyes.

"Well, it appears you've got a dilemma," Anton told him. "You can travel all the way to the Capitol and take the risk that Kravnik's note won't be honoured, meaning you'll come out of this escapade next to penniless. Or you stay here and wait for Leopold to send the cash and pray our troops get here ahead of the nosferatu.

"I don't see either prospect appealing to your treacherous associates. They want gold and they want it now. How long do you think it will be before Quintz slits your throat or Johann puts a bullet in your brain? Whatever way you look at it, I'd say, right at this moment, Sergeant Drubrick, you're in as much jeopardy as I am."

Anton tensed, anticipating a burst of violence. What he wasn't expecting was Milosh to suddenly cock his head to one side.

"Do you hear it?" he challenged.

Anton concentrated, puzzled.

Then a moment later the sound hit him. Coming from the stables. Roaring. Ferocious roaring.

CHAPTER 37

It was one of the few compensations of this benighted, unforgiving time of year. The sun set early. From her window, Kristina Modjeski watched in excitement as the blazing red orb slowly disappeared below the horizon, the last flickers of daylight fleeing before the omniscient darkness. It was barely 4pm.

Finally!

Below, the courtyard burst into life, figures scurrying, shouting, her warriors unwilling to wait those last teasing minutes to absolute safety as they rushed to their mounts.

The stables were flung open. Inside, loud excited whinnies rang out as the steeds greeted their riders and sniffed at the air, the sleek, shimmering white horses sensing the anticipation, the pulsating adrenalin.

Snorting, pawing at the ground, they twitched and flexed, blue eyes the hue of marsh flames blazing with supernatural brightness. Each knelt to allow a saddle to be placed upon its back, each horseman leaping up in a fluid motion, before their mounts cantered out into the open.

The wide stone enclosure filled rapidly as, raising their forelegs into the air, the demon herd rose up as one, shrieking to the Heavens, nostrils flaring, expelling dense clouds like a dragon's breath.

"Magnificent," Kristina murmured, as she ventured out onto the balcony to gain a closer view.

"It is no wonder the sight instilled such despair in our foes," Viktor agreed, appearing at her side. "Why so many armies turned and ran."

Yes, she recalled, even before her blood riders had charged into view, the banshee cries of their nightmare horses had often been enough to make the quivering mortals flee in terror.

Alas, they couldn't count on that now. Not where they were going. Not against him.

Hooves clattered in a deafening tattoo as the castle's main gates opened and the first forces dug in their spurs and surged forward.

"The messengers have their orders. To rally our forces and bring them here with all haste," Viktor reported.

Startled, she glared. "What! You are sending them away!"

"To gather all those loyal to our banner," he replied defensively, not expecting her ire. "If we are going up against the slayer we'll need all the warriors we can assemble."

"There isn't time," she chided. "We must strike now. We must ride for Brejnei before anything worse can befall Stefan at Yoska's hands."

She felt anger fill her heart, sharp irritation at her consort's over cautiousness. She knew part of him was deeply worried by the thought of battling the old enemy again. Viktor would rather they gave up on Stefan than face the one mortal whose legend intimidated nosferatu kind.

She wouldn't allow it. She couldn't contemplate turning her back on her favourite. She would rescue Stefan no matter the risk, no matter the cost.

"Stand to," she bellowed to the riders still within the confines of the courtyard. "Stand to, I say. I have new orders for you. You will accompany me. Ready my carriage."

Viktor couldn't keep the alarm from his voice. "You are going to Brejnei!"

"Of course," she replied. "Did you think I could stay here while my son suffers? I must lead the attack."

"But the danger!"

"I will go there proudly, at the head of my troops," she repeated, and held her palm reassuringly to his face. "This is something I must do. Our enemies must see I am not afraid."

Her eyes flared as powerfully as the cyan fires of her thoroughbred battle steeds. "And I want to look into Yoska's eyes as he dies. I want him to know he perished at my hand."

CHAPTER 38

Sliding to a halt in the entrance to the bear's stall, Anton quickly processed what he was seeing. The beast was leaning over his master, alternately bellowing and whimpering, padding about in distress. The dwarf was bloodied, not moving, face down in the straw.

"I thought you said the creature doted on him," he said accusingly to Milosh.

"It does," the bounty hunter replied. "I don't get it."

Spotting them, Samson reared and bared its teeth, its roaring doubling, causing the horses nearby to whinny in alarm.

Behind him, Anton was aware of Irina and Johann rushing inside, Irina unable to stop herself from emitting a loud shriek, which made the creature even more agitated.

"Is the freak dead?" Johann asked.

Unsure, Anton whispered: "It's impossible to tell from this far back." Cursing, he realised the only way to get near the prone dwarf was to put himself in the path of the beast's angrily swiping paws.

Milosh was spellbound, unable to work out what to do.

Glancing around, Anton spotted two discarded pitch forks and instructed the men to grab one each. Neither sought to hide his discomfort as he instructed: "Keep the beast occupied. Fend it off. I'm going to see if I can drag Quintz out of there."

For the first half dozen attempts, the beast knocked the poles away easily, becoming even more animated and irate, until the duo got into a rhythm and both aimed above its neck at the same time. The bear reared back to avoid the sharp prongs hitting its face and Anton spotted his opportunity. In one blurred movement he sprinted forward, grabbed the dwarf by the feet and pulled him clear.

The bear immediately went berserk, and tried to charge at him. Thankfully, the chains held, otherwise Anton knew he'd have been mauled to death.

The animal's incensed bawling grew in strength as Johann and Milosh kept it at bay.

"Quintz is breathing," Irina exclaimed, kneeling over her fallen comrade. Flipping him over, she was surprised when the small man coughed violently and began to stagger to his knees, demanding: "W-w-what's going on?"

"The bear attacked you," Anton reported, but Quintz wasn't listening. He leapt up, throwing himself against Milosh and Johann, crying: "Leave him alone, you bastards. Stop poking him."

He caught both off guard. They stumbled, dropping their make-shift weapons.

"Samson didn't attack me," Quintz rumbled. "It wasn't him. It was Kravnik!" And, putting his palms out, he began to cautiously approach the shaking, distraught mountain of fur and fury.

"Shhhh," he said in a low, sing-song tone. "Shhh, my deadly darling. It's okay. I'm okay. Be still. Be still. Relax."

At first the words appeared to have no effect, then gradually the beast calmed, sitting back on its haunches, nostrils opening and closing rhythmically.

Judging it safe, Quintz knelt beside him and began to stroke its pelt as the animal nuzzled him and made a low moaning growl.

"It's over. It's over. Now, now. Calm, my brave boy, calm. There's nothing to be afraid of."

Casting a glance back at them over his shoulder, he explained: "Kravnik was stealing a horse. I tried to stop him and got clobbered for my troubles."

He touched his head gingerly and grimaced, bringing his fingers away stained crimson. "Samson was trying to protect me."

Both Anton and Milosh shared a thought at the same instant and rushed out into the courtyard, skirting the wagon, swearing as they felt the cold blast of air and saw one of the two heavy gates lying wide open. It was snowing heavily outside, fat flakes blowing in.

"The son of a bitch has done a runner," Milosh said through gritted teeth.

"Yes, but how?" Anton asked. "He couldn't have got that gate open unaided."

"I can answer that," Gregor announced as he and Pavel appeared. "The cook is missing. Our dear Count unlocked the larder and let her out."

Anton couldn't help a grim smile. Knowing Kravnik it was inevitable the woman would have done the lion's share of lifting the cumbersome crossbar.

"Ah, if it was the cook, that would explain this." Quintz held up the piece of wood that had been used to cosh him, a rolling pin still covered in flour.

Milosh seemed almost amused as the Marshal at the audacious nature of the escape.

"Seems like your protector has gone," he declared, with a glint of triumph. "Now we'll see how brave you really are."

Anton showed no sign of alarm. "Perhaps, but I'd have a think before I got too smug," he counselled.

"Why?"

Anton pointed down the street to where a large crowd of Brejnei citizens holding blazing torches, scythes and hammers were marching determinedly through the fast lying snow towards the jailhouse.

"It appears Kravnik put the cook in the picture about our unwanted guest and she's just announced it to the whole population," he said, signalling for the gate to be barricaded with all haste. "And, much as you intimidate the locals, it looks like our vampire frightens them more."

CHAPTER 39

The sea of burning sticks flickered and whipped in the howling wind. The crowd huddled together against the twilight chill, yet for all their cold faces and shivers, an icy determination blazed within them.

"We know what you've got inside. Bring out the monster right now or we'll burn the place down," a voice bellowed up to the parlour window where Anton was standing, carefully scanning the agitated throng.

"Can they do that?" Irina whispered. "Set the place on fire?"

"Probably not," Anton said over his shoulder. It's a stone building. All the same, I wouldn't want to see them try."

"Stop stalling, Marshal. Haul the abomination out so we can kill it," a tall figure at the other side of the mob boomed.

Opening the window, Anton shouted back: "I can't do that. Stefan Modjeski is my prisoner. He's going to stand trial. Until then no one is going to lay a finger on him. There's nothing useful you can do here. Disperse. Go back to your homes. I'll deal with this."

"Like you dealt with the Lucens brothers?" The shout dripped with derision. "You promised them they'd be safe. Now you're promising us the same thing. Forgive us, Lord Marshal, if we don't believe you."

"You're putting us all in mortal danger," a woman added, fear clear in her trembling, determined voice. "If that devil creature gets loose it will slaughter us all."

Anton sensed Milosh's anger building. "Maybe it will, maybe it won't, but I'll slaughter them for sure if they don't bugger off back to their stinking hovels," the bounty hunter threatened, pushing past to train his shotgun on the confusion of bodies below.

The sight of Milosh sparked an immediate response. A hail of stone and bottles arced upwards, ricocheting off the walls with thuds and a shower of exploding glass.

The gang leader brought the gun sight up to his eye. Immediately Anton touched his arm.

"It'll only make matters worse," he warned.

Milosh's eyes darted maliciously to the mob and back to Anton. His chest heaved alarmingly. For several apprehensive moments it was uncertain what the burly man was going to do.

Then, seeing the alarm in Anton's eyes, Irina interceded, touching Milosh's face, calming and soothing him, murmuring: "They'll get bored, lover. We don't need to do anything. A few hours standing in the snow will cool their enthusiasm. They're just ignorant, carrot crunchers."

With each sentence, each gentle caress, Milosh slowly began to relax, shoulders loosening. Anton couldn't help noticing how much the technique mirrored Quintz calming the raging bear. It did little, however, to reduce the tension levels in the parlour.

Glancing restlessly at the darkening sky and the increasingly heavy snowfall, Johann pointed out: "We don't have a few hours. By then it will be too risky to start out. We've got to go now. Shoot our way out, splatter a few of these shit-brain yokels till they get the message."

Stone faced, Anton cautioned against it. "This morning Milosh caught the mob off guard, and there were only a dozen or so. This time they're ready for you, and the whole town is out there."

Johann shrugged indifferently, as though he'd relish the confrontation.

"So what do you suggest?" Milosh demanded.

"Irina has the right idea," Anton answered carefully. "The people out there will grow tired and hungry. Eventually they'll give up and go home. Wait until then. Better still, overnight here. Set off at first light before anyone is fully awake."

Gregor grunted from his position across the room. "It's an attractive prospect," he urged. "I, for one, welcome the prospect of a soft bed and warm food. It's dangerous enough to be blundering in the dark with the creatures searching for us. The last thing we need is to compound our troubles by venturing into a blizzard. I say we stay put."

"And you?" Milosh asked Irina. "What do you think?"

"Makes sense to rest up as much as possible," she concurred. "We don't need the hassle of a gun battle. Besides, the snow may have stopped by the morning."

Milosh screwed up his face, clearly undecided.

"It would give Quintz time to get over that thump on the head," Gregor suggested.

It was uncertain which way it was going, but after a few moments Milosh blew out his lips, declaring: "We'll stay put till morning. Come first light we're out of here." He tapped the gun meaningfully. "And no one, lawman or peasant, is going to get in our way."

Gregor clapped contentedly while Johann kicked the leg of his chair. "This is a massive frigging mistake," he complained, but by that point no one was listening.

Outside, more rocks flew up, interspersed with threats and taunts. Stealing a quick look at the hotheads who were trying to attack the solid wooden gates, Irina grinned.

"Watching all that energy being expended is making me hungry," she declared with a sensuous sigh. "Did someone mention hot food?"

CHAPTER 40

It was an exaggeration to describe it as a munitions store, more a forgotten and ramshackle corner of a long-disused, damp cellar, and as Anton stared incredulously at the meagre contents he recalled it had been ages since he'd last checked the arsenal. Now he saw the subterranean room was barely a tenth full, the wet, lime scale encrusted walls holding a dozen or more ancient muskets balanced on rusting bent nails. Some of the rifles looked as though they hadn't been fired in eons. On shelves nearby, ammunition boxes were just as depressing, empty or bearing a few layers of metal balls, covered with the dust of ages.

In the far corner, under a torn tarpaulin, a line of gunpowder barrels offered the only cause for hope but only if the clamminess of the basement hadn't seeped in, making the powder useless.

Hardly enough weaponry for normal law-keeping duties, he comprehended; definitely not enough to provision an army. Not for the first time, he gave silent thanks that the nosferatu shunned the use of guns as beneath their dignity.

Closing the door, he determined not to tell the others how empty the arsenal was. He didn't want to give the bounty hunters another excuse to depart.

Heading upstairs he reminded himself there was one weapon he hadn't counted in his tally, and minutes later stood in the hallway, staring at it hanging above the grand fireplace.

The old crossbow was a constant source of curiosity to Pavel and he knew the young deputy would have given anything to hold it just for a minute; provided he could support its punishing load. He never tired of quizzing about all the nosferatu it had destroyed.

Anton hadn't used the weapon in years. It had become a mere ornament, a gruesome household decoration surrounded by a fan shape of metal bolts. Yet as he studied it he could sense the instrument of death still exuding an air of menace.

Reaching up, he gently stroked the walnut handle and felt the callous coolness of its metal mechanism.

The clock chimed interrupting his thoughts, reminding him he hadn't looked in on his captive for two hours. Entering the cellblock he spied Nicku, face sullen and taut, seething, as only inches away Quintz made no attempt to conceal the fact he was guarding the deputy just as much as the vampire.

It was a necessary insurance policy. They'd all witnessed how easily Nicku's mind could be invaded and Anton didn't want the supernatural hostage to trick the deputy into harming himself or others.

No such worries about Quintz. The diminutive fighter presented more of a challenge - sharp minded, determined, strong-willed. And as the bandage around his head demonstrated, thick skulled. The creature wouldn't be able to use him for sport.

Hearing his approach, the small man nodded a greeting, as Nicku scowled, complaining: "My hand hurts like buggery. I told you I needed a physician. This wound needs proper treatment not some of that senile monk's poxy ointment."

Anton was unmoved. "We have more pressing things to worry about. And even if I felt like summoning the doctor, do you think your fellow citizens would let him through?"

Quintz edged towards the deputy, holding his knife under the whining man's widening eyes.

"If your hand is bothering you, I can always cut it off," he suggested brightly. The deputy flinched, grasping the bandaged limb close to his chest.

Anton hid a smile. "Our friend been behaving himself?" he enquired, jerking his head towards the cell and its malicious occupant.

"Good as gold," Quintz replied. "We haven't heard a word out of him for hours. Model little prisoner, aren't you, bloodsucker?"

The dwarf made an obscene gesture towards the cell. Putting his eye to the spy hole, Anton noted that the captive was sitting in a pose of meditation, boredom oozing from his aristocratic pores.

"Come to see if I am showing signs of fear? If the thought of being at the mercy of the notorious Anton Yoska has me quaking?" Stefan challenged.

"And are you?"

The vampire chuckled softly. "With what I know about the helplessness of your plight? Why would I be concerned?"

The truth of the words stung.

"Yet it is still not too late to change your fate," Stefan remarked, rising effortlessly and coming closer to the door until his eye was only inches from Anton's. "I have a suggestion, a proposition for you, slayer."

"Let me guess. If I let you go, you'll shower me with riches? Give me more wealth than I could possibly spend?"

The eyes behind the metal slots filled with amusement.

"I wouldn't insult your integrity. We both know greed isn't what motivates you. However, I can furnish the one thing you desire beyond all other Earthly enticements."

He waited, letting suspense build. "The life of your wife," he whispered.

Anton rocked back. "What!"

"I can save your darling, sad Sofia from the impending appointment with her maker. I can take away her malady."

It was all Anton could do not to swoon.

"That's impossible. She's beyond salvation. The best medicines have no effect. What makes you think I'd believe for a moment you can achieve what the doctor cannot?"

Stefan sighed at the lawman's childish naivety. "I mentioned nothing of potions and pills and other quack remedies. I speak of a cure that goes beyond man's fleeting mortality, that removes frailty and vulnerability to pestilence forever."

Anton felt the ground suddenly unsure beneath his feet. "No!" he gasped. "Not that!"

"Don't be so quick to dismiss my proposal. Just consider. Your doomed Sofia has only hours to live, unless she joins our kind. She can become nosferatu, a Modjeski; a princess amongst the Undead."

Anton didn't trust himself to reply. The notion was abhorrent, sacrilegious, unconscionable, and yet it flooded his heart with hope.

"If you truly loved her, you'd agree."

"But—"

"And I offer you the same release from your tribulations," the vampire purred silkily. "You can be with her. The devoted couple. Together. For all eternity. All you have to do is let me go. Let me finish what I began at Ossiak..."

At the mention of the battle, Anton shuddered, ice shooting through his veins, instantly coming to his senses.

"Very clever," he conceded. "It almost worked." Turning to Quintz, he instructed: "If this thing gives you any trouble, stick the bear in the cell with him. We'll see how funny he finds that."

As he crossed the courtyard, he heard the Modjeski prince's taunting laughter reverberating, underlining that Anton's fragile control over himself and the situation was a fantasy.

CHAPTER 41

"There's something I still don't understand about vampires," Pavel said, brow furrowing.

Around the dining room the others stopped mid-mouthful to gawp disbelievingly at the deputy. They'd found a pot of half congealed stew in the kitchen, and had coaxed the immense range's fire back to life, only succeeding after a half hour struggle and a lot of cursing. Since then all had been too distracted, wolfing down the thick gooey broth, to speak or even look at each other.

"He's fascinated by bloodsuckers, this one, and that's a fact," Gregor remarked, letting his spoon drop into his now empty bowl. "He has more questions than the inquisition and is just as relentlessly insistent."

Across the room, Johann sucked through his teeth, informing the youngster: "All you need to know, kid, is how to kill the fuckers. Anything else is irrelevant."

"I thought I'd already told him how to do that," Gregor answered pointedly. "Apparently I left something out."

Pavel blushed. "No, I get it about staking and holy water and all that stuff. What is puzzling me is why the prisoner keeps referring to the Modjeski as his family. Surely the creatures can't be related? Do they... reproduce?"

Gregor, Milosh and Johann all coughed melodramatically and turned to Irina, gesturing for her to answer. She rolled her eyeballs in exasperation at having to be the one to explain the birds and bees to the gauche youth.

"It's a good question," she conceded. "The leeches can't procreate. They can't give birth. They are sterile although, ironically, it doesn't seem to stop them having an insatiable liking for sex."

The glint in her eyes suggested that indulging carnal desires was something she approved of.

"They can only increase their numbers by transforming victims into more of their own kind, turning humans into the Undead," Gregor explained, giving Irina a censorious glare.

If any of it made sense to Pavel, he didn't show it. Biting his bottom lip, he repeated: "But why call themselves a family?"

Stretching, Milosh ambled over to the pot and sloshed another portion of the meaty casserole onto his plate. "Because it makes them feel less like the unnatural, disgusting abominations that they are," he volunteered, ripping a chunk of bread in two and dipping it in with forceful jabs. "It's like everything they do - a travesty, a mockery of the living."

The explanation was clearly confusing the deputy even more. Sighing, Gregor got to his feet, grasping his jacket lapels like a schoolmaster. "Think of it this way," he began. "By referring to themselves as families, thinking of themselves as great noble houses, it makes the nosferatu tribes easier to organise into a cohesive host. You could say it has been one of the reasons for their dominance and success over the centuries.

"Collectively they are known as The Brethren, an alliance of families, each clan led by an elder, with all those within it taking the surname of the chief."

"So Stefan wasn't always a Modjeski?" Pavel deduced.

"Correct. Whatever Stefan's real surname was in his life before, he took the Modjeski appellation when he was assimilated."

The old man waited, watching the youngster absorb the information, spotty face twisting in concentration, before he added: "It is confusing because in many respects the creatures look upon each other as kin; as brothers and sisters."

"But that doesn't stop them fornicating with each other," Irina interjected and immediately put up her hands in mock apology at Gregor's disapproving glance. "Okay, okay. I'll shut up."

Getting up, she doled a generous portion of stew onto a plate and made for the door.

Gregor was about to launch into the next section of his lecture when Milosh cut across him. "Where are you going?" he asked the woman suspiciously.

"I won't be long," she replied, with a teasing wink. "I've just remembered I've some unfinished business to take care of."

CHAPTER 42

He headed for his parlour, desperate to lie down and give his throbbing temples time to calm. Entering the room, Anton instantly saw the idea was impossible.

"Why, Marshal, there you are. I thought you'd snubbed us," Irina said teasingly.

"I had important chores to attend to," he replied.

"A lawman's work is never done?"

"Something like that." He nodded to the plate of stew near her: "Is that for me?"

"I thought you could use it." She pushed it towards him. "By my reckoning you haven't eaten all day."

Or even the day before, he remembered. Grabbing the spoon he shovelled mouthfuls into his mouth. Although barely lukewarm, it tasted better than anything he'd had in ages, hunger indeed being the best seasoning.

"I'm grateful but must admit to being a little surprised," he confessed, between chews. "You don't strike me as the domesticated type. I wouldn't expect you to go running around after any man."

Irina chuckled. "Because I travel with a band of bounty hunters? Because I'm good with a gun?"

"Because you're independent. Self-reliant. And don't need to be at any man's beck and call."

She edged closer. "That depends on the man."

Despite himself, Anton found himself leaning towards her, eyes closing as her heady scent wafted over him. It was Sofia's perfume, stolen from her dressing room. On this woman, it smelt different; earthier, beguiling, hypnotic. It drew him in like some enchanted love potion.

"But Milosh?" he protested. "You're his woman—"

"Not for a long time," she murmured. "He hasn't touched me in months. Not like that. Not that it would make any difference if he did."

She reached out, her soft, slender fingertips brushing his unshaven cheek and as much as he wanted to push them away, he felt his fingers encircle hers. It was as if she had him under her spell.

"He can't keep it up." It was said with stinging rancour. "My so-called lover... It's the drink. The gallons of alcohol he pours down his throat. It's made him all but impotent. Stupid, selfish bastard."

Anton couldn't believe what he was hearing. "I didn't know..." he began but her fingers were now touching his lips.

"Shushhh," she urged.

She brought her mouth to his. Immediately, he felt himself about to surrender to the sensual promise, wanting to force open her mouth and thrust his tongue deep inside.

His pulse quickened, pictures filling his head: of himself ripping her blouse, buttons popping as they burst violently from the material; of her brushing across his groin, feverishly seeking to free his already stiffening penis, her suddenly naked to the waist, her small pointed breasts pushing against him, brown nipples hard and enticing, her dragging out his manhood and running her nails along its length, teasing the head.

He imagined her demanding 'Fuck me' as he dropped to his knees, bringing her right breast towards his mouth and running his tongue roughly over its milky whiteness.

In the back of his mind he knew he should fight, resist the lust-filled images. He was betraying Sofia, going against every moral and code he'd ever lived by.

No, he told himself, no. This is *wrong!*

She must have sensed his struggle because Irina cupped his face and pulled him closer. And at that moment he would have been overwhelmed, save for the noise suddenly filing the room.

Both rushed to the window, to see what was causing the unexpected commotion.

In the street below he saw the crowd pointing, running in all directions; a stampede of panicked individuals crashing into each other, frantically scrabbling to get away.

Those who didn't move seemed spellbound, watching in terrified fascination the blazing, fast-moving blue dots appearing between the trees, cyan sparkles of intensity cutting through the falling snowflakes.

"What is it?" Irina whispered, elbowing her way in to see for herself. "What's going on?"

"It's the Modjeski," he said hoarsely. "We're out of time. They're here."

CHAPTER 43

The glistening snow swooped and gyrated, the cruel strengthening wind whipping the sparkling flakes into a dense, dancing curtain. Peering through the white blanket, Anton couldn't see farther than twenty yards but could hear hooves thudding across the wooden bridge. Wheels too - a carriage, its axles squeaking rhythmically.

The inhabitants of Brejnei had fled, running for whatever shelter they could. Centuries of fear, terror so engrained it passed from generation to generation, had sent them running headlong from the impending threat. Anton knew it was futile. There was nowhere safe, not even the ramshackle church on the hill.

Gripping the crossbow tightly, he cautioned himself that it was lunacy to think he could prevail, no matter how much the bulk of the weapon and the evil solidity of the metal-tipped bolt gave the illusion of protection.

For an instant he remembered how it had felt to let fly, the deadly yew shaft cleaving clean through its yielding target as if the weapon were alive, possessed, vengeful.

Soon he knew he'd feel that terrifying exhilaration again.

Glancing sharply to his left, he studied his only companion on the slick, wet jailhouse steps. Milosh's eyes glinted with excitement.

"Just like old times, eh?" the hunter remarked, their enmity temporarily put to one side.

Except we had a large troop of experienced soldiers with us, Anton remembered. The odds infinitely more favourable, and even so we lost...

The shroud-like curtain parted, snapping him out of his thoughts. Flickers of colour appeared, shapes bursting through the milky flurry.

He heard Milosh gasp: "Christ!"

Before them were five, no six, outriders. Towering. Hooded. Gaunt-faced warriors on mighty stallions, the horses like nightmarish griffins, sapphire eyes glowing, steam billowing from their nostrils. The riders were dressed in the Modjeski livery of crimson and purple, each decked out in a long, flowing cloak.

Without breaking pace, the pale riders parted to take up position in a semi-circle, silent, staring disdainfully through the defenders.

"How many?" Anton whispered. "Your gun - how many can you hit?"

Milosh replied simply: "Not enough."

With a portentous grace the carriage finally appeared, gliding to a halt in the middle of the group.

The majestic vehicle was lavishly carved, its ebony coachwork perfect in every detail, from its gilded wheels and shining brass handles to its team of six white horses magnificently poised, each adorned with a black feathered plume.

But it was the carriage door and its coat of arms emblazoned in silver and gold that held Anton's focus. To the uninitiated it could appear simply another heraldic montage: shields, badges, mythological beasts; a gaudy sign of the wealth and self-regard of the family who deemed themselves aristocratic enough to warrant such an ostentatious show of pride.

To him it meant much more. This crest and its motto *None Shall Deny Us* had haunted his troubled dreams for years. The Modjeski. The most sadistic of all the predator clans. Few cast eyes on this coat of arms and lived to tell of it.

The presence of the coach could only mean one thing. *She* was here in person. Kristina Modjeski , the supreme nosferatu in Europe. She had come to personally settle the score.

Silently, a footman climbed down the side of the carriage - his movements swift, effortless. He strode crisply through the white carpet to the side of the coach and unclipped the wooden steps, letting them drop into place inches above the ground. Then, bowing, he swung the door wide open.

The emerging figure paused for a moment, sniffing the night air like an animal seeking the scent of prey, regally holding out her gloved hand. The servant took it, helping the woman from the carriage. Closing the door behind her, he took up a respectful distance three paces behind as she progressed towards them.

Even if she hadn't been six feet tall, with silver blonde hair, skin the hue of fine porcelain, perfect crimson lips and shining, dark, intelligent eyes, Kristina Modjeski would have commanded the complete attention of any man. There was a raw, elemental sexual power that danced around her like Saint Elmo's fire. She was reputed to be at least a hundred and seventy years old, yet possessed the features of a beauty of just forty.

Under the flowing cape, there were ample clues to her slender figure, full breasts and long, delicate arms.

She was stunning and, despite his intellect telling him it was only to be expected, Anton was amazed that she hadn't aged since that fateful occasion when he'd last encountered her - the day The Brethren had surrendered to a stunned Mankind; to generals still unable to believe they had triumphed against this most implacable of foes.

"Lord Marshal Yoska," she said, halting ten feet away and dipping her head in acknowledgement. "It has been some time."

He mirrored her bow. "Eleven years."

"And an unexpected reunion for us both. Unfortunately, I cannot say it is a pleasure. Not in these regrettable circumstances."

"Circumstances not of my making or desire," he pointed out.

Regarding Milosh with repugnance, she murmured: "So I see." For a moment he was aware of her reading the bounty hunter's aura, trying to find a way through the impenetrable layers of hatred, deceit and treachery.

Glowering, she refocused her attention on the lawman.

"I shall come straight to the point. You have Stefan a prisoner, chained in your cell block."

She raised a warning finger to indicate Anton shouldn't bother denying it.

"I sense him, not fifty feet away. He is manacled, in pain. He has been denigrated and tortured. For that I should take your life. Nevertheless, I see in your companion's thoughts that you are not the architect of this outrage, nor a willing participant."

She gave Milosh a look of pure loathing. "It appears my quarrel is with this pitiful animal and his cohorts so I will make you, Lord Marshal Yoska, the most generous bargain you will ever receive in your benighted existence.

"Hand over my son, without fuss, resistance or conflict. Release him immediately and I will leave you, your family and staff unharmed."

Anton couldn't help himself. Part of him urged his conscience to be quiet and comply with her demand. The primal urge for self-preservation was irresistible. It wouldn't just be himself he was saving. Co-operating would protect the town and save Tomas, Pavel and Nicku. And Sofia...

At the thought of her, his heart lurched and he remembered Stefan's enticing offer.

The inner debate must have been displayed across his features for he heard Milosh grunt and felt the big man tense.

"What about us?" the gang leader challenged. "What about me and my companions? Do you leave *us* alone and unharmed. If you get your son back does your unexpected generosity extend to us too? Or do you expect Yoska to step aside and let you do what you want with us?"

The question immediately stilled the raging argument in Anton's head. He waited expectantly, even though he knew the sickening certainty of what the Modjeski matriarch was about to say.

"You are doomed whatever happens," she told Milosh. "I cannot permit your heinous rabble to live after what you have done. How can I? You have challenged my authority, carried out this affront to my family, abducted my son."

Fixing Anton with a chill stare, she said: "They are a scourge. Vermin. Extortionists. Rapists. Spreading chaos, discord and despair. Surrendering them to me would be a service to the world."

"I can't argue with that," he conceded, "but it would be murder. Pure and simple. And I can't allow it."

"Would you just listen to the bitch," Milosh barked. "These bloodsucking parasites slaughter, maim and terrorise for fun and she has the fucking audacity to call us vermin!"

He levelled the cannon, taking aim. "We'll see how high and mighty you'll be when I blow your face off."

Anton had to move fast and stepped into the line of fire. Ignoring the bounty hunter struggling to shove him out of the way, he informed Kristina: "It doesn't matter who you offer to spare. Nothing you say makes any difference. I won't give up Stefan. He is my prisoner, legally arrested and facing charges. No one is getting near him."

It was difficult to tell who was more incensed, Milosh or the nosferatu queen.

"You dare refuse me!" she raged. "I thought you, of all mortals, had more sense."

"I have taken an oath to uphold the law. Stefan Modjeski will stand trial for his crimes. He is in my custody." He motioned with the crossbow. "If you want him you will have to go through me."

Kristina regarded him with measured pity. "If that's how you wish it, Lord Marshal, I am happy to oblige." Her horseback troops moved determinedly forward. "As you can see, I have superior numbers."

Anton whistled once - a long, shrill note. Around the street, windows flew open. Lines of muskets poked out. The deputies and gang members were deployed exactly as he'd ordered.

"And as you can see, I have you and your men caught in a deadly crossfire. Make a move and you'll be cut to pieces."

Despite the revelation, Kristina swiftly regained her composure. "Ah, clever slayer. So you haven't forgotten any of your tricks." Surveying the firepower, she observed: "It would appear we have a stand-off."

He nodded. "So go now and I guarantee safe passage. No one will fire on you. Leave and never come back."

Inside, his guts churned. It couldn't be this easy. You didn't just bluff the Modjeski. She'd be sizing up the odds, working out if she could cleave his throat in the first seconds.

Even with Milosh's multi-shot gun, enough of the supernatural riders would survive to overpower them.

After several nerve-shredding seconds, the woman cocked her head challengingly.

"Safe passage? How unbelievably generous of you, my old adversary. You are bold, and no mistake." She pretended to consider. "Such an enticing notion. Sadly, I cannot accept, for there is one factor you have overlooked."

Now it was her turn to give an unexpected signal - the elegant raising of a gloved hand.

The coachman strode to the vehicle and reached inside, pulling hard, and in a heartbeat, Anton knew it was over. His bluff had failed.

CHAPTER 44

At first nothing happened beyond a loud squealing from within, then the coachman pulled again, even harder, and a bedraggled, blood-stained, bundle of clothing tumbled out into the snow, turning the virgin white deep vermilion.

The shape scrambled on all fours to get away; animal howls emanating from within the despoiled finery. Without pity, the servant grabbed the bleeding form, effortlessly hoisting it high in the air.

There was no mistaking the voice whose shrieks rent the air.

"I believe you know Count Kravnik," Kristina said, as calmly as any hostess introducing a vague acquaintance at a party. "We bumped into him on the way here. It's amazing whom one can run into on the highway. He was disinclined to accompany us at first, but we persuaded him."

Anton gasped so deeply he feared his lungs would burst. The aristocrat was barely identifiable under the bruises and the vicious cuts covering his face. The arrogance had been stripped away and only a shaking, terrified human remained.

"Yoska," he gasped. "Christ Almighty, give her what she wants. They are going to devour me if you refuse. Please, please, I don't want to die. Don't let them kill me. Co-operate, I implore you."

He wept loudly, each sob accompanied by an explosive shudder, and Anton remembered how much he detested the envoy, feeling no pity even in this moment of the man's abject terror.

"You heard him, Lord Marshal," Kristina pressed. "We will feast on him before your very eyes. He's fat and bloated. I wonder how many pints of blood he holds. Shall we find out?"

"For God's sake, Yoska! I'm begging you. Hand over your prisoner," Kravnik croaked. "Give her that bastard son of hers."

Anton was aware of Milosh just out of his eye line, leaning over, whispering menacingly: "Don't you fucking dare. The second she gets what she wants, we're all dead."

Anton ignored the warning. What the bounty hunter really meant was the moment the nosferatu leader got what she wanted, Milosh's gang would have forever lost their shot at riches.

Instead, he focused solely on the violently trembling, sobbing nobleman.

"You ran out on us," Anton said levelly, "so why should I bother to save you now?"

"I-I-I went to get help. I went to raise the alarm. You must believe me. I am no fighter. I-I-I wouldn't have made any difference, only got in the way. I was riding to alert the Imperial Cavalry."

The words rang false.

Voice hardening, Anton told Kristina, "Go ahead. Slaughter him. You'll be saving me a chore."

The Count's eyes went wide. "No, no, no," he pleaded. "You can't do this. You can't sacrifice me. I am a personal friend of the Crown Prince. I am an important member of the Government. I am—"

"Surplus to requirements," Anton interrupted. "Just another preening coward in fancy clothes who thinks he's better than the rest of us." He stared coldly. "How would you put it, Count? It's just that some lives are worth more than others."

Kravnik barely had time to scream before the coachman pulled him in close and in a single motion tore the noble's ear clean off, chewing furiously at the brutalised face.

What happened next seemed to occur to Anton in slow motion, different actions erupting at once.

As Kravnik dropped to the ground, shrieking like a stuck pig, Milosh aimed at Kristina Modjeski, firing a spread of musket shot that threaded through the air, dozens of tiny metal balls hurtling towards their target. But as the deadly spheres approached, the woman demonstrated just how incredibly fast the nosferatu could react and dodged each with ease, her body seeming to flow around them. An instant later the deadly cascade thumped noisily into the carriage, sending splitters of wood spitting outwards.

As the outriders charged, Anton swung the crossbow to chest height and pulled the trigger. The bolt took out the lead rider, who fell backwards from his horse, his face shattered by the impact.

The defenders opened up from the upper windows, a volley of lead knocking two other riders from their steeds. Then it became pandemonium as Milosh fired again, this time into the galloping warriors, smashing the legs of the stallions; the falling animals screeching in pain and surprise.

Anton couldn't remember reloading, drawing back the taut bowstring and grabbing a second bolt from the quiver on his back; it must have been ingrained impulse. Spotting the projectile sitting in place on the weapon, he acted, sending it thwacking into the coachman, the missile bursting through the servant's torso, throwing him six feet backwards through the air.

Then a rider was upon him, leaping from the saddle and Anton knew it was the end, as the force brought him to his knees and powerful hands grabbed his shoulders, pulling him in. Although he tried to struggle, the grip was too tight and looking into the face of his attacker, he saw the warrior's lips part and the dripping incisors gleam.

Inside, Anton felt no fear, just a sense of relief. After all this time finally, finally he could rest.

CHAPTER 45

A wave of pleasure coursed through her, each nerve-ending trembling with anticipation. She'd dreamt of this, of course, and now as Kristina Modjeski watched the slayer overwhelmed it was all she could do not to howl in delight.

Yoska was limp, the warrior's teeth grazing the side of his face, as it licked and tasted, relishing the moment of absolute triumph. The Marshal was making no attempt to fight back. It was as if he welcomed what was about to happen.

"Do it," she urged, "do it. Bite him!"

The warrior paused, suspicious at the lack of resistance, and she thought of rushing over and claiming the prize for herself. Would that not be fitting? The final revenge for all the suffering Yoska had inflicted upon her kind; should she not enjoy the ecstasy that was hers by right?

Musket balls whizzed past her head. She paid them no heed. Her attention was entirely on her trapped enemy. Enthralled, she watched as her dark fighter pulled Yoska's head to one side by the hair, exposing his throat and, deadly teeth protruding, attacked.

For a divine, teasing instant, it seemed her desires were fulfilled. The warrior plunged his fangs down ferociously only to unexpectedly stop before making contact; all motion frozen.

What!

What was happening?

She reeled in shock.

The warrior's head slumped and she saw the knife protruding from the back of his skull. Following the line of trajectory, she identified the thrower. From his position at the parlour window, Quintz gave her a mocking wave.

Kristina was conflicted, debating whether to finish Yoska or scale the side of the building to dispatch the leering sprite. The moment's indecision was all it took, allowing Milosh the opportunity to aim his reloaded shotgun straight at her and mouth a single word: "Surrender."

Although her fury made her willing to charge at the bounty hunter, she knew it was futile. There were too many guns, too many opponents.

"Desist!" she shouted. "Desist, I say!"

Whether she was addressing her own troops or the jailhouse defenders, she didn't know. It was a cry of frustration. However, it instantly halted the fighting, the air becoming spookily still.

Helping Anton to his feet while keeping the shotgun trained on the vampire leader, Milosh sneered at her: "So we're not the pushover you were expecting, eh?"

Kristina said nothing. Drubrick was already food for the worms, she consoled herself. He just didn't have the wit to comprehend it yet.

Anton was tapping his head with the heel of his hand, trying to clear his thoughts, and for an instant she could have sworn there was regret etched on his features, dismay at being rescued.

"I promised you safe passage and I will honour that pledge," he declared. "Nothing has changed. Stefan stays here under lock and key. You must leave immediately. Go and never come back."

She waved away the idea. "That is impossible. As you say, nothing has changed. I will have my son. And I will destroy anyone who tries to prevent me."

Gesturing at the fallen bodies, she conceded. "You have me at a disadvantage, Lord Marshal, and for now I shall withdraw. But be assured I shall return with my entire force to wipe you and your loathsome companions from the face of the Earth."

Ordering her remaining warriors to form up, she headed towards her now despoiled carriage. She knew turning her back on the jailhouse defenders was taking a risk, but she needed to make a defiant gesture. I fear you not. I am Modjeski and you cannot touch me.

Stepping into the coach, she halted as Milosh's taunting voice rang out.

"Before you go, Your Majesty, I have a way of ending this *unpleasantness*. The Crown Prince has posted a thousand-crown reward on your bloodsucker son's head. Double it, give me and my associates two thousand gleaming golden crowns and he's all yours. We'll even help you spring him."

Turning slowly, she faced the gang leader. "If I were to agree? What about Lord Marshal Yoska?"

"We'd eliminate him or stand aside while you did."

"And after that you would naturally expect me to allow you and your thugs to simply ride off into the distance, unharmed."

"Naturally," Milosh replied. "So what do you say, Ice Queen? Tempted? Want to make a deal?"

She didn't need to consider it. To co-operate with criminals, blackmailers and assassins would embolden other vermin scum to challenge her might. "What I say is that the Lord Marshal should choose his allies more carefully," she answered.

Shaking her head at Anton, she observed: "Only minutes ago you refused to allow me to mete out the punishment these callous animals so richly deserve, and what gratitude do they show for your protection? They would slit your throat in a heartbeat."

The lawman sighed wearily. "Of that, I've never been in any doubt. But they aren't my problem at this precise moment. You are. So go. Go now. Before I change my mind."

He motioned to Milosh, to the menacing gun the bounty hunter was clutching lovingly. "Before *he* changes his mind."

Drawing her cloak tight, Kristina slowly arced her unrelenting stare from window to window, inspecting each defender.

"Your heads will all adorn the entrance to my castle," she promised, "as a warning to others."

She began to climb into the carriage.

"One last thing," she said, pausing defiantly. "Please ensure Count Kravnik is given a decent burial, befitting an eminent member of the establishment. I wouldn't want the Crown Prince to think we didn't show proper respect."

CHAPTER 46

Anton supposed he should be elated, at least relieved. He felt neither, just numb, aware he hadn't won a victory, only a reprieve.

Listening to Milosh's voice booming from the parlour, it was clear the gang leader considered the nosferatu taken care of. Barely twenty minutes on from the defenders regrouping in the residence, he was holding court, grasping a vodka bottle, declaring to anyone who'd listen: "Didn't I say? It's all fairy stories to scare little children. The Modjeski are no better than all the other cowardly bloodsuckers. Stand up to them and they turn and run."

From the doorway, Anton saw the others didn't share the beefy man's jubilation. Huddled in a corner, Johann and Irina whispered animatedly, frequently glancing at their extrovert leader, while Gregor mouthed words, slowly rotating a set of rosary beads, and Quintz, the enigmatic Quintz, cleaned his knives tenderly, using long, deliberate swipes of a beautifully embroidered but blood-stained handkerchief.

Even the two deputies seemed subdued. Nicku regarded the others with ill-concealed scorn, flexing his injured hand as though the exercise would magically banish the pain, while Pavel leant over the fire, lost in his own thoughts, too preoccupied to pester anyone with more questions.

In the centre of the gathering, Milosh - three quarters drunk and absorbed in his rant - was blissfully unaware.

"Did you see the bitch's face when we sprang the trap?" he exclaimed with a lop-sided grin. "It was a fucking picture. I thought I'd shit myself laughing."

He took a swig, smacking his lips. "One thing's for sure, she's learnt not to mess with me." Gesturing to the assembly, he generously included his companions. "Not to mess with *us* again."

No one reacted; distracted by the sight of Anton walking purposefully into the room, carrying a large axe.

For a moment Milosh failed to register the abrupt silence. "Know what I reckon, they should put up a plaque to me. The bold defender o—" He whirled around.

"Do go on," Anton urged. "I'm fascinated to hear about how we should commemorate your heroics."

He strode forward. Milosh immediately took a stumbling step back, eyes locked on the hatchet.

"Look, let's not be hasty," he offered, with a hollow laugh. "I didn't mean what I said out there. It was a bluff. I was goading her. That's all."

"Bluffing?" Anton spat the word. "You could have fooled me." He took another step forward.

"What is it you always say?" Anton prodded him with the axe head. "It's nothing personal, just business. Well, tell me - how am I supposed to take you offering my head as part of the deal?"

Without waiting for an answer, he summoned the deputies to his side. "Nicku, go fill two storm lanterns," he ordered.

The grizzled man made a face: "But—"

"Do it *now!*"

Muttering, Nicku left without looking back.

"Pavel. Go to the armoury. Start bringing up the gunpowder kegs. We're going to need them. This isn't over, no matter what our drink-sodden friend seems to think."

Pavel scanned the room worriedly. "But I can't leave you here on your own."

"I'll be fine. Now go."

At the young man's departure, Milosh tensed. "Getting rid of the witnesses?" he suggested, nodding meaningfully to the shining weapon still jabbed into his stomach.

It was a tempting idea.

"I don't need to lay a finger on you," Anton scoffed. "Your compatriots will do it for me, soon as they find out how badly you've duped them. I have other uses for this axe tonight."

Switching his attention to the preacher, he ordered: "Father Mathias, grab your bag of tricks. You're with me."

The old man looked surprised, then pulled himself together, putting away the rosary and gathering up his things.

Irina's brow creased. "What does Yoska mean, duped us? What is he talking about, Milosh?"

Her lover didn't answer.

"Marshal?" she challenged.

Ignoring her, Anton told the heavily jowled man: "Maybe if you hadn't been so greedy, Milosh, the Ice Queen might have gone for it. Brave though, doubling the stakes like that when it was your last throw of the dice."

The others frowned in confusion. Anton made no attempt to explain. They'd figure it for themselves soon enough.

On the surface she appeared in icy control, but fury surged through Kristina, as she chided herself over and over. How could she have been so stupid, so criminally reckless? She knew better than to rush into battle unprepared, to let her over-eagerness for the fray get the better of her.

She should have anticipated Yoska would have some trick up his sleeve. Plus, the knowledge she'd never have blundered into the ambush if it had been anyone else but Stefan, her darling Stefan, in the odious slayer's cell, made it all the worse.

It added to the stinging humiliation she felt, recalling Viktor's warning. He'd been right to be cautious, and she'd been a fool to ignore his counsel. Now five of her fighters were gone while the Marshal had not lost a single man.

Peering out of the carriage window at the passing forest, she decided she'd come a safe distance, and thumped on the roof for the driver to stop. As the servant opened the door, she stepped out, surveying the acres of ghostlike trees, bent alarmingly with the powdery load on their branches, and judged it the perfect place to wait until her main force arrived.

A tentative tendril of psychic energy pulsed out from her mind, as she focused on the Undead army's approach and grunted in annoyance that there was no sense of them yet.

However, she comforted herself with the knowledge that other allies, much nearer, were at her disposal.

Looking up towards the mountains, she called out in silent mental command and immediately they replied, the night filling with terrifying howls as one by one their shadow shapes began to pad hungrily through the wilderness.

CHAPTER 47

Irina wasn't going to let it go. "What the hell did Yoska mean by last throw of the dice?" Her face was set hard. When she was this determined, she was more intimidating than any man.

"Nothing," Milosh dismissed. "He's just making mischief." He tried to walk away, steps unsteady, but she placed herself in his direct path.

She probed deeply into his black, devious eyes. She didn't need to read auras to know he was lying.

What was he hiding? What made the lawman think he could use it to his advantage?

Her mind raced through the various possibilities. "It's the reward, isn't it?" she deduced quickly. "There's a problem with the bounty!"

She grabbed the leather money belt around his ample waist, wrenching it free. Upending the pouch, she sent a cascade of gold coins rolling across the wooden floor.

"Where's the rest?" she said, voice icy. "There's barely a hundred crowns. There's supposed to be a thousand. Where's the gold!"

In a second Johann and Quintz were by her side. "Answer her," Johann ordered. "Where's the gold? What have you done with it? If you've tried to cheat us—"

Milosh's temple twitched as his scar-faced cohort curled snake-like to pounce. Irina could see him thinking fast, his alcohol befuddled brain trying to work out how to defuse the danger.

"Don't worry, there's no problem," he declared, taking a gulp of vodka. "What you see is simply a down payment."

"A what? A fucking down payment? Where's the rest?" Johann snapped.

Milosh's hand moved swiftly, and automatically Johann reached for his gun.

It was half out of its holster as Milosh soothed: "Whoa there. Hold up. I'm simply getting this out of my pocket." He produced a crumpled ball of paper, proffering it to anyone who'd take it.

Snatching the parchment, Quintz smoothed it out. For a moment he said nothing, then chortled with bitter humour. "You've got to be kidding me." He passed it over to Irina.

"What is this nonsense?" she exclaimed. "Why have you got a bloody treasury note?"

Milosh had the decency to look shamefaced. "It wasn't my idea. There wasn't enough to pay the full bounty in gold. The blue blood gave me that as a guarantee for the remainder. We just need to take it to the Capitol. No one's been cheated. You'll all still get your cut."

Johann regarded him like he was a particularly backward child, and grabbing him roughly, bundled the big man over to the window.

"No problem, hey? I'll tell you what the frigging problem is." He pushed Milosh up against the glass. "See that bastard lying dead out there. He signed it. Without him to honour that guarantee, it's worthless."

Irina took a second for the full implications to sink in. "You're telling me we went through all this danger for nothing. We took on the bloodsuckers, rode halfway across the country, got ourselves trapped in this dump - all for some lousy loose change!"

"Yeah, that's exactly what I'm saying," Johann agreed, eyes flaring. "We've been royally shafted. Our fuckwit leader has let his old mate run rings round him. From the moment we got here the Marshal has been making fools of us."

He leant in close to Milosh. "I said to kill Yoska quick and simple. There was no need to kidnap the leech but no, you had your ingenious master plan all worked out - the grand, retribution drama. Well, guess what? It's all turned to crap. The big pay day has evaporated, Theodore's dead, and we're going to join him if we don't get the fuck out of here."

Quintz stroked his chin thoughtfully. "Do you know what? I think you're wrong," he advised Johann, ignoring the answering scowl. "It's not Yoska who's been making a fool of us. It's him." He motioned in Milosh's direction. "Don't you think it odd our normally meticulous chief didn't check whether there would be enough gold to pay us before dragging us all the way to the middle of nowhere?"

He pointed an accusing finger. "You know what I reckon - Milosh didn't care if Brejnei jail had enough cash to pay us. It's never been about the reward, just his damned revenge. The gold was simply a lure to con us into helping."

At that revelation Johann banged Milosh's head against the pane. "Is that right, fat man? You been playing us all along?"

The gang leader mumbled, speech slurring, but Johann wasn't listening. Thumping Milosh's head even harder, making the window rattle alarmingly, he warned: "You have five seconds to tell me why I shouldn't smear your brains all over this glass."

CHAPTER 48

Outside, a hard frost had turned the snow to powder, crunching underfoot, the thin dusting on the strewn bodies of the vampires taking on a twinkling iridescence.

"Do you want me to pray for them?" Gregor asked, taking the proffered lantern and holding it high, the yellow light adding a sickly glow to the sinister scene.

"It's a bit late for that," Anton said, moving his own lantern in a wide arc, grunting as the light pushed the darkness grudgingly into the corners. "They forfeited their souls years ago."

"Then what do you require of me?" Gregor asked, as they approached the twisted figures scattered haphazardly across the ground like a pile of smashed statues.

Anton nodded to the cleric's bag. "You've got a supply of stakes?"

"Yes, but the fiends are already slain."

"You may know a lot about nosferatu folklore and legends, Father, but I fought them up close, witnessed things I can't explain. We know precious little about their powers of recovery. I don't want to take any unnecessary gambles."

Gregor blinked. "Yes, of course."

Rummaging, he produced a fat bundle of yew pegs, each sharpened to a menacing point, plus one other item.

"What's that?" Anton asked.

"A little mixture of my own making," Gregor replied, removing the cork from the small bottle. "Olive oil infused with garlic. I normally use this in my culinary pursuits." He set about smearing the greasy mixture over the coarsely planed shafts. "But as you so rightly point out, we don't want to take any risks."

For the next ten minutes they moved methodically through the nosferatu corpses, following the same ritual: Gregor holding a slippery stake to each chest, Anton using the flat end of the axe head to hammer it in deeply with a squelching crunch. Satisfied they'd punctured the heart, Gregor made the sign of the cross over each body.

It was grisly work, but they made an effective team and eventually only the devil steeds remained to be disposed of. Gregor held his bag wide to show his supply of whittled pegs was now exhausted.

"It doesn't matter," Anton divulged. "I have something else in mind for them."

Opening his storm lamp, he poured kerosene over the carcases of the equine monsters, ensuring each was drenched. Herding Gregor back to safety, he lit a match and tossed it on to the charnel pile, which erupted with a whoosh.

Staring into the flames, the holy man mused. He had a nagging sense that he'd failed to note an important fact, something vital he'd seen or heard in the last few minutes, but no matter how much he concentrated, he couldn't force it to the front of his mind.

He gave up, remarking: "You're certain Milosh is wrong? The Modjeski will return tonight?"

"It's guaranteed." Certainty gave Anton's voice a steely edge. "Milosh is deluded if he believes Kristina will desert one of her kin, especially her favourite. All we've fought is the opening skirmish in the battle."

The cleric peered anxiously into the distance as if trying to spot the approaching enemy. "How soon?"

Anton consulted his fob watch. It read twenty minutes past ten. "An hour, maybe less," he estimated. "The main force can't be far behind her."

"In that case, we must make preparations to flee while we still can."

The Marshal shrugged. "You can try but it won't do you any good. Run, hide, fight, surrender - it makes no difference. The outcome will be the same."

The priest's head jerked in surprise. "I can't believe that. I won't believe it. We can't be completely powerless."

Anton touched the man's arm but with little reassurance. "We have options but don't confuse that with having power. The game is in play, events are already spinning out of our control. The only say we have left is to choose where we die."

He studied the slaughterhouse glop leaking from the sizzling, melting equine forms, adding: "And how quickly."

"Do me in and any hope of getting the reward vanishes forever," Milosh warned in a hoarse croak, face squashed so hard against the windowpane that his features distorted. "You need me. I'm your only hope."

There was something about his tone that made his cronies hesitate. Where there should have been panic, desperation, he projected confidence belying the perilous nature of his situation.

"What are you blabbering about? There's nothing left to get," Johann snapped back, shoving even harder. "The reward is history or are you so frigging drunk the news hasn't worked its way into your thick, stupid skull yet."

"You're wrong. I can still get you the gold," Milosh wheezed. "No one but us knows Kravnik is dead. If we can make it to the Capitol before word gets there, we can—"

Irina flinched at the vehemence of Johann's sudden snort and the homicidal grin twisting his mouth and before she knew it she'd yelled "No!" and grabbed his arm, desperately pulling with all her might.

"Don't do it!" she yelled. "This is crazy. Can't you see, this is what Yoska wants, us at each other's throats, bickering?"

She whispered soothingly: "We haven't got time for this. Our cunning host wants to keep us here, arguing until it's too late to escape, so we'll end up having to face the bloodsuckers with him."

The warning did the trick. Almost at once, Johann's anger abated. Stepping back, he slowly let go of Milosh's head.

"We'll finish this later," he promised, curling his lip, "but right now Irina's right. We need to get moving. The snow's stopped. The yokels have buggered off. Yoska's occupied and the bloodsucker bitch is licking her wounds miles from here. It's time to make a run for it."

A reproachful expression appeared momentarily across his visage. "Like I said this afternoon before the leeches showed up, but no bastard would listen."

Milosh didn't speak, rubbing at the blotchy redness spreading across his bruised temple. Irina could sense him rapidly sobering up, stunned that he'd been usurped and figuring how to regain control.

"I'll get Samson into his cage, ready for travelling," Quintz volunteered, heading out the room.

Johann shoo-ed him with an eager wave. "Go to it, half measure. We'll be right with you. The sooner we get out of here the better. The moment Gregor finishes playing with his crucifixes and comes back inside, we'll hit the road."

He waited until the dwarf had left, before shaking his head. "Trusting little fucker, isn't he?"

Irina's expression darkened. "What do you mean?" she glared suspiciously. "What are you up to? What nasty idea are you hatching in that scheming little brain of yours?"

He met her stare. "Simply getting rid of the dead weight. Thinning out the gang."

"Dead weight?"

"We'll need speed if we're going to get clear of the leeches. That means taking the stallions and galloping full pelt. Gregor can't ride and Quintz won't leave his flee-bitten bear behind. They'll insist we take the wagon, and that's out of the question, so the solution is obvious. We dump them here to take their chances alongside Yoska." He grinned. "It's no loss. They've outlived their usefulness. Besides—"

Milosh was already ahead of him. "Besides, a three-way split is more attractive than a five-way split."

Puffing up his chest menacingly, he added: "And in case you're thinking of making that a two-way split, I'd have a good hard look at that IOU."

Johann glanced at the parchment.

"You'll see it's made out to me personally," Milosh pointed out, and Irina instantly understood why he'd been so sure of himself. "Only I can cash it, so you'd better make sure I come along, and that I stay good and healthy."

A look passed between both men. A temporary truce being called. But how temporary? she wondered.

Johann gave a meaningful nod to the gang leader and turned to her questioningly. "What'd you say, sweet thing? Just the three of us. We blow out of here and leave the freak and the senile old sod to rot."

Irina's mouth opened but no sound came out as, without warning, Johann gasped, stiffened, and abruptly crashed to the floor.

CHAPTER 49

There was still one diabolical task to complete. Sombrely, Anton and Gregor regarded Kravnik's mutilated remains. What was left of the nobleman lay face down in the centre of a ruby-tinged pool three feet wide.

"Poor soul," Gregor grunted. "He didn't deserve to go that way. No one does."

Anton didn't respond. As far as he was concerned the envoy had brought his terrifying demise upon himself. Even so, he understood that they couldn't simply leave the carcass for scavengers to devour. As Kristina had mockingly pointed out, they had to show some respect. Not for the aristocrat's rank, Anton determined, but for the basic human dignity due to all men.

Kneeling, he slowly turned over the cadaver. The illumination from the lantern made Kravnik's glassy eyes shine like a porcelain doll's. He moved the noble's mauled features to get a better look, and frowned.

Under the mottled skin there was a barely perceptible twitch.

"Oh shit," he spluttered. "He's still breathing. The bastard isn't dead."

"Are you sure?" The old man dropped urgently to Kravnik's side. "With this amount of injuries it doesn't seem possible."

"Feel it for yourself. There's a pulse. Faint, but regular."

Snatching hold of Kravnik's wrist, the cleric concentrated. "Good Lord, you're right. Pass me my bag. I think I have something that can hel—"

The Count's battered form suddenly vibrated violently, eyes turning nightmare black, as a gasp of foul air exploded from his mouth. Surging upwards, he grabbed Gregor's shoulder with one hand while the other grasped the back of the cleric's head and drew him in with easy strength.

Gregor yelped and tried to scramble against the iron clutch, feet skittering frantically through the snow, as the nobleman bared his now deadly teeth; molars rapidly lengthening as they creaked and cracked, sharpening into a ridge of fierce serrations.

Kravnik's lunge was fluid, a blur of speeding precision. So was Anton's. The axe swung down, catching the exposed neck as the reanimated envoy thrust hungrily forward.

The blade detached the aristocrat's head in a clean slicing cut, sending it flying high into the night air, hitting the ground with force several feet away. It rolled across the snow, tumbling over and over like a discarded plaything.

For a long time neither startled man could move.

"Good Lord, that was too close. It was fortunate you got to the axe in time," Gregor gasped.

Disentangling himself from the headless corpse, he reran his miracle escape in his mind and immediately appreciated that providence had nothing to do with it.

"You knew that was going to happen, didn't you?" he accused.

Anton shrugged unconvincingly.

"I suspected," the Marshal admitted. "It was likely that when he was captured Kristina would have forced the

Count to ingest her tainted blood. She'd have intended him to transform the moment our guard was down. The perfect Trojan horse."

Moving over to examine his grisly handiwork, he nudged the severed head with his boot, making it roll even further away.

"She knew we'd have to move the body," he added, "and gambled we'd be in such haste and confusion that we wouldn't take proper precautions."

Gregor swallowed hard. "You've seen this ruse before?"

"Yes," Anton recalled, body going taut, "once before." He paused for a strained moment. "At Ossiak."

"What happened?"

He glanced suspiciously at his companion. "You must know. I thought everyone knew."

"Not the details. Just rumour, supposition, half-truths." Gregor leaned in eagerly. "Tell me. It's the least you can do after what you just put me through."

What to say? Anton asked himself. Admit the massacre was entirely his fault? How a naïve young lieutenant led his men to their doom?

"It was standard procedure," he began, heart quickening. "We'd patrol during the day, hunting out their nests and slaughtering them as they slept, then taking shelter in a monastery as soon as dusk fell. It was supposed to be fool proof, ensuring we'd overnight somewhere the nosferatu wouldn't dare attack."

"But something went wrong at Ossiak?"

He nodded. "I was over-excited, eager to prove myself. I should have called off the hunt earlier but we'd been tracking a group of Undead warriors for days and we'd just located their hideout. By the time we'd dispatched the creatures, twilight was upon us."

After that, they'd galloped like the devil was on their heels, racing the impending darkness, he explained. The soldiers were edgy, fear growing, but they trusted their leader implicitly despite his relative inexperience.

When, finally, the seminary at Ossiak hove into view, they'd relaxed. The lights in the tower blazed a welcome, displaying the correct sequence of colours for that day's security signal. All thoughts turned to a hot meal, soft beds and the sweet brandy wine the monastery was famous for.

"It looked so unthreatening. There was nothing to alert us that anything was wrong. Until we rode up to the gates and found them wide open."

Anton paused, head dipping. When he spoke again it was difficult to hear what he was saying, his voice tight.

"The monks were dead, no one spared, the monastery grounds littered with the defiled corpses. It was only when we dismounted and began to examine the bodies that we realised the truth."

"The truth?"

"It was a trap. Every last one had been infected with nosferatu blood. Before we could react, they reanimated and fell upon us. We fought like men possessed, battling for our lives. Who knows, we might even have triumphed. But at that very moment the main Modjeski force rode in. It was over in less than five minutes. We were annihilated. Those who were lucky died first..."

Gregor studied the lawman, waiting for him to go on; to answer the mystery that had beguiled and haunted so many for years.

"But you didn't die," he said softly. "You escaped. How on Earth did y—"

The shout from above was panicked. Both men looked up to the open first floor window. Irina was beckoning frantically. "Gregor, come quickly. Bring your potions and bandages. It's Johann. He's been stabbed."

CHAPTER 50

The iron mask remained motionless, its occupant not bothering to raise his head as Anton looked through the spy hole.

"No guard?" the voice said in faux disappointment. "I am insulted. Are you now so confident of success, slayer, that you no longer feel the need to keep watch on me? Foolishly thinking that you have triumphed?"

Anton's tone betrayed his weariness. "Nothing could be further from the truth. I simply can't spare the manpower. Besides, we both know a guard is no longer required now your kin have found you. You don't need to do a thing but sit smugly and await liberation. Trying to break out at this stage would be an unnecessary waste of effort."

Stefan chuckled softly. "True. Soon I will be set free to re-join my family. Yet, that fact begs the question: if you know I will be on my best behaviour, why have you come in here? It cannot be to gloat. That is not your way. Nor do you torture or torment. You piously leave that to others, like the bounty hunter rats who even now prepare to abandon you in your time of need. There can be only one answer, you have at last come to your senses and reconsidered my proposition?"

Anton knew there was no point feigning ignorance. The offer had been eating away at his resistance for hours, like a worm burrowing into an apple, corrupting the goodness.

"My answer remains the same," he replied with more firmness than he felt. "I'd rather lose Sofia than let you change her into one of your filthy kind. I won't condemn her to eternal damnation."

"Pity."

The mask swept upwards and Anton felt the intensity of the raw malevolent energy.

"You have no concept of what you are rejecting, slayer, for her and for yourself. What it is like to cheat the reaper, deny the grave its measure and enter a world where you have dominance over all crawling mortals; becoming a lord in reality, not just in empty title."

For a fleeting moment Anton allowed himself to picture it.

"Never!" It was just as sincere as the first time he'd uttered it but there was less vigour in the reply, the volume betraying an uncertainty. An uncertainty the vampire noted with an amused shrug.

"Time ebbs away for you, my defiant friend. Do not leave it too long to submit to the inevitable. Once my mother returns, it will be out of my hands."

The creature communicated with an idle sigh that it considered the conversation over, the audience no longer of any interest.

At once Anton had a flash of insight. The creature's bribe - no matter how disdainfully expressed - was a sign of weakness, an inadvertent admission that Stefan Modjeski believed it possible his kin just might fail in their rescue mission.

He felt a spring return to his step. On the threshold of the courtyard he paused.

If he believes I can win, why shouldn't I? he thought, and immediately knew the answer.

Because to win the coming battle, I must become more of a monster than the ones I'm battling... and condemn myself to an eternity of perpetual darkness.

It took three of them to hold him down. "The sick little creep tried to kill me!" Johann hissed, grimacing in agony as he tried to get to his feet to attack the dwarf, and fell back, clutching his side with red-stained fingers.

Tutting, Gregor told him: "And if you don't hold still, he may still succeed. Now be quiet and stop moving, or I won't be able to stitch the wound." With a rough shove, he forced his fellow bounty hunter back onto the parlour couch, causing his patient to cough harshly.

His examination didn't take long. It was clear what had happened. A single, deep, stiletto wound to the lower back, expertly administered.

"You've lost a fair amount of blood," he observed, telling Irina to push the towel even more tightly to stem the flow. "Fortunately, the blade doesn't appear to have pierced any major organs."

Over on the other side of the room, Quintz grinned and cleaned his nails with the knife he'd used minutes earlier.

"Good fortune has nothing to do with it," he announced to Milosh, ignoring the big man's glare. "If I'd meant to murder him, he'd be stone cold by now. I just wanted to teach our comrade a lesson about loyalty."

He jerked his head at the healer busy at work then out the window to where the wagon stood below, ready and waiting, the bear already asleep in the far cage. "I heard him all set on abandoning us but now it appears he suddenly requires a skilled physician and wheeled transport if he is to escape. What serendipity."

He jumped from the chair and padded over, standing far enough away from his bleeding victim to be safe from retribution. "I'd have thought you'd have learnt by now, Johann," he jeered. "The one thing I'm not is a trusting little fucker; quite the opposite. That's why I always make a point of eavesdropping. Just as well, eh?"

"You're a nutter, you know that," Irina barked at Quintz, angrily shoving her hair from her face. "As if we haven't enough bloody shit to deal with, you pull this stunt."

She went to slap him. Something in his cold expression made her stop.

"Now, don't be unfriendly, Irina darling. You know how much it diminishes your charms. You should be thanking me. Now he won't be dumping any of us," he taunted. "And if anyone else is thinking along similar lines, this is a demonstration of how unwise it would be."

He showed her the blade, angling it so the light reflected into her eyes, making her squint, and added: "Be assured, I have enough knives to go around."

The threat hung in the air.

"I'm going to gut you, you pint-sized freak," Johann promised, the words difficult to make out through his clenched teeth. "Soon as I get the chance, you're fucking dead. Do you hear me!"

The dwarf yawned exaggeratedly.

Gregor couldn't hide his disgust. Perhaps Anton was right, he thought, the gang seemed to be unravelling by the minute.

"I need clean sheets to rip up for bindings," he announced. "I'll also require twine and a large needle. As clean as possible."

Nodding, Irina left to find the items.

Addressing Milosh, he added: "And as I don't have any suitable ointment left, I shall require alcohol to disinfect the cut. I'm sure you won't mind sharing some of yours."

Milosh surrendered the vodka bottle as unhappily as a mother giving away a new born child.

"I'll make sure you get it back when I'm finished with it," Gregor assured him and, firing Quintz a reproachful glare, ordered: "And you can help put right some of the mayhem you've caused. We're going to need something to use as a stretcher. See what you can rustle up."

"A stretcher?" There was incredulity in the dwarf's voice. "Where am I going to find a stretcher?"

Gregor scrunched his nose. "I don't know. Or much care, for that matter. Use your ingenuity. Improvise. As you've just demonstrated, you think quickly on your feet."

Quintz didn't budge for a few seconds, then he broke into a crooked grin. "Sure thing, *Doctor* Mathias. Whatever you say. Your wish is my command."

With a jaunty bow, he too vanished from the room.

Sighing, Gregor regarded the remaining members of his group. What was it Kravnik had called them? *More resembling a rag-tag troupe of travelling players than reckless desperadoes.*

How correct he'd been. Except this unfolding drama was no place for clowns and that's all they seemed capable of playing.

Irina came back first, followed minutes later by Quintz holding a table top over his head, swaying side to side under the load until Milosh grudgingly helped him.

Transferring their patient to the sheet of wood required all of their strength. Johann emitted a string of obscenities at each bump and fumbled move.

Eventually he was positioned to Gregor's satisfaction and, lifting the long darning needle Irina had located, the old man plunged it into the fire long enough for the tip to start to change colour.

Blowing on it, he threaded the twine through its large eye and walked deliberately towards the wriggling, swearing man.

Nodding to Milosh to drench his precious vodka over the wound, then force open Johann's blaspheming mouth and pour copious amounts down his throat, Gregor gave a short blessing.

Then he jabbed the needle into Johann's flesh and the resulting shriek vibrated around the room.

"Oh, I'm sorry," he said, insincerely. "Didn't I mention? This is going to hurt. Quite a lot."

CHAPTER 51

Tight lipped, Nicku watched the cart rumbling down the main street, the bounty hunters loaded precariously on board, Quintz at the reins, Milosh and Irina riding alongside. They didn't even give the jailhouse a backwards glance, he noted with anger. Bastards.

"I don't believe you just let them go. You must be off your head. We need them," he protested.

Anton gave a small grunt, neither agreeing nor contradicting. "They're free agents. They can come and go as they like," he reminded the greying deputy. "They haven't broken any laws. And in case you'd forgotten, they outgunned us. I don't think we'd have enjoyed much success insisting they stayed."

"But they're dumping us in the shit. They're running away, leaving us to die."

They're trying to, Anton thought calmly, but it's not going to be as easy as they assume.

Ignoring Nicku's censorious tirade, he tracked the wagon's steady progress, wondering how far they'd make it. With an injured man hampering their getaway, makeshift stretcher hanging over the tailgate, they'd have to stick to the main trails. They'd be easy meat.

He suspected they were doing what Kristina wanted, heading straight into her web.

Waving Nicku away, with a barked: "Go find something to do. Help Pavel clean the muskets or something," he let his attention switch from the vanishing rig to the church on the hill.

Most of the community would be sheltering there, he guessed. Among their number would be men who'd served in the vampire wars, veterans who knew their way around a firearm. Not as proficient or as ruthless as the group who'd just fled, granted, but potentially useful.

In a heartbeat he dismissed the idea. Even if they'd be any use, they wouldn't agree, and not just because of their dread of the Undead. Kravnik's arrogant insistence on executing the poachers had set the whole of Brejnei against the Marshal. No one would raise a finger to help him.

"You thinking what I'm thinking?" Nicku asked, gesturing towards the chapel.

Anton almost jumped. He'd been so wrapped up in his thoughts he hadn't noticed the man was still there. "What?" he snapped. "What are you wittering on about?"

"The church," Nicku repeated, rolling his eyeballs. "I'm saying we should be getting the leech out of the cell and hauling it up there. It's the perfect solution. The bloodsuckers will never dare attack sanctified ground, so we simply relocate there. It's common knowledge they're scared to go near a place of worship."

Tell that to the poor victims at Ossiak monastery, Anton thought savagely.

"The Modjeski aren't scared of anything," he pointed out. "They'd attack a cathedral if it contained something they wanted. All you'd be doing is making the church a target. You'd be putting every single soul in Brejnei in harm's way and we're supposed to protect the people, as it laughingly says in your job description."

He indicated towards the cellblock. "More to the point, you haven't explained to me how the three of us could move Stefan without him tearing us apart. It was dangerous enough when he was drugged and we had back-up. What have you in mind?"

Nicku didn't reply, his antipathy increasing until Anton felt it like a physical presence.

"Well, we could... we could... Oh, I don't frigging know!" He jiggled with frustration. "You're the expert, the famous vampire slayer. You work it out. There must be a way."

A gun fired far off, followed quickly by another and another, a barrage of shots tearing through the night.

Tensing, Anton searched the horizon and saw the flashes.

"What the fuck!" Nicku exclaimed.

Anton was aware of the deputy twirling, running back towards the safety of the building.

He told himself he should be doing the same but couldn't budge, mesmerised.

It didn't take long for the musket shots to come to an ominous end.

Sighing grimly, he murmured: "So not that far at all."

The bear was the first to sense the impending peril. Awakening suddenly, Samson sniffed the air and growled, climbing up the inside of the cage, paws gripping the bars.

Quintz tensed. "What is it, boy?" he asked. "What do you smell?"

The animal's volume increased, as it became more agitated, rocking from side to side.

"What the hell is wrong with him?" Milosh shouted, spinning his horse around.

"There's something out there," Quintz replied, scanning the trees ahead. "Not too far off."

They both squinted into the darkness. Without Johann riding point they were without a lookout, his keen eyes able to spot dangers long before they threatened the group.

"I say we stop," Gregor urged. "Long enough to get a clear idea what's ahead."

Milosh looked up into the sky. The moon was still as round and bright as the night before, but clouds had drifted across it, diminishing its welcome illumination.

He did a quick reckoning. Halting went against all his gut feelings, especially as they were only two-thirds of the way over the wooden bridge. They'd be trapped. Better to press on a little further and hope the visibility improved. He noted wryly that his group already had flintlocks at the ready.

"I'll ride on ahead," Irina volunteered.

Milosh frowned.

"There's no sense us bungling into an ambush," she cautioned. "I'll be careful. I'll scout half a mile or so ahead. Any sign of trouble and I'll hightail it back to you."

Grunting unhappily, he agreed, but even as she departed, he knew it was a bad idea. Johann clearly thought so too, struggling to sit up, he immediately swore in pain.

"It should be you doing that," he told Milosh accusingly, but got no response.

The wagon lumbered forward, Quintz throwing the reins to Gregor, and clambering over to soothe his restless pet, the preacher complaining bitterly.

For all they'd been through, nothing changed, Milosh thought with a moment of humour. The smile died on his lips. The clouds had parted and he could see Irina, wheeling her horse, yelling, racing back, and behind her, rapid movement.

The bear went crazy.

In the gloom Milosh spotted silvery disks, dozens of them, moving in loose formation and instantly identified them. Eyes - predators' eyes catching the moonlight, glinting, seeming to hover disembodied in the darkness. Wolves.

The gang opened up, guns roaring, and in one sickening moment, he knew they'd fallen into the trap Irina had worried about. Just as terrifying, he realised they had no choice but to carry on into the attack. There was no room to turn the wagon until they made it to the far bank of the rumbling crossing.

The leading attackers leapt, and were brought down by musket shot, hitting the ground with stunned yelps. A large male chased after Irina, making the mistake of targeting the horse rather than the rider, found himself mere inches from her flintlock as she pulled the trigger, exploding his face.

Two others paused, baying to the sky.

Within seconds the wagon was clear of the bridge, Gregor fighting to keep the terrified team of horses under control, the cart banging and tipping as it began to describe a wide circle, wheels skidding deeply in the snow.

Wolves approached from all sides, more cautious than before, wary of the guns but still determined. The braver raced alongside, snarling, not giving up as they were picked off one by one. The others bided their time, waiting for an opportunity to pounce.

Milosh watched in awe as Quintz swung over the side of the wagon, hanging upside down, knife between his teeth. He couldn't understand what had possessed the dwarf. For Christ's sake, it made him easy prey.

The wolf that went after him thought the same until, grabbing a handful of its fur, Quintz whipped the blade from between his lips and slashed across the animal's throat.

The wolf was dead long before he released it, towing its carcass through the deep white blanket before letting go and delighting as a section of the pack broke off to hungrily investigate the sudden bounty.

"We've got to get back to the town," Milosh yelled, as the wagon completed its precarious curve. From the back, Johann blasted away, his twin flintlocks scoring hits.

Moments later they were back on the bridge, rumbling towards the mocking lights they had only just abandoned.

It was only then that Milosh registered that the wolves were no longer following. The pack had halted and calmly settled in the slush. They showed no interest in the fleeing gang.

Their mission had been accomplished. Brejnei was bottled up tight.

CHAPTER 52

Anton exhaled in a long slow breath, as he saw the wagon return with all the gang alive. So Kristina had other plans for them. He was relieved. Even squabbling and treacherous, they were still his only hope of surviving the coming storm.

All looked drained, finally understanding their perilous future was inextricably wound up with his.

Gregor was the first to speak, mouthing a single word: "Wolves."

Anton nodded. He needed no further explanation.

Standing hands on hips, he regarded Milosh. "You seem to make a habit of running out on me, and it never goes the way you expect."

Milosh gave a weary acknowledgement. "Touché," he replied, as he dismounted. "Though I think this makes us even."

That was debatable.

"Right, listen up," Anton said with authority. "Whether you like it or not, we're all trapped and the Modjeski main force will be here any time. If you want to come out of this alive, you'll start doing what I tell you. From now on, I'm in charge. No arguments."

There were no dissenters, or at least they'd decided to co-operate for the meantime.

"So you're our new master?" Irina said dryly. "Leading us fearlessly into battle? Well, you can't make any more of a mess of things than our last one."

Milosh scowled warningly.

"What do you want us to do?" she asked.

Build defences, he told them, start barricades, set up shooting positions.

Gregor raised an eyebrow. "Surely not me? I'm not as young as I used to be. There must be something else I can do?"

Anton thought for an instant. "Yes, you're right. Take over from Tomas. The poor lad must be exhausted. He's probably asleep. If he is, wake him, tell him to grab whatever he can from the kitchen and report to me out here."

"You're asking me to keep watch over your wife?"

"Will you do it?"

"Yes, of course." The old man gave a kindly smile. "You can rely on me. I'll see she stays as comfortable as possible."

Nodding thanks, Anton waited until he scuttled away, then turned his attention to Quintz.

"I'll put the wagon back in the courtyard," the small man volunteered, "and see that Samson is securely chained. He's a sensitive soul and he's already been upset enough."

Anton couldn't believe his ears. The last thing he considered the huge bear to be was sensitive. He studied Quintz for a moment to see if he was joking, but the dwarf was deadly serious.

"No," he countermanded, "don't do that. If things go the way I expect, we're going to need you, the big brute and the wagon."

Quintz's eyes narrowed. "Me and Samson I can understand, but why the cart? You've just seen how useless it was trying to get out of here. Who are you intending to transport? And where?"

Anton visualised his next move, hoping his strategy wasn't as crazy as he feared it would sound.

"Not who - what," he said. "We're going to use it to move as many gunpowder kegs as it will carry." He nodded back in the direction the gang had just come from. "Over there."

"The vampires? You're going to blow them up?" Milosh exclaimed.

"No," he replied, cryptically. "I'm going to blow them down."

Tomas stumbled out of the jailhouse, one hand rubbing his eyes, the other clutching a ham sandwich, which he munched greedily. Anton ruffled the boy's hair. For a split second he considered telling the lad that Kravnik was gone for good and would never again try to molest him. However, that would involve explaining how the nobleman had met his end and he didn't want to inflict the details on the impressionable child. Tomas would have more than enough to fill his nightmares in the coming hours. Which is why getting him out of there was crucial.

Hunkering down, he said: "I'm sorry I left you alone all day. It wasn't my intention. Things got a little..."

He risked a glance at the gang members, busy hammering sections of scrap wood over the insides of the first-floor windows. "...complicated."

The boy spoke with his mouth full, crumbs flying like shrapnel. "It's okay, Lord Marshal. I didn't mind. I was happy to sit with the mistress. It was no hardship."

"And she'd be so grateful," Anton replied. "When she's better she'll tell you herself."

Don't lie to the boy. He doesn't deserve that. Don't get his hopes up.

"But what I do know is she'd want me to make sure you're safe."

"Is there going to be trouble?" Tomas asked, brow scrunching up.

"Yes, and soon."

"Is it the man with the scar? Is he the reason? Is it something he's done?"

Anton was going to say no, but thought about it and admitted to himself that yes, Johann was the reason. Him and the other bounty hunters, and their criminally stupid get-rich-quick scheme.

"Perhaps. I can't fully explain. I said it was complicated." A change of tack was in order. "All you have to know is that I want you as far away from the trouble as I can get you."

"Master?"

He drew the lad closer, spinning him to face the church. "See up there. I want you to run there as fast as your legs will carry you. Tell the people inside that I said they were to keep you safe."

Tomas hesitated. "But I don't want to leave you. If there's danger, you'll need me. I can help."

"And you will," Anton promised. "Once you're inside, I have a task for you, an important job. When no one is looking I want you to climb up to the top of the bell tower, lock yourself in, and keep watch. When you see riders, I want you to ring the bell and keep on ringing it like your life depended on it."

It was inevitable the boy would ask the obvious question. How would he know it was the right band of horsemen?

"You'll know them when you see them," Anton stated with certainty. "They'll be riding steeds with blazing blue demon eyes, galloping faster than you ever believed possible, and there'll be dozens of them."

The gang buzzed through the jailhouse making preparations, Anton ordering them to different tasks with brusque commands. Johann felt like he was back in the army. He'd hated the army.

"The lawman thinks he's a frigging general," he complained to Irina. If there'd been one thing he'd loathed more than the army, it was preening, pompous officers.

"Don't play up," Irina told him, pretending to scold but not quite managing the proper schoolmarm tone. "He's doing his best. I don't see you making much of a contribution."

That stung. Wriggling on the stretcher, he seethed through the pain. They'd pulled out a table from the dining room, complete with dirty plates from earlier and set up his makeshift gurney on it, propping him up with pillows so that he sat fairly upright. The lash-up was shoved over to one side of the ground floor corridor, giving him the opportunity to observe while being unable to participate. It was maddening.

"What am I supposed to do," he argued, "laid up like this?"

Irina shrugged.

"Yeah, precisely. You've got to help me," he said. "I need to get up and about."

"You heard the old man. If you move the wound will reopen."

"Bugger the old man, bugger the wound. I need to be doing something useful."

"When the Modjeski attack, we'll move you over to a window. You'll be able to fire at anything that approaches," she promised.

"I want to do something now. I'm injured, not a cripple." He looked pleadingly at her. "If you'd bundled me up in bandages, wound them round as tight as possible, I might be able to stand."

"Why don't I just get you a corset," she teased, then regretted her levity.

"Don't mock me. I don't deserve that." He meant it to be harsh, but it came out as self-pitying. "Please, you're the only one who can patch me up."

She chewed her lip, considering.

Even though she knew it was a mistake, she nodded wearily and, ten minutes later, helped Johann to shuffle into the office where the lawman was outlining his battle plan to Milosh and Quintz.

Anton looked astonished to see Johann on his feet but said nothing. Milosh gave Irina an interrogative glare and Quintz tutted, muttering: "I obviously didn't stab him hard enough. I'll know for next time."

Inching himself into a chair, back burning as though being jabbed with red-hot pokers, Johann finally settled into a position that hurt less than any other and the briefing resumed. Even so, he struggled to focus through the throbbing.

"Even if we wanted to defend every opening to the building, there just aren't enough of us," the Marshal insisted, sitting on the edge of his desk, facing them. "So we pick key firing positions where we've got a good line of sight and board up the rest. The ground floor here isn't the problem, most windows and doors have iron bars and dead bolts fitted anyway. It's the first floor that's the concern so that's where we'll locate the majority of firing positions. Plus, shooting downwards will give us an advantage."

"What about the roof?" Milosh asked.

"I'm putting Nicku and Pavel up there. It will be a tricky climb up from the attic dormer windows, the tiles are thick with ice, but it'll offer a sniper's line of sight, nearly three hundred and sixty degrees around the building."

"Why two men together," Irina queried. "Surely we need to spread ourselves out as much as possible?"

Anton gave an acid laugh. "You don't want to leave Nicku on his own, believe me."

"And what about the rear of the building?" she pressed.

He nodded to Quintz and a look passed between them. "We have that covered," he promised.

No one spoke for a moment. In the background, they could hear the frantic sound of hammering as the deputies boarded over windows in the rooms above.

"But barricading is only half the story," Anton announced, "I have an idea for taking the fight to the Modjeski before they get anywhere near."

Outlining the plan, using a roughly scribbled diagram, he explained what was expected of each of them. They listening sceptically and Johann reckoned Yoska was either mad or brilliant. Either way, he wanted in on it.

He heard himself say: "One amendment, lawman. I'm going to help Milosh with the ambush, not you. I can ride out with him."

Anton gave him an unconvinced look.

"You can hardly sit up so just how do you think you'll be able to stay on a horse?" he said. "It's out of the question. I won't allow it."

"It's not far," Johann argued, "I only have to ride a few hundred yards. I was in the Imperial Cavalry, for Christ's sake. I can do it."

Milosh coughed dubiously. Irina pursed her lips, cheeks pinching. Only the treacherous sprite welcomed the idea.

"If he says he can manage, I say let him," Quintz remarked. "If he wants to play at being a hero, it's his look-out."

"His funeral, don't you mean," Irina snapped back.

Quintz grinned, unconcerned.

"You'll be in a lot of pain," Anton warned Johann. "It won't be easy. You'll suffer."

"I'll suffer whatever I do," he snapped back.

The hammering above abruptly stopped. In the silence both men glared at each other, a stand-off with no obvious resolution, until Pavel appeared, clearly unhappy.

"We've run out of wood," he announced. "And half the windows aren't barricaded yet."

Sighing, Anton got up, telling them to follow. He led the defenders to the largest room in the residence and, pulling out a large iron key, placed it in the lock.

The interior felt musty, unused. It was only when the lamps were lit they saw with astonishment that it was lined with oak benches and panelling along its entire length. At the front, facing the rows of seats, a high elevated padded chair sat grandly, under a wooden canopy emblazoned with the Crown Prince's coat of arms and the motto *All Equal Under The Law*.

Anton sighed cynically at the inscription. I wonder who dreamt up that witty little gem, he thought. It had a whiff of Kravnik about it: a sop to the despised populace, balancing idealism and hypocrisy while providing just the right amount of fake hope.

"They hold the quarterly assizes in here," he announced like a museum guide. "That's when the authorities even bother to go through the motions of pretending to give the accused a fair trial. Mostly, it's for show."

Irina whistled, gazing at the witness stand, the jury box, and the fine drapes hanging on the walls. "You've been holding out on us, Marshal. You never mentioned having your own personal court. If I'd known I'd have curtsied."

She did one now, a pantomime performance with grace and poise. Ignoring her antics, Milosh kept his eyes on Anton.

"What is it with you?" he challenged. "Always wanting to haul me into courtrooms? Well, I have news for you, my former Lieutenant. There won't be time to play at judge and jury before the bloodsuckers show up. When that happens, we'll all be facing the death sentence."

Anton didn't answer, but produced the axe he'd used earlier on the stakings. Johann noted that it was still splattered with Kravnik's gore. He wondered for a moment if the Marshal was going to threaten Milosh again with the blade but, with a whizzing swing, Anton smashed it into the nearest bench, splitting the timber.

"We need wood for barricades. This room is full of it and something tells me this court has heard its last testimony," he announced. "Strip the place, rip everything out. Don't leave as much as a matchstick."

Pulling Quintz to one side, he said: "It's time you hitched up the wagon and got busy elsewhere." And beckoning Pavel, told him: "Go with the knifeman. Soon as he's set up, fetch the cart back and see it safely stowed."

It took the rest of them twenty minutes to pull the courtroom apart, removing the wood and ferrying it upstairs before hammering for all they were worth.

Taking one last look at the empty shell, Anton felt a satisfaction he couldn't explain. A moving shadow caught his attention.

It was Gregor, grim-faced.

Anton's heart quickened.

"Is it Sofia?" he demanded. "Is she—?"

The old man didn't answer. Instead he tugged worriedly at his beard and asked: "Who's Gretchen?"

CHAPTER 53

The pall bearers floated above the ground. Six, black, evil crows. None spoke, faces partly hidden by their top hats, each sporting a crepe weeper ribbon dangling from their back like oily tail feathers.

She chased after, begging them to wait, to stop. There'd been a mistake, a terrible, terrible mistake, she pleaded. It couldn't be true. But they wouldn't slow their eerie stately progress, the tiny child's coffin weighing nothing on their shoulders. No matter how much she wept, they paid no attention, floating relentless up the hill towards the newly dug grave and the wet, squirming soil piled high by its side.

"But there's no body," she yelled. "She can't be dead. There's no body, damn you. Why won't you listen?"

At that, one inky shape turned, tilting its head in empty contemplation, and she gasped, realising it had no eyes - just two deep chasms. It regarded her for a moment, then, with no change of expression or pace, turned slowly back.

"She isn't dead!" she yelled even louder, fighting the gasps that compressed her chest more surely than any vice.

Yet the nightmare procession wouldn't deviate from its grisly path.

Suddenly he was there. Her darling Anton. Standing in front of her, in his mourning clothes, shaking his head with pitying sadness at her delusion and the torture it was putting them through.

"You have to let her go," he said, voice breaking with emotion. "Sofia, you have to face this. Please, please, my love. Accept it for you own sanity if not for my sake. We've lost her. Our daughter is gone."

But she couldn't, wouldn't, accept it. Not ever.

"Gretchen!"

Her wail carried on the wind.

"We searched for days, hundreds scoured the woods. The only trace they found was a ripped shawl, a blood-stained shawl," he reminded her, holding out his hand beseechingly. "Please. Don't make this any harder than it already is. If she'd been there, if she'd been alive, we'd have found her. You know that."

She felt her face crumpling.

"Gretchen!!!"

This time it echoed, the words a summons to the Heavens.

The crows halted without warning, the fragile casket tumbling to the ground, their swirling shapes flapping and cawing, looking for escape and, with a skywards leap, they flew.

The coffin rolled over and over, thudding towards her... and in her terror she flinched, feeling Anton's arms wrap around her, yanking her powerfully out of its way.

And the voices started again...

"You're sure it was Gretchen she said?"

"Clear as anything, Marshal. She kept repeating it. She seemed distressed. I didn't know what to do."

"No, you were right to fetch me."

"Sofia, Sofia. Can you hear me? Squeeze my hand if you can hear me."

Shaky, unsure, baffled by the fuzziness washing over her, she tried to do what he said.

After a moment she heard him exclaim: "She did it. Just then. I felt her. She squeezed. Sofia, Sofia. Wake up. Oh Lord, please wake up."

With an effort she tried to blink.

Her eyelids wouldn't budge.

The second time she struggled to find more strength and was blinded, coloured dots dancing in front of her pupils, the light stinging.

"That's it," he urged her, excitedly. "Come on. Just a little more."

With a moan, she forced her gummed lids fully open and saw him, and with bone dry lips, whispered: "I've had the strangest dream, my love," and burst into floods of tears.

They gave her some of Gregor's foul-tasting pick-me-up. She swallowed it quickly and vomited most of it back up just as rapidly.

At that, the old man tried to hide his concern, but even so she spotted the weary futility in his body language.

"It's okay," Anton said, dabbing at her mouth with a piece of linen. "There's plenty more where that came from."

She shook her head. "Maybe later. Just some water for now." The effort of moving her skull hurt badly and she lay back on the pillow, shivering.

She didn't know much about healing and illness, just enough to understand the fever that had imprisoned her had broken, but the infection burning inside hadn't given up. It was still lurking, draining limbs of vitality, making every organ ache, waiting to triumph.

But she couldn't let on. Anton's face looked so happy, such expectation and faith radiated from him. It would be a new cruelty to dash those hopes. The stranger - Anton had called him Gregor - wasn't fooled. She made fleeting eye contact with him, and they exchanged a look of understanding.

"I think you two deserve some privacy," he announced. "You must have a lot to say to each other. There's plenty to catch up on. I'll be just down the corridor, if you need me."

He left, Anton instantly cuddling Sofia, kissing her on the forehead in a flurry of affection.

Putting as much command into her voice as she could muster, she said: "Tell me what's going on. All of it."

"Why ever now? There's plenty of—"

"Because something terrible is happening," she interrupted. "I don't know what but I recognise that haunted look. Stop pretending, Anton. How big is the mess you're in?"

She said nothing for a full minute after he finished, unsure whether she could believe what she'd just heard, or whether she was still in the fever-fuelled dream and it was all a terrifying fantasy.

"There's no way for you to escape?" she checked.

He made a face. "Brejnei is sealed off. And even if I could find a way out, I'm not leaving you."

She smiled, love merging with pride and annoyance. "Then you're a brainless, romantic fool."

"That's fairly much what Kravnik told me," he replied, "although I don't think he meant it quite so kindly."

Fatigue overwhelmed her. "Then there's only one other alternative," she whispered, though it was not a suggestion but an instruction.

"No, don't ask that of me," he beseeched. "I vowed I'd never be that man again."

"I'm releasing you from that promise. Do what is required, become what is needed. Too many people are depending on you."

"But I'd be letting you down."

With an effort she brushed his cheek with her hand. "You could never do that," she murmured and felt her eyelids close.

She could hear his voice fading away, pleading, upset... Then the crows were back, circling in the sky. Harbingers of what was to come.

Below their stark black forms, a church bell was tolling, ringing frantically in a clatter of hurried peels.

Her last thought before the greedy sleep claimed her was that it was tolling too quickly for Gretchen's funeral, and was oddly muffled, as though the manic ding-dong, ding-dong was being sounded some way off.

CHAPTER 54

It was as if the very earth had come alive. On the south bank of the river, the ground quaked and tremored, the horsemen churning the terrain in unison as they galloped towards the town's sole entrance.

Wedged in his hiding place down amongst the bridge's icy piers, Quintz guessed from the frenzied shaking there must be at least forty Modjeski riders. The vibration was so furious he feared being tossed headlong into the freezing waters below.

Wrapping both arms tightly around a rough-planed stanchion, he glanced anxiously over his shoulder. The four gunpowder kegs he'd attached to the underside of the structure were still in place but only just. One had already slid a few inches, only the rope looped around it preventing it from dropping. The other small barrels looked just as precarious.

Well, there was bugger all he could do about it now, he thought and, forcing himself to ignore the cramp building in his shoulders, clung on, concentrating instead on the approaching army.

He'd known the task of setting the explosives would be his alone. None of the others was small and agile enough to weave their way through the restricted space between the numerous criss-crossed supporting columns. Nevertheless, he couldn't help a sense of unfairness that he was being asked to take on a risk none of the others shared, especially when it meant creeping about in order to avoid attracting the attention of the wolves still standing guard on the opposite side of the river.

He'd urged blowing up the bridge from a distance but had been overruled.

"Too much could go wrong," Yoska had cautioned. "Maybe if we were simply destroying the crossing to deny them access, but I have something else in mind. And that involves setting the charges at the last possible moment."

The dread steeds were slowing now, the massed ranks dropping to an impatient trot as they lined up with the tight opening. As Yoska had predicted, the bridge's narrowness created a pinch point, forcing them to cross only two abreast. And as the rickety, uneven boards above Quintz's head rumbled and dirt-despoiled snow dropped in showers he knew this was the moment he'd been waiting for.

The lawman's words echoed in his mind. "She'll be in the middle of the group. Kristina will ensure the carriage is protected back and front. You must catch her midway across. Destroy her and the others will be leaderless and confused. It'll give us a chance, albeit a slim one."

Quintz counted the riders passing overhead. Twelve, fourteen, sixteen... It must be soon. Gritting his teeth, he struck the match. The spark looked insignificant, hardly enough to do the job. Touching it to the cotton length, he watched as the fuse caught and began to burn, the tiny flame zipping along the wire with a spitting fizz.

For an instant he was engrossed, as the eager sizzle came to the junction with the other fuses and one dancing spark became four points of madly moving light. Then self-preservation broke his reverie and he scrambled to get away.

As more horses pounded above, he climbed out of concealment and, arms protesting in fiery torment, swung to the outside and began clambering from pylon to pylon. Six stood between him and dry land.

Behind, the barrels swung like pendulums, all threatening to plummet, the bridge juddering and twisting with the heaviness of the crossing company. It would be a miracle if the makeshift fixings held.

There was no point worrying about it now.

"You've done your bit," he muttered. "Time to get your arse out of here."

The last pier loomed, beyond that the steep town-side embankment. Although only feet away, the stanchion didn't seem to be getting any closer. Troubled, he realised he was slowing.

His heart banged loudly, competing with the crashing coming from the rattling planks. Just as he stretched out to grab the last pillar a new vibration shook the bridge as the first of the homemade bombs ignited.

The detonation was ear-splitting, yet nothing compared to the shouts of the startled riders, and the frightened snorts of their steeds; the procession immediately skidding to a standstill.

The pier shuddered and Quintz began sliding downwards, digging in desperately with his heels and the insides of his arms, tearing cloth and scraping his skin.

Before he could move again, the second and third barrels erupted and he felt himself flung towards the embankment as the force wave pushed out, bringing a choking cloud of dust and spinning splinters.

He landed hard on the snowy slope, the impact winding him. Dazed, he glanced back and saw confusion and panic on the faces of the trapped nosferatu. There was another emotion too. Bafflement. They couldn't figure out why the gunpowder had been located so far below that they'd been unharmed by the blast.

The last keg triggered. Instantly they had their answer. One by one the central stanchions split with an ominous crack, the midpoint of the bridge beginning to collapse.

"We haven't got enough powder to blow them up, but we can do the next best thing," Yoska had declared. Now as Quintz clambered up the slippery bank to level ground, he understood what the Marshal had intended. Trapped, unable to move, warriors yelled as more and more planks gave way plunging horses and riders into the glacial river below.

Nine fell, their cries filling the air before being cut off as they were instantly submerged. The dwarf knew none would drown. A fate much worse awaited them as, breaking surface, they burned and melted, screaming, flesh greedily stripped from their bones.

"Jesus Christ," he exclaimed, his mind refusing to process the evidence of his eyes. He'd heard the legend that the leeches could be destroyed by immersion in running water. Yet, this was beyond belief. The stream was as deadly as if filled with acid, eagerly devouring muscle and tissue, transforming the normally serene tributary into a churning, bubbling cauldron.

Even with his strong constitution, Quintz felt bile rise in his throat. Forcing it back he noted with disappointment that Kristina Modjeski's coach had made it safely beyond the collapsed section of the bridge and, together with some twenty or more warriors, was again on the move.

It was time to make himself scarce, he determined, just as the approaching group spotted him. The nearest rider pointed and yelled. Quintz broke into a sprint, going as fast as his short legs could carry him back towards the jailhouse.

Pumping his arms, gasping as he fled, he lurched forward, half stumbling. He daren't look back because he knew with chilling certainty what lay behind. Immediately he heard hoof beats, a moment before he was hoisted up and swung around.

The galloping nosferatu fighter held him suspended in his outstretched arm, oblivious to the dwarf's weight, bringing him in closer with each stride. There was cold amusement in the unstaring eyes, contempt shaping the vampire's features.

The derision didn't last.

In one sinuous motion, Quintz reached inside his tunic and produced a blade, swinging it out in a swishing curve, before digging it deep into the horse's neck. The animal instantly reared and, as he twisted the knife, it bucked and stumbled, crashing towards the ground, neighing, skidding, nostrils flaring in pain.

The warrior fought to keep control as he was pitched forward. Struggling not to be thrown over his mount's wildly thrashing head, he failed to notice as Quintz brought out his second weapon. There was an unexpected stab of agony as the dagger went straight through his eyeball, deep into his brain.

Horse and rider crumpled into a dying pile, and Quintz rolled across the ground for several feet before springing up and running again. He knew his actions had granted him only a temporary reprieve. The others would soon give chase.

In fact, he was counting on it.

Barely twenty-five yards on, a phalanx of fighters caught up with him. To their amazement he stopped sprinting, instead throwing himself sideways as they hurtled headlong into a length of rope that abruptly sprung up in their path.

On either end of the hidden cable, Milosh and Johann, both on stallions, gave a mighty pull, tugging as hard as possible on each end of the line, transforming it into a rock-solid barrier.

Without time to react, the pursuers were sent tumbling, their mounts' legs swept out from under them.

Watching in awe, Quintz observed Milosh point the cannon towards his foe and fire a volley into the confusion of flaying bodies, both equine and *infernal*. While he reloaded, Johann kept up the attack, firing two pistols into the thrashing mob.

In disarray the ambushed riders fought to escape, crashing into each other, the carnage increasing as Milosh took precise aim with individual head shots.

Quintz wondered if his homicidal leader would attempt a second reload of the merciless firearm but a summoning wave from Milosh told him there wasn't time.

Over to his left, Johann hesitated momentarily to clutch his wounded side, gritting his teeth in pain. The scar-faced hunter gave him an accusing scowl, before digging in his spurs and riding off.

Johann would have discarded him without hesitation as revenge for the stabbing, Quintz was sure. Luckily Milosh was there and as the dwarf darted forward, the gang leader leant towards him. In a motion identical to that of the nosferatu moments before, he hoisted Quintz up, flinging the small man into the saddle behind him.

Head down, clinging to Milosh's coat belt for his life, Quintz risked a fleeting look at the sickening mayhem they'd just wrought and knew they'd done all they could. The only thing that mattered now was getting away.

Bawling at the top of his lungs, he urged Milosh on as the remaining warriors broke away from guarding the carriage and raced after them.

Ahead, the relative safety of the jailhouse beckoned, the other defenders in position, ready to give covering fire. Yet, as he glanced at the determined faces of the warriors just yards behind, he couldn't help a surge of panic.

The Modjeski horde was gaining on them, their fiendish chargers covering the ground three times as fast as the bounty hunters' stallions.

"How near are they?" Milosh yelled.

"Close," Quintz gulped. "Too close."

While he spoke one of the chasing pack broke clear of the others and sped down on them, so near he could have reached out and snatched the dwarf.

At once Quintz knew with surety that they weren't going to make it.

Anton was out of the jailhouse before the last explosion had faded, running headlong down the main street. If the plan had gone well, the Undead invaders would be in

301

chaos, leaderless and without purpose. Had it failed, gone wrong in any small detail, he knew his help would be crucial.

Indeed, it didn't take him long to see the bounty hunters were in trouble. Making a rapid computation, he brought his crossbow up to his eye. One shot, he told himself, just one. He had to make it count.

Even at full gallop, Milosh's and Johann's speeding horses were still far off, as were the steeds of their pursuers.

He must wait, Anton reminded himself. Each second the pack came closer improved his odds of a solid hit. It was an effort of extreme will to ignore the nagging urge to fire blindly.

He heard a muffled shout - Johann yelling at him to do something. "Not yet," he shouted back, certain his words would be lost in the wind.

Both defenders' horses moved so swiftly they appeared to be floating, hooves barely brushing the ground, before leaping again; straining every sinew. In other circumstances, he'd have found the sight stirring; poetic. Here and now it was terrifying.

He could make out Milosh, teeth gritted, pushing his mount to its limit, driving it on by sheer will alone. Only just a few feet behind, Johann's face was twisted in agony, his riding becoming increasingly erratic, pace faltering.

Making ground with every stride, the Modjeski fighter was nearly upon them. Anton knew at any moment the vampire would leap.

You're out of time, a voice in his head, bellowed. *Do it! Shoot the bastard thing.*

Dropping to one knee, he focused, lining up on the pursuer and felt the crossbow tense, demanding to carry out its deadly mission.

His fingers applied the merest hint of trigger pressure and he sensed a thrill of electricity as the bow snapped forward, propelling the metal tipped shaft from the cradle.

It sliced through the air as Milosh and Johann swung their chargers to either side, out of the line of fire. Anton barely had time to take in the look of alarm on the attacker's ghostly face, observing his frantic attempts to swerve too, before the bolt arrived at its target.

And missed...

CHAPTER 55

Disbelief. Disgust. Raw, stinging emotions overwhelmed her, urging her on to more rash and dangerous moves to prove her invincibility and power.

In her troubled mind Kristina Modjeski fought to regain control of her emotions, to find calm and reason from inside the turmoil. She had allowed herself to be outplayed a second time, and if she didn't regain her chill, forensic detachment, she knew further defeat was inevitable. Her fury was what Yoska was counting on; had exploited to devastating effect so far.

But to hear the lung-bursting screams of her dying soldiers was maddening beyond endurance. She hadn't dared look back at the source of the inhuman keening. She didn't need to. She could picture the nightmarish kaleidoscope of gore, terror and suffering swirling just feet away, as the last remains of her proud warriors fought vainly for survival in the unforgiving torrent. She knew their tortured cries would haunt her for years to come.

Every impulse urged her to rush forward to the jailhouse, avenge their slaughter, to feast and destroy. Except to do that invited doom.

She needed focus, to make a swift assessment of her losses and ability to fight on - and to count her blessings. Yes, even in this maelstrom of confusion. The demolition of the bridge had been intended to eradicate her. If the explosions had taken place just seconds earlier, her carriage would have dropped into the river. There would have been no possible escape.

A mistake by the slayer's defiant scum.

And Viktor, her darling consort, still lived. Despite his protestations that he must lead the attack, she had insisted he remain safely towards the rear of the force. Having him up front presented too attractive a target, she'd counselled.

Gradually serenity stilled the storm in her brain. As long as Viktor survived, the losses they'd experienced were acceptable. There was the bonus that he still had a number of warriors under his control, all safe, cut off on the other side of the half-destroyed crossing.

Closing her eyes, bringing her fingertips gently to her temples, she probed out with her brain waves...and immediately connected, recoiling as Viktor's consciousness shouted, booming in excitement and bewilderment.

ARE YOU ALL RIGHT? HAVE THEY INJURED YOU? WHAT ARE WE GOING TO DO?

She waited until he became less agitated, letting her thoughts and emotions enter his cranium, soothing and reassuring.

I AM UNHARMED, MY LOVE. BE CALM. STILL YOUR CONCERNS.

BUT I THOUGHT I'D LOST YOU, he insisted, shuddering.

THEN GIVE THANKS TO THE INCOMPETENCE OF YOSKA'S FORCES.

Looking through his eyes, she scanned the fighters at Viktor's disposal. More than half their original force remained. Excellent.

I SHALL CONTINUE THE ATTACK, she announced. *PROBE FOR WEAKNESSES IN THEIR DEFENCES.*

WITHOUT ME? MY TROOPS?

FOR NOW ONLY, YOU MUST FIND A WAY TO RE-JOIN US. GO DOWNSTREAM, FIND ANOTHER BRIDGE, CROSS IT, AND RETURN ALONG THIS BANK.

BUT IT COULD TAKE HOURS, he pointed out. *THERE'S NO TELLING HOW FAR THE NEXT CROSSING POINT IS.*

It was true and she was well aware of the implications. *SO YOU HAVE TO HURRY. GO NOW,* she said, resolutely.

Sensing him about to argue, she severed the mental link. Instead, renewing her focus, she made contact with another mind, malicious, sly and alluring.

MOTHER, AT LAST! I FEARED YOU HAD ABANDONED ME.

NEVER. YOU MUST BELIEVE I WOULD NEVER TURN MY BACK ON YOU.

She made her thoughts more insistent, impossible to defy. *I NEED YOUR ASSISTANCE. I REQUIRE A DISTRACTION. SOMETHING TO KEEP YOSKA OCCUPIED.*

She drank in the tingling sharpness of Stefan's delight, the notion filling him with excitement.

LISTEN CAREFULLY, MY SON. THIS IS WHAT I WANT YOU TO DO...

Anton was shocked but not as much as his intended target. The vampire warrior had flinched, certain of being hit. Instead, the bolt passed harmlessly over his shoulder so closely it slit the material of his cloak before embedding with a shuddering thud in a nearby shop front.

Grabbing a second shaft from the quiver, Anton loaded as fast as his trembling fingers could manage.

Despite being dazed by his miraculous reprieve, the dark rider came swiftly to his senses and leant in to the neck of his skittish steed, urging it on to greater speed.

Whether the fighter spotted Johann was struggling to stay upright in his saddle or could smell the blood rapidly soaking the hunter's coat as the wound stitches gave, it made no difference. Ignoring Milosh and Quintz, it dashed after the bleeding man, closing the distance in a heartbeat. Without pause, he leapt, barrelling into the faltering defender, sending them both tumbling into the snow.

Johann produced a knife from inside his boot and plunged it towards the attacker's head, only to have the vampire clamp his wrist powerfully, easily intercepting the weapon in mid thrust. The creature continued to apply pressure, forcing the blade to drop uselessly and, pulling back his lips to bare his teeth, positioned himself to bite.

Milosh was wheeling around to charge, roaring in frustration, but it was clear that even at a gallop the gang leader couldn't save his confederate.

The incisors dripped with drool as they tore into action. Normally a nosferatu would aim for the neck, gnawing at the throat's vulnerability. On this occasion, the gash in Johann's side was a more enticing prospect.

Desperately Johann thrashed, kicking out wildly. It was hopeless. The warrior bit through the sodden riding coat and Johann shrieked, over and over, a strange pleading, echoing cry devoid of hope or manliness.

Just then, Anton let fly with his second bolt. Eagerly, he tracked its trajectory as it hurtled across the distance; the crisp, snapping twang of its release more aggressive than any battle cry.

Even if Johann hadn't been weakened from the weeping wound, he was no match for the vampire's strength and couldn't prevent the mauling. Twisting its head towards Anton, the creature's eyeballs went black with bloodlust, and it tore viciously from side to side, tearing off chunks of flesh.

Then, abruptly, both victim and attacker shuddered. Johann went into spasm, his body racked with convulsions, rebelling against the atrocity being inflicted upon it. His attacker quaked too, even more violently than his prey, as the top of its skull exploded, cleaved by the crossbow's bolt.

Anton felt no triumph at dispatching the rider, only a spreading melancholy as Johann's violent tremors grew slower and slower.

It was unlikely anything could now save the stricken hunter, but no one was able to try. As the stunned defenders looked on, wondering what to do, the nosferatu pack fell upon him.

In an instant Johann was gone, disappeared under the black, churning mass. There was no sound, only an eerily silent feasting.

Anton's head dipped as he appreciated that he should have used his bolt to dispatch Johann, putting the bounty hunter beyond his unimaginable suffering.

Recriminations would have to wait, he decided, and began running back to the jailhouse as Milosh rode past, roaring in fury. His contorted face was demon red, but that wasn't what most disturbed Anton. It was Quintz's calm demeanour as, watching the nosferatu pack devour his former comrade, he smirked.

CHAPTER 56

Hurling himself through the main entrance to the residence, close on Quintz's heels, Anton felt the oak door slammed shut behind him; Irina turning the key a split second before frenzied darkened shapes pounded at it.

"Stand clear," she instructed, as both she and Milosh levelled muskets and fired through the small ornate glass panes at the top. Two of the crazed figures outside dropped, only for others to take their place; clawing, snatching, pulling at the door with enough force to make it bend within its frame.

Both Anton and Quintz grabbed the guns proffered and the four fired in unison; the volley sending more attackers reeling. The assault continued for several more seconds until, at some silent command, the invaders retreated.

While the creatures leapt back onto their mounts, shots rang out from the rooftop as Pavel and Nicku opened up, winging one, knocking him to the ground. Their firepower was boosted by a shot from the open window of Sofia's bedroom, the crawling, wounded, rider inert in the filthy slush. Gregor, it seemed, was as proficient with a flintlock as a rosary.

"What happened out there?" Irina demanded. "Where's Johann?"

Anton's silence told her all she had to know. Gasping, she turned to cover her face.

Shoving hefty bolts shut on the top and bottom of the door, Anton ordered the others: "Quick. We need to get to our firing posts."

Irina made no move. He said her name gently but with urgency. Snapping to, she nodded, wiping her eyes with the heel of her hand and made for the stairs.

Quintz regarded the locked access wistfully, pointing out: "We're trapped in here, you do realise that?"

Anton shrugged. "Believe me, you don't want to go outside. The only place you're safe is in here - and that's relative."

"You told Kravnik this place is a fortress," Milosh said accusingly.

"It's harder to breach than most buildings, but the Modjeski won't rest until they fight their way inside."

"So what's the point?" Quintz asked. "Why did we bother with the barricades?"

"Slowing the attack. Splitting them into small groups we can tackle. Taking the initiative." Anton's look was steely. "Staying alive as long as humanly possible."

Not waiting for a response, he too headed for the stairs, shouting back over his shoulder. "I'm going to check on my wife. You better make yourselves as comfortable as possible. It's going to be a long night."

Entering the bedroom, he saw Gregor was at the window, head bowed, leaning against his musket. He appeared to be in silent prayer.

Keen not to interrupt, Anton moved quietly over to the bedside. Sofia was again in a semi-coma, mumbling incoherently and moaning. The sight filled him with an emotion he hadn't expected. Envy. He wished he too could be unaware of what was taking place.

Leaning over to kiss her clammy cheek, he chided himself for the unworthy thought. Nothing was worse than this half life she was experiencing, drifting in and out of consciousness, dreams filled with phantasms.

Much like our own predicament, he thought and, joining the elderly man, asked: "What's going on outside. Any sign of movement?"

Gregor pulled the curtain to one side. Squinting through the smeary pane. "They're up to something. I can see them creeping about but they don't look about to attack. Not yet, anyway."

Anton took a look for himself, unable to discern any details in the gloom, just vague outlines flitting backwards and forwards, their movements jerky and difficult to read. Then his eyes adjusted and he could make out individual figures and a sense of purpose in their furtive activities.

"They're rounding up the stallions," he announced. "What the hell do they want with them?"

Discarding the horses had been necessary. When they'd planned the details of blowing the bridge and springing the ambush, it was agreed there wouldn't be time to close the heavy courtyard gates on their hasty return.

But what use could the animals be to the Undead?, he wondered. They had their own steeds, infinitely faster and stronger. And there was no chance of turning the beasts into more demon mounts. That involved *infernals* infecting pregnant mares with their tainted blood, the bite ensuring the mother died but the foetus inside transformed.

Then, with a gasp, it dawned on him.

Just near enough for him to witness, yet too far away for him to accurately reach with musket fire, the warriors dragged the struggling stallions into the middle of the street. With silent, malicious determination they began dismembering the terrified animals; long, razor nails digging in - pulling, snatching, cleaving, stretching, revealing muscle, tendon, veins with each bloody eviscerating slash.

Both steeds reared, screeching in blind panic, infused with stomach-churning pain and bewilderment. Their cries were bowel-loosening, more disturbing than anything Anton had ever heard.

He wanted to look away, wipe the charnel house images from his consciousness. Despite that he looked on, mesmerised, his repulsion doubling, trebling, as the warriors stood over the pile of wet, shiny gore and butchered the body parts remaining. He watched unfalteringly as they dipped their fingers deep into the bloody mound, drawing the disgusting slime over their faces in thick parallel lines.

"What in the name of creation are they doing?" Gregor whispered.

"Putting on war paint."

"What!"

"It's their tradition," he replied, voice dull and level. "They believe adorning their faces with the blood of the vanquished makes them even stronger."

"But why slaughter defenceless beasts? Why commit this Godless atrocity?"

"As a graphic illustration of what they are capable of. To frighten us. To break our resolve."

"Well, they needn't have bothered," Gregor confessed. "I'm already terrified beyond reason."

There was worse to come, Anton sensed, and after the warriors applied their crimson markings, they led their own steeds over to the festering heap of slaughter and laughed as the nightmare horses smelt the carnage then ate hungrily.

Behind him Gregor retched.

"I'm going down to the kitchen to fetch water," Anton announced, a new urgency in his voice.

The man looked puzzled. Anton didn't explain, dashing out only to come back five minutes later with a large pail, water sloshing over its edges. Watching him setting it down with a clatter, Gregor remarked: "If you intend to bathe your wife's brow, surely we don't need this much?"

Looking wretchedly at Sofia, Anton replied: "It's not for her." And motioning to the priest's deep pouch, said: "You'll need a crucifix."

Gregor recoiled, startled, quickly guessing what was intended. "You want me to convert this into holy water?"

"Yes."

"It's impossible. I'm no longer a cleric. I don't have the authority."

"That may be but you're the nearest thing I've got. So a quick blessing, if you please."

Giving Anton a disbelieving look, he did as he was instructed, lips moving swiftly, repeating the well-worn mystical incantation.

"This won't work!" he insisted.

"Why not?" Anton challenged. "Isn't it merely a question of faith?" With that, he upturned the quiver on to the floor, emptying more than a dozen and a half crossbow bolts at Gregor's feet.

314

"Dip the heads in the water."

Tutting, the preacher obeyed.

"Now pass me one."

The bolt gleamed in the kerosene light, flickering with a constantly changing multi-coloured glow. Anton grunted. That was good. Bracing himself, he touched the arrow tip with his fingertip.

The heat was intense. Searing.

Just what he needed.

Gregor regarded him with awe, new questions on his lips. At that second the night air was split by a sharp battle cry followed by answering shots from the roof. The main assault had begun.

CHAPTER 57

No matter how much his teeth chattered in the bitterly cold church tower, Tomas daren't budge, unsure what reception he'd get from the citizens below. When he'd tolled the bell to sound the alarm, panicking fists had hammered at the locked entrance to the rickety staircase, yelling at him to stop; that he was putting them all in danger. It was likely if he opened up now, he'd get a sound beating - or worse.

Eventually, the thumping had stopped, a new sound replacing it - hymns being sung out of tune, hushed, as though the frightened crowd was hesitant to make too much noise lest it brought the creatures down upon them.

It struck him as odd the congregation should be praising God, yet be so uncertain of his almighty power and ability to protect them that they daren't raise their voices above a murmur.

If anything was going to save the townspeople, he reasoned, it was their faith. If they doubted the Good Lord and had hardened their hearts against the Marshal, then who would come to their aid?

Lips pursed, he glanced back at the jailhouse. Loud cracks issued from various windows as guns fired, while dark sinister shapes flitted about, unearthly howls both from those hit and those still attacking. All this interspersed with moments of flaring incandescence which, he guessed, was the creatures catching fire.

It was impossible to tell who was prevailing. The defenders seemed so few against the voracious foe; the nosferatu warriors undeterred, even when several of their number fell. They swarmed over the front of the building, climbing with unbelievable dexterity. It could only be a matter of time before they gained entry.

Kneeling, Tomas tried to pray, covering his ears, trying to block out the chaotic medley of cries, bangs and hypocritical worship. But if God was listening to his desperate entreaties, the Almighty gave no sign. Tomas felt no comforting response, no warmth, kindness or hope. Just cold, empty indifference.

It was as if Heaven had turned its back on Brejnei, content for the community to suffer whatever desolation awaited.

There was nothing for it. Tomas knew he had to act. The Marshal may consider him a mere child to be mollycoddled and protected, but the master was wrong. Being here, being unable to help, was torture.

There was plenty he could do, Tomas told himself: reloading guns, fetching powder, nursing and defending his mistress. More than that, he could fight. He wanted to fight. It was his duty!

In the distance Milosh's cannon fired, the boom bursting into the night. It felt like a signal. Getting up stiffly from his vantage point and rubbing his limbs to get the circulation going again, Tomas crept down the winding, wooden steps.

At the foot, he halted, putting his eye to the keyhole. He saw rows of white-faced souls holding hymnals, staring up at the plaster statues hanging over the altar, some of the makeshift congregation weeping, others crossing themselves, all lost in their own thoughts as they sang in desolation. No one was looking at the door to the tower. No figures waited to pounce.

Carefully he inserted the key, gingerly pushing the door open a crack. Heads immediately turned and, aware he had barely a second or two to make his move, he threw the door wide and ran for it.

He'd always been nimble and sure footed, faster than any of the other boys, and adrenalin gave him an extra boost. Ducking under snatching hands, jumping over bundles blocking the aisles and weaving in through the startled figures, he raced towards freedom.

"Stop him!" a voice yelled.

"Quick, block the way out. Don't let him get away."

But they weren't fast enough or determined enough, and with a final sprint, he leapt over one pursuer and slid between the legs of another and was up and pelting through the main entrance, aware only of the snow and the gruesome fireworks display ahead.

He didn't stop, heading towards the explosions and battle screams, not even hearing the woman who pleaded: "Tomas come back. Come back" and collapsed to the floor, arms outstretched, racked with uncontrollable tears.

Fire, reload, fire again. Swiftly pouring the black powder into the muskets, placing each shot on the paper disk, ramming it down the barrel. Feeling the weapon grow hot, too hot. Switching to the next rifle, all the time aiming at the supernatural forms that moved and dodged with impossible speed; hitting a few, missing most.

In the mêlée the defenders lost any sense of time. All around the Undead assailed; ripping at the barricaded windows and doors, clambering up the front of the jailhouse only to be brought plunging downwards by point-blank gun fire.

And still they came.

If Gregor was perplexed that Anton should think it necessary to dip already potentially lethal crossbow bolts in holy water, he soon understood the reasoning as those shafts that didn't instantly kill caused the creatures to spontaneously combust moments later, transforming them into screaming balls of flame.

How many *infernals* it dispatched, Gregor couldn't tell. It seemed so effective that no Modjeski should be left standing. Yet still they came. Still the muskets discharged their flying balls of lead.

Quiver empty, Anton had patted him on the shoulder, saying: "There's nothing more I can do here. I'll join the others."

"What do you want me to do?"

"Keep the window manned, shoot at anything that moves. And pray." He offered the cleric a sad half smile. "Pray for the dawn. It's the only thing that can save us now."

Even though it's still three hours away...

On that worrying note, he turned to go. He was part way out of the room when Gregor reached into his pocket and shouted: "Here, take this with you" flinging a small object. It spun in its arc and he saw Anton go to catch it then whip his hands back, face blanching. The bible fell to the floor with a thud.

"I thought so," Gregor muttered triumphantly. "I wasn't certain until now, but the clues were there."

The Marshal regarded him warily. "Clues? What are you talking about?" They both knew he was lying.

"You sensed heat in the holy water," the priest explained softly, "and earlier something bothered me when we were staking the fallen. I couldn't figure it out then but it finally came to me. As soon as I'd smeared the shafts with garlic oil you wouldn't touch them."

Anton considered telling the old man he was mistaken, indulging in crazy fantasies, but he knew it wouldn't do any good.

"Very observant," he conceded. "And what does that tell you?"

Gregor's cheeks pinched in concentration. "That there's more to you than any of us ever dreamt. That there was good reason for you to suspect Kravnik would be transformed, because that's what happened to you. But it didn't work, did it? Or at least something stopped it. I wonder what?"

Anton felt the room lose all its air, the walls closing in on him. "Do the others know?" he asked. "Have they worked it out?"

Gregor shook his head. "No, they're too stupid and distracted fighting amongst themselves, and I won't tell them, for now. Your secret will remain between just the two of us, if you grant me one favour."

Anton didn't need to ask what it was.

"Tell me how you survived at Ossiak," his companion demanded. "Tell me everything..."

CHAPTER 58

Reloading with practiced ease, Irina placed battle-ready muskets beside Quintz and Milosh, snatching up the recently fired guns and refilling them with sure movements. Over and over, she worked, hardly bothering to look at either man as they aimed and fired.

It was as perfect a system as possible in the circumstances. Not a constant fire, she acknowledged, but shots closely enough spaced to keep the monsters at bay.

The only thing that would have made it more effective was having a third man firing, and instantly she thought of Johann. Picturing him lying butchered just yards from the jailhouse, she couldn't help a tear running down her cheek.

She didn't believe in love. It was a silly notion for children and fools. Yet, his passing had affected her more than she could explain. It wasn't the idea of him being devoured. No matter how sickening, it was just a death and to her one death was as hideous as any other, no matter what form it took.

No, it went deeper. She cared about him more than any man and only now, with him forever snatched from her, the truth was dawning on her.

"Irina!"

Milosh's rebuke snapped her from the unsettling revelations.

"I need a weapon. What's wrong with you, woman! Why have you stopped?"

Trembling, she became conscious she'd stopped reloading. He signalled to her in irritation to fill another musket, but she couldn't move.

"Why didn't you save him," she whispered, accusingly. "You could have saved him."

Quintz frowned, clearly puzzled, but Milosh understood.

"There wasn't time," he answered flatly. "It was all over in a moment. If I'd ridden towards him, the creatures would have got me too." He jerked his thumb at the dwarf. "And him. All three of us would have ended up as food for the leeches. I'm sorry but there was no other way."

Without being aware, she was grasping a flintlock; loaded, ready, pointing straight at him.

"You're lying. You deliberately sacrificed him."

"Why would I do anything so stupid when we need every man we can get?" Milosh's voice was calm, but his brow shone.

"Revenge," she spat.

"For roughing me up earlier? Christ, I've done worse to him over the years." He took a step forward.

She raised the gun level with his head.

"You know what for," she said.

Both of them looked at Quintz, unwilling to say more in front of him. "Make yourself scarce," Milosh ordered. "Fetch more ammo."

Quintz didn't need telling twice. He took off, with a backward glance that suggested he was working it out and didn't want any part of what was about to erupt.

The door slammed shut, a signal for Milosh to gaze witheringly at Irina, shaking his head like a reproachful parent.

"I don't want to disappoint you, my unfaithful dearest, but I've known about your squalid rutting for ages. Do you think I wouldn't notice you and Johann, the looks, the way he panted after you like a dog in heat?"

Irina gulped, knocked off centre.

"If I was going to kill him for pawing you I'd have done it long ago."

"You're lying," she said, voice uncertain. "You only found out today. Your ego wouldn't have let you ignore what was going on under your nose."

He gave a mocking laugh. "Oh, poor deluded Irina. Everyone's whore. Theirs for a kind word and a pat on the backside. Fluttering your eyelids at anyone who'd notice. The reason I didn't kill him is that I didn't care. I've long since given up caring who you screw."

Her finger twitched on the trigger.

HE MOCKS YOU, CALLS YOU WHORE! BLAST HIM BETWEEN THE EYES!

"You're a bastard," she spat at Milosh. "A limp-dicked, apology for a man. If you hadn't been so determined to pour drink down your fat throat, maybe you'd have been able to get it up more than once a month. And I wouldn't have had to look elsewhere."

Milosh's forehead was gleaming, a tell-tale trickle of sweat trailing down his nose.

FINISH HIM OFF!

She fired.

Milosh ducked, and the musket ball raced through the air, and he had a split second to comprehend that it wasn't going to hit him. Instead it smashed with deadly force into the caped figure looming at the window, sending it reeling backwards.

323

Irina shook, her tears flowing freely. "You know what, you drunken bastard, you're not worth a bullet," she told him, throwing the flintlock to the floor.

As she stormed out, in the front of her brain the punishing voice scolded: THAT WASN'T CLEVER, MY PAINTED POPPET. NEVER MIND, I HAVE OTHER USES FOR YOU. USES MORE SUITED TO YOUR TALENTS.

Not comprehending why, she began to tread purposefully towards the cellblock.

CHAPTER 59

The insidious chorus crept around the edge of Anton's consciousness - the gossiping, needling, incessant whispers, goading...

"How you didn't perish is something I'll never understand. You were drained, a bloodless husk. Another few seconds and you'd have been wormfood."

"People talk. They say he betrayed his men, made a deal with the bloodsuckers to save his own life - was probably in league with them all along..."

"Tell me how you survived... tell me everything."

Closing his eyes, he surrendered to the dark refrain, one evil voice hissing over all the others: "All you have to do is let me finish what I began at Ossiak... began at Ossiak... began at Oss—"

With a sudden shudder, Anton felt himself pulled back in time, feelings raw, immediate, terrifying...

He was deep in the grip of the metamorphosis, the evil transformation seeping through each atom of his body, seeking out the last vestiges of his humanity. It was beyond any sensation he'd ever experienced - as though thousands of spiders swarmed through his veins, biting and tearing, spreading their acid venom, burning away all that had been mortal.

All the while his brain urged him not to fight. Give in, it exhorted. Accept the inevitable. Soon the torment will be over and you will have become a god. An eternity of unimaginable power awaits.

But one stray isolated thought broke through: *the eternity will be an infinity of damnation. You will spend centuries prisoner to a constant hunger that can never be sated, a blood lust always demanding one more sacrifice, one more atrocity. Is that what you desire?*

With that, what little human remained within him rallied and struggled, engaging every fibre of his depleted strength.

Better to die than allow this violation to run its course, he reasoned, as he rolled on to his side and scanned the ground nearby. The saddlebag was several feet away. Reaching it took focus and bloody-minded determination. An eon passed before his fingers gingerly touched the buckle and he pulled it back and opened the flap, teeth clenching so hard they crunched.

He searched the interior by feel alone, sobbing with the torture of forcing his protesting limbs to obey. After a minute and a half fumbling he was ready to give up, convinced what he sought wasn't there and he was doomed.

Just then he made contact with the two items he required, and began to tug them from their concealment.

Inch by inch, he pulled his treasures towards him, looking around in dread lest the milling feral monsters spotted what he was doing. By fluke of circumstance all feasted, lost in a frenzy, unaware. Even Stefan, the creature that had infected him, had moved on to other targets.

The powder flask had a tight lid. He could barely grasp the metal, but eventually he managed to unscrew the cap, fingertips worn raw and bleeding with the effort. He shook it, most of the fine gritty particles scattering uselessly over his uniform. Yet enough landed where he intended, the spray stinging madly as it made contact with his bleeding neck.

The pain was intense, but nothing compared to what must come, he knew, and juddering uncontrollably he grabbed the second item and smashed it into the wound. The sharp edges of the crucifix sliced him, flesh parting easily, but there was no time to consider the damage as the icon made contact with the gunpowder and ignited it in a roaring, blue-green flare of light.

Screaming loudly enough to be heard at the very gates of Hell, he held the blackening metal cross in place, pushing it harder and harder as the hungry flames sizzled, searing, devouring, melting his skin. It was beyond agony, beyond torment, an ecstasy of anguish that transcended suffering, and in that moment of almost religious rapture, he died.

And was reborn...

CHAPTER 60

Up on the roof ridge, Nicku blinked, unable to believe it as the attackers suddenly halted and quickly withdrew, some taking cover behind water butts and empty crates further down the street, others on horseback sheltering behind the carriage.

"Looks like the bastards are taking too many casualties and have pulled back to have a rethink," he said, hope rising, firing a test shot at the nearest target, the musket ball puncturing the barrel, producing a trickle of water that spread slowly across the boardwalk, but failing to clip any of the warriors.

"And that's our cue," he announced.

Across from him, Pavel frowned. "Cue?"

"To get the fuck out of here. Before they start up again."

The boy recoiled. "What! Flee? We can't do that. What about the others?"

Nicku gave him a sour look. "Bounty hunters? Killers? Hoodlums? Who cares about them. This is their fight not ours. If we stay they'll get us killed."

"But the Marshal? He's depending on us. We can't abandon him."

At the mention of Anton, Nicku spat. "I don't know why you worship him. It's his fault we're in this mess. Him and those cut-throats he calls friends."

Pavel glared, but Nicku didn't care.

"Look, Kravnik had the right idea," he pressed. "Hanging about here is suicide. I don't intend to let one of those inhuman bastards make a meal of me."

He held up his bandaged palm. "I've been hurt enough, thank you so much."

Pavel looked unconvinced. "But trying to escape didn't do Kravnik much good. He barely made it out of town before he was captured. Now he's lying out there with his head chopped off. Anyway, even if you could get past the vampires, there's still the wolves to deal with."

Nicku snorted. "Who said anything about leaving Brejnei? I told you, this is a private war. The leeches don't care about any of us. They just want Yoska and the bounty hunters. We're small fry. We could make a dash for the church. We'll be safe there."

He gave the young man an encouraging grin. "What'd you say? Hey, Pavel? We can head out the back of the building and up the hill before anyone knows we've gone. Five minutes from now this nightmare could be over. Like it never happened."

Pavel didn't consider it for a second, declaring: "No, no way. Whatever you say, I'm not running out on the Marshal. I won't let him down."

Nicku moved without warning, bringing the stock of his musket thudding against his companion's head. Pavel cried out and pitched backwards, almost falling off the treacherous slope.

"Sod you and your beloved Marshal," Nicku hissed. "I'm getting out of here, kid. If you had any sense you'd come with me."

He was part way down to the open dormer when he heard the tell-tale click. Turning, he registered the flintlock in Pavel's shaking grasp; the determination in the pain-filled eyes.

"No," the younger deputy insisted. "You're not deserting. I won't let you."

He swayed, grimacing, the gun dipping a fraction. It was all Nicku needed. Scrambling upwards, he threw himself on top of his colleague, grasping at the firearm.

The two scuffled, skidding for purchase as they slid down the tiles, heading perilously towards the roof edge and the forty-foot plunge to the ground.

Despite his injury, Pavel had surprising strength. Even so, it was no match for Nicku's cunning street fighting blows and within seconds the flintlock was pointing downwards, Pavel's grip weakening.

Then, to both men's shock, the gun suddenly jerked upwards and fired.

It took a moment for Nicku to comprehend what had happened. Both faced off, still holding the smoking weapon, still struggling for control.

Until Pavel looked down to the growing scarlet stain spreading across his stomach. He mouthed *Nicku,* part admonishment, part plea for help, as his feet gave way and he slithered downward, out of control.

But Nicku wasn't listening. He was already making his escape, climbing back into the attic without a second's regret.

Irina knew it was madness but the compulsion to obey was too strong - the insistent voice in her head urging her onwards, coaxing, enticing, wrapping its will around her own and crushing it.

DON'T BE SHY. COME TO ME MY TEASING TROLLOP. COME TO ME.

Standing on the threshold of the cellblock, she dithered, vainly rebelling against the alien feelings infesting her brain.

THE OTHERS HAVE SPURNED YOU.

It was true, she thought. Milosh no longer desired her. She was not a lover, not something to be cherished. He hadn't even bothered feeling jealous about her infidelity with poor dead butchered Johann.

THE SLAYER REJECTED YOU.

Oh God, was she so repulsive that the lawman should prefer his fading husk of a wife? How could he be so callous when she'd offered him her body, her devotion, her carnal skills, sexual delights any normal man would sell his soul to experience.

The insult stung, twisting in her like one of the dwarf's blades.

I WILL NOT REJECT YOU. COME TO ME.

Her fingers trembled, rattling the cellblock handle, the vibration shooting up her arm, making her gasp. In an instant she remembered other gasps, other moans, blending, melding in a kaleidoscope of lust; images of uncontrolled orgasmic climax flooding her sight.

I KNOW WHAT YOU DESIRE, THE ECSTASIES YOU CRAVE, THE WANTON PURITY ONLY I CAN PROVIDE.

At once she heard her own voice, the words she'd uttered on the night of the creature's capture as she'd watched his unbounded licentious indulgence with envy.

"I'm told they can mate for hours on end, just imagine that. Climaxing again and again and again and never tiring."

Instantly her body calmed, the inner conflict gone. Her destiny decided, she sighed languorously and ventured inside.

Without haste, or self-doubt, she entered the deputies' room and reached across to take the bunch of keys hanging on the wall, moving each around the ring until she found the ones she needed.

The atmosphere immediately changed; intensifying. She felt the excitement, the waves of anticipation emanating from the confines of the only occupied cell.

THAT'S RIGHT, MY LOVE. NOT LONG NOW AND WE CAN BE TOGETHER.

Tingling, she approached the maximum security cell, unlocked it, pulling the metal door open with a shiver that coursed down her spine.

Stefan's predatory grin widened as he rose to meet her.

It was as if she'd left her body, observing herself from afar, unable to connect with her feelings of self-preservation. In a trance she grasped his head, rubbing her face across the mask, murmuring, her tongue lashing out, trying to taste his through the reinforced mesh.

Then, without hesitation, she was searching through the keys on the ring, grunting when she located those that undid the padlocks. Fingers working nimbly, she unlocked each in sequence, letting them clatter to the floor and reached to the back of the cowl.

She wrenched it off.

Stefan gulped air greedily, like a drowning man bursting to the surface.

"The straps," he commanded, shaking the straitjacket impatiently. "Undo the straps. Free me from this diabolical contraption."

It was impossible to refuse, nor protest when he flexed his aching body, stretching and unbending his limbs, and huskily whispered: "Now, my doxy, remove your rags."

His kiss was silk - velvety, sweet and intensely cruel. He made sure her tongue went deep into his mouth, drawing her in, guiding it so it ran along the edge of his incisors. She felt panic, tried to pull away but his laughter was inside her head, her lips held captive.

With distain he ended the embrace and, with hands so powerful she feared they'd break her, he pushed her towards his groin.

"First I shall keep my promise," he said harshly into her ear, "and take you to levels of sexual bliss you could only dream of. But later - much later - I shall use your wretched mortal body in ways that will make you beg to die."

Irina tried to scream but it was already too late.

CHAPTER 61

A hammer. Where was the bloody hammer? Nicku searched frantically through the scraps of wood and nails left over from the rushed bout of fortification. He knew he had only moments to get the wooden planks off the exit and make good his escape.

There was no doubt in his mind. Yoska and the bounty hunters would shoot him without hesitation for leaving his post, especially when they learnt what he'd done to Pavel. It was a shame about the kid. He shouldn't have got in the way. He wondered if his fellow deputy was still alive, immediately banishing the thought. The only thing that mattered was getting away.

He kicked the loose debris, sending several pieces clattering across the floor, and there it was - the hammer he'd used only hours before. Grabbing it eagerly, he stuck the head under the nearest board, levering with as much force as he could muster. The nails held stubbornly firm but the timber cracked then sheared off noisily.

Repeating the exercise, he prised plank after plank, booming crack after crack, until the doorway was exposed. He pulled back the bolts and turned the key. Cold air hit his face as he shoved his way through and it felt like a caress on his sweating forehead.

His first reaction was to run blindly, flee as swiftly as his legs would carry him, but a sixth sense made him check the way was clear before venturing outside.

The back yard of the jailhouse was darker than the main street and treacherously uneven. For a moment he cursed not having a lamp to light his way but realised it would be a beacon for the creatures to home in on.

Waiting for his eyes to adjust to the murk, he dashed from outbuilding to outbuilding, using their cover to keep himself hidden. Far away, he could make out the outline of Kristina Modjeski's coach with three warriors guarding it. There was no sign of the bitch so he assumed she was safely inside it, planning, plotting her next move.

Halting on the corner, he tried to work out whether they could spot him if he sprinted across the road. Perhaps it would be better to crawl, moving slowly and hugging the ground, he reasoned.

It might be the logical thing to do but the idea of being out in the open any longer than absolutely necessary rankled and he decided to make a dash for it.

Bracing himself, he breathed in deeply and gagged as a stink unexpectedly washed over him, a sickening animal stench. Spinning he was assailed by hot breath, and a gigantic mud-encrusted paw swiped across his face, slicing his features into five deep grooves.

Although he tried hard to conceal it, Gregor knew his face betrayed his shock. The Marshal's revelations had appalled and amazed him, and he guessed there was worse to come.

"I blacked out after that," Anton recalled, expression hardening. "I'm told I was found wandering about forty miles away three days later. I have no recollection of what transpired during that time; where I went, what I did. It's a total blank, except..."

"Except?" Gregor prompted.

"The troopers who brought me back to the fort said I had a bag of heads slung over my shoulder. Eight vampire heads. They'd all been ripped off and my fingernails were clogged with blood."

Gregor edged back a few inches. "Good Lord above. No wonder the nosferatu feared you."

"The patrol also reported that I looked remarkably well nourished, perhaps even a little plump, as though I'd recently feasted."

And that explains why you terrified your fellow soldiers more than the enemy did, Gregor thought. What are you, Anton Yoska? What feral beast lurks inside you? Just what savagery are you capable of?

He watched as Anton leant over to caress his sleeping wife's lank hair, guiding it tenderly from her eyes, seeming far removed in temperament from the monster Gregor pictured. But was it all an act?

Without looking up, Anton said: "I know what you're thinking. How dangerous am I?"

Gregor denied it quickly, too quickly - but Anton didn't press the point. "The answer is, I don't know and that's the truth," the Marshal admitted. "But by the end of this long night I suspect we'll all know, one way or another."

He pulled the blanket tightly around Sofia, causing her to moan, struggling to free herself from the unwanted extra heat.

"What I do know is in their bungling arrogance the *infernals* created a devil more terrifying than themselves," he said starkly. "I embodied the darkest, most brutal elements of man melded with the vindictiveness and cunning of the nosferatu; an inhuman ogre guaranteed to exterminate without hesitation, devoid of pity."

For a moment the old man remained silent, struggling to process what he was hearing, thinking it a cruel fairy story. He sat heavily on the chair in front of the dressing table, inhaling hard, energy seeping away. He risked a glance in the mirror. Not to view his own troubled condition but to check that his companion still possessed a reflection. Seeing the Marshal in the looking glass, he relaxed a fraction.

Anton got up, moving over to the window, pistol ready, watching for any movement outside. It was quiet for now, he noted, the Modjeski warriors regrouping out of sight.

"I rejoined my regiment vowing to wipe the bloodsuckers off the face of the Earth and for a long time I made a remarkably good job of it," he said, resuming his account. "I revelled in the slaughter, thrilled at the chase. It was all I craved. Nothing else had meaning but dispatching the abominations."

He blew on the glass, misting the surface and drew his fingertip through the film, lost in concentration. The finger travelled determinedly, slowly building a picture, lines connecting. After a few moments, Gregor recognised the image emerging - a tombstone. But whose?

"And it was fortuitous for us all that you did kill so many of the enemy," he suggested. "I've heard the stories, what they say about your exploits. Without you, I believe we'd have lost the war. The foul creatures would have enslaved us, turned this world into their larder."

Anton looked unconvinced. "Perhaps. I don't know. One should never believe legends, particularly your own. We had many brave officers and men. We all played our part."

Grunting, he wiped the smudged glass, obliterating the macabre sketch and declared: "But it was different for me when the conflict ended. Unlike my comrades, I no longer had a purpose. I was a killing machine with nothing left to kill. And it didn't take me long to see I was a growing concern to my superiors. Why continue to keep a mad dog when it could turn on you? There were muttering, whispered suggestions..."

He didn't elaborate. Gregor could imagine.

"I faced a stark choice. Wait to be slain by the very people I'd served or annihilate the beast myself. Banish it forever, force it so deep inside my core it could never again threaten any living thing. Disappear from view, try to become the man I'd once been."

"So you strived to revert from monster to meek mortal," Gregor deduced. "Renounced violence, dodged conflict."

"It took years, making myself as unthreatening and inconspicuous as possible. And until you and your gang arrived, I thought I'd succeeded. Now I don't know how long I can keep the darkness inside me caged. Or even if I want to."

Chilled, Gregor wondered how much nosferatu blood coursed through the Marshal's veins, just how far through the metamorphosis Anton had gone before the contagion was halted.

Most worryingly, if the lawman's control snapped, would the process re-engage, reaching its inevitable diabolical end?

The bedroom door shuddered, an echoing bang on the other side making him jump half out of his skin. He looked questioningly at Anton, but the man was already rushing across the room.

Another thump, but much quieter.

Aghast, Gregor watched as Anton turned the handle and Pavel's bloodied body fell into the room.

CHAPTER 62

Gazing into his ammunition pouch, Milosh cussed, kicking the makeshift barricade he'd been sheltering behind, sending one of the stacked chairs tumbling. It fell heavily, breaking into three jagged pieces.

"Oh great," he muttered. "Just great."

Looking at the shattered fragments, he thought grimly about the possibility of the bible basher fashioning it into more stakes. The way things were going, they'd need more. Dozens of the frigging things.

He was convinced the leeches were recuperating faster than he could shoot them. Sure, injuring the beasts put them out of action for a while, but later they came back, full of fight, venom and speed, as though nothing had happened. Not that he could tell them apart, male or female. They were just a series of cloaked figures to him, all with the same graveyard pale faces lined with thin blue veins, empty bloodlust eyes and slavering, snapping mouths. Just shapes to shoot at, soulless ghouls to blast into smithereens. Shapes that strengthened with every passing hour.

And now he was out of musket balls.

Where the hell was Quintz?

He snorted as he recalled thinking those same words just 24 hours before, when they'd battled Stefan, when it had seemed they'd all be slaughtered right there in the mill house. Until the sprite had shown up with Samson, their brown saviour. An eternity ago, in a different life.

340

The dwarf had been away for ages, he fumed. He couldn't wait for him to return with more powder and shot. The cessation in the battle couldn't last. The leeches could resume their assault at any moment, and it would be the end if he was by the window, alone, with no way of firing the shotgun.

"You little twat," he murmured. "You're always showing up too late." And, picturing what he was going to do to the tiny man, he slung the heavy gun over his shoulder and headed out of the room. For an instant, he wondered about Irina, but pushed her from his mind. Teaching her the importance of fidelity could wait until later.

Right then, bullets were more important than bitches.

He approached the armoury cautiously. The door was ajar, shadows moving frantically about in the lamplight as the room echoed to crashes and thuds.

For a moment he feared the building had been breached and the enemy was destroying the weapons. But as he rushed inside, he spied Quintz clambering over the shelves, the small man leaping perilously to the top ledge, grabbing at boxes, peering inside each before discarding them.

"What the Hell are you doing?" he challenged.

If the dwarf heard him, he didn't respond but kept searching, recklessly scrambling to the next ledge.

"Quintz! What's going on?"

With a string of profanities, his companion replied: "We're screwed."

"What?"

Quintz picked up a box, upending it to demonstrate its emptiness.

"They're all like this," he announced, shoulders dipping. "There's only one box of musket shot left, and it's barely a quarter full. We're almost out of ammunition."

It was Milosh's turn to curse. He'd known their stockpile was meagre but had no idea they'd go through the precious bullets so quickly. There were less than fifty metal spheres remaining.

Factoring the cannon into the equation their supply wouldn't last an hour. Enough perhaps to fight off one more concerted attack. After that...

Quintz motioned towards two barrels of gunpowder lying uselessly in the corner.

"I suppose we could always turn these into grenades if we collected up all your empties and filled them," he said, snidely.

Milosh gave Quintz an evil look. Then, almost immediately, his mood softened. The dwarf had meant it as an insult but the joke gave him an idea.

"Help me shift these kegs outside," he instructed.

Quintz didn't move, gesturing that he needed a good reason to go near any more powder barrels, the memory of his near miss at the bridge still fresh in his memory.

"We're going to booby-trap the cellblock," Milosh revealed. "When the Modjeski break in, it's the first place they'll head for. I intend to give them a welcome they'll never forget."

"But it'll kill Stefan Modjeski," Quintz countered. "Yoska will never agree to it. You've heard all that nonsense about the prisoner being in his care."

"That's why we're not telling him," Milosh said darkly. "It'll be our little secret. And with a stroke of luck he'll be the first bastard in the line of fire when the whole lot goes boom."

Anton gently cradled the boy, his heart breaking. The young deputy was barely alive, his eyes opening a flicker, just long enough for him to give the Marshal a faint look of acknowledgment, before choking, coughing up a stream of crimson flecks.

"Nicku has gone. I-I tried to stop him," he mumbled, "I really tried, Marshal but he was too strong. I'm sorry."

"Shhhh, it's okay, lad," Anton said. "Don't worry. You did your duty. I'm proud of you. Lie still. It's going to be okay."

He flashed Gregor a beseeching look. The priest shook his head.

God, how determined must the boy have been to drag himself in off the roof and stumble down from the attic in that condition.

He forced an encouraging grin to his rictus-tight lips. "You'll be up and about in no time," he lied, squeezing the boy's hand. "And when you're well again I'll teach you how to use the crossbow. You'd like that, wouldn't you? We'll make a slayer of you yet."

Pavel tried to move wincing in agony. "But the vampires? The battle? I want to help."

His trembling body slumped, eyes instantly glazing, trapped forever in their look of helplessness and pain.

Anton leant forward to kiss the young man's forehead and with the lightest of touches, closed Pavel's eyelids. Inside, he felt the darkness stir and, overtaken by a primal urge, let out an animal roar of uncontrollable sorrow.

Gregor stumbled back. He'd never witnessed a death ritual at once so eerily human, so riven with raw emotion, yet also so alien.

Ending the cry, Anton leapt to his feet. Without a look at his companion, he rushed for the main staircase.

"Where are you going?" Gregor shouted.

"To catch Nicku," Anton snarled over his shoulder. "I'm going to tear the murdering bastard into a thousand pieces."

His footsteps thundered, making the staircase wobble.

"But you can't go out there after him. It's suicide," Gregor shouted. The Marshal wasn't listening. The only thing to do was rush after him.

Cursing the slowness of his ageing limbs, he was gasping desperately when he reached Anton, already busy scouring the back entrances to the jailhouse for the doorway the deputy had used as an escape route.

He grabbed the Marshal's arm. "This is madness! He's got too much head start. You stand no chance. All you'll do is make a present of yourself to the creatures."

"I don't care," Anton said, and pushed the priest away, spotting the door lying ajar, wind whipping in.

He was almost through it before Gregor could yell: "Stop! Look!"

Despite his fury, Anton halted, gazing in shock. Nicku hadn't got far. He lay only yards away, his battered and bleeding body being repeatedly bitten and pummelled by a mountain of fur and fury.

344

His mouth was open in a silent scream.

His glassy eyes made direct contact with Anton's, pleading for help.

But it was too late.

With an effortless, almost playful, tug of his massive paws Samson dragged Nicku across the ground, leaving a wide bloody track. Without pause, it roared in the mauled man's face, put its mouth around his head and bit down.

Gregor fumbled in his waistband for his flintlock, bringing it up to his shoulder, aiming at the creature.

Anton stayed him. "Don't! We need the bear."

"Then at least let me put the poor wretch out of his misery."

"No," Anton replied coldly. "He chose his fate."

Gregor looked away, unable to stomach what was about to happen. Anton's intense stare remained fixed, not flinching as Nicku finally expired; Samson's jaws crushing his skull like eggshell.

Neither man said anything as Anton calmly relocked the exit and began to repair the barricade. Studying him, Gregor shivered. The Marshal's anger had evaporated, but had been replaced by something much more frightening - a cold, callous ruthlessness that shone through his darkening eyes.

CHAPTER 63

Tearing off the sodden lace gloves, discarding them with disgust on the floor of the carriage, Kristina gazed at her hands, shocked there was a deep trench slashed into each. Her immaculate nails had dug in with force causing blood to well up, seeping through her fingers. She hadn't felt a thing, hadn't noticed that she'd balled her fists so tightly in her frustration at the inability of her troops to prevail in the battle.

This wasn't how things were supposed to play out. By now her warriors should have smashed the defences, storming the jailhouse and slaughtering all the mortals inside. Instead, it was her fighters who perished. She who was running out of precious hours of darkness.

It was impossible. Unthinkable.

She would not let it stand. Leaning out of her carriage window, she scanned the entire length of the building, searching for weaknesses to exploit. Window by window she surveyed, analysing the points from which flashes of gunfire issued, looking for unprotected spots, areas where the makeshift barricades were less robust. After a few moments her attention travelled upwards, at once spotting what she sought. The rooftop was now unmanned, the deputies nowhere to be seen.

She couldn't believe her good fortune.

A sense of relief crept across her as she realised the approach to the rear of the jailhouse was no longer in the line of fire. Looking to the ground, she spotted a colossal bulk padding about and hissed. A bear! So not so unguarded after all.

The beast made her uneasy, but it would be dealt with. Not by her warriors - a more fitting force was required, and closing her eyes for an instant, summoned other predators equally as feared and loathed by Mankind.

On the far bank of the river the wolf pack stirred and bayed, making for the water, plunging into the icy torrent without hesitation. Thrusting, kicking out, heads held above the surface, they swam easily - their strength and the webbing between their toes making their traverse effortless.

Halting only to momentarily shake their pelts dry, the wolves came padding down the main street in ones and twos.

As Kristina watched, the pack gradually gathered before her, putting back their heads and howling like a choir from Hades. Their eyes sparkled with malice, muscles rippled, and in a deadly rush they obeyed her will and attacked.

The bear roared, rearing to its full height to meet the onslaught and easily batted away the leading animals, smashing wolf skulls, sending their bodies flying lifelessly through the air.

But numbers were against it, and as Samson twisted and battled, the pack surrounded. With a mad fury they leapt upon the bear, drawing it down, biting and clawing until, with a fading bellow, he disappeared under a living sea of hate.

Satisfied, Kristina sent out one more mental command. Silently, swiftly, her fighters moved past the frenzied wolves and began to climb the rear of the building, ascending with balletic grace, heading upwards towards the now vulnerable and unaware guardians within.

The old man was loath to leave his side. But much as he welcomed the company, Anton needed Gregor to go back to guarding the bedroom.

"Sofia must remain your priority," he stressed.

"But I am frail, barely able to wield a weapon. I won't be able to protect her."

There was truth in that.

"I need you to do something more crucial than fight," Anton said, voice heavy, "if the creatures break in..."

He didn't finish the sentence. He didn't have to. Gregor shrunk back in abhorrence.

"If she must die, I want it to be at your hands, not theirs. You must promise me that. They can't be allowed to feast on her. Do you understand?"

"I-I can't. It's not right," Gregor replied, appalled. "You're asking me to execute her, to violate God's law."

"I'm asking you to show mercy and save her soul. You were a priest once, isn't that what you're supposed to do?"

Gregor sucked in air and Anton saw the old man's eyes filling, face about to crumple with the enormity of what was being asked.

Behind, footsteps sounded with Milosh and Quintz appearing from the basement, each carrying a powder keg. They halted, their conversation ending mid-sentence, clearly startled to see anyone there.

"What are you doing with those?" Anton challenged.

The two exchanged a meaningful look, fidgeting under his reproachful glare.

"Seemed stupid to leave them downstairs when we'll need them soon enough," Milosh answered. It was a careful selection of words, a mask of honesty concealing the true meaning.

"You know, Milosh. I'm too tired to put up with your scheming any more. I don't even want to know what evil mischief you intend with them," Anton told him. "Just put the barrels down."

"But—"

"Put them down - right now." He meant his tone to be calm, but the order came out as a guttural, aggressive rasp.

Suddenly wary, Milosh licked his lips. "Whatever you say." He nodded to Quintz to do the same. "See, no problem. Happy to oblige, oh wise leader."

Both backed up from the barrels, and above, an abrupt crash made any further confrontation pointless.

The four looked up instinctively.

More thuds followed.

"It's the bloody leeches. They're breaking in," Quintz gasped. But the other three didn't pay him any attention. They were already rushing towards the staircase. He took after them, flintlock in hand, wondering whether to mention the ammunition problem, and decided the lawman would soon find out for himself.

Anton was racing ahead, grabbing his axe from where it lay abandoned by the courtroom entrance, the old man moving surprisingly fast behind him.

Quintz heard the Marshal tell Gregor: "Lock the bedroom door, wedge whatever you can in front of it.

We'll try to keep them back as long as possible but when the time comes, you know what's expected of you."

"I do," Gregor replied, "and may the Lord forgive me."

The desolation in the old man's voice made Quintz shiver.

He increased his pace, short legs swaying like a sailor's. By the foot of the stairs he caught up with Milosh, the big man unexpectedly halted and looking conflicted.

"What's the matter?" he asked. "Why have you stopped?"

Milosh's brow creased. "Irina," he murmured. "Where the frigging hell is Irina? I've just realised she's disappeared."

Anton was waving at them to catch up, yelling: "Get up here. We haven't much time."

Milosh wouldn't move.

"What are you playing at?" the lawman bellowed. "C'mon, we need you."

The bounty hunter didn't look frightened, but perplexed. "Irina is missing," he shouted back. "Have you seen her?"

Anton hadn't set eyes on her for nearly an hour. In fact, none of them had. "Finding her will have to wait," he snapped.

Quintz pushed past, quickly climbing to the top of the steps, heading along the corridor towards the danger.

Milosh remained where he was. "I'm going to look for her," he declared. "Something's not right. I can sense it. She's in trouble." And before anyone could stop him, he'd doubled back, vanishing into the darkness.

At that second, the window at the end of the corridor creaked, vibrating under the frenzied force being unleashed from outside, fragments splintering inwards as hands ripped and punched through the wood with inhuman strength.

Dropping his axe to the ground, Anton cocked his flintlock. Quintz levelled his gun too. "It makes sense for you to aim high and me to aim low," the dwarf suggested out of the corner of his mouth.

Anton blinked, non-plussed. He hadn't expected gallows humour at a moment like this. Smiling, despite himself, he agreed.

Further banter wasn't possible. With a resounding crash, the window fell in and the first of the frenzied intruders was upon them.

CHAPTER 64

Racked with worry, Milosh ran, unable to block out the terrifying images flooding his mind's eye. He couldn't explain how he knew Irina would be in the cellblock. It was more than an assumption, or guess. He just knew. The certainty of it pulled him across the cobbled courtyard, his heart pounding. He knew what he'd find wouldn't be good.

Yanking open the outer door, he sensed the electricity in the air, the atmosphere fizzing with tension, and rushed forward, swinging his cannon into a firing position.

He called her name, his shout echoing off the walls. There was no reply, just a silence that twisted malevolently.

His second yell was even louder, but not as booming as his roar as he pulled up short, staring in horror at the open cell and the scene of sadistic depravity revealed beyond it.

Irina was naked, dead, throat ripped asunder. Draped across her bare corpse, Stefan Modjeski lay licking blood from her breast, swirling it around his mouth like a fine wine.

He made eye contact with Milosh and smiled with mocking indifference. "I've had better," he said cruelly, "but never gifted with such desperation to please."

And moving his head downwards, murmured: "The sweetest blood is always found below - the snatch is so succulent. The tastiest of treats. It must be all the juices."

Milosh couldn't speak, lips quivering, waves of rage and torment crashing over him. It wasn't a time for words, but action. Pulling the trigger so hard it nearly tore his finger off, he fired the cannon.

The first warriors plunged through, the remnants of jagged wood catching their cloaks, slowing their progress. Ten feet away, waiting for the optimum moment, Anton and Quintz fired in perfect synchronisation. The first two intruders came crashing down.

The defenders ran forward, discarding the spent guns - Anton grabbing the axe and Quintz producing the most vicious knife in his arsenal, a hunter's weapon, with teeth more jagged, pointed and sharp than that of any vampire.

Barging into the clamouring bodies, the Marshal's blade swished as it dug deep; Quintz singling out a victim, his knife hand jabbing back and forth, stabbing into the same yielding area, the action neat and relentless like a crazed automaton.

Their Undead opponents snarled and stumbled. Anton freed his hatchet from the tumbling nosferatu with a brutal tug, taking a large chunk of flesh with it. The creature's torso pumped blood but it paid little heed, rising upwards, intent on getting its drooling mouth up to his neck.

Swinging the cleaver in an arc, Anton grunted with satisfaction as it made contact with the side of the attacker's head, smashing cheek bone and jaw, demolishing one side of its face. Stunned, the figure went rigid and collapsed.

Anton didn't falter, finishing it with a third deadly blow. Stealing a glance to his side, he saw Quintz wasn't faring as well.

The dwarf had his back against the wall with a warrior towering over him. Both grasped the knife handle between them in a battle of strength and wills; the tiny man struggling but losing the contest, the weapon being turned back towards him.

Yelling, Anton swung his weapon into the vampire's back. Immediately releasing its grip, the creature pivoted, roaring in pain, to see who had attacked it. Turning around was a mistake. As it faced Anton, the dwarf slashed at the creature's unprotected rear, catching it across the back of its legs. The *infernal* went straight down. It kicked and scratched wildly as both men laid into it, splattering its gore in a wide semi-circular rain until the overwhelmed fighter finally lay immobile and mangled.

"I owe you," the small man gasped in thanks, as more shapes appeared in the breech and leapt in.

At that point Anton surrendered himself to the red mist - all became a blur of blood and spinning blades. He gouged, slashed and chopped, barely completing one violent motion before launching another. He was vaguely aware of the small man fighting beside him, stabbing and piercing, his knife so sharp it severed fingers, slashed to the bone and pierced vital organs.

Yet, even in his homicidal rage, Anton knew they couldn't keep up the defence.

"It's no use," he told Quintz. "There are too many of them. Run, get away, save yourself."

The diminutive knifeman gave him a disapproving look. "And miss all the fun? No bloody way."

More figures appeared in the opening, climbing through, but that wasn't what dismayed Anton. It was a sudden wail; so loud, agonised, and bestial it made him stagger with its force.

Reeling, feeling the world tumbling away, he sensed it freeze his core and understood that he hadn't heard it with his ears but his mind. And, as Quintz looked at him in puzzlement, Anton felt his consciousness travel a vast distance.

He was looking through other eyes - Stefan Modjeski's eyes. Milosh was towering over him, face crimson, swearing as he lashed out cruelly at the vampire; punching, smashing and kicking over and over. Panicking, Stefan was trying to fend off the brutal blows, overcome with intense pain.

Then the mental link abruptly severed.

In an instant, Anton knew that defending the first floor didn't matter anymore. The only priority was saving his prisoner. If her son died Kristina's wrath would be uncontrollable. It would no longer be a private war. She'd murder every living thing in Brejnei.

"We've got to get to the cellblock," he shouted, pounding down the stairs, jerking his head for Quintz to follow.

The dwarf looked anxiously at the fighters heading along the corridor towards Sofia's bedroom. "But the old man? We can't leave him," he protested.

Anton hardened his heart.

"He knows what to do. No one can help him now."

Without another word, Anton took off, lungs threatening to burst, unable to shake the last image he'd seen - Milosh advancing with homicidal intent, holding the metal cowl high over Stefan's head before swinging it down with all his might.

CHAPTER 65

Gregor's wrinkled hands trembled, each outspread finger quivering. Only the thickness of the soft pillow in his grasp prevented the shaking from taking over his whole upper body.

The woman hadn't responded as he'd gently lifted her head to slide the cushion from underneath but, in his troubled heart, Gregor wished she had. If only she'd awoken, seized his wrist, prised the bolster from him, he'd have been spared this agony.

It was unfair of Anton to demand this heinous task of him. Looking upon Sofia, he appreciated how trapped both of them were - she held prisoner in tormented slumber, him immobile, sickened, paralysed by his abhorrence at this terrible thing he must do.

Along the corridor, the cries and crashes continued. It could only be moments now until the creatures overwhelmed the outmatched defenders, he judged. Soon the nosferatu would be right outside and the bedroom's insubstantial lock would yield.

Anton's words pounded in his memory: "If she must die, I want it to be at your hands, not theirs. You must promise me that. They can't be allowed to feast on her. Do you understand?"

Oh, he understood all right, but he also knew that Anton had no concept of the enormity of the request, no matter how merciful and loving in its intent. It endangered Gregor's soul, threatening to damn him for all eternity.

Murder was a mortal sin in the eyes of the Lord, he reminded himself. A priest was a channel of goodness and hope, not destruction.

Yet, he reasoned, to allow one of the Almighty's precious creations to be devoured, to be abused by the craven servants of the darkness, wasn't that a sin of equal guilt and cowardice?

The crashes suddenly stopped, the silence more terrifying to him than the battle noises had been. He knew the time for dithering had passed, and he could only trust that the Lord would forgive him.

Forcing his hands to steady, he pushed down and balked, stumbling back as the woman's eyes flickered open.

He yelped. "Oh my God. Forgive me. I didn't..."

He couldn't find the words. The pillow tumbled to the wooden floor.

He could see in her eyes she knew he'd intended to smother her. He searched her sweat-slicked countenance for anger but saw none.

She gave a weak smile, beckoning, her finger barely rising more than an inch. He knelt by her, shame coursing through him.

"Why did you stop?" she whispered.

He gulped, a half whimper. "I could not... I am no killer," he muttered and the tears began.

"I need you to do this," she instructed him.

"But—"

"I am doomed. The infection..." She gasped, as her stomach spasmed. "I am already destined for the grave."

His voice quavered. "I haven't got the courage. I won't - I can't."

Now irritation showed in her gaze.

"You must, old man. While I breathe, Anton is weak, indecisive, afraid to do what he must. Free him. He has a purpose to fulfil. I cannot be part of it."

He froze, unable to think.

Her finger lifted, pointing towards him. "Please."

Crossing himself, he reached for the cushion. This time his fingers didn't shake as they gripped its edges.

He held it above her face, the shadow obscuring the pain lines. She smiled and mouthed: "I forgive you."

Muttering the first lines of the Lord's prayer, he thrust down - just as the door burst open, the frame shattering, and two nosferatu warriors entered.

For a second Gregor was torn between finishing his grisly task and fighting the intruders. Years of training took over. Dropping the pillow, he reached for a crucifix.

He held it at arm's length, causing the creatures to recoil, snarling, repelled by the potency of the iconography. They kept their distance, sizing him up.

It wouldn't hold them off for long, he knew and he dashed across the room towards the bucket by the window. They followed, swooping on him as he reached it.

The relic fell from his grasp, useless.

He shuddered as the first bite dug deep. The second stung like molten brimstone. Then he lost count of the wounds as the creatures started to devour his wrinkled neck.

Looking across at Sofia he thought with despair: *I've failed her.* And, with a bellow, he thrust his hand into the pail, splashing a wave of the glimmering, multi-hued liquid over their three colliding bodies.

The warriors caterwauled, instantly lost in a frenzy of pain, as their faces began to sizzle and melt and a dozen or more orange tongues flared where the droplets had landed. Locked in blazing, struggling confusion, the trio wrestled, over-balancing, pitching headlong towards the window before making heavy contact.

The pane smashed, glass exploding, and Gregor had the momentary sensation of wintery air whipping the flames away as they plummeted; a giddy, stomach-wrenching moment of vertigo. Then all was numbness as they hit the ground.

Pinned under the twitching, burning *infernals*, Gregor tried to continue the Lord's Prayer but was forever silent before he'd uttered three words.

Christ, it was incredible how much punishment these abominations could endure, Milosh thought in awe as he lashed the iron facemask violently back and forth, slashing flesh, making the creature's head snap back one way then the other; each blow eliciting a bone-crunching crack.

Despite taking a beating that would have killed any mortal ages before Stefan still struggled; bellowing, slashed, torn, but defiant.

"You just don't know when to stop," he told it, as it lurched towards him, reeling and unfocused and he easily sidestepped the move, binding the metal contraption around his fist and punching upwards, delighting as Stefan's nose finally snapped and the vampire fell to the ground.

"Not so smug now, eh?" he jeered at the prone figure, kicking it hard in the stomach. "What's wrong? Not so fast and elegant with five musket balls in your gut, eh?"

Kneeling, grabbing him by the hair, he hauled Stefan's head level with his own and spat straight into his tormented eyes.

"How'd you like that, you animal?" he goaded. "Maybe now you'll stop thinking you're a fucking overlord."

For an instant he considered the thrill of murdering the *infernal* there and then, a musket ball or two to the brain to finish things, a fitting retribution for the violations it had performed on poor, desecrated Irina.

But a thought stopped him. *Maybe there's a way to get out of this. Play it right, keep your nerve and the bloodsucker could still be your ticket to salvation.*

"Time to go for a walk, leech. We're going to have a friendly little chat with the ice queen," he mocked, manhandling the suffering vampire across the courtyard.

The gates were closed, the sturdy timber cross-brace in place. Milosh didn't worry. It was a minor concern.

"Lift the beam," he instructed.

Stefan hesitated, disorientated, muttering: "Never."

Milosh removed his shotgun from its harness across his back. He couldn't kill the bastard, but there were other ways to put the gun to good use. Grinning, he hit Stefan squarely with the gun butt, landing a blow directly in the kidneys.

His captive fell to his knees, howling, all potency and resistance gone.

"Don't worry," Milosh soothed in his ear, "mummy will kiss it better. Soon this nightmare adventure will be over and you can crawl back to your stinking reservation. All you have to do is pick up the frigging beam!"

He threatened with the gun butt. Swallowing hard, Stefan obeyed, swaying as he got unsteadily to his feet. Straining, he got both arms under the heavy oak section, heaving it upwards with such force that it clattered to the cobbles several feet away.

"Good boy," Milosh purred with a brutal pat on his prisoner's raw, tattered cheek. "See how much easier it is when you do what you're told. Now push open the gate, my preening prince, and let's go find out how much you're really worth."

CHAPTER 66

It took all her strength to climb out of the bed, even the effort of pulling the damp linen from her skin draining what little reserves she possessed. Dots danced before her eyes, nausea rose in her throat, the room spinning like a fairground ride but Sofia knew she couldn't give up. Lugging herself towards the mattress edge little by little, she swung her legs and leant over, her feet touching the floor for a second before giving way.

Grasping the blankets, she arrested her fall, lying part slumped, wheezing madly. Inside she felt the heat increasing, as though she was being roasted, and knew the fever was returning, its grip redoubling.

She sensed the chill breeze coming from the gaping, jagged hole where the window had been, and felt a stab of sadness for the old man she'd known only minutes, the stranger who'd sacrificed his life to protect her.

Your name was Gregor, but I know nothing else about you, she thought, except that you were brave and moral and all too ready to put the welfare of others before your own. And yet, you travelled with bounty hunters - and it was the end of you.

Suddenly, she had an irresistible urge to see his body. Wiping her hand across her sodden face, she gritted her teeth and used the bedding to pull herself up, grabbing the bedstead for support as she almost swooned.

A short rest, then she stumbled her way across the room, grabbing one piece of furniture then another until she was wrapped in the crisp wind. The dizziness faded a bit and she felt a little steadier - balanced enough to hold the narrow window ledge, poke her head through the gap and look below.

The sight caused her to give an involuntary sob. The mound of twisted flesh below had little form, the two nosferatu bodies blackened and smouldering. Underneath, barely visible, Gregor's face was in repose, as if just sleeping. She felt as though she could rouse him from his slumber with a gentle shake, but she knew it was a cruel illusion. He was dead.

The noise was slight, but enough to make her turn back to the room. Her eyes met a glaring pair of midnight black pupils, unblinking, hypnotic, devoid of all warmth or pity.

Their owner was a young female, barely more than a child, spread across the doorway, hands outstretched, fingernails long and sharp digging into the woodwork. The female tilted her head, questioningly, smelling the air, drinking in her prey's scent.

Fear seized Sofia. There was another sensation too - confusion. For a single shining moment, she thought the girl familiar.

"Gretchen?" she whispered, holding out her hand.

In her mind, the crows cried out in alarm, their wildly fluttering wings making her cringe.

The female took a half step forward and immediately Sofia saw her mistake. The girl's features became clearer in the lamplight, nothing like her lost daughter's.

You fool, you desperate fool, Sofia chided herself, always clutching at phantoms and crazy hopes.

The female fighter moved nearer, no longer wary.

They hadn't broken their stare, and as Sofia kept looking she saw the expression change in the girl's eyes - caution replaced by scorn and growing hunger.

The next thing she knew, the girl was rushing towards her, mouth opening, fangs ready. There wasn't time to think, to analyse her plight. Instead, Sofia acted on impulse and did something that took them both unawares.

He moved cautiously, ignoring the gnawing cold eating into his young bones, waiting up to ten minutes before changing position - staying immobile until he was certain he wouldn't be spotted then edging forward in a crouch. It was maddeningly slow, but he daren't risk going any faster.

Since reaching the bottom of the hill, Tomas had darted from one piece of cover to the next, constantly inching towards the jailhouse aware that the slightest noise or sudden movement would draw the attention of the besiegers. He didn't know if it was true but he'd heard stories: that the creatures had superhuman hearing and sight; that they could smell your fear over unbelievable distances. He couldn't take any chances.

Filling his lungs with a single precious gulp of air, then holding his breath, he moved again, crawling under the boardwalk, inching towards his destination. From the new angle he saw that the creatures had breached the building and he almost wailed out loud. He was too late. All his efforts had been for nothing.

He pictured the Marshal, the mistress and the two deputies, tried not to image what horror had befallen them. He felt his eyes tear up, and wiped them roughly.

Gazing around, he saw bodies strewn across the street, men and horses, mangled and torn. Some were still moving, twitching in agony, making strange sounds that were neither animal nor human.

Away to the back of the building, a mound of fur lay as though a hunting party had prepared pelts for market, and as he focused he saw the hides belonged to wolves, dozens of forest beasts, piled haphazardly on top of each other, many missing limbs, others with heads twisted and partially severed. None lived.

Sickened, he went to avert his eyes but halted with a shiver, aware that a movement, tiny, almost imperceptible, had made the mount quiver slightly. The pile began to part, and from deep underneath a single large, blood-encrusted paw emerged, sending wolf corpses rolling down the mound.

Tomas blinked, unable to believe what he was witnessing, as the badly injured head of a bear broke surface, scratched and torn, snout quivering. Samson flexed his mighty muscles and the heap rose with one last protest, and fell apart.

He clambered out, unsteady as any drunk, and with a barely audible grunt began to lick his many wounds.

Unsure what to do, the boy wanted to rush across to comfort the battered and suffering animal, but was immediately distracted by another sight. One of the courtyard gates had opened and slowly the vampire prisoner emerged, being pushed by the beefy bounty hunter, his shotgun jabbing into the creature's back, the reins of his stallion in the other hand, the horse stepping timidly behind.

"Kristina Modjeski," Milosh shouted, bellowing coarsely, "come out, come out wherever you are. I've got something you want. Come and see what I've got for you, Your Majesty."

Nearby, the window opened in the carriage and Tomas saw the vampire matriarch lean out, gasping at the sight before her.

"That's right," Milosh agreed with wicked humour. "I've got your son, all bashed up and hurting. The poor lamb's not feeling so big and brave any more. He needs his mother's love. Do you want to have a look?"

The carriage door burst open and she appeared like a typhoon.

Even from that distance Tomas could sense her fury, an anger that radiated crackling waves of malice, and he marvelled as she seemed to grow taller, standing more upright, body stiffening.

"You dare taunt me," she challenged, striding towards him, her long dress trailing through the snow. "I will pull your puny body apart with my bare hands, vermin!"

Milosh held his ground, grinning slyly. "Amazing what a good beating will do. Before, your boy was so full of himself, the great vampire nobleman. Now, he's nicely humble and compliant," he scoffed, "Unfortunately, the thrashing means he's not so pretty anymore."

She charged, hissing, and he thrust the gun up to the nap of Stefan's neck, advising: "That's near enough. You don't want to make me nervous."

The two enemies faced each other across a distance of ten yards, Tomas watching as other nosferatu approached, forming a semi-circle behind their leader.

"The same goes for them," Milosh warned. "Anyone takes a step closer and laughing boy perishes in a heartbeat."

Tomas could see her calculating if she or her cohorts could rush the gunman, before deciding it was too far.

"So what do you want, scum?" she demanded, voice so tight it reminded the boy of a pressure cooker lid about to blow off. "What are your demands? What will it take for you to hand over my son without further injury?"

Milosh pretended to consider. "Hmm - you wouldn't believe what I want, just how much it's going to cost you to stop me spreading his brains all over the snow." He sighed exaggeratedly. "We'll begin with your jewellery. The necklace, the earrings, the sparkling diamond buckles you're wearing. I want it all. There must be thousands of gold crowns' worth. We'll call it a ransom, shall we? Or a finder's fee, if you prefer."

Kristina gave a bitter snort. "Trinkets! Baubles! Is that all your tiny, criminal mind can comprehend? They are meaningless and will do you no good. You will not live long enough to exchange them."

He shrugged. "Perhaps, but I'll have them all the same."

She didn't move to comply.

"Right now," he yelled and smashed the shotgun against the back of Stefan's skull, making the vampire moan and stumble. "This is the last time I'm going to ask politely."

The assembled host twitched in fury, and Tomas thought the provocation was going to tip them into action but, to his amazement, the matriarch slowly unclipped the jewellery, piece by piece and threw it, the gems landing at Milosh's feet.

"Now that's more like it," he said happily, forcing his prisoner to pick them up and pass them to him. The items disappeared under the fur coat into the recesses of his voluminous waistcoat.

"Earlier this evening I offered to let you buy him back for just two thousand crowns but you refused. Guess what, Your Majesty, it's just cost you more than that. Ironic, isn't it? And you could have saved him so much humiliation and pain into the bargain."

Although she didn't answer, Tomas sensed her anger building to a new level.

"You have what you demanded. You have your riches. Now give me my son." She spoke slowly, emphasising each word, making them resonate with danger.

Milosh wrinkled his nose mischievously. "Not so fast - we're only getting started. He's not leaving my side until I have everything on my list and my safety is guaranteed. Until then this gun is staying pressed against his precious head."

Tomas was mesmerised. He couldn't tell how the stand-off was going to unfold. However, he did spot that no one was looking in his direction and, sliding out from his hiding place, began to creep to behind the coach and, reaching it, climbed onto the back and hunkered down.

He was about to congratulate himself on his stealth when Milosh's voice rang out. "My next demand is simple," he boomed. "You're going to lend me your carriage."

Even though Kristina's response was muffled, Tomas sensed a tone of incredulity in her words.

Milosh's amused reply was clear. "For my getaway, of course. I'm heading out of here, in your very own wheels, Your Bloodsucking Highness. And guess what? Poor, sad, hurting Stefan is coming with me."

CHAPTER 67

Sofia didn't know what possessed her. Perhaps it was divine intervention, a delayed answer to the holy man's dying prayer. She grabbed the half empty pail determining to fling the remaining holy water over the girl, but a subconscious impulse made her stop. And instead of flinging the iridescent liquid at her attacker, she held the bucket over her own head and tipped it upside down, yelping with the sudden icy jolt of the drenching water.

Nightdress soaked through and quaking with cold, she remained immobile, aware that the nosferatu fighter had abruptly halted inches away, bemused and suspicious, unable to figure out what trickery this was.

Lifting her head, Sofia smiled at the girl. The would-be assailant flinched, but held her ground, body awkwardly twisting in its desire to escape.

So let's see what happens if I do this, Sofia thought and reached out. Her hand was outstretched, palm up, unthreatening, yet the female fell backwards as though struck by a powerful blow.

It was impossible to determine if it was some element of the holy water projecting a repellent force or the female *infernal's* fear of the divinely combustible fluid coming into contact with her skin. In reality, it didn't matter. All that counted was that it worked, Sofia decided.

Stepping forward she headed towards the door, driving the growling girl before her; the nosferatu scrupulously keeping a yard or more between them, clearly wanting to maul and destroy her prey yet unable to get near enough to achieve her desire.

Pausing only to pick up the oil lamp Sofia pushed on into the corridor and in the yellowy illumination saw a huddle of the heathen creatures by the top of the stairs, regarding her with the same flabbergasted expressions.

Maybe this is why I didn't throw the liquid, she told herself. I'd have immolated one vampire but this way I have some protection against them all.

Trembling, she moved forward, reaching them in five weak steps. The group instantly parted, pressing to either side of her, hissing as they fought to hug the wall and banister, leaving a wide gap in between.

She ventured tentatively into the cleared path, proceeding downwards between the creatures. Immediately, they moved behind to fill the gap, following at a safe distance.

Sofia's thoughts raced, as she tried to decide what to do with this bizarre gift that fate had unexpectedly bequeathed her. She couldn't fight the invaders, merely staying on her feet was making her exhausted and giddy. She couldn't banish them from the building, all she could do was herd them like malevolent sheep. Yet, she knew there must be a way she could use her blessing to help Anton and his dwindling band to survive. She must think, think...

Reaching the ground floor, she shuffled onward, pausing only to check that her supernatural escorts were still in place. They remained steadfastly attached.

Turning back, she tripped. Not a full stumble but enough to make her wobble and almost drop the lamp. She thrust the pale light high to see what had stubbed her toes, and instantly had the answer she'd been seeking.

A swift depressing glance into the cellblock told Anton what he feared, that he and Quintz had been too slow. It was deserted. The prisoner was gone, his straitjacket discarded on the floor, the cowl nearby, smeared in blood, sticky to the touch. There was no sign of Milosh. Only Irina lay there, her lifeless brutalised remains a testimony to the contempt and violence at the heart of all vampires.

He heard Quintz murmur: "God bless the poor bitch. May she find the love in Heaven that eluded her down here." It was as good a eulogy as any, he decided.

In the courtyard the gate lay wide open, and he and Quintz edged towards it. For a moment Anton tensed, believing the warriors he could see through the gap were about to pour in.

But even as he brought the axe up in readiness, he quickly became conscious that they were paying no attention to the undefended entrance, engrossed by the exchange taking place in the street outside.

Milosh's voice suddenly rang out. "For my getaway, of course. I'm heading out of here, in your very own wheels, Your Bloodsucking Highness. And guess what? Poor, sad, hurting Stefan is coming with me."

Bemused, Quintz gave him a questioning look, and Anton shrugged in answer, jerking his head to indicate they should creep to the opening to take a better look. What greeted them made Anton curse. The damned fool!

The gang leader held Stefan in front of him at gunpoint, the prisoner befuddled, barely able to stand, his pounded and battered face deformed. Across from them Kristina and her remaining troops lined up, straining, ready to rush forward at the slightest opportunity. The space between the enemies crackled with unseen electricity, the air churning with malicious intent.

"You are even more dim witted than I supposed, bounty hunter. What you propose is impossible," Kristina scoffed. "The bridge is destroyed. My carriage cannot ford the river; the raging water would melt the horses on contact should you attempt to wade them across. You witnessed the horrific effects for yourself earlier tonight. Your cowardly escape cannot happen."

Milosh laughed long and hard as though it was the funniest thing he'd ever heard. "That's the trouble with you leeches, so frigging arrogant. You never credit mortals with intelligence and ingenuity. I've already thought of that problem..." He nodded to his own stallion, anxiously pawing at the snow behind him.

The Modjeski matriarch's face revealed her puzzlement. "But that mount is a thoroughbred built for speed, it will be too weak to pull a heavy carriage. Even a team of such steeds would be insufficient."

"Who said I'd be crossing the river in the poxy carriage?" He curled his lip. "I'll be riding across on my own horse. The carriage is to transport your snivelling son away from here. He's my safeguard, my hostage, to make sure none of your minions tries to interfere. Soon as I reach the river, I'll leave the carriage and its passenger unharmed."

He purred with satisfaction. "You'll have your son, I'll have my loot and you can do whatever your cold horror-filled heart desires with Yoska. I can give you a few suggestions if you like."

She nodded in unhappy acceptance of the logic. "And you will have triumphed. We will have to watch while you cross the river, certain in the knowledge that we cannot follow; there is nothing we can do about it. Unless—"

Flexing her mind, she gave a psychic order; the line of followers edging forward.

"No, no, no!" Milosh warned, hitting Stefan even harder than the time before. "That's near enough. The tricks won't work. We do it my way or he dies. Understand? Now summon the coach over here."

Head dipping, she waved for her coachman to comply.

The carriage slowly rolled towards them, halting to the side of Milosh. At his instruction the driver jumped down and joined the line of warriors.

In a fuzzy, half conscious movement, Stefan looked up through his lank, blood-matted hair and held his hand towards Kristina. "Mother," he croaked plaintively.

Milosh used the shotgun to guide him clumsily towards the vehicle, snapping: "Tie my horse to the back."

Anton knew he couldn't stand by and do nothing. Spotting the pistol wedged in Quintz's holster, he asked: "Is that loaded?"

"No, but I have powder and musket ball." The dwarf reached into a pocket and produced both. Anton took the firearm and hurriedly slotted in the metal sphere, pouring in the gunpowder.

"It won't do you any good," Quintz insisted. "You'll have only a single shot. There are too many of them."

"One shot will be enough for what I intend," he answered, and to the small man's horror, stepped outside.

Kristina showed no astonishment at his sudden arrival. Gesturing towards Milosh, she declared: "I said they were vermin, Lord Marshal, and this is what comes of allowing such scum to live. So much destruction and death. So many loved ones lost by both you and I, and yet this *specimen* survives. There he stands, unharmed, untouched, laughing at us. This cur, this foul, loathsome animal."

Milosh raised an eyebrow. "Laughing at *us*? So you and the ice queen are now on the same side?"

Anton breathed in angrily. "I'm not on anyone's side. I told you that right at the start." He strode towards the bounty hunter, deliberately keeping the Modjeski force in his sights, ready to fire at any warrior who moved.

"This has never been my fight. I never wanted any part of this madness. I've only ever had one intention, to carry out my duties as Lord Marshal, and that's what I'm doing now."

He swung the pistol, ramming it savagely into Milosh's ear. "Drop the gun!" he said, as all about him gasped.

CHAPTER 68

"Have you gone completely fucking mad?" Milosh spluttered, spit flying from his lips.

"No, quite the opposite, old friend," Anton assured him levelly. "I've come to my senses."

He edged carefully around the bounty hunter, increasing the pressure on the weapon, forcing it tighter against the man's reddening ear.

"Stefan Modjeski is in my custody, my prisoner, and I am still Lord Marshal - sworn to uphold the law, and that law says he stands trial. You're not taking him. You're not trading him. The only place he's going is back to his cell."

Anton risked a glance over at the nosferatu horde and saw they were as amazed as Milosh. Kristina watched in rapt attention, trying to work out if this was a ploy.

"In case it's escaped your notice, we're all screwed," the gang leader said through clenched teeth. "The bloodsuckers have won. Understand? They're ready to feast on each and every one of us. The only thing that's stopping them is this cannon trained on her precious son."

Kristina nodded solemnly. "What he says is true. The battle is lost. You are all destined to die horribly and Drubrick will be the first to be devoured." She closed her eyes momentarily, letting her tongue lick her lips. "He will be the sweetest of meats. Treachery gives the flavour such piquancy."

Anton didn't doubt her sincerity or how doomed they all were, but that altered nothing. "I need you to put down the shotgun," he repeated. "I won't ask a third time."

"So this is your revenge, is it?" Milosh challenged. "I schemed to have you killed, so you're determined to do the same to me. Whatever happens, you're going to stop me escaping?"

He snorted. "Just like before, all those years ago at the court martial. Playing the noble man of virtue, pretending it's about principle when all you actually want is vengeance."

Anton sighed wearily. "Believe what you like, Milosh. You always do. As far as I'm concerned you can escape, get as far away from here as you can run, but you're not using my prisoner to make it happen."

He wasn't prepared for what the bounty hunter did next. Boiling over with frustration, Milosh roared up into the Heavens, eyes filled with incandescent rage.

"You're out of your mind!" he bellowed. "You want to die, is that it? You want us all to die? You're a lunatic. The moment I lower this gun, they'll charge us."

Snarling, he ordered Stefan: "Climb up onto the coach, bloodsucker. We're getting out of here and you're driving." And part turning his head, he warned Anton: "If you're going to pull that trigger, you better do it now, lawman. It'll be a quicker, cleaner end than those fuckers will give me."

With that, Milosh moved forward, face screwed up in anticipation, ready for the musket ball to smash into his brain.

But there was no gunshot.

Anton's hand trembled, fingers refusing to move.

If anyone ever deserved to die it was Milosh, he reasoned. It wouldn't be murder, more like culling a dangerous animal.

Yet he couldn't do it. For in that one act, he knew the caged monster lurking inside him would burst free, and the world would never again be safe.

His hand dropped to his side still clutching the unfired pistol.

"I thought so," Milosh growled. "You're all talk, Yoska. I knew you didn't have the balls."

He motioned gleefully towards their foe. "Well, I hope you all have a merry old time of it. Looks like I win after all. Be assured I'm going to treasure this memory for the rest of my long and depraved life."

The hunter chuckled, backing up, cannon aimed at Stefan as the battered hostage stumbled towards the carriage. At that instant Anton expected the vampires to act. He was wrong. Kristina swiftly put out her hand to hold them back, and much as they hissed and snarled, they obeyed.

Good lord, you must really love that boy, he thought.

The words that suddenly sliced into the night were a female's, but not Kristina's: "No, Milosh Drubrick, you're not going to live. Not for another minute. You have an appointment with the devil and I'm here to make sure you keep it."

Anton gasped as he saw Sofia.

CHAPTER 69

The residence door was gaping wide, Sofia framed in the entrance, shivering and swaying in her wet nightdress, face plastered with sweat. She seemed so pallid, frail and ephemeral that Anton could have believed her a ghost.

Immediately behind, four furious Modjeski warriors growled in frustration, reaching with grasping fingers, contorting, straining to snatch her to them but unable to touch her trembling body. There was desperation, panic even, in their frantic struggle. And letting his gaze slowly travel down, Anton saw the reason.

One of Sofia's bare feet rested on a small wooden cylindrical shape. Even at this distance he recognised it as a gunpowder keg. Beside her, a second lay upended.

He felt his stomach lurch. *Oh Lord no... don't do this...*

With an effort that made her wince Sofia kicked the barrel, sending it rolling through the doorway. It got as far as the top step and wedged.

"What the hell?" Milosh exclaimed.

She kicked again and the second barrel followed the first, thudding into it and Anton saw that its cork bung had been removed and black powder spilled, piling in a heap.

"I'm dying and you're coming with me," she informed the bounty hunter icily. "You and all these heathen abominations. It's time for us to meet our maker."

With that she hoisted the oil lamp high.

What happened next occurred in less than ten deadly seconds.

Roaring, Milosh dropped the shotgun, his fat arms and legs pumping as he tried to put distance between him and the coming judgment. Kristina moved too, speedily turning away from her fighters, all her normal grace lost in the urge to survive. Distraught, she glanced over her shoulder at her dazed son and, in the deepest recess of his mind, Anton heard her telepathically bellow: *STEFAN! SAVE YOURSELF! RUN!*

Befuddled and crippled, the vampire prince lurched to the side.

Anton couldn't move, frozen in anguish and disbelief. Fixing him with a compassionate gaze, Sofia smiled and mouthed: I will always love you, my darling. Please, please forgive me.

Then she dropped the light.

The nosferatu behind her screamed, fighting to escape back into the building as the lamp smashed, spewing flame. Sofia was instantly engulfed, yet even as the voracious orange tongues lapped greedily at her, her smile didn't falter.

Anton barely had the time to bawl "*Nnooo!!!*" before he was aware of small feet scuffing behind and two strong arms grabbed his legs, forcing him downwards.

A split second later, the kegs ignited.

The bang was louder than he could have believed, drowning out all other noise as the explosion blew outwards, blast travelling in all directions. Pummelled and smashed, Anton felt his lungs empty, as the very air around him shuddered and rolled, flexing and pulling apart in its destructive surge.

He managed to glimpse sections of the jailhouse walls disintegrating, windows shattering, before the street became a churning maelstrom of dust, metal, stone and glass; obscuring everything in an impenetrable, choking fog.

Hard on its tail a curtain of fire whooshed over his head, scorching like a dozen suns, racing outwards, engulfing all in its path.

And then there was an eerie, unnatural, bewildering silence and a part of Anton's brain registered that the cacophony of destruction was continuing but the blast had damaged his ears, robbing him of all hearing.

Befuddled, he peered through the slowly falling debris and saw the enemy fighters had been annihilated, only scattered, blackened, twisted bones remaining. Nearby, Kristina Modjeski lay disoriented, half conscious. She'd managed to dodge the firestorm, but not the force wave and her face was sliced and bloodied. She tried to get up, but fell back, eyes rolling.

To Anton's right, the entrance portico was now a large, gaping circle of black. Where the walls had been, piles of rubble smoked. Of his wife and the vampires who'd been guarding her there was no trace and in his breaking heart he knew there never would be.

Letting his dazed, disorientated gaze travel further along the building's ravaged frontage, he saw most of the ground floor ripped and exposed, the scattered contents of the rooms no more than firewood. Beyond that the open courtyard gate had been blown off and the other hung at a crazy angle, its heavy top hinge smashed.

And directly before them a nightmare scenario made him want to vomit. The Modjeski coach had been slammed full force and now lay on its side, blazing, its coat of arms and motto blistering, smashed wheels still turning. The petrified demon steeds, out of their minds with terror, were piled upon each other, rearing, kicking in panic, foaming at the mouth, fighting to break free as the flames licked towards them. As he watched them scream in macabre mime, Anton gave thanks that he couldn't hear.

But he had other horrors to contend with. Only feet away a deadly skirmish raged. Milosh and his supernatural captive, both encased in flame, were locked in a deadly embrace, clawing at each other's throat. Awestruck, he watched their murderous struggle, man and monster's bloodlust so great, their determination to exterminate the other so overwhelming, that they were oblivious to the conflagration roasting them alive.

It was a terrifying sight, and yet it had a sickening beauty too. A purity of hatred. Violence and carnage as art form.

He made no move to intervene, wondering with a chilling detachment who would triumph, if either could prevail before the ravenous fire claimed them both.

The question was answered with a blade. The knife thudded through the air, spinning over and over, landing deep in the back of Milosh's melting skull. The bounty hunter went rigid and hung there for several seconds before toppling forward to the ground.

From inside the courtyard Quintz appeared, his immaculate clothing in tatters, and stumbled forward. Halting by the gang leader's corpse, he stared emotionlessly, face as inscrutable as ever, save perhaps a twinge of satisfaction at a job well done.

He slowly turned to Anton and spoke. It was difficult to be sure through lip reading alone but Anton imagined the dwarf declared: "I made a promise to myself a long time ago that no one would kill the bastard but me. I always keep my promises."

Nearby, Stefan too was on the ground, rolling madly in the snow, trying to extinguish the raging combustion. He looked pleadingly towards Anton.

Unmoved, the lawman shook his head.

YOU SHOWED ME NO MERCY AT OSSIAK. Anton projected the thought straight into the dying creature's skull.

YOU SHOWED IRINA NO COMPASSION.

YOUR WHOLE EXISTENCE HAS BEEN A BLIGHT ON MANKIND.

I WAS WRONG TO SHIELD YOU. MONSTERS DESERVE NO PROTECTION.

For a second, he could have sworn the vampire smiled.

AH, THE OLD SLAYER HAS RETURNED, the answering thought told him. *I CONGRATULATE YOU, ANTON YOSKA. AT LAST YOU'VE STOPPED RUNNING FROM YOUR DESTINY. I SHALL TAKE THE CREDIT FOR THAT.*

With a triumphant gasp, Stefan went still.

Anton looked at the vampire corpse, stunned, unable to take it in that his old foe was finally gone. It didn't seem possible.

His hearing returned abruptly with a sharp pop, in first one ear then the other, and a demonic chorus of cries, crackles and shrieks flooded in.

Lying by his feet he saw a small body, face down, splayed out, unmoving. Turning it over, he inhaled sharply as he saw it was Tomas.

What on Earth?

In all the mayhem he'd had no opportunity to check who had flung him to the ground immediately before the detonation, assuming until a few moments before that the small pushing hands had been Quintz's.

Now he realised his loyal serving boy had been the one to save him. But, oh God above, had the lad paid with his own life for the bravery?

"Tomas, Tomas. Wake up!" he yelled, shaking the boy. "C'mon, lad, be alive. Breathe, breathe, damn you!"

In a trice, Quintz was running over, grabbing his arm. "It's no good. He's gone. Leave him be."

Then, to both men's amazement, the body twitched. Tomas coughed harshly, grimacing in pain.

Anton grabbed the boy and held him tightly to his chest, aware that he was shaking with relief.

Even Quintz grinned.

Tomas' eyes opened a flicker but instead of joy they showed alarm, and yelling, he warned: "Marshal, behind you!"

CHAPTER PO

Anton had no time to react, snatched backwards with unbelievable force and thrust high into the air. He didn't need to see who had grabbed him to comprehend what was happening, and kicked backwards with all his might.

His lashing feet made contact, to no effect, his heavy boots failing to injure his attacker or even slow her for an instant. She spun him and the sight was so astounding he gasped. Kristina Modjeski was transformed.

It wasn't just the slashes and bruises from the explosion. Her face was contorted, all its beauty stolen by uncontrollable wrath; rage stripping away any pretence of youth, revealing the true ravages of her age and the evil that dwelt in her black heart.

"My son is dead!" she bawled. "You have killed my son! You have murdered the only thing I have ever cared for. And you are going to pay with your blood!"

Anton flinched, tensing, expecting her to lunge at his throat. But it wasn't going to be that quick.

Roaring, she threw him one handed, hurling him like a rag doll. He flew across the devastated street, jolting every bone in his body as he skidded across the ground for eight yards or more, crashing against the already wrecked boardwalk. Moaning, he tried to scramble to his feet, legs failing to obey and collapsed, aware of her standing over him, eyes flashing, screaming abuse in a torrent.

She snatched him up and slammed his frame through the remnants of the raised walkway - again and again, using him like a sledgehammer, shards of wood stabbing into him.

Away in a woozy, barely coherent corner of his consciousness he told himself it should be her feeling the agonising sting of stakes, and for a moment he giggled in madness, unable to control himself.

If anything the demented, insensible laughter drove her to a new level of violence. Before he could fathom what she intended, he'd been thrown against the store front; bursting through the wooden wall and landing amongst glass, bales of dress material, broken tailor's dummies and his own leaking life-force.

Without halting, she grabbed him by his feet, dragging him back into the street, his head smashing against each step, his arms stretched out like a crucifixion victim.

Leaning in close, she hissed: "Time to die, slayer."

He couldn't move or speak.

She bit down and he shrieked as her incisors broke through his collar, plunging deeply into his throat, and then she was gnawing, chewing like an animal possessed.

The sudden boom was nothing compared to the detonation before, but loud enough to gain her attention. She halted in mid bite, and turned.

Tomas was trembling, his trousers turning dark as he wet himself. Yet he held his ground, didn't blink, as he again pulled the trigger on Milosh's shotgun.

Stunned, Kristina looked down slowly at the second red circle spreading across her chest.

The gun spat out a third time. Through his haze of suffering, Anton tried to find the energy to cry out to the boy that it wasn't working, and he must flee. No sound escaped his lips.

The musket ball connected just as she began to hurtle towards the lad. Anton sobbed in desolation. This was worse than Ossiak; the result more cruel. *Not a child, please God!*

There was a slight jerk as the bullet impacted, but it did nothing to slow the nosferatu queen's charge.

Not Tomas, Lord. Take me. Take me instead, save him...

Kristina reached out to grab the boy. But unexpectedly Tomas threw himself to the ground, rolling away, and something much larger and aggressive than any vampire grabbed her instead; a powerful paw pulling her in, the second slashing with unforgiving accuracy.

Anton struggled to take in what he was seeing. Kristina Modjeski was held firm, flinching as claws lacerated and slit; trapped and unable to fight free of the creature that toyed with her.

Quintz appeared, pulled the boy to his feet and, almost as an afterthought, turned to the bear, ordering: "Samson, destroy!"

CHAPTER 71

He must have lost consciousness for the next thing Anton knew the sky above was beginning to lighten, the darkness grudgingly edging back, and he found himself propped up on the bounty hunters' wagon with Quintz finishing wrapping a thick wad of ripped bed sheet around his neck as a makeshift bandage.

"I'm not as good a medic as the preacher man," the dwarf informed him, "but it should stop the wound becoming infected."

"What happened?" he asked groggily.

"You passed out. Loss of blood."

Or maybe my brain refused to make me watch the atrocity that took place, he told himself, saving me from the nightmare of seeing someone being literally torn into shreds, even if that someone was a hated creature of the night.

"Is she definitely—?"

"Dead? I hope for her sake she is. Samson was very hungry," Quintz said, with an unsettling delight.

Looking around, Anton saw they were some distance from the jailhouse and that the building was burning. For a second he frowned, puzzled, convinced that although it had been badly damaged by the blast the structure hadn't combusted. Then he saw the figures in front of it, celebrating, bottles in hand, dancing and cheering.

"Charming lot, your friends," Quintz said. "If I hadn't pulled you clear, I suspect you'd have ended up on the bonfire."

Of that, Anton had no doubt.

"I'll consider that a vote of no confidence," he said, with a wan smile, wincing as his neck suddenly throbbed. "I wasn't exactly a popular person in Brejnei before all this happened. In many ways I don't blame them. I was a terrible lawman. My heart was never in it. They deserved better."

Quintz offered a dubious look. "Far as I can tell they deserved nothing. Ungrateful inbreeds."

He grunted, turning sombre. "I'm sorry about your wife. You have to believe me, she was never supposed to be involved in any of this."

But without her sacrifice, we'd all be dead now, Anton thought, forcing back a gasp of woe. She deserved better too and I let her down. I didn't even say goodbye.

He paused, lost in angst and recrimination, watching in silence as the residence's interior blazed.

"What are you going to do now?" Quintz asked.

For a moment Anton couldn't answer. Then he sighed and gave in to the inevitable. "There's really only one job that I'm still suited for."

"Vampire hunter?" the dwarf ventured, but it wasn't really a question.

"If you don't mind me tagging along."

The tiny man shrugged, then grinned. "I've had worse companions. And you seem to know your way around a crossbow. Speaking of which..."

Leaning down, Quintz produced the weapon from under the seat, blackened but otherwise intact.

390

"But how?"

"I had a helper find it for me," the small man replied. "Very keen he is."

He pulled back the canvas over the cage and revealed Tomas, snuggled up with the bear, gently stroking its blood-matted fur.

"Samson is an excellent judge of character and he seems to have taken to the lad."

The bear growled softly.

"And he's prepared to tolerate you."

That, Anton told himself, was a relief.

Letting off the brake Quintz gave the reins a sharp tug, the horses unwillingly moving forward. "What about the rest of the Modjeski fighters?" he asked, over his shoulder.

Anton had a mental picture of the remaining forces, some way off, reluctantly abandoning their mission rather than risk immolation by the morning sun.

"It'll be dawn soon," he replied. "The town is safe, for the meantime. And if I'm any judge of things, the nosferatu will be in chaos for a while. Kristina will be a difficult leader to replace. They'll go back to the reservation to argue it out amongst themselves. We're all safe for now."

But inside he knew it was a lie.

Brejnei may be secure but he and Quintz would never be safe as long as any of the clan remained alive. Vengeance was the Modjeski stock in trade, and this night's work meant the jailhouse defenders would be targets forever.

Five minutes later, they reached the river's edge and halted to look at the wrecked bridge. The centre had completely vanished, its timbers long lost in the torrent below.

"I did a damn slick job with the gunpowder, if I say so myself." Quintz beamed, as he admired his handiwork. "But it does mean we're going to get wet."

Flicking the whip, he coaxed the unhappy horses into the icy water, the wagon submerging up to its axles as it began to cross.

The cold was intense, but Anton barely noticed. Opening his coat, he unfastened the Marshal's badge from his waistcoat and, running his finger across its rough, ragged edges, tossed the tin star into the water.

He didn't watch it sink. He already had his focus locked on the uncertain future and what dangers lay ahead...

The end

Made in United States
North Haven, CT
12 September 2022

24002591R00243